PATRIOTS
THE REDROCK LAND WAR

A Novel by
Mark A. Taylor

*For Jim
Best Wishes
Mark A. Taylor
—06*

OXIDE BOOKS

Salt Lake City

First Edition

ISBN 0-9770424-2-1

Text copyright © Mark A. Taylor

Cover design © Jamie Chipman
Photo Jeremy Woodhouse, Getty Images

Dedication poem
"News of Death for Tom Charlotte" from *Where Many Rivers Meet* by
David Whyte. Copyright © 1990 by David Whyte.
Used by permission of the author and Many Rivers Press.

This is a Juniper Press and Oxide Books product,
published by Juniper Press.

Book/Cover Design: Jamie Chipman
Cover photo: Jeremy Woodhouse/Getty Images

Printed and bound in the United States

Library of Congress Cataloging-in-Publication Data

Taylor, Mark A., 1949 –
Patriots: The Redrock Land War, 2005

Last night they came with the news of death

Not knowing what I would say.

I wanted to say, "A green wind blows over the fields

Making the grass lie flat."

I wanted to say, "The apple blossoms flake like ash

Over the orchard wall."

I wanted to say, "The fish lie belly-up in the slow stream

Stepping stones to the dead."

They asked me if I would sleep that night.

I said I did not know. Of this loss I could not speak.

The tongue lay silent in a great darkness.

The heart was strangely open.

The Moon had gone.

It was then when I said, "She is no longer here."

It was then that the dark night put its arms all around me

And the white stars turned bitter with grief.

David Whyte.

Ten years later and I love you more than ever.

For my mother, June B. Taylor
January 27, 1923 - September 11, 1995

ACKNOWLEDGEMENTS

Thanks go out to Jamie Chipman, Phil Sullivan, Grant Bassett, Shon Burton, Steffie Chambers Von Bank, Michael Von Bank, Roger Chapman, Jeffrey Grathwohl, Mary Dickson, Duncan Wallace, Michael Hullet, David Holbert and Margo Taylor.

This book would not have been possible without the love, support and understanding of Lonnie Burton. Thanks for all the kisses Ms Gracie

CHAPTER ONE

By the time Garrett Lyons arrived in Page, Arizona it was already dark so he drove to the end of Navajo Street, rented a room at the Sidewinder Motel and collapsed on the bed. Garrett found it easier to arrive in Page after nightfall so he wouldn't be slapped with the new commercial development that sprung up since his last visit.

He woke before dawn, unable to move, paralyzed by sadness. A soft, warm breeze came off the desert and caught in the room's curtains, gently billowing them in and out as if they were lungs. They are all gone, he told himself, and they aren't coming back. Why can't I just accept it? He watched the curtains dance until the wellspring of tears ushered up from deep inside his chest. Please, he muttered, I can't go it alone.

At half-past eight, Garrett rose, dressed and left for the Bonanza Cafe a few blocks walk away. Outside, the new day was already hot and he pulled his baseball cap down to shade his eyes. The sky was a washed-out blue and a dirty haze lay at the horizon. A wave of weakness swept over him as the dry heat filled his lungs and baked into his bones.

In the parking lot of the Bonanza Cafe, Ateen's dusty four-wheel drive sat next to Joey Nez's shiny red Cadillac. Nez was an important Dineh elder and owner the Bonanza Cafe. Since Garrett's last visit, Nez had landscaped the parking lot median areas with black bark and garish-looking plastic Christmas trees bought on sale at Ace Hardware.

Joey Nez could always be found at the front door welcoming his mostly Dineh customers or standing at the end of the counter near the kitchen door where he watched the Navajo women and girls who ran the restaurant. With his long, slicked-back gray hair and silver and turquoise jewelry he made quite an impression at the door, but when Garrett pushed through the entryway only the escaping rush of refrigerated air was there to greet him.

Garrett stood in the foyer, letting his eyes adjust before spotting Brigham Joseph Ateen standing down between the counter and a row of red tuck-and-roll leather booths at the end of the aisle. Ateen stood at attention in front of the U-shaped corner booth where six Dineh elders including Joey Nez drank coffee. When Ateen finally noticed him, he moved quickly toward him, frowning and raising his eyebrows at the same time.

"You got my message," Ateen said.

"Yeah, we need to . . ."

"Not now," Ateen interrupted. "Important business. Wait here."

"Good to see you, too," Garrett replied, throwing his arms around his friend and slapping his back. Garrett's arms could barely reach around the six-foot-seven and three-hundred-fifty pound Ateen. Garrett, at six-foot-two, was no shrimp but he was dwarfed by this native American giant. Ateen's movements were slow and deliberate, and hinted of his tremendous power. The first time they met, Ateen reminded Garrett of Ken Kessey's character, Bromden, the giant mute Indian in *One Flew Over The Cuckoo's Nest*. Garrett once joked, "A hundred years ago you would have been a great warrior, fighting my greedy little European ancestors and taking their scalps." Ateen frowned, but Garrett continued, "I can just see you defending the tribe against Kit Carson and the U.S. Cavalry when they came through here in the 1870s." Ateen responded in deadpan, "Are all you Anglo writers so full of shit?"

Ateen and Garrett met by accident twenty years earlier when Ateen wore the uniform of the American homeless - a worn-out U. S. Army fatigue jacket, a filthy wool stocking cap, a pair of oil-soaked trousers and some grimy ill-fitting mock-leather sports shoes. After being drafted at age nineteen, and then serving as a Special Forces ranger in Vietnam where he killed many enemies, Ateen's victims came back in his dreams. "I took the scalps of some men and their spirits come back to haunt me," he once told Garrett.

Ateen now dressed in the uniform of a modern Dineh elder, what Garrett called cattleman chic: fancy hand-tooled cowboy boots with rocket nose cone tips, black Levi's, starched long-sleeved Western shirts, mirrored aviator sunglasses and at least one oversized turquoise and silver necklace. Some topped the look off with an expensive Stetson but Ateen only wore an occasional baseball cap, generally wearing his shoulder length salt and pepper hair in two thick braids parted down the middle.

After Vietnam, Ateen ended up in San Francisco living in an alleyway with other drunks for nearly a decade before returning home to the reservation. Garrett and Ateen met on the day Ateen arrived back home. It was

2

1985 and Garrett was on the reservation to cover the Hopi - Navajo land dispute for a news magazine. Ateen was panhandling at the Circle K as Garrett used the pay phone to call his editor. A few hours later, Ateen saved Garrett's life when a group of drunken bucks, consumed by hatred for white men wanted his scalp. Now, twenty-years later, the two were bonded by a devotion to a harsh, contemplative land. Ateen had taken a long and difficult route into his true manhood and wisdom. He was now a respected elder, a voice of reason, a man of tremendous character and strength.

Garrett dropped in a nearby booth and ordered eggs and beer. He knew the Dineh did not measure time against a clock so he could be in for a long wait. Ateen returned to the elders' table standing there as if he were a bodyguard or a junior partner who wasn't worthy of a seat yet. Garrett recognized some of the men, Joey Nez, Tomas Soulburner, Mark Maryboy from over in Blanding, Leon Kills Small, who wasn't a Dineh at all but a Sioux from South Dakota who married into the Crank clan, Nat Tahonnie, and Natani, a secretive and powerful medicine man. Except for Ateen, they were all in their sixties or seventies and adorned with silver and turquoise rings, bracelets and heavy necklaces. Ateen stood with his arms folded, rocking slightly from heel to toe.

Garrett pretended to watch the other patrons but he was really interested in the elders. Their expressions were placid and unflinching yet he sensed an underlying tension. He was struck by the beauty and sheer size of their heads. Some faces were handsome and distinguished, others were fleshy and round, but each was mapped with a sensuous mantle of wrinkles.

Garrett tried to read the wrinkles. If any faces on earth could be read for their true meaning, he said to himself, it must be the Dineh. The men's wrinkles told that something of great importance was happening. Perhaps it was a death in the tribe or a dispute over money or property. Perhaps it was the turning away of Dineh youth from traditional ways, choosing instead Anglo drugs, music, sex and video games.

These were important clan leaders, heads of large families, shamans, medicine men and big honchos. To some they were more powerful than the elected tribal council in Window Rock. They represented the Dineh spiritual center of Navajo Mountain - the home of the Gods. Garrett believed he was watching Dineh justice at work. The elders were deliberating. One man spoke and suddenly everyone raised their eyebrows, sending rainbows of wrinkles arcing up and away over endless expanses of vermillion-colored foreheads. A moment later, they went snake-eyed and pursed their lips tightly, creating sharp spines radiating out from their mouths. When the spines finally softened, crows feet appeared splaying out from the corners of their obsidian eyes and they were transformed back into sweet old men.

They fell silent, some sitting ramrod straight and resting their hands in their laps, others leaning easily on the edge of the table. They no longer acknowledged the sounds or movements in the cafe. It was as if they were inside themselves, meditating perhaps. They could even have gone somewhere else, Garrett considered, vacating their bodies as wise men are said to do and traveling out across the land, searching for some wild truth. Perhaps, he mused, only the shell or husk of these great wise men remained sitting there at the Bonanza Cafe.

Garrett glanced around but no one acted as if anything was out of the ordinary. Am I the only one to notice that something strange and powerful is happening?

Later, after the Bonanza council concluded, Ateen and Garrett left Page, heading north for the outback of Utah's Grand Staircase National Monument, the site of the most recent crime and the reason Garrett was there. Neither man spoke.

It all started two days earlier when Ateen left a telephone message saying someone burned down the famous cowboy line shack at the foot of Fifty Mile Ridge. They shot more than twenty-five mangy cows grazing nearby. Garrett wasted no time loading his camp equipment and truck. After a sleepless night, he left Salt Lake City before dawn. They would meet at the regular place, the Bonanza Cafe, in Page, Arizona.

Ateen's message arrived at a good time and Garrett was glad for an excuse to get away. He always liked the highway leaving the city, taking him away from the houses and schools and work places of one million people he had little in common with, except perhaps for a mutual disdain. This departure was even sweeter because on his way out he passed the house of his most recent ex-lover, a woman he would never understand, especially her insistence that she loved him. How can she love me, he wondered, she must be a fool.

Once out of the city, the highway passed through some mountains, then opened up onto some high flat lands where endless desolate-looking rolling hills covered with sagebrush and burnt June grass mixed with worn-out farm fields.

The drive south gave Garrett time to consider the destruction of the line shack and the killing of the cows. The crimes were just two in a growing list of recent weird sandstone incidents. Individually, they made little sense, but together they seemed to form a pattern - and a mystery. It began with the cutting down of road signs, then someone damaged some grading equipment and then it escalated to the harassment of environmentalists by a group of cowboys. Campers in the Grand Staircase reported shots fired into their camps at night, and a wave of petty vandalism rocked ranchers in surrounding towns. Garrett and Ateen decided if the incidents continued they would get to the bottom of it. This latest crime cranked up the intensity and had ominous implications, it marked the first time blood - albeit bovine - was spilled. The long simmering feud pitting locals and ranchers against the growing environmentalists appeared to be heating up.

At a favorite rest stop, Garrett sat on a rock and visualized the old line shack. To him and many others, the ranch shack was more than just a historic piece of architecture lost out on a remote and spectacular land, it was a monument to another time, one of the last true statements of the authentic old West. Simple, unadorned, homely. It became part of the land, and strangely, part of him. He admired its staunch, rugged and defiant posture. Destroying the old line shack was an act of hatred and its message was clear: the old West and the new West had just collided head-on. One way or another, he promised himself, I'll get to the bottom of this. He knew it wouldn't be easy. Like the land itself - with its colorations, nuances and contradictions - the truth of this mixed-up land dispute would be hard to decipher.

Back on the road he thought about a comeback book. This incident could be exactly what I need, he thought. If all hell breaks loose and somebody ends up dead, who better to tell the story? I'm not saying I want bloodshed, but if it's going to happen I should be the one to get the story. I've paid my dues! He had another reason as well, it would help reclaim the life he lost, the life some people concluded he simply threw away.

Hours later, he spotted red cliffs many miles to the south. He always liked the way the outcroppings jutted upward, lifting their chests to the sky as if trying to break free and rocket away. Settling back into his seat, he rolled down the window and took his foot off the accelerator. He had survived long enough to return.

5

Garrett Lyons always enjoyed departure. He liked the packing up and the gassing up and especially the part where he turned his back on his vacuous life in the city. Not long ago, he told Ateen, "Even though this is my home town, there is nothing for me here anymore. The city has been torn down and replaced by something I don't recognize; it scarcely resembles the place I was raised." There was no bitterness left in him. "Strange," he asked Ateen, "is this the way it is supposed to be?"

"Your soul is homeless," Ateen answered in the voice of a Dineh medicine man. "You need a place."

Late in the afternoon, Garrett arrived at Zion National Park, just as the towering cathedral tops burned with the last rays of the sun's light. Cool, obelisk-shaped, shadows crossed the canyon to meet great ponderosa pines standing on the pink and white shoals of the grand Checkerboard Mesa. The scale and beauty and colors and magic struck a nerve of hallowed melancholy within him.

Garrett no longer visited Zion, except to pass through it on his way to the deep outback. "Last year three million cars passed through the park," he told a half-filled auditorium during a reading of his last book, "and I was not in any one of them."

When he first discovered the park years ago, Zion was empty and he broke his pride against its quiet majesty more than once. He wrote, "Zion is one of those special places on Earth where you can stand alone, yet be in a rapturous communion with the larger family of life." Garrett loved the spires and monuments of Zion, but now searched the remote back to find the lost and broken pieces of his soul.

After meeting up with Ateen in Page, the two men started north to the crime scene at Fifty Mile Ridge. As the crow flies, their destination was only sixty miles away but because of Lake Powell and the impenetrable sandstone landscape surrounding it, they were forced to take a circuitous route, more than 160 miles across two famous dirt roads. From Page, they drove to Big Water, Utah then north on the wild and remote Smokey Mountain Road. This unmaintained track climbed Kaiparowits Plateau at the dangerous Kelley Grade before crossing the backbone of the one-hundred-mile plateau, slicing through the heart of the new Grand Staircase National Monument.

From Big Water, the Smokey Mountain Road cut across a barren oxide-blue plateau with enormous bronze-colored boulders standing like eerie goblins on the flat surface. The road worked across the second or middle level of a three tiered plateau, each tier separated by thousand foot cliffs. Below them was Lake Powell, its beautiful blue tentacles reaching into every gold canyon, and above them the towering escarpment of Kaiparowits Plateau - thousands of feet above.

"What were the elders talking about at the Bonanza?" Garrett finally inquired.

Ateen turned to him slowly, "Football."

"Come on!" Garrett exclaimed, "Get real! I saw what was going on. I know it was important."

"You want answers but are never satisfied when you get them." Ateen nodded and pointed to Garrett with his lips, "What are you afraid of Anglo?" His voice originated from deep inside his barrel chest. Garrett knew that when Ateen called him Anglo his patience was thin, so he just kept quiet and watched the road.

"What do you think, my friend," Ateen asked, straight faced, "Should the Washington Red Skins football team change its name?"

Garrett squirmed but remained silent.

"You are not an Indian but if you were an Indian, would you be offended?"

Silence.

"You asked," Ateen said smiling. "I am just telling you."

"What did they decide?" Garrett finally took the bait.

"That is Indian business and I cannot say." Ateen stared out the window, his massive frame impassive.

Fifteen miles north of Big Water, the road cut straight for the dangerous Kelley Grade and the threatening escarpment of the Kaiparowits. Blazed by cowboys a century ago wanting to move cattle to high grazing, the Kelley Grade snaked up an improbable path following seams and cracks in the cliffs and then up a series of steep switchbacks cut into sheer cliff faces to its top. In many places the roadway was only wide enough for a single vehicle. Nearing the grade, Garrett sat straight up, gripped the steering wheel and shifted into four-wheel drive. Ateen shifted as well, from one bun to the other, glancing at Garrett several times but not wanting to be noticed. Finally, he offered some encouragement, "Watch what you're doing here."

"Right arm." Garrett quipped, never taking his eyes from the road.

The first thousand feet were the easiest but after cresting a small ridge and making a hairpin turn to face the valley and lake, the grind became steeper and more narrow. On the inside, a wall of eroded rubble made of giant boulders stacked atop each other appeared so fragile it looked as if a minor disturbance might bring it all down. On the outside, the path was so narrow the truck's wheels rode inches from the crumbling edge and thousand foot drop-offs. The tires dug for traction on a bed of deteriorating gravel and marble-sized rocks.

Garrett kept as far away from the edge as possible; riding the clutch with one foot and the accelerator with the other - it was imperative to keep the engine's RPMs racing. A stalled engine meant certain death, before he would be able to restart the engine, the vehicle could slip back over the ball-bearing rocks and slide off the cliff. Twenty years earlier, the driver of a flat bed truck loaded with boy scouts missed a shift and stalled out. Before he could get the truck restarted, they went off the edge backwards, eight-hundred-feet to their death.

The last thousand feet to the top of the grade were the worst. The road serpentined back and forth across an exposed sandstone cliff face so narrow only one vehicle could go at a time. It was impossible to open either door here: on the inside was the cliff wall and on the outside, a two thousand foot drop off. Garrett held his breath and sped up, worried someone might start down from the opposite direction. Ateen straightened his legs, lifting himself up and filling the cabin.

Cresting the plateau they were relieved but did not speak. There was no reason for talk and they sat quietly, satisfied to watch the hypnotic dirt road wind endlessly ahead through cedar forests, around rock outcroppings, up and down washed out drainages, skirting around deep canyons, and along endless sagebrush flats. In some ways, the Kaiparowits is more inhospitable and more difficult than other places in sandstone country. Garrett liked to view the Kaiparowits from some far-off mountain or mesatop where he could see it in the distance - large, dark, mysterious and foreboding. It reminded him of Tarzan's escarpment in Edgar Rice Burroughs' books - an unknown and forbidding world surrounded by high cliffs where only the most foolhardy or adventurous risked exploration.

Garrett finally felt at ease. He looked at a faraway monolith at the horizon and saw his dead friend Mick's face carved into it. In the vast emptiness and rolling hills he saw the silhouette of Nancy's breasts and shoulders and hips lying supine across his bed. At the distant horizon, where the land and sky meet and are neither, he felt his mother watching him. They are all out there waiting for me, he lipped silently, somewhere in the misty blue horizon.

The two men stopped at a favorite turn-out and walked over tabletop sandstone to a rock outcropping where they could see one hundred-seventy-miles to the east. Garrett stood unmoving, spellbound by the scale and scope of the landscape. A few miles further, the road dropped into a deep intestine-like drainage where the canyon walls were so narrow Garrett felt claustrophobic and agitated. "These are the worst for me," he told Ateen. Ateen nodded. "I feel I can't breathe!" They worked along the canyon bottom for an hour before climbing out and being delivered onto a high ridge where new visions awaited.

"I'm glad the President established the national monument," Garrett commented, relieved.

"He has no authority here," Ateen shot back.

"What would you rather have, a monument or the coal mine?" Garrett was referring to Anaxalrad, the Dutch mining company, who planned to develop a rich seam of coal found under the plateau until the President's proclamation killed it.

"This land is more than a President or coal mine. It possesses power of great significance but your people do not see or feel it."

"I do!" Garrett protested, then asked, "My people?"

"Over there," Ateen pointed with his lips to some ridges off to the West, "The Hopi have been gathering ceremonial herbs for a thousand years. The monument will come and go but the Hopi will still gather there."

"Where's the monument going?"

"Its days are numbered." Ateen smiled, "Just as your days are numbered, my friend."

"What of the Dineh? Are its days numbered, too?"

"The Dineh and the Hopi and the true people will remain." He explained, "There is no ownership of this place. The land is just the land, as the Creator made it. The Hopi and Dineh respect this. Only the people who understand this will remain."

"Personally my friend, be that as it may, I'm glad no strip mine will be here . . . so you and the Hopi will not be bothered by it." He paused, thinking. "What I worry about is the new monument will bring families with kids. In a couple years, the entire god-damned place will be overrun with screaming kids and disposable diapers. There'll be RV pads, California morons, idiot tourists, and Mormon masses. Every goofy religious zealot will be saying it's their spiritual homeland."

"You mean people like you?" Ateen grinned.

"Hey! Fuck you, Ateen."

Garrett wanted to complain, to tell him how frustrating it's been being run out of all the national parks - Zion, Bryce, Arches, Capitol Reef, Canyonlands and the Grand Canyon - just ahead of the noise, the traffic and the tourists, but he decided to keep quiet. Ateen and his people faced their own abuse.

"The way you think," Ateen went on, "everything and everyone will be gone soon anyway. You are temporary. Your people are a temporary people. Be at peace with it, at least you won't have to worry too long."

"Until then," Garrett warned, "I'll tell everyone about the insects and snakes and dirt and especially about the stinkin', untrustworthy Injuns down here. I'll say, 'don't turn your back on 'em, they'll steal you blind.' They'll stay away in hoardes."

They laughed.

From the high places, the torrid sandstone sea of rock and sweeping vistas brought a sense of peace. They could even see the curvature of the earth. Years ago, this phenomenon troubled Garrett. It was easy for him to believe he was at the center of all creation, the biggest guy on the block, but when confronted with this colossal metric - the   ball-shaped Earth rolling through space - the significance of his insignificance frightened him.

As they moved through it, the land changed from rolling hills to deep canyons, from towering cliffs to forested flats, from slanting ridges to barren shelves, from dry washes to mesas and from steep drainages to petrified sand dunes. The land evolved, morphed and transformed. It repeated itself; beginning or ending something new; finishing or starting something old. It was unpredictable yet predictable, different but the same, unique but uniform.

Hour after hour they worked across the lonely plateau and every time the road turned south to face Navajo Mountain, anchoring the horizon many miles to the south, Ateen shifted in his seat, folded and unfolded his arms, and rocked from side to side. The Dineh Gods live on the mountain, and he was raised on its eastern foothills where the Ateen clan had lived for hundreds of years. He once told Garrett if everything else was destroyed, the mountain and Kaiparowits would remain untouched. "We will fight you Anglo," he told him, "if you come anywhere near them."

The sun arced across the heavens and the monuments and buttresses sundialed through time casting shadows across great expanses of hills and the lesser canyons that populate this land. This territory is a secret rock garden of Homeric pursuit; it is a place Cyclops and the Serene of Silence could breathe free and where lesser souls are humbled by its vast unadorned grandeur. In the late afternoon, they followed an old side road and camped in a hidden grove of cedar and juniper trees.

They arrived just as dusk settled in the cliff eddies and the silver fairy dust mixed with the umber, vermillion and golden oxide of the sandstone. At this time of day, the green of the high desert forest turned black and the tops of the blue sagebrush colonies in the chaparrals glowed as if by magic.

The pleasure of a good companion is one of life's greatest gifts, Garrett thought, and he enjoyed being with his friend again. We come from different worlds, but share a kinship to this place. Garrett collected dead wood while Ateen brought enormous stones - some weighing nearly a hundred pounds - to make a perfect fire ring. It was a silent choreography, a dance of camp set-up they had performed with an elegance and an economy all its own. From the pile of wood, Ateen chose only the right pieces and built an Anglo fire.

"I will build an Anglo fire - just for you," he said without looking up. "It will be big because you Anglo are small and afraid of the dark. An Indian fire is small - just right."

"Uh huh."

The burning wood filled the air with a heady perfume of cedar, juniper, frankincense and a touch of sage. Not far from camp was a high, plump, chocolate colored, breast-shaped dome, and as the golden sunset ripened, they trekked to its top to get a good look. The valley below was all shadows and silhouettes, hips and shoulders, bellies and buttocks. They sat in silence and watched until Ateen nodded his head and pointed with his lips to a tree at the base of the dome. "He is watching us," he said.

"What? Who?"

"Coyote. He is watching. There. He is the spirit of this place. I spotted him near camp. We are in his territory."

"Where? Oh yeah, I think I see him. Is he gone now?" Garrett could not get a fix.

Back in camp, they lost themselves in the campfire. When the flames died down Ateen added more wood. "Are you afraid?" he asked.

"Only when I see your face," Garrett answered.

Ateen nodded and pointed with his lips. Out in the darkness, two red eyes gleamed back at them. "Coyote," he whispered. For a while the three of them fell into the trance of the fire, each looking deep into its core.

Sometime around eleven, the sound of vehicles carried to them from some far off place. The sound drifted in and out, sometimes growing louder and seeming only a short distance away, other times fading out completely.

"Not my people," Ateen claimed, "they do not come here at night."

A few minutes later it was back, the sound of engines revving came from their left - but no road existed to the left. In the city, the sound of a single vehicle goes unnoticed, but in this place of great stillness, it reverberates off the sandstone and is amplified a hundred times. Suddenly, headlights illuminated a stand of cedar trees on a hilltop above them. Whoever it was, they were creating their own road, ripping the hillside apart, tearing through stands of sagebrush. The headlights grew more intense until suddenly a vehicle crested the ridge opposite them and rolled forward just enough to throw light down into their camp.

"Sons-of-bitches!" Garrett swore, standing.

Ateen disappeared behind a cedar tree.

Two vehicles joined the first at the top of the ridge, motors idling loudly. Over the wail of the engines came a mix of confused sounds - doors opening and closing, country music spilling out, men shouting and laughing and then glass breaking. Garrett and Ateen felt vulnerable, their unwelcome guests looking directly down a rocky hill and into camp.

After a few uncomfortable minutes, the unwanted visitors cut their engines and headlights but turned on a powerful spot light instead. They directed the beam into the forest and it illuminated everything with an eerie interplay of light and shadow. It moved back and forth systematically across the hillside until it finally came into their camp. Garrett stood in full view and flipped them the finger, "Turn that fucking light off!" he shouted.

The light moved off quickly, continuing to scan back and forth across the hill behind them. They were searching for something and after a long time they must have found it because the light stopped in an open area between some cedar trees. It was the coyote! The large mature male stood on the hill side hypnotized by the light, its red eyes gleaming back at them.

Cupping his hands Ateen and shouted, "Go! Go! Get out of here!"

An instant later, a deafening gun shot cracked out and the coyote winced, cried out in pain, circled itself once and then again - as if trying to get at its behind - before it curled into a ball and died.

"Muther fuckers!" Garrett screamed at the light.

"No!" Ateen whispered, "Get down. Don't let them spot you." He was now behind a rock. His obsidian eyes looked dead and his flat native features appeared warlike. Garrett moved into some bushes as the light flooded back into camp, searching back and forth, going from the truck to the campfire to the tent and back again.

"No good," Ateen said. The light moved away in ever larger concentric circles as the two men moved further away, into an impossible rock jumble where, if necessary, they could escape into a side canyon. Surprisingly, the spot light was turned-off and they heard doors closing and truck engines starting. From behind some trees, they watched the coyote killers leave, moving off in the other direction, down the hillside and into another section of country.

Back in camp, Garrett got a beer from the cooler and Ateen retrieved an ancient .22 caliber rifle he brought for protection. His gestures were those of a warrior making ready to fight. His wide fleshy face glowed in the firelight and Garrett saw a familiar determination and outrage. For a moment, Ateen was an Indian brave of the old West, defending his land against evil white men, and then a moment later, he was a U. S. Army ranger moving silently through the jungle of Vietnam.

Suddenly, before either realized what was happening, three trucks rounded the hillside on the dirt road and descended into their camp, coming to a skidding stop and throwing up a wall of dust and dirt. Garrett moved back behind the vehicle and opened his beer with a defiant gesture. Ateen stood at the center of the cloud in front of the truck, legs spread apart, rifle positioned in the direction of their unwelcome guests.

"Seen any coyotes?" a man shouted from the lead vehicle.

Ateen said nothing, impassively looking at them.

"Just the one you killed." Garrett called out.

Three men bailed out of the lead vehicle. They did not approach but stood several feet apart, near the truck. They wore working ranch wear and cowboy hats.

"Care for a beer?" the driver asked politely, retrieving several cans from a cooler in the bed of the truck. He moved forward holding a can out but Ateen did not move and the man stopped abruptly short.

"Beer?" he asked again, holding it out.

No answer.

"We've got our own," Garrett finally replied. "Lookin for more coyotes?"

"We're always lookin' to kill varmints," he answered, "but tonight we're hopin' to find bigger game, some goddamned cattle killers."

"Yeah . . ."

"Yeah, some son-of-a-bitchin' environmentalist muther-fuckers shot a bunch of 'em over on the Hole in the Rock and left 'em to rot."

"We heard. . . "

"Burned a line shack down. . . "

"Yeah," Garrett tried again, "We . . . "

"Been here long?" the man interrupted.

"Since this afternoon."

"Campin'?"

"Right."

"Huntin'?" he asked, looking at Ateen and his rifle.

Garrett had seen Ateen's posture like this only once before - the day Ateen saved him. It was the posture of brave men who have heard enough. It was time to stand their ground; their next move was often lethal.

Ateen did not answer.

"No. No, we're not hunting," Garrett answered, moving a few feet toward the men, "We're not hunting anything - except some peace of mind maybe. . ."

"What caliber is that rifle you got there?" The man asked.

"You the law?" Ateen barked, almost shouting.

"Nope, ain't the law," the polite cowboy answered, shuffling his feet back and forth, pushing dirt into little piles. He wore expensive lizard skin boots. His hands were on his hips, near an old West styled revolver and holster. "Nope. I ain't the law," he repeated. His eyes were hidden under the brim of his hat.

".22 caliber," Garrett answered, nervously. "And yours?"

"Colt .45," the cowboy answered, looking down proudly at his holstered side arm. "You can't hit shit with that .22 pea shooter you got there," he said in a half mocking voice. "That thing's only good for pingin' targets."

"I can hit shit all right. . ." Ateen said, his voice deadpan. "Right between the eyes."

There was a long and uncomfortable silence and everyone stood motionless. Ateen did not take his eyes off the coyote killers, but moved back out of the headlights and into the darkness. He stood near a wide cedar tree where he could see the men better. Garrett stayed put and engaged in small talk. The two other cowboys looked anxiously back and forth as if waiting for someone to make a move.

From inside one of the other trucks someone shouted, "Come on Cody! These ain't the ones. Let's go. I'm leavin' - back to town." Without waiting for a reply, the driver barreled off, churning up a cloud of dust and spraying rocks as he raced away. The second vehicle followed.

"Alright," the polite cowboy said, tipping his hat, "Sorry to bother you. . . guess it's time for more beer."

Ateen and Garrett said nothing. They stood in the roadway listening long after the coyote killers were gone.

The next morning, they went out to find the coyote. It was not dead, it pulled itself into the brush and laid out to die. The cowboy's bullet severed its spinal cord and its back legs hung lifeless behind it. There was nothing they could do. The coyote panted and looked terrified as they approached. Garrett leaned over and slowly poured water from a bottle over its muzzle. The beautiful creature lifted its head, licked with its tongue to drink. For a moment, the coyote seemed to relax as if it knew they were wanting to help. Before Garrett could stand and move away, Ateen stepped past him and finished the coyote off with a single shot from his rifle to its head.

CHAPTER TWO

An armada of cumulus clouds sailed southwest on a ocean of blue sky, their polyp bottoms tinted red by the sandstone below. The men drove the last twenty-five-miles to Escalante in an uneasy silence. The image of the coyote made it difficult to acknowledge the serenity, the blue sky or the heralding sandstone formations.

This section of the Kaiparowits was dry and dusty and defeated. The high desert forest of cedar and juniper lay in ruin, as if some angry retreating army, determined to kill everything in its path, destroyed it. It wasn't an army but loggers who destroyed everything for a few marketable trees, then ranchers followed up by chaining what remained so their cows could graze. Great piles of root balls and debris were scattered here and there, dotting the landscape like the discarded bones of enemies.

Working down the plateau's gradual decline into Escalante they spotted a few outlying homesteads and feed lots and garbage dumps and sagebrush flats dotting the hills.

"Doo Doo, look! There!" Ateen nodded, pointing with his lips. "A badger. Gold and black."

Garrett saw something disappear into the sagebrush as they passed.

Doo Doo was Garrett's Indian name. The complete name was "Makes Doo Doo in His Pants." The name was bestowed upon him by Jack Crank, a fearsome Navajo warrior who hated all whites and most everyone else as well.

Jack Crank came up with the name Thanksgiving night a few years earlier after a traditional turkey dinner when Garrett and a group Navajo men crowded into a small sweat lodge. An hour or so later, Garrett developed terrible gas. No one said a word but looked around, each raising his shoulders as if to say, it wasn't me. "Whew!" Crank finally said, "I know who did it, it's Anglo stench." Crank turned to Ateen, "It's your friend, Ateen, Makes Doo Doo in His Pants." The gathering broke into laughter, they rocked back and forth, slapping their knees. Garrett was embarrassed, but mostly relieved Crank was not angry.

"Good eyes, Fry Bread." Garrett answered. He gave that name to him when he learned that Ateen couldn't stomach the traditional Navajo staple.

"Seeing a badger is a good omen." Ateen added, smiling. "Something important is going to happen." Ateen's heaviness departed. "Tell me, Doo Doo, is it easier to break wind then straighten your pants or straighten them first?"

"Come what may," Doo Doo answered, "my pants fend for themselves."

It was a great honor for a white man to be gifted an Indian name, especially by such a feared and respected warrior as Crank. Jack Crank was crazy in the old Navajo way, his famed courage was really a disguise for a kind of wild recklessness. Many Dineh who displayed this same bravado were killed when the long rifles of the U.S. Cavalry arrived in Indian country 150 years ago. Crank hated all white men; his family was nearly wiped out by Kit Carson's army eight generations ago.

"I'm wondering, Fry Bread," Doo Doo went on, "are you still investigating people who hang out at the fry bread stands in Tuba City?"

"I only investigate you, Doo Doo," Fry Bread answered. "We Dineh have decided to keep an eye on you. . . we have a rich tradition of helping ruminators . . . to help keep their pants clean."

Garrett smiled and sat forward. "That reminds me, speaking of keeping things clean, I've been wondering, since your people profess to love Mother Earth so much, why do you pile junk cars and old refrigerators and garbage in your front yards?"

"For us, when a thing's usefulness is finished, it no longer exists. It is irrelevant. We don't see it."

"You expect me to believe that?"

"We do not expect you to believe anything. We are not the Jones or the Smiths or the Doo Doos. We do not have expectations. . ."

" But Fry Bread, it looks bad . . . it's . . ." he stopped, turning to face Ateen.

"Perhaps," Ateen said with an Asiatic look," you should point that same discerning eye inside yourself. Criticizing the Dineh will not make you feel better."

"I see. I get it," he replied, rounding a corner, "Point well taken . . ."

Coming out of a tight turn, they saw smoke coming from the large

17

elaborately carved wooden sign welcoming visitors to the new monument. Not only had someone torched the sign but they pushed over the cement foundation. The wood sign still smoldered and Ateen and Garrett doused it with piss and water from their canteens.

Until recently, the community of Escalante slumbered in a one-hundred-year-long isolation. Wedged in a valley surrounded by desolate outback, Escalante was so far out of the stream of events it developed its own unique way of doing and seeing things. The townsfolk of Escalante didn't accept the new monument. Outsiders showed up in expensive SUVs and bought the best lands. They built fancy houses and log cabins, fenced off acreage, posted no trespassing signs and then they left, coming back only occasionally for a weekend. The entrepreneurs arrived too, pouring cash into long-closed buildings on Main Street and hawking tee shirts, postcards, cheap Indian jewelry and coffee lattes to monument visitors. At either end of town, new fancy gas station/food marts opened, selling beer and killing business on Main Street. For the first time, residents locked their front doors and took keys from car ignitions.

Garrett and Ateen gassed up at Thompson's, the oldest gas station on Main Street. Ateen noticed one of the coyote killer's trucks parked across the street at the Golden Loop Cafe, next to a line of Garfield County deputy sheriffs' Chevy Blazers. The deputies sat in a window booth, drinking coffee lazily and gazing out the grease-covered window, watching the few cars move through town. If nerves were on edge about the cow killings and the arson it wasn't noticeable.

Two miles outside of town, they turned south onto the Hole in the Rock Road. It was good to be on dirt again and they settled in for the long drive. Sixty miles later, at the foot of Fifty Mile Ridge, they turned on a side road leading into the hidden box canyon where the famous line shack stood for more than one hundred years. Nestled against the base of the two-thousand-foot ridge, the cabin sat in one of several sandstone folds that reminded Garrett of the cascading gowns Michelangelo draped over his models and chiseled from marble. The box canyon was a natural amphitheater with perfect acoustics, every sound and vibration echoed and reverberated again and again.

Garrett loved this place and a special energy seemed to reside here. In the mornings and at dusk, time slowed down and magic was suspended in the air. He often camped next to the shack, laying on his tarp and gazing up, transfixed by the towering Fifty Mile Ridge and the stars above it. But now, all that was left of the shack was a rectangular-shaped pile of burned and blackened rubble. Neither man exited the truck, they just sat staring, shocked at the sight.

"The door was never locked," Garrett said, finally climbing out. "But I never went in."

Ateen nodded.

"Inside sat a simple wood table covered with a calico tablecloth, two iron frame beds, a small desk and an old wood burning stove. I could see it all through the window."

Only the bed's iron headboards now stood above the rest of the blackened rubble around it.

"Mountain goat and deer horns hung on the walls over there," Garrett pointed.

"You never went in?" Ateen asked, looking over the scene.

"I didn't want its essence to escape. It was enough to look through the windows. Dorothea Lange, the famous photographer, stayed here in 1935 when she came looking for her friend, Everett Ruess, who disappeared nearby."

Ateen nodded, "I know his story." He walked the perimeter looking for clues.

"I would stand right here," Garrett went on, "at the front windows and look inside. I would imagine Lange standing on the inside of the window, just few feet away and looking out. I imagined the sadness and the searching in her eyes."

"You loved this woman?" Ateen asked without looking up.

"Love her? She died before I was born."

"You profess to love 'em all."

"Yeah? I loved the idea of her being right here at this exact spot just two feet away but separated by sixty years."

The Anasazi Indians lived in the box canyon for a thousand years before the line shack was built. The canyon walls were covered with pictographs and steps chipped into the sandstone climbed hundreds of feet to unknown destinations. On his first visit, Garrett climbed some steps high above the canyon floor until he realized his precarious position and froze. One misstep meant falling to certain death so he pressed himself against the sheer rock wall and lowered himself down - spread eagle - one step at a time.

The two men walked around the structure again and again. There was nothing they could do but they didn't want to leave. Garrett sat on a sandy hill and replayed every detail of the cabin in his mind. It may be gone, he thought, but I will remember it exactly as it was. It will live within me - as all my loved ones do.

Back on the road a mile or two further where the trail juts up against Fifty Mile Ridge, they spotted the cow carcasses. They looked like dark round stones standing against the gold and vermillion rock on either side of the road. Some were shot just a few feet from the road, others not far away on a hillside. Some appeared as if they tried to run while others fell where they stood. The carcasses were neither bloated nor deflated, inside a toxic mix roiled with fly larvae and feasting insects. Garrett moved in closer but was repelled by the smell. He covered his mouth and nose with his shirt and tried again, but it was no use. Ateen moved past him, going from one carcass to the other, searching and chanting in Dineh. Garrett looked on from a distance.

"Scavengers will take care of them," Ateen reassured him as he crossed the road to look at those shot on the hillside. Back and forth he went, tracking this way and then that way, disappearing over a ridge, reappearing back on the road some distance away, disappearing again.

Garrett retrieved a bottle of Scotch and took a big, cleansing swallow then drenched a paper towel and covered his nose and mouth. He sipped Scotch, happy to do nothing except consider the mysterious situation and wait. When Ateen didn't return, he drove to a nearby campsite and got comfortable.

Out of the long dusk, Ateen appeared coming up the road.
"Something's wrong," he said, shaking his head, "it isn't right."

"I should say not," Garrett answered, quite drunk by now. "Why would someone . . . "

"Listen," Ateen demanded, "the tracks, the shell casings, the slugs, the tire prints, none of it makes sense."

"Yeah?"

"The story of the killing is all wrong."

"I don't get it." Garrett was excited.

"It is not as I was told. It makes no sense. "

Ateen explained that the sheriff in Page told him it appeared that some environmentalists traveling in one vehicle killed the cows with cheap assault weapons, probably tech nines. He told Ateen they were bad shots and missed more times than they hit. In some cases, instead of taking the cows with a single shot, it appeared they were shot multiple times as if the shooters were amateurs.

"What did you find?"

Ateen handed Garrett a single shell casing and several slugs dug from the bodies. "No amateurs. No tech nines," he said. "This is a military round. A restricted military round. High power. Armor tipped. Civilians never see these." Garrett held a slug between his thumb and forefinger and examined it.

"Security forces only." Ateen went on. "Delta Force. Secret Service. NSA. CIA."

Garrett laughed as if Ateen just told a great joke. "Secret Service? CIA?"

"I told you it wasn't right." Ateen raised and lowered his shoulders. He went to a container of water and gestured for Garrett to pour water over his hands.

After sharing bread, cheese and canned fish the two bedded down on a tarp Garrett spread over a flat area. Lying on their backs, arms behind their heads, they watched the Milky Way fill in the sky with starlight. The night was moonless and the light from the Milky Way illuminated Fifty Mile Ridge with an unreal light.

Before dawn, Ateen left camp and much later Garrett awoke to the sun in his eyes. At first, he pulled his hat over his face, turned onto his side and continued his alcohol-induced slumber. It wasn't until the sun's heat and insects droning above awoke him that he sat up and looked around. His mouth was dry and without fully knowing what he was doing, he got to his feet and stumbled to the truck for water.

It was already hot and he plunked down in a fold-out chair. He spent most of the day sleeping, writing and thinking. In the late afternoon, the heat and silence combined with the solitude and suddenly, Garrett thought he heard the voice of his best friend, Mick Tripp, calling to him from somewhere out on the land. He jumped to his feet, turned in a circle and searched the horizon. He suddenly realized that he was standing in the exact place where, ten years earlier, his friend Mick told him he loved him. Garrett looked down at the ground, searching for Mick's footprints but they were gone. Just one month before Mick killed himself, the two escaped the city and took refuge here. For many days they hiked fast without destination or stopping to rest; they searched every alcove and hidden

21

draw, every slope and amphitheater. They dropped stones into canyons and climbed high onto the shoals of Fifty Mile Ridge.

During a cavalier moment, as the two friends stood surveying a fine prospect of land, Garrett told him, "I believe the face of every man, woman and child who has ever lived can be found out here in the sandstone cliffs and shadows."

Turning to him, Mick gallantly replied, "If that is so, my friend, then I, too, shall one day reside here."

Since Mick's death, Garrett has seen his face three times out on the land. The first time he was watching a magnificent sunset above Arch Canyon when out on the serrated horizon, the silhouette of Mick's face appeared. It was perfect to a minute detail. The next time, he was atop Grandview Point in Canyonlands when Mick's face took shape in the morning shadow of Junction Butte below; it moved across an expanse of sagebrush flats until it twisted, contorted and became unrecognizable. The last time he saw Mick's face, it was rendered on a palette of rain-soaked, vermillion-colored Kayenta sandstone above Davis Gulch, a half mile from where he and Ateen were now camped.

"Hey Mick," Garrett shouted into the unattached solitude, "You out there?"

From behind him, below in Davis Gulch came a reply, " Down here!"

Garrett ran down the sandy hill toward the canyon some distance away, stopping every few feet to listen or to call out - but there was no reply. At the canyon edge, he searched the darkened narrows. More to himself than to Mick, he asked, "What am I lookin' at on the other side, bro'? Are you still alive?"

From somewhere below Mick shouted back, "Lyons, the only thing waiting for you is an icy black river of night!" There was a brief silence then Mick cut loose with his famous horse laugh, the one Garrett loved to hate when Mick was alive.

Ateen showed up late and looked beat. He held up his palm, "Yutahey, Doo Doo."

"Yutahey."

Ateen retrieved a gallon of cold water. He was exhausted and perplexed, but could see something strange in his friend's face. "Dancin' with your dead friends again?" he asked.

Garrett ignored his question, "Find what you were looking for?"

"I found what I wasn't looking for."

"How so?"

"I found nothing. This was a professional job. A thorough clean up. It is not what we think."

"What then?"

Ateen's shoulders slumped and his head moved back and forth. "Can't say."

The next morning they packed and left, traveling past the rotting carcasses and the burned out line-shack back across the difficult road. Ateen stopped at every side road, checking for recent tire tracks.

At one road leading to the spectacular but little visited place named Egypt, he spotted tire tracks he had seen at the crime scene. Garrett knew this road well, Egypt was one of his hiding places. For years he base-camped on the cliff edge of Egypt and hiked into the deep maze of the Escalante River where few ever go. He loved this section of land but ultimately moved on after the BLM built a small parking lot and placed sign-in sheets for hikers.

They decided to investigate. The area's name came from a group of remarkable white and pink freestanding Luxor-like towers and pharoah-shaped sandstone formations sitting among some red hills along a ridge. Garrett hadn't been there in years and felt the strange sense of homecoming. Why did I ever leave this place? he asked himself.

At the road's end, where the cliffs drop into the Escalante River drainage, they found a beautifully preserved old VW camper bus. It sat in a campsite surrounded by cedar trees and hidden by a ridge of boulders. No one was around so they checked the vehicle's tires.

"This is it. This VW was there," Ateen declared.

"Colorado plates," Garrett added.

"Two people carrying heavy packs. Leading to the trailhead," Ateen told him, pointing to some tracks in the sand. "A man and woman."

"Check this," Garrett said, pointing to a bumper sticker, "EarthIsland - Activists Against Destruction."

"I've heard of them," Ateen said. "From Colorado or Oregon."

"Anarchists, right?"

Ateen shook his head. "What are they doing here? This is not their country."

"They're out of their element."

After checking the VW out, they doubled-backed a half mile to a campsite with a commanding view of the massive Escalante drainage and the VW campsite. The next day they waited, squatting under a centuries-old cedar tree, trying to keep out of the oppressive heat. In the late afternoon, three vehicles traveling caravan-style rolled into the trailhead parking area.

Garrett watched with binoculars as the motley crew of men and women piled out and set up camp. They parked near the VW and some cupped their eyes against its windows to get a look inside. It appeared they were searching for the VW's owners. Some wore long hair and others shaved heads, some wore baggy shorts and flip flops, others military-style fatigues; still others stripped down and went naked. They pitched tents, gathered firewood and prepared to cook. The sound of drums floated up to Garrett and Ateen.

Three more vehicles arrived, adding ten or fifteen people. By late afternoon, a total of eight trucks and vans congregated at the VW camp. Ateen counted twenty-eight people and half as many dogs. It looked like a rainbow family reunion: as each new group arrived, everyone greeted the newcomers with hugs and handshakes. They drank deer, passed pipes, played hackey sack and frisbee, and danced to the drums.

Deciding to find out what was going on, Ateen crept through the trees and rocks and bushes until he was behind their camp. He climbed a house-sized boulder and crawled on his stomach to a place where he was right above them. At about the same time, a group of men standing near one vehicle moved into an open area. To Garrett's amazement and horror they were carrying military-styled assault weapons. Some looked like Kalisnikovs with no stalk and large banana-shaped clips, others were long barreled rifles with sniper's scopes. They passed the weapons back and forth as if showing them off.

"Come on, Ateen." Garrett said, to himself nervously. "Get the hell out of there." Garrett was worried, if Ateen hadn't seen the guns, he needed to somehow alert him. Stay put, he told himself, you'll only make matters worse. Without warning, one of the men stepped away from the group, pointed his weapon to the sky and let go a burst of automatic machine gun fire. The others followed, squeezing off hundreds of rounds into the air.

Garrett looked back to the rock where Ateen was hiding but he was gone. He scanned the rocks and trees and could not see a thing. For a moment, he panicked, fearing Ateen was discovered and taken hostage. Luckily, Ateen appeared moving quickly back to camp.

"We'd better get outta here," Garrett blurted out.

"How? They will hear us. We can't let them follow."

"Who are they?"

"Dunno. License plates from Utah, Colorado, Oregon, Washington, Delaware, Minnesota. . . All EarthIsland."

"Bumper stickers?"

"Yep. They don't like cows or cowboys."

"Doesn't surprise me."

"They bitched about being framed for killing the cows. They want to find out who really did it. They are afraid and angry. They're supposed to meet up with the people in the VW - someone important - but they are worried someone snatched them. . . They think the cowboys shot their own cows. "

"Why?"

"To start a fight. To get public support. To collect the insurance."

Later as night fell, they watched the congregation gather at a bonfire. They beat drums and danced, sometimes linking hands and moving in a circle. Their celebration continued late and in the firelight, they looked like scarecrows moving in herky-jerky movements and casting long shadows that stretched out into the darkness. Some drank alcohol and took turns leaping over the fire until one fell into the flames and had to be pulled out by the others.

CHAPTER THREE

Garrett awoke to find Ateen standing over him. He never intended to sleep but once the late-night party ended he slipped off laying atop the boulder. Ateen motioned him to follow. At a stand of junipers atop a nearby hill they stopped.

"We need to get out," Garrett insisted.

"Can't! Not without them knowing."

"We'll chance it, they're asleep now."

"Too dangerous."

"What then?"

"We need a plan," Ateen answered. He believed the newcomers would definitely find their camp that day and when they did it would mean trouble. He had seen men stoked-up by gun play in Vietnam and knew how things could get crazy.

"That's why we need to get out," Garrett told him. "Before it gets ugly."

Ateen nodded.

"Think they did it?" Garrett asked, pacing back and forth, "killed the cows?"

"The guns make it look bad - but they talked like it wasn't them."

"What about the people in the VW?"

"Right."

"If I had proof, I'd get the sheriff. . . "

"What would that do," Ateen interrupted, "other than start a blood bath? We need proof."

"If I could just talk to them. . . "

"But how do you propose that, Doo Doo? Walk on down there and introduce yourself? You could say, 'Hey, by the way, we noticed you have some guns down here, did you shoot those god-damned cows and burn the line shack?'"

"It's an idea."

"A bad idea."

After a long time Garrett had another idea. He outlined the plan to Ateen who listened, nodded and smiled. Back to camp they loaded food, water and sleeping bags into backpacks and headed down to the cliff edge. They hiked in the opposite direction of the EarthIsland camp. To avoid leaving tracks, they hop-scotched from one piece of tabletop sandstone to the next wherever possible.

Years earlier, Garrett discovered a dangerous Anasazi Indian trail leading down off the plateau and linking up with the main Escalante trail some distance away. He used the nearly eroded-away trail only once, concluded it was too dangerous and never used it again. At the place where he remembered the trail started he searched back and forth along the cliff line until he discovered a small pile of rocks. "Here!" he called out, excited. "I piled the rocks myself."

The trail was barely distinguishable and looked very dangerous. Back and forth it wound down the two-thousand-feet escarpment, cutting across nearly impossible areas where water and wind had nearly worn the narrow groove away. In some places the trail was nothing more than a rounded niche in the smooth stone. Luckily, at the most dangerous and frightening places, the Anasazi carved handholds and deeper steps.

By midmorning, Garrett and Ateen rested on a shaded shelf below the cliff before starting across a cedar covered ridge that intersected with the main trail a few miles away. Scattered along the way, they discovered pottery shards and an occasional Anasazi burial mound. The solace and peace were undisturbed in this seldom visited place, few white men ever came here. They worked through the trees and boulders and hills and hidden drainage canyons in a meandering fashion, taking time to relish the solitude. The silence satisfied both and they loved wandering in an aimless fashion, able to muse with little thought of destination or time passing.

Ateen scanned the surroundings, moving his head back and forth methodically as he walked. It was a practice that saved his life - and many others - time and again in Vietnam. As a child he was taught to keep his eyes moving and unfocused as he walked the forests of his beloved Navajo Mountain. It was at the periphery that spirits and apparitions appeared and one could only spot them by unfocusing and keeping the eyes moving. His fellow Army Rangers were convinced he had special powers because he was an Indian.

Passing a small ravine, Ateen spotted an old Navajo man sitting on a flat rock next to a tangle of uprooted cedar trees. When he looked again the man was gone. This old man, who he was convinced was his great- great grandfather, appeared to Ateen many times over the years. The first time it happened was when Ateen was a child and lost on the mountain with his dog. The old man stepped out of the trees and told him of a secret cave nearby where he could rest before going home. The old man told him that the ancestors once practiced important ceremonies at the cave. The cave's walls were covered with beautiful paintings and the bones of many people were lined up in rows where someone stacked them. The old man told him that great sacrifices were made there and only the most pure of the Dineh knew of its existence.

Later, after the old man showed him the path home and young Ateen asked his granny about the old man and after describing him, she became excited and cried. She told him the man was most likely her great grand-father, a man who went onto the mountain and never returned. Over the years, people claimed to have seen him or even talked to him but, all these many years later, he must be long dead. "He disappeared eighty years ago," she told him through her tears, "when I was just fifteen- years-old." Ateen returned to the place his great-great grandfather showed him the cave but it was gone. For many years afterwards, he searched for the cave but never located it.

Over the years, his great-great grandfather appeared time and again. Once, when he was in the jungle of Vietnam, Ateen and his company were sweeping through a dense rain forest at the center of VC territory when he appeared in a clearing right before a terrible fire fight. He held a finger to his lips and waved his arms back and forth alerting Ateen that an ambush lay ahead. Ateen instructed everyone to get down and averted the ambush, saving many lives. Another time, he appeared in San Francisco when Ateen was drunk in Golden Gate Park. "I do not come to chastise you," he said, "but to tell you that your path may be difficult and painful, but it is a test - it has great heart and will lead to wisdom and leadership." He then placed his hand on his great-great grandson's shoulder and told him, "Son, it is time to go home."

At the juncture where the old Anasazi trail intersected the main Escalante trail, they rested in a stand of cedars near some unusual rock out-croppings that looked like a half-buried spaceship. They were tired and sat in the dappled shade drinking water. Garrett pulled tuna, cheese, crackers, nuts and dried figs from his pack. Using his Swiss army knife, he opened the tuna and sliced cheese. From where they sat, it was three miles to the Escalante River going east and, in the other direction, a half mile to the base of the cliff and the trail up to the trailhead where the EarthIslanders were camped. Garrett's plan was to fool the gun-toting radicals into believing they were backpackers just returning from the Escalante River below. He figured that by the time they descended the cliff, made their way to the main Escalante trail and then hiked back up to the trailhead, the EarthIslanders would have found their vehicle and would have no idea they had been spying on them. Once at the trailhead, they would ask questions. This ruse was not without risk, but its merits could produce the information they needed.

Sitting with his back to a knarled tree trunk Ateen nodded to Garrett that someone was coming. Garrett turned to see two backpackers coming from the direction of the Escalante River. At first, the man and woman seemed to recognize them, as if they expected to find someone waiting. They smiled and waved but as they neared their expressions turned to surprise and even concern. The man was tall and handsome and strong looking, his stride across the tabletop sandstone was long and confident. He was shirtless, wore shorts and well-worn high top leather boots; he carried a large, heavy-looking backpack whose straps pulled tightly across his muscled shoulders. Behind him, the woman was petite and athletic looking. She was sunburned and tanned, her face hidden under the shade of a long brimmed cap except for her smile.

"Greetings," Garrett called out.

"Greetings to you," the man responded, smiled and stopped on the trail a few feet away.

"Water?" Garrett asked, holding out a large container.

"No," the man answered straight away, "that's very generous but we can't do that."

"Do what?" Garrett hopped to his feet and extended the bottle, "We have plenty. Runnin' low?"

Garrett learned years earlier to recognize people in need of water. These two were classic cases, as soon as he mentioned water, he saw their Adam's apples move up and down.

"You have enough?" the man asked.

"Plenty. Always carry extra. Never know when you'll need it."

The man stepped forward, took the container and passed it to his companion who hesitated at first then took a drink and passed it back. He tipped his head back, brought the bottle to his lips and drank deeply.

"Thank you," the woman said politely.

"The truth is," the man admitted, wiping his lips, "we finished our last drink - what we'd been saving for the hike out - an hour ago." He extended his arm, trying to hand the bottle back.

"No, no." Garrett insisted and sat down, "Go for it. We have plenty. Fabulous day, isn't it?"

"Thanks," the man bowed, passing the bottle back to his friend who did not hesitate this time.

"It's important if you're thirsty." Ateen added.

Over the years, Garrett helped many people with water. This landscape was famous for making destinations appear closer than they really were. Hikers were drawn out onto the land and then ran out of water.

The couple passed the bottle back and forth. "You just comin' in?" the man asked.

"We're heading out," Garrett motioned to the cliff top behind him. "We camped over in Coyote Gulch."

"You can get to Coyote from here?" the man asked.

"Yeah. Anasazi trail. It's wild. It meets up right here." He pointed toward the trail and changed the subject. "You heading out?"

"We're coming from the river. We spent a two days exploring. . ."

"Have you ever been there?" the woman asked Garrett, interrupting.

"A few times," Garrett smiled.

"It's truly entrancing," she exclaimed. "It's the most magical place I've ever been. It is so quiet . . . and we found ruins and pottery shards and corn cobs. There's a hidden spring ten-feet-deep filled with ice cold clear water in a secret cleft in the canyon wall. It's totally amazing."

Ateen nodded, but kept his eyes lowered.

"For a second, we thought you were our friends," the woman confided coming closer, standing in the shade.

"Seen anyone?" the man asked.

"Nope. You're the first in days."

They were Jonah Sandborn, a photographer from Colorado, and Petra Greenfield, a graduate school political science major at an East Coast ivy league school. Jonah was intense and straight forward, at the same time, he was polite but couldn't take his eyes off the Indian, Ateen. Petra was enraptured with the land and its power and could hardly contain her enthusiasm.

Ateen stared into the trees or at some stones near his feet. He possessed an Asiatic look that seemed to say that he knew what was on the other side of things. Garrett sliced more cheese and retrieved apples from his pack. As he did, his cell phone dropped out.

"That thing work?" Jonah asked.

"Sorry you had to see that," Garrett said, truly embarrassed. "I hate the fucking things - for emergencies only. Won't work down here but up on the mesa it might." Garrett put the phone back in his pack. "You meeting friends?"

"Uh huh," Petra said, "friends."

"Any cars at the trailhead when you came in?" Jonah enquired.

"Just a VW camper."

"That's us," Jonah responded and seemed surprised. "No one else?"

Ateen stretched out along the rock, gazed blankly into the forest then darted a look into Jonah's eyes. Garrett shook his head negatively and acted as if he heard nothing unusual.

"We got here early," Petra went on, "we wanted to do some exploring and enjoy the peace and quiet."

"People are coming from around the country," Jonah added. "Most have never been here. It will be interesting."

"What's the plan?" Garrett asked, "Hiking, camping, sightseeing?"

"Good question," Jonah answered, quizzically. "We'll see. Time will tell."

"It's best to come alone," Ateen added. "This is a place to be with yourself. No one else."

"I'm sure you're right," Jonah agreed. "But it's too late now. At least we had a few good days."

For a half hour they shared figs and water and cheese and crackers and apples and Garrett kept slicing as they ate. Jonah, who at first seemed cautious, was friendly now. He talked about the land's magic and how glad he was to visit. Everyone deserves to come here and find this place as undisturbed as it was when it was created million of years ago, he told them.

After eating they decided to hike out together and pulled on their packs. Jonah peppered Garrett and Ateen with questions about the places and distances and roads and terrain. He realized his hiking companions were the real deal, desert rats whose spirit or personality brought them to this wilderness. He sensed they possessed a wisdom and knowledge that

31

came from many solitary journeys here.

Garrett told him about the young poet Everett Ruess and his disappearance near here in 1934. He also told him about the early explorers including Charles Bernheimer, the last of the Victorian explorers, who tried unsuccessfully for two years in the 1920s to circumvent the sandstone maze surrounding Navajo Mountain and find a land route to Rainbow Bridge. Finally, at the end of the second expedition funded by the National Geographic Society, Bernheimer used dynamite to blast through a series of sandstone fins opening a route to the famed Rainbow Bridge. Jonah and Petra had never heard of the expedition or of the Bernheimer Trail.

"The trail hasn't been used in forty years," Ateen told him. "Not since the dam filled Glen Canyon. People float to Rainbow Bridge. No need to hike."

"Too bad about the dam," Jonah added, shaking his head and glancing at his companions to gauge their response.

"I hate the son-of-bitch," Garrett said.

His response excited Jonah, "Someone needs to do something about it."

"Like what?" Garrett asked

"Blow it up?" Ateen queried.

"It's not a bad idea."

"Be patient," Ateen offered, "this dam will be gone one day."

"As will all of us," Garrett countered.

"No need to worry," Ateen went on. "Time will do the work."

"I know people who don't want to wait," Jonah added. "They believe it represents a danger for today and tomorrow."

Neither Garrett nor Ateen responded, it was not that they did not have anything to say but they had arrived at the base of the difficult trail climbing to the top of the escarpment. As they rested before making the ascent, the sound of voices echoed down. The voices came from the cliff edge more than fifteen-hundred-feet above. Someone was calling out greetings to Jonah and Petra.

"It's Llan and Isis and Ronin," Petra said, looking up. Cupping her hands she hollered back, "Hellooo. . . We're coming!" A volley of salutations came back, bouncing and reverberating down off the rocks.

Turning to his companions, Jonah asked, "Have you heard of EarthIsland?"

"Once or twice." Garrett shot back, "Seen their bumper stickers.

Environmentalists?"

"Right."

"You one of them?" Ateen asked.

"Yes," Petra answered smiling, happy to hear the voices of her friends above. "Jonah is the leader, he organized the group."

"What do you stand for?" Ateen inquired.

"We believe it is time to take a stand - on things like the dam. We confront those who pollute and destroy the land for profit. We take the initiative where others - the more established groups - work through the system." He went on, "We are a coalition of sorts, a bunch of different groups rolled into one, an offshoot really - of people dissatisfied with the pace of the movement."

"What are you doing here?" Garrett asked.

"A retreat," Petra answered, enthusiastically. "We came here to contemplate and clear our heads. Most of us have heard of this place for years, so we decided to meet here."

"What about grazing?" Ateen interjected.

Jonah took a deep breath, "There are good places to graze cows. There are millions of acres, in fact, but unfortunately none of them are located here on this particular landscape. Yesterday, we saw some cows standing in a creek that feeds into the Escalante. We watched them take a dump in the water wildlife depend on to drink. Cows destroy the streams so fish and birds and animals can't use them. Cows are products, hamburgers for meat-eaters and profit for those who raise them. We have no fight over that - but they should not be out on the public land, destroying it just so some fat cat can make a few bucks. This place is the wrong place."

"What about the new monument?" Garrett countered, "It's a good start."

"It does nothing about grazing."

"For one more generation, then it is over."

"It needs to stop now." Jonah changed his approach, "Tell me, do you trust your politicians to take care of the problem?" Without waiting for an answer, he continued, "Time for waiting has run out. It is now time to do whatever is necessary to get the cows off the land."

"Like shooting them down in cold blood?" Ateen asked, looking eye to eye with Jonah.

"I guess that is one solution, but we won't go that route."

"No? Not by any means necessary then?" Ateen said in his elder's voice.

"If it came to that, I guess we'd choose to truck them off."

"There is an honorable pathway," Ateen said forcefully and Jonah gave him a questioning look. "Do not choose a fool's way," Ateen concluded.

"I respect your advice, Ateen," Jonah told him honestly. "Each of us follows our own conscious. For us, the time has come to do something."

The group fell silent, the hike demanded their attention. It was slow going, switch-backing again and again to the top. The entire time friends of Jonah and Petra called down, offering bits of news and encouragement to hurry up.

Cresting the escarpment, Jonah and Petra were surrounded by the group. They hugged and greeted each other warmly, and the gathering was festive now that their leader had finally arrived. While a sense of relief permeated the gathering, the worry was over but not the problems.

"Finally, you're here!" one man said. "We found your van but had no idea what happened."

Another added, "We thought they kidnapped you . . ." Still another added, ". . . if you hadn't arrived by sunset we were going looking for you."

Jonah went from one person to the next, shaking hands, looking into their eyes, listening to what they told him. At the same time, Ateen and Garrett were largely ignored and moved a few feet away to a place they could observe. Ateen spotted something lying in the sand and without anyone noticing, leaned down and picked it up. It was a shell casing from the previous day's gun play.

Since Garrett and Ateen's early morning departure, another four or five vehicles including a converted school bus carrying ten or more people arrived. It was an unlikely group of men and half as many women, most in their twenties or thirties and dressed in baggy shorts, bandanas, shirts and sandals. One man was at least sixty and wore a rainbow coalition tee shirt, he stood with a group of worn-out looking hippies, some totally naked.

One barrel-chested man stood with arms folded at the edge of the crowd. He huffed and puffed and postured and pulled his enormous chest even further out. He wore a long bowie-styled knife from a belt attached to his leather shorts, no shirt and heavy, high-top leather combat boots. Across his back was slung a AR-15 military assault rifle and ammo belt. He was tattooed from head to toe and his shaved head possessed a striking blue and red spider's cobweb. Several armed men stood at his side. The man did not move to welcome Jonah, he stood his ground and waited for Jonah to make his way to him. On the surrounding hilltops, Ateen spotted lookouts with assault-styled weapons. He motioned to Garrett to look, then started up the hill toward camp.

"Wait!" Jonah hollered, breaking away from the welcoming committee. "Don't leave!" He pushed through the crowd, who, for the first time, focused on Ateen and Garrett.

"You've got your hands full here," Garrett commented, smiling. "We need to get to camp and get this gear off."

"Okay, right." Jonah agreed, looking at both of them earnestly. "Promise you'll come back later, when you're settled in."

"Too many guns," Ateen said in a deep resonating voice so they could all hear.

"Yeah," Jonah said, noticing the lookouts above and then looking back to the group, "Yeah, it is a bunch of people. . . good people. . . dedicated people. . . Look," he started, almost apologetically, "the guns are for protection. . . If you get a chance come back down, okay?"

Turning quickly to the group, he explained, "These are good people. Friends. They helped us."

Petra shouted, "Come see us, please."

Garrett smiled and Ateen nodded. Jonah turned to the tattooed man - whose name was McVey - and who leered at the two outsiders suspiciously from a few feet away.

Back at camp, Garrett kept an eye on the group below while Ateen loaded the vehicle. He watched Jonah move easily though his people, going from one group to the next. It was clear there were several different factions and he needed to talk to each separately. The tattooed man and his followers pitched their tents away from the rest and entertained themselves by throwing hatchets and knives at a cedar stump.

At dusk the drums started beating. At first it was a single slow deep drum that sound like a heartbeat, then others joined in, adding rhyme and tempo and color and depth. The group gathered at the bonfire where they played hackie sacks and ate a communal meal. They talked and shouted and laughed and drank. But one thing was missing from the previous night - there were no guns anywhere.

As darkness fell, the fire was lit and people linked hands, swayed back and forth and sang songs. Jonah addressed the group with an evangelist's zeal. He raced round the fire, making points by thrusting his hands up into the air or clasping his hands together as if in prayer. Once, he appeared to be fighting some invisible serpent that he ultimately defeated and then cast into the flames. His followers were entranced and cheered wildly. Throughout it all, a drum beat out a resonating cadence and because of it Ateen and Garrett could make out little of what he said. Something about sacrifice and courage and belief and consequences. He used the word peace and resistance many times.

As the meeting continued, Ateen and Garrett slipped into their vehicle and without turning on the lights sped away. Garrett knew the road well and drove while Ateen sat in the truck bed, his trusty old .22 rifle resting in his lap. In the environmentalists' camp, Jonah and Petra and all the others heard them leave.

CHAPTER FOUR

Back in camp Jonah was hit with bad news. He was informed of the line shack arson, the shooting of the cows, the previous night's gun play and the most worrisome problem of all, one of his key lieutenants and best friends, Ian, failed to show up at Egypt and was now long overdue. If that was not enough, local authorities were stopping and detaining people who fit the environmentalist profile. They believed radical environmentalists were responsible for the crimes. In a country where at one time cattle rustling could get a man hanged, the cold-blooded slaughter struck at the heart of ranch life.

Jonah was founder of EarthIsland but his was a coalition of factions held together from necessity. It was a strong alliance under his direction but faction leaders were largely strong willed, vocal outcasts of other main stream groups. They were either hardened veterans, myopic fundamentalists or testosterone driven eco-warriors; and all were impatient and competitive. They wanted action - now. Among them were a few antinuclear activists with Green Party roots from Germany, some anti new-world economic order crusaders and even animal rights extremists once affiliated with ELF who supported the coalition out of self preservation. They had been investigated and imprisoned and hounded. The largest contingent were the individualists who, by definition, were non-joiners and whose histories were checkered with protests, confrontations and arrests.

The most dangerous were the ex-EarthFirsters!, the old growth forest activists from California, Oregon and Washington who fought pitched battles with the logging industry and law enforcement in the Northwest. This contingent, lead by McVey, was the most frightening. They gravitated to violence and guns and were ready to stand toe to toe with anyone who stood in their way. They were specialists at sabotage. And finally, there was the loyal cadre of Jonah's followers. Most worked with him at other organizations and possessed a rabid devotion to their charismatic leader and defended his interests without question or hesitation.

The majority were exiles of old guard mainstream environmentalist groups who had grown tired of waiting for action and were dissatisfied with top-heavy leadership that had grown fat, ineffective and enamored with their public persona. EarthIslanders wanted action, not rhetoric or compromise or protracted lawsuits. They no longer believed in the legal system and hated the established fabric of activists groups. They were closer to an anarchist's ideology than one based on consensus building. All this made Jonah's job complex; he was forced to switch from leader to diplomat many times a day. He decided they meet in the Grand Staircase because it was neutral territory, a place they didn't know but one famous for its solitude and contemplative value. They were there to have a pow wow retreat, to strengthen their coalition and to plan the next year's strategy.

"First things first," Jonah said moving around the bonfire, "we need to clear the air. Who did the cabin and the cows?" He stopped in front of McVey, the tattooed man.

"No, man, no! Not me!" McVey jumped up. "I thought it was you! We all thought it was you." He motioned to the group, "You told Ronin you were going down to Hole in the Rock!"

"It's not my style, besides I don't even have a gun."

"It's my style?" McVey defensively asked.

"You've been begging to shoot something or someone since the day I met you!"

McVey laughed and sat down, "Yeah, but if I offed the fucking cows, I'd tell you about it. Man, I'm telling you straight up - me and my men had nothing to do with it."

McVey made sense, Jonah knew that McVey was a famous blowhard who wouldn't be able to keep his mouth shut. "Okay," Jonah said, turning to the group, "Who did it? The deed is done. We can't take it back. We need to talk about it."

Each looked with anticipation at everyone else but no one spoke.

"Alright," Jonah said, slowly, "If none of us did it, could it have been someone else, one of your people? I want you to vouch for your people."

A chorus of testimonials went up, everyone speaking at the same time, denying involvement of their supporters and assuring Jonah of their sincerity. Everyone was fairly certain that no one present committed the crimes, but they couldn't be sure about the people who had not arrived yet. Surely, there were those within their sphere whose judgment could easily be called into question. It was most likely an outsider, one offered, an independent flying no flag, but supporting the cause. As the others spoke, Jonah thought to himself that someone was lying. He had no proof but his intuition was telling him something. There were petty intrigues and constant power plays enough for him to consider this a real possibility.

"You were at Fifty Mile Ridge," one asked Jonah, "didn't you see anything?"

"We didn't see or hear anything. We camped above Davis Gulch on a ridge where we had a stunning view - it was awesome. We could see Navajo Mountain to the south and the white tabletops of the Escalante drainage north. We were totally alone."

"Apparently," another added, "they were shot at Fifty Mile Ridge."

"We went by there coming and going out but didn't see a soul. We did see some cows near the road."

"They were killed right next to the road." McVey offered.

"Not when we were there. We'd have seen them."

"You could have missed them."

"It must have happened after we left. . . on Monday."

McVey gave Jonah a quizzical look, "You didn't see anything?"

"Hey man, look around. " Jonah turned, arms outstretched, "For all we know, there could be an army just over the next ridge and we'd never know it! This is a big place. Just because we didn't see any thing doesn't mean they weren't out there."

"So, now what?" McVey asked.

"Until we find out where Ian and the others are, we need to sit tight. We need to . . . "

"My bet," McVey announced, interrupting, "the cowboys did it themselves!"

"Killed their own cows?" Someone asked.

Standing and strutting, he continued, "What better way to make us out to be the bad guys! They'd raise support for themselves and at the same time blame the nasty old radical environmentalists. How does it read? Honest ranchers face financial devastation today after environmentalists murder the hamburgers of tomorrow."

Everyone laughed.

"They got insurance, too," he added. "They'll collect big time and get the publicity coup. Look, I see it this way, they are out-manned, out-financed, outsmarted and now with the new monument, they gotta do something." McVey knew this terrain well. It happened to him two years earlier when a logging company employee vandalized some of the businesses own equipment then pointed the finger of blame at McVey. He was arrested, held for a week, then after bailing out was hounded by the FBI. The charges were ultimately dropped when the employee was found out.

"Okay," Jonah concluded, "it doesn't look good. We are sitting on top of a keg of dynamite - too bad we didn't go to the Wind Rivers like we talked about. Here, we are out of our element, at a distinct disadvantage.

"We need to get a communiqué out, denying any involvement." Turning to Shon, the resident communications expert, "What's the status on an uplink?"

"You've got it. Right now. We can go when you're ready."

"We need a public statement, and an encrypted one for members."

"Of course," Shon said looking down, embarrassed for Jonah. Why did he have to ask for encryption? After spending his teenage years haunting hackers' conventions and building a formidable reputation as a bold and even reckless world-class hacker, Shon founded an internet company at eighteen. Multinational corporations hounded him with six digit salaries to assist them build anti-hacking security systems, but ultimately, he soured on the whole lot, the money, the chumps, the hours, the suits, the booze, the plasticity. He cashed out - before the crash - and dropped off the face of the earth.

Turning to McVey, Jonah pointed a finger and attacked, "What in the hell were you trying to accomplish shooting off your guns? Everyone is freaked! We got some nonviolent people here, my friend. We don't need no Terminator - we need cool heads! Remember our agreement, defense and protection only, remember?"

"Right!" McVey answered, "that's exactly what it was all about. Defense. Someone has gotta protect us. Look around, we're out in this fucking desert surrounded by cowboys and pigs - looking for us."

McVey stood, pushed his hands into his lower back and thrust his fat, naked tattooed stomach out. He rocked from side to side, "when we heard what happened and then couldn't find you, we got a little concerned. Can you dig it? We were wigged out! That's all that happened, man. We needed to take some off the top." In what was as close to an apology as McVey ever got, he added, "Look, call it a case of nerves, call it excess, call it any thing you want. It was a mistake."

"What if someone heard?"

"Fuck 'em. They didn't!"

"No next time, understand?" Jonah moved close to McVey, stood sideways and looked down over his shoulder. "We aren't starting a land war. If it gets ugly, we can never fire the first shot. Get it? It's the moral high ground thing, understand? Defense only. Got it?"

"Security is my specialty," McVey spit out, swaying from side to side rhythmically like a poisonous reptile. "I've heard a lot of talk. Talk about standing up and fighting. What's happening to you Jonah? You running scared? You better strap on some balls."

"Yeah, I'm scared . . . only a fool wouldn't be. I'm afraid some fool will do something stupid and blow everything we've worked for. As for my balls, they're right here," he pointed to his crotch. "I don't need to carry a gun to prove I'm packing."

"It's the old boy scout motto, 'Be prepared.' Nobody's going to get the better of me."

"It's not about you, McVey. That's your problem, you think it's all about you. It's not . . . it's about objectives and reaching them."

McVey tensed and doubled-up his fists, "I've had enough of you, and your holier-than-thou bullshit." He shouted, "Maybe it's time someone else take over."

"Right here," Jonah hissed. "You want a piece of me, have at it." McVey did not move. "I'm calling the shots here. Period. It's a free country, and if you don't like it, get your sorry ass outta here."

McVey smiled and shook his head, never taking his eyes off Jonah. He sat down and turning to the others, reported, "He's with us." Looking at Jonah, he explained, "You see, my friend, some of us have been questioning if you ain't lost your edge. We needed to test you. You're calling the shots, for now. What's next, Captain?"

Jonah relaxed, "We wait. We need to find out what happened to Ian. Whoever shot the cows didn't do us a favor. No matter who did it, we're the most likely suspects."

CHAPTER FIVE
Outside Panguitch, Utah

"Cody," Lonnie Bullock, called out for her son as she crossed the dirt and gravel yard behind the barn toward the tack room, "You in there?"

"Yes, ma'am?" Cody replied.

Lonnie stopped short of the front door, placed her hands on her hips and leaned away slightly, "Cody, I need you to go over to the irrigation canal and open the gate - full. We can't afford to lose the alfalfa now."

"Yes ma'am."

Cody appeared in the cedar door frame wiping saddle soap from his hands with an old towel. He smelled of leather and his shoulders filled the door frame - just like his father, Mack.

"Finishin' up Dad's saddle," he said in a soft voice, never looking at his mother, "an hour or two and it'll be done. It's been two years since it had a good moisturizing."

Lonnie nodded and looked past Cody and into the long wooden shed. Passing her on his way out he crossed the dusty yard, climbed the old log corral his grandfather built a hundred years earlier and disappeared into the back field.

With the tack room door wide open Lonnie could see the walls covered with harnesses and lengths of leather strap, metal buckets filled with horse shoe nails, wire curry brushes and blacksmithing tools. It was all there in neat rows where Mack put it. After Mack's accident, Lonnie couldn't bring herself to go into the tack room so she had Cody lock it up. After four generations of use, first by Mack's grandfather, Randolph Woods Bullock, who homesteaded the place in the 1880s, then by his father, Mack Sr., longtime Garfield County Commissioner and the most successful rancher in the state, and finally by Mack himself, also a county commissioner, the tack room had a new purpose. It was transformed into a time capsule, an air tight and sealed cedar-wood cask of her late husband Mack's essence. It was the one place his scent and resonance still could be found.

She stood there looking and her sadness floated with the dust that hung in the air, illuminated by the rays of sunlight pouring in the windows. The dust swirled and floated in and out of the sunrays and she was lost in a reverie.

The tack room remained locked for nearly two years until Cody cracked it open one day and began to use it again. When she returned from town to see the door wide open, her heart pounded and she cried - but she did not protest. She cried in private; Cody had as much right to use the tack room as she had avoiding it. The 6000 acre ranch was his too, and every year he was more like his father and his grandfather before him. Standing at the entryway, Lonnie was simultaneously drawn forward and pushed away. For the first time, she admitted how much she missed the place, some of the best hours of my life were spent in this stupid old shed, she thought.

Long ago, she stood out of the way watching a shirtless Mack pound and shape red hot metal into horseshoes and parts for broken equipment. It was a work space where sweat and muscle and experience and truth forged and fashioned the ranch into what it was. It was in this very shed twenty years earlier on a late autumn evening that Lonnie finally knew she loved Mack Bullock and wanted to spend the rest of her life with him. Because of her feisty independence and history of "loving 'em and leaving 'em," she never believed she'd feel this way about another cowboy.

For an instant, she was transported to that exact moment in time - the fragrances, the sound of the bellows, the heat from the fire, the white hot sparks rocketing away from his hammer, the golds and browns of the broken bales of hay, and the passion as they fell back onto them. Then, her recollection was over just as quickly as it as it came and she was back in the present with a strange taste in her mouth, like the taste of a tin coffee cup. Six months after that fateful night in the tack room so many years ago, she and Mack were married. It was a mating the Bullock family fought to stop, considering Lonnie's troubled past and her worthless alcoholic father. But within a year, she had earned her place and became the compassionate heart of the Bullock clan.

Cody had waited two years to use his father's saddle. He was patient, knowing it was still to early for his mother. Still, he was his father's son and while he would wait forever if necessary, he wanted to sit in his father's seat, to take the reins, to know the ride as his dad had.

He, too, had grown up in the tack room. For Cody the tack room was not the only place he could still be with his dad. Since he had been old enough to ride, he and Mack rode the silent sandstone country searching for strays and secret watering holes. They explored Anasazi ruins and visited places few white men go. Now, when Cody needed to be with his father, he rode deep into the outback and camped alone. Out in the emptiness, he felt especially close and when night fell and the stars of the Milky Way galloped across the heavens, Cody sensed his father's presence. It was sad and joyous at the same time, the bittersweet of life. A good life, his father often said, is made up of equal opposites. Only by contrasting the good with the bad can you truly appreciate life and what you have. Back then, Cody had no idea what his father meant, but now with his longings and memories, he knew.

From the center of the alfalfa field Cody railed against those who destroyed the line shack and killed the cows. I'll kill 'em if I find out who it was, he thought. The dirty sons-of-bitches! He could just imagine watching his father's response to the crime. 'By god,' he would shout, 'let's find the sons-of-bitches and string 'em up!' Cody had good reason to be furious, his grandfather, old man Randolph, and a half dozen area ranchers, built the shack. He stayed there many times, helping his dad bring in the cows and get ready them for shipping. Just weeks ago, he spent a night there. I wish I'd have been there, he said to himself, the low down bastards would have never gotten away with it.

Lonnie stood at the threshold of the tack room, the smell of leather and saddle soap and metal oil and organic decay floating out to her. After a long time, she pulled the door shut and walked across the yard and into the house. The phone was ringing.

"Hello, this is Lonnie."

"Commissioner Bullock, Sergeant Sherm Bangerter, sorry to interrupt. . ."

"Of course not," she answered, in a friendly but businesslike voice. "What is it?"

"We need you in town. We got Bradshaw and his bunch wantin' to talk to you."

"About what?"

"The line shack and the cows. They're all riled up. The chief told me to call."

"Who else?"

"Well, that's why we need you to come into town. There's a whole bunch, mostly ranchers from out on Circle Cliffs. You know the ones."

"Thanks, Sherm." She knew the ones, in her mind she referred to them as the Circle Jerk Crew. They were hotheads mostly, old-school Sagebrush Rebellion folks; they hated everyone, especially outsiders and always thought someone deserved to be tarred-'n-feathered. Some were outlaws, men who should have been born a hundred years ago and forever trying to circle the wagons and recreate the old West.

Slowing to round the wide curve into Panguitch just past the welcome sign, Lonnie was shocked to find a line of dead coyotes impaled up through the anus and mounted on the roadside markers. For an instant, she couldn't fathom the scene, but it was real; a cinematic nightmare, one frame after another - each coyote's belly facing the roadway with its legs spread apart like a Thanksgiving turkey. Some were covered in blood while other were pristine and spotless as if alive. Their heads hung either forward or to the side slightly and some had blue bloated tongues protruding. They looked like marionettes, and again for an instant, Lonnie questioned what she was seeing - am I going insane?

In the parking lot at the county courthouse, Sheriff Andy Anderson was waiting for her.

"You seen the coyotes?" She nearly screamed, getting out of the car.

"Yeah," he said shaking his head, a smirk on his face. "Bradshaw and his group! Their calling it, 'Coyotes on a Stick' and braggin' it up all over town."

"It's a disgrace! Those asinine fools!" The commissioner was beside herself. "I want them down and I want it right now!"

"Yes, ma'am."

"What is the meaning of this. . . this. . . inhumane act?"

"They want to tell everybody - the BLM, the tourists, the outsiders, and especially the radical environmentalists, that they are in control."

"Control?"

"Basically, all outsiders, ma'am." Anderson liked to watch women squirm and struggle with anger, especially Commissioner Bullock. He was pleased with himself.

"We'll see about that!" she said, making for the door. "I want those coyotes down - off those poles - now."

"Gerome's on his way, he'll get to it first thing."

Anderson pulled his shoulders back and struck a military pose, "Ma'am we've had another arson - out at the Bailey place. Shed burnt down. They left a gas can behind."

Lonnie Bullock, Garfield County Commissioner, who took over to complete her husband's term, stopped.

The sheriff continued, "Ten miles away at the same time, someone pulled down a length of corral on Cottonwood Canyon. Fifty head of cattle, on their way to the auction in Richfield, are out."

"Thompson's cows?"

"Thompson's."

She tripped into a moment of disbelief, like when she heard Mack was dead. "Those cows are Angela's college money. . . " She reached for Anderson's arm and stammered, "Wait, what did you say . . . Never mind, I heard you. . . ." She went on, "We need to get some men out there to help. Who in God's name would do such a hateful thing?" She gazed into the sheriff's starched gray shirt, incredulous and searching for reason and clarity.

"What are they plannin'?" Bullock suddenly asked, referring to Bradshaw and his bunch. She nodded to the building and started off toward it.

"They're jumped-up, hot mad. . . I'd say homicidal. Vigilante talk."

Bullock entered the building with Anderson following behind to find Bradshaw and fifteen ranchers standing in the hallway. She moved quickly toward them, forcing the much taller Anderson to quick step.

Pointing a finger in Bradshaw's face, "The coyotes are coming down. Now!" She could barely contain her rage. "You know better than a stunt like that, John Bradshaw! What is wrong with you? What about all the women folk and children we got living here, John? I can't believe you'd pull such an asinine, stupid prank. You got anything between your ears?" She held an index finger to her temple. "What in the world are you thinking about?"

"Don't you go takin' sides against us, Lonnie," Bradshaw, a longtime Marine and Sagebrush Rebellion devotee answered defensively, "We'll roll right over you and anyone who stands in our way."

"Or, are you wanting to show the world what a stupid hick you are?" she exploded, not quite finished.

Sheriff Anderson pushed his chest out and moved in front of Commissioner Bullock, "Don't go threatening the commissioner there, John. I'll have you behind them bars faster than you can pop a Budweiser."

Pushing Anderson aside, Bullock stepped up, "I don't need help from the sheriff here. I'm the Chairman of the County Commission and you better remember it. I know for a fact that we've got laws on the books right now that can put you behind bars for that stunt. I have a mind to have the sheriff lock you up until you settle down!"

Bradshaw glared and stood his ground. Another rancher stepped forward, "You arrested the people who killed the cows yet?"

Another asked, "You heard about the Thompsons?"

"You know we haven't," Anderson answered. "We're working on it. Give us some time. And yes, the commissioner has been briefed about the Thompsons."

"What about the line shack?" Bradshaw asked.

"What about it?" Bullock countered.

"Any suspects?"

"If I did," the sheriff answered, "you'd be the last to know."

"Anyone come onto my property, burning my buildings or killing my animals . . . or sabotaging my ranch . . . or trying to hurt my wife . . . or one of my kids, will be shot - dead."

"Don't say something that might get you in deep trouble," Bullock countered, turning to Anderson, "Sheriff, if anyone ends up dead in Garfield County, under any suspicious circumstance, I want you to arrest Bradshaw here . . . for suspicion."

"Yes, ma'am. My pleasure," the sheriff answered.

Turning to Bradshaw, she continued, "The sheriff here knows where to find you."

Another rancher jumped in, "We have worked hard, we can't have somebody coming in here and destroying what's ours." The crowd added their support. "We need to protect ourselves."

"And you have every right to," Bullock answered. "We are in this together - don't forget it. I got as many cows as the rest of you. But let's not go off halfcocked.

She placed her hands on her hips, "Now, we have got a problem. Some crazy is on the loose out there and we need to get . . . "

"Crazy?" Bradshaw interrupted, "Looks mighty systematic to me. We're talking arson. Destruction of private property. Theft. "

"Someone is attacking us," another added, "attacking our way of life."

"Okay, what if it is true?" she asked, "Should we fall apart and go off creating more problems for ourselves - like the coyotes?" She flashed a glare at Bradshaw. "The question is, do we play right into their hands or keep our cool and act responsibly? Let's not make it worse on ourselves. There is a right way and a wrong way to be dealing with this."

"What?" Bradshaw demanded angrily, "You want us to sit back and take it? We've had it!"

The group sounded their agreement.

"We've lost control to the feds, the god-damned radical environmentalists, the new monument people . . . What are we supposed to do?"

"Don't you be swearin' in my presence!" Lonnie shot back. "Remember me? I didn't want this job. I was happy ranchin' just like you. I've got a business to run, but I got drafted into it, by most of you standing right here. I'm just doing the job you hired to me to do."

"Say what you want," Bradshaw added, "but we better see arrests. In this country we got a tradition of taking care of things on our own, our own way."

"Don't you go making threats and don't go telling me about historical tradition. My family's granddaddy was here before yours were born and our tradition is to be law abiding citizens . . . I will hear none of your vigilante crap." In an official tone, "I will treat anyone who engages in any act of vigilantism the same as those who shot the cows."

"You all know me as a man of my word," Bradshaw said slowly, turning to the group, "I'm tellin' everyone here just so you all know, if the sheriff and the commissioner and all the powers that be can't put an end to these terrorist attacks, I will do whatever is in my power to protect myself and my neighbors."

"Save the speeches and proclamations for your cows, John. We don't need them," Bullock scolded. "We need level heads and cooperation. If you can't be part of the solution you better not be part of the problem. Go home now, mind your own business, leave law enforcement to us. "

Speaking to the other men, Bullock went on, "I want you boys to get in your trucks and go help Lester and Dorothy Thompson. Their cows are all over the mesa and some probably have gotten down into the narrows. Bring your trucks. We need to get them rounded up and over to Richfield for the auction."

The next morning a photograph of the "Coyotes on a Stick" splashed across the morning front page edition of Denver's Rocky Mountain News. In large bold type, the caption read, "Protesting Ranchers Impale Environmentalists' Icon." The image showed three impaled coyotes in the foreground and a new, smartly designed "Welcome to Friendly Panguitch" sign behind it. News services around the world picked up the grotesque image and broadcast it. The governor of Utah made a personal call to Bullock to enquire what was going on, and animal rights groups denounced Garfield County, calling for an investigation.

CHAPTER SIX

Garrett and Ateen slept in the truck in a hidden canyon off the main road. In the morning they followed a steep mining trail built during the uranium days of the 1950s leading to a narrow shelf halfway to the top of the western slope of Kaiparowits. From their perch they had a commanding view of the Escalante drainage including the Hole in the Rock Road snaking north and south, and the road to Egypt as it rolled across the flats and hills at the eastern horizon. No one could come or go without them seeing.

Over the next two days they spotted only five vehicles. Three went down the Hole in the Rock Road, disappearing into the Escalante drainage and then returned before sunset. The other two took the Egypt turnoff and did not return; they concluded they must be more EarthIslanders. On the second day Ateen spotted a flash of reflected light away from the road and coming from a roadless side canyon. Using the binoculars he made out four dark gray SUVs and one windowless gray van tucked strategically under a large sandstone overhang - as if hiding. Nearby, a Desert Storm era camouflage command tent and small gas powered electric generator sat among some broken down cottonwood trees. The windowless van was fitted with an array of antennas and a satellite dish uplink.

"Probably monument vehicles," Garrett offered, "but what are they doing where there's no road?"

"Not the right model, color or size for the feds," Ateen responded. "Maybe an oil exploration party."

"The only thing wrong with that theory," Garrett offered,

"is that the new monument put an end to that, didn't it?"

Ateen watched as four men moved from the tent to the vehicles. "Same clothes, same height, same hair cut." He reported, handing the binoculars to Garrett.

"Expensive outfits," Garrett commented. "Most likely some rich muther fucker and his entire entourage - traveling undercover." Handing the binoculars back, he added, disinterested, "Probably Robert Redford and his tree hugging desert loving groupies."

Ateen laughed through flared nostrils, "That's a good one, Doo Doo."

"I've seen him here before," he said.

"Looks like military to me."

"It always does," Garrett added.

Ateen scanned the road again and sat straight up. Hanging in the air above the Hole in the Rock road coming from the town of Escalante was a huge cloud of dirt churning up into the air. "Looks like we got company," Ateen announced. "Somebody's coming - lots of them." He focused the binoculars. "Can't tell how many, fifteen maybe more. Twenty miles out, near Harris Wash."

"Can you make them out?"

"Big dust," Ateen responded. "Definitely not good."

"Yeah?"

"Looks like ranchers. Work trucks maybe. Ten to twenty of 'em."

Garrett jumped to his feet and strained to see, "Here we go . . . what happens if they head to Egypt?"

"Not good," Ateen said, expressionless. "Could be a big problem . . ." He passed the binoculars to Garrett, "Whoever it is, they are moving slowly."

"If they make the turn to Egypt and meet up with Jonah and his bunch it's going to be war."

The two men nervously watched as the phalanx of trucks undulated forward, moving along the winding trail below. When the vehicles were five or six miles out, they could see fourteen in all and they recognized the lead vehicle, it was the polite cowboy who killed the coyote.

"Remember the time," Garrett asked, without bringing the binoculars down, "during the land dispute when you and Russell Means and some of your defense force took over the trading post at Kern Canyon on the Hopi reservation? What a trip! I'd been listening to the scanner and arrived about the same time as the Hopi BIA police. That was a scary muther fucker. . . You had us all pinned down. . . bullets flying . . . I thought I was dead meat. . . I'm still amazed no one got shot."

"Doo Doo, nobody got shot because no one on either side wanted to hit anyone. We intentionally shot over each other's heads - on purpose."

"Don't gimme that, Fry Bread! Everyone was scared shit-less including you and your Dineh warriors."

"Indians are the best actors in the world," he said smiling. "We are born talented . . . we should all be in Hollywood. Just like you Anglos and lying, you have an affinity for it. We naturally know how to act, you naturally know how to lie."

"It was an act?"

"The Dineh and the Hopi are brothers. It was important to take a stand but it did not need to go any further than that. We did not want to hurt anyone. We got what we wanted."

They took turns with the binoculars, watching the cowboys approaching from the north, then checking the road from Egypt to make sure no one was coming from that direction. If the convoy kept going south on the Hole in the Rock and did not turn at the Egypt turnoff everything would remain as it was - peaceful. But, if they went toward Egypt the chance of a full scale bloody shoot-out was high.

More than a half-hour after first spotting them, the convoy was directly below at the Egypt turnoff. As the lead truck neared, it slowed and came to a complete stop.

"Gawd, no!" Garrett shouted.

"No, no, no." Ateen muttered, as if a mantra.

"Are they turning?"

"Don't know. We'll have to wait and see."

"Anyone coming from Egypt?" he asked.

"No. I can't see anyone."

After what seemed like a long time, the driver of the lead truck, the polite coyote killer, bailed out as did everyone else.

"What are they doing?"

"Taking a piss break."

"Deciding to go to Egypt or not?"

"Could be. Maybe they'll break up into pairs, each pair searching a different road."

The men stood leisurely talking in a circle, some leaning on the trucks, others stretching their legs in the roadway, some sitting on the pile of dirt at the road edge. They looked relaxed, obviously not in a hurry and from what Ateen could see, no one was carrying a gun. They continued talking when Ateen spotted something.

"LOOK!" he said, shoving the binoculars at Garrett. "Coming from Egypt. . . " He nodded and pointed in the direction with his lips. Sure enough, there was a dust cloud rising up above the Egypt road several miles out and coming this way.

"Worst case scenario!" Garrett muttered, sounding like a parrot.

"Ten, fifteen minutes away - can't tell," Ateen added.

"Here we go. I knew it!" Garrett jumped up and started pacing. "What can we do?"

"We will be the witnesses."

"That oughta do some good," Garrett answered, sarcastically.

He stopped and looked down at the ranchers. They hadn't moved, they were still talking. Handing the binoculars to Ateen he moved from the cliff edge and paced back and forth. "Don't tell me what's happening. I don't want to know."

"Okay, Doo Doo. I won't tell you." Ateen answered, and then went on, "They're still talking, no one has moved. Who ever is coming will be here in five minutes."

"I told you not to tell me."

"Small dust. One vehicle maybe. Going slow. We'll see it soon."

Moving back to the edge, Garrett took the binoculars. "It's going to be nasty."

Garrett focused on the cowboys and saw one move off, in the direction of his truck. A good sign. They seemed to be breaking up, first a few men then the entire group started back to their trucks. It was going to be close. From their vantage point, the vehicle coming from Egypt came into view crossing a high flat area covered with sagebrush. Its headlights were turned on and its chrome bumper reflected the afternoon sun. It was still a few minutes away.

"They're finally leaving!" Garrett cried out.

"Not too late?" Ateen said.

"Come on. . . come on. . . Get going. . . Quit stalling. . . get outta here," Garrett chanted. Their eyes went from the vehicle to the convey and back again, over and over.

By the time all the men were in their trucks, the car came into full view crossing a high point. It was white or off-white and looked like a station wagon. It was moving across the wide flat area with no vegetation. The only thing between the convoy and approaching station wagon was a series of small hills. It didn't look good. The car was coming faster than they thought, it would be there soon.

"Remember the first time we met," Garrett asked, "at the Circle K?"

"So what?"

"You saved my life."

"If you didn't get those hotheads drunk, you wouldn't have had a problem."

"Just being polite."

"Your heart may have been in the right place, Doo Doo, but your head was up your ass."

"As I remember it, so was yours."

It happened nearly twenty years ago in 1986 when Garrett, working as a journalist, spent a week with two hundred fired-up Dineh activists and their supporters from the American Indian Movement (AIM) at Big Mountain, Arizona. The braves were hot and itching for a fight with the Bureau of Indian Affairs after threats were made by authorities to forceful-ly remove them from the mountain as mandated by the Hopi - Navajo Relocation Act. Garrett was in Kayenta standing outside at the Circle K making calls at the pay phone when he and Ateen met.

"Spare change?" Ateen's deep voice asked from the sidewalk.

Garrett was startled to find a buffalo-sized Navajo standing there. His oversized army-style camouflage jacket barely accommodated his tremen-dous shoulders and fifty-gallon barrel girth. An alcohol-induced   stupor deadened his eyes.

"Yutahey," Ateen said, slowly. He was unsteady and wavered like a great tree in the wind.

Garrett automatically retrieved the contents of his front pocket and dropped it all into a grizzly bear-sized hand. Along with some quarters, dimes and nickels were several gum wrappers and pieces of wadded-up wastepaper. Ateen patiently picked out the trash from among the coins and dropped it to the ground. He turned and walked away without a word.

A few minutes later, he was back. "Spare change?" he said again, this time standing at attention, like a military man. "Yutahey," he said clearly. His voice was clear and resonant.

"I gave you all I had," Garrett pleaded.

"Not enough."

"For what?"

"Mad Dog." He stared at his open hand as though it would tell the story. The coins lying there looked like miniature counterfeits.

"No more spare change," Garrett said resolutely but suddenly felt anx-ious. I am an outsider on foreign soil, he thought. The reservation was a sovereign nation and he had just spent a week witnessing the anger of some dangerous natives.

"Look," Ateen said in perfect English, "I am drunk. I will be sober tomorrow. I have just come from San Francisco. I am alone." His huge chest rose and fell with sadness.

"You don't live here?"

"It was my home once - Navajo Mountain - long ago. I am here because my great-great grandfather told me to come. I will go home tomorrow but tonight I need to get drunk." He pulled the long hair away from his face and looked down at Garrett.

Garrett was speechless.

"I will get sober tomorrow," he said again. "Help me buy some hooch. I will share it with you."

Thanks," Garrett answered, "but no thanks. I am waiting for someone." He pulled his wallet out, "How much for MD?"

"I knew you were a good man," Ateen responded, sincerely. He reached out to grab Garrett's shoulder in a gesture of goodwill but instead lost his balance and nearly fell. For several uncomfortable moments, the two men danced around together, trying to stay afoot. Ateen smelled of bitter layers of sweat, alcohol and motor oil.

Again, Ateen disappeared into the Circle K then reappeared, this time carrying a brown paper bag pushed into his midsection, like a fullback protecting a football. He turned to Garrett, raised the bag over his head and hollered something before disappearing around the corner.

A few minutes later he was back again. He had circled around the back of the building and was standing at its corner. He nodded and pointed with his lips.

"What?" Garrett said, now impatient and not caring about the reservation and the Navajo sovereignty.

"Over here."

"No. You come over here."

Ateen made a few tentative steps forward then stopped. Nodding to the bottle and then to the street, he whispered, "Federales."

For the very first time, Ateen really looked at this white man standing before him. "You a Vietnam vet?" he asked, spraying Garrett with wine and saliva.

"Aren't we all?" Garrett snapped a sharp salute.

Ateen lifted the bottle out and away from his body, arcing it in a wide circle. "We are all veterans of this Vietnam and of this heartless muther-fucking world!"

He stood at attention and saluted. "Corporal Brigham Joseph Ateen, reporting for duty, sir."

"At ease, soldier," Garrett answered.

"Eighty-second Airborne. Two tours in Nam. The Ashua Valley." He saluted again, this time with the bottle to his lips. He held the bottle out and Garrett instinctively grasped it. He put it to his lips and took several long pulls.

"We can't talk here," Ateen said, taking the bottle quickly away. "Around back."

Behind the store, four young Navajos were sitting on the hardened, oil-soaked ground. Thousands of sharp pieces of green, brown and clear glass from broken bottles surrounded them. Ateen and Garrett sat on a mound of dirt and talked. Night fell and occasionally the errant headlights of a car out on the highway caught the shards of glass and transformed them into sparkling jewels.

"I took the scalps of some gooks" Ateen told him, "and it made me go crazy. The doctors said it was battle fatigue or Agent Orange but I took the spirit from these good men and I have been paying for it ever since."

One of the young men nearby took the bottle from Ateen and drank from it. He then performed a flawless Michael Jackson moon walk across the carpet of glass to his friends who were waiting there. They helped themselves until the bottle was finished off.

Garrett gave Corporal Brigham Joseph Ateen enough money for two more bottles and when he returned Ateen continued telling his story. He was raised on Navajo Mountain and left for the first time when he was drafted into the army. "This is the first time I've been home in thirteen years." Ateen broke down and cried. He covered his face and rocked back and forth, then side to side. His pain was hard to watch and Garrett want-ed to put his arm around him for comfort but did not.

The four young Navajos joined them. They cracked open the third bot-tle of Mad Dog and sent it around the circle. Just as Ateen was telling about his uncle Larry, a code talker in W.W.II - a name given to Navajos who befuddled the Japanese radio transmission code breakers by speaking Dineh - and who had been killed by stepping on a land mine shortly after the end of the war, one of the young Navajos piped up,

"Why do your people take everything from us?" He glared at Garrett.

His friends joined in with magnificent war whoops.

"Your people," he went on, "killed our ancestors, stole our land and now you keep us out here. There is nothing here! Nothing!" His voice was high-pitched, nasal and shrill. "You kill our fathers, take our sisters and turn our brothers into this!" He pointed at Ateen.

"He did nothing to you!" Ateen shouted.

Unable to contain his fury, the young man jumped to his feet and threw the nearly empty bottle of fortified wine against the back wall of the building. Boom! Glass and wine rained down on all of them.

"You think you can assimilate us - but you can't!" He screamed and reached down, finding the broken neck of a bottle on the ground. "No one gave you permission to be here on our land!"

Ateen stood, "He is with me!"

Realizing the situation was going to get ugly, Garrett stood to fight. He knew how to defend himself but they were all drunk.

"You have taken everything from us, but you cannot take my life - only I can do that!" The man extended his arm and drew the sharp glass down along the soft skin of the inside of his arm. His friends staggered around, screaming.

"You can try to save me," he challenged, gallantly, "but it is no use. I am as good as dead."

Neither Ateen nor Garrett moved to help, the thought never entered their minds.

He held out his arm to show his blood, but surprisingly there was nothing there. His friends took a closer look. An expression of shock came over his face and his friends cried out to the heavens.

"Sit down and shut-the-fuck up!" Ateen demanded.

"We will drink ourselves to death then," the young man said, "we are the Dineh, The People."

Suddenly, with broken bottle in hand, he rushed forward, lunging out at Garrett, but before Garrett could move to defend himself, Ateen - the ex-U.S. Army Ranger - stood between them, knocked the bottle away and absorbed his tribesman's anger. "Go! Quickly!" Ateen said, "Go, my friend from Nam."

That was years ago now and in the intervening years, Ateen grew strong and was now a respected elder and teacher. He was finally the man he might have been had he not descended into the flames of war. The two men became close friends, often sharing the solitude of the high sandstone desert. He told Garrett once, "I took the long way home. I left for Vietnam and didn't know I was on a journey to find my manhood until my great-great grandfather came to me in a vision in San Francisco."

The polite coyote killer and friends were all back in their trucks and the procession moved forward. One by one they passed the turn off to Egypt proceeding south. Just as the last truck cleared the turn off, the vehicle coming from Egypt descended the last small hill that blocked the view to the main road. It was an old station wagon and Garrett and Ateen recognized it from the EarthIsland camp.

"He's seen him," Ateen said to Garrett. "The last truck, he's slowing down. He must have seen him. Looks like he's stopping. Wait . . . wait."

"I can't believe it!" Garrett shouted, "Gawd damn it!"

The truck slowed as the rest of the convoy moved off leaving him behind.

"Wait. . . no . . . he's leaving! We lucked out!" Ateen proclaimed, "He's going. Outta here."

"He's not stopping?" Garrett asked incredulously, looking down to see the truck speeding off.

The station wagon descended the hill and stopped at the stop sign. It idled for several minutes, the dust from the cowboy convey still hanging heavily in the air, before it turned north toward town.

The phalanx of ranch trucks continued south until they reached Fifty Mile Ridge, stopping at the burned out line shack. Cody had organized the search after learning someone salted the watering trough up Soda Springs Gulch, but when they checked it the water was pure and clear.

Most of the twenty or so men were young, like Cody, and came from ranching families whose fathers and grandfathers eked out an honest living raising cows, mining for uranium in the 1950s, cutting a few trees on the high mountains to the north, and learning to be jacks-of-all-trades. Cody and his friends were the next generation and were determined not to be the last.

Cody pulled an oversized blue cooler from the back of the truck and passed out ice cold beers. "It's hard to figure," he told them, looking at the burned out shack, "how someone could think they could come down to our land, do this kind of destruction and think they would get away with it. Don't they know we're going to fry their asses?"

"They're morons," one man with a small head and large hat proclaimed. "The other day, I sat in my truck and watched as some campers, pulled onto my property, leaving the gate wide open, and set up camp in my front yard. Stupid fuckers! I wanted to blow their heads clean off."

One of the Circle Cliff cowboys added, "I've helped 'em and before me, my daddy helped them, but hell no - I won't any more. They come down here thinkin' they own the place; like it's some God-damned Disney World or something, and thinking we're some kind of actors all dressed up and ready to give 'em a do-si-do."

"Cock suckers!" the big hat answered. "We need to put up a fence around every son-of-a-bitchin' city in the country. Keep the pricks out the country!"

Everyone laughed.

"Ever notice," Cody asked, "how they never come prepared. This is the goddamned desert. They don't even carry water!"

"Or the way they drive their SUVs out into the sand dunes thinkin'' they won't get stuck cause the god-damned vehicle cost 'em fifty grand."

"Simple fucks!" Cody shrugged. "But ya know," he said in his philosophical way, "I'm convinced some of 'em want to be like us."

"Who wouldn't want to be?" one asked.

"We lucked out." The hat admitted, "I know I ain't livin' in no big city! I'd put a bullet in my head first."

The more beer they drank the uglier they got. They knew what all cowboys knew: you couldn't be a cowboy without getting into some kind of outlaw mischief. The sun went down and they built a fire, stoking it with hatred. They boasted endlessly about what they would do if they found the damned radical environmentalists or their shit-head, city-folk friends who did it."

"How will we know 'em when we see 'em?" one drunk cowboy asked.

"We don't need no evidence," the Circle Cliff cowboy told them.

"I'll know 'em when I see 'em."

"Wish I had just five minutes with one of 'em muther fuckers right now. They'd have to scrape him up with a shit shovel."

Cody was drunk and fell silent. He listened, smiled and laughed. They took pot shots at a Glen Canyon Recreation road sign a few hundred yards away, destroying it.

The beer ran out about midnight and one announced, "I can't sit here all night. Got cows to fed in the morning."

"Me too," another added. "My wife is going to kick my ass."

"Pussy whipped son-of-a-bitch!" The hat sang out.

"I need to finish grading to the top of Colette Top," one added. "I need to bring the herd down."

"If I had your wife," a skinny, cowboy added. "I'd be a going home, too. I'm so fucking horny I feel like a two peckered hoot owl. I'd like to get myself a piece of one of those horny enviro bitches. I'd teach her a thing or two."

The group broke out in laughter and with the exception of Cody, they all moved toward their trucks.

A few minutes later they were all gone. Cody sat at the fire ring for a few minutes then staggered to the cab of his truck. He spun around to face the shack and amphitheater, "I'll get 'em, dad. You can count on it!"

CHAPTER SEVEN

At dawn, Ian's old Volvo station wagon rolled into the EarthIsland encampment. His girlfriend Lana was behind the wheel and Summer, her best friend, sat in the passenger seat. Within moments the entire camp was out of bed and running to greet them. Since they were three days late everyone feared they had been arrested and detained by local police.

Lana did not speak and clung onto the steering wheel as if in a trance. She was naked and her head was swollen and bleeding from a large gash on the temple. She was covered from top to bottom with blood and dirt. Her beautiful face was nearly unrecognizable. "Ian," she finally said, sobbing, "in the back. Please. Help. Hurry."

Ian sprawled unconscious on the back seat, laying on a blood-soaked blanket. Blood pooled under his head, coming from his ear. He had a large open wound on his scalp, a broken arm and his hand lay backward against his forearm. Summer was nearly naked too, her tank top was torn and she was propped up between the seat and the door. She neither moved nor acknowledged anyone. Her eyes were blank and dead-looking. Dried blood coagulated in her hair and on her nose, which was obviously broken. Blood dipped from her nose over her swollen upper lip and down across her chin.

Everyone swarmed over the car, aghast and shocked and trying to help. After getting a good look, many turned away, standing flatfooted and crying openly. Some ran to pack their bags while others retrieved guns and raged with hatred, shouting for revenge.

"Get Ian to the medic's tent," Jonah ordered, peeling Lana's hands from the steering wheel and wrapping her in a blanket. He carried her to a nearby tent and laid her on a futon. Petra and Terri, a one-time emergency room nurse, helped Summer to the futon.

"Who did this, Lana?" Jonah asked, searching her face.

"Please help Ian." She kept muttering and refused to look at him.

"Tell me? Who was it?"

She didn't answer and seemed to nod off.

He shook her arm, "Lana, for Ian, tell me. Who did it?"

"It's important," Petra pleaded softly, "Please Lana. For Ian."

"Cowboys." Lana blurted out, frightening everyone and then broke down sobbing.

"What happened?" Jonah repeated.

"Tell us, Lana." Petra asked, rubbing her arm.

She finally nodded, "Cowboys in trucks. They had a roadblock. We tried to back out and get away but they blocked the way." Her voice was shaky and almost inaudible, "They had guns and dragged Ian out and started beating him. They took turns hitting and kicking him; they hit him in the head with a metal bar." She collapsed back onto the futon and Jonah waited silently, burying his face in his hands.

"Every time he started moving," she finally continued, "they beat him again. They were drinking whiskey and started slapping and punching and beating me and Summer. One punched me in the stomach and I couldn't breathe. I knew we were going to die. They called us sluts and cunts and city whores."

Lana, a tall beautiful, willowy twenty-five-year-old, looked at Jonah, her lips red and puffy, one eye swollen shut. "I kept hoping you'd come save us, Jonah."

He fought back tears of guilt and rage.

"They tied us up and kept saying they were going to kill us." Holding her wrists out, she showed them where the rope cut deep into her skin. "Is Ian going to be all right?"

As near as Terri could tell, Ian suffered a serious head injury, several broken ribs, a fractured wrist and arm, some broken fingers, and his back, neck and buttocks were covered with black and blue welts from being kicked or hit with some object. He was in shock and unconscious.

Petra cradled Lana's head and tried to comfort her.

"Every time Ian moved they beat him again. It seemed like it would never stop." She swallowed hard, trying to control her emotions. Turning to Petra, "They grabbed me and slapped and punched me. They were squeezing me so hard," she cupped her breasts in her hands, "pinching me. They kept telling me what a whore I was and pulled my hair and forcing me to kiss them."

Jonah couldn't standing it, squirming and wincing. He tried to comfort her, "It's okay Lana, no one is going to hurt you anymore."

She stared at him defiantly, "Don't you want to know what they did to me? I knew they were going to kill us." Her voice quavered and she shook softly. "I felt like I was in a movie. You know that feeling, like everything is unreal, like you are actually in a movie?" She blinked wide-eyed at Jonah, who had a look of utter shock on his face.

"They took me to the back of a truck and took turns raping me. The truck smelled like cow shit, it's all over me now. They stuck it in my mouth and pushed it so far down I couldn't breath. I knew I was going to die. Please don't," she begged, replaying it in her mind, "please, please don't hurt me."

Petra stroked her face, gently. "Come out of it! It's over Lana. You are safe now! Come on, it's over."

"But they did it anyway. They didn't care. They wanted to kill me. You know what I mean?"

She fell silent and Jonah sat defeated, transfixed as if the corrosive nature of each description was destroying some inner vision and strength within him. "Fuckers!" He suddenly screamed out, "Muther fucking cock suckers. They will pay for this!"

Lana covered her face and sobbed, rocking back and forth. "One started strangling me and like . . . I played dead so he would stop. When he quit, he told the others he killed me and they all laughed like it was a big joke. He told them he was going to hang me from a tree and gut me out like a deer - cut me from here to here and leave my guts for the coyotes to scavenge. They would leave my body where it would be found, as a warning."

"It's okay, sweetie," Petra told her, crying. "You're safe now. You don't have to say anymore."

Lana drank some cold water and continued, "They thought I was dead and talked about killing Ian and Summer so there wouldn't be any witnesses. When I started coughing up blood he put a gun in my mouth and told me to die or he'd blow my head off."

Laying next to Lana on the futon, Summer started to sob gently. Terri hovered over her, stroking her forehead, asking if she were all right but she did not acknowledge.

"Summer begged them to stop," Lana bravely went on, "but they just kept torturing her. There was nothing I could do. All I could do was be glad it wasn't me." She broke down, sobbing uncontrollably. "I'm so sorry. . . I want to die. . . I just hate myself. Summer cried and pleaded and they just laughed, 'Ride em cowboy.'"

Summer curled into the fetal position and pulled a blanket over her face.

"That's all I remember," Lana quietly said, rocking back and forth, then went on, "Somebody - another one - drove up and there was a big fight. They said they were going to kill us and he told them that no one was killing anyone. They put a gun to my head and cocked it. . . It was like I was in a movie . . . like slow motion; but I really didn't care anymore. I wanted to die. . . I couldn't stand it." She coughed, wiped her nose and sat straight up. "They started fighting and screaming but I don't know what happened next. . . I guess I was passing out. . . Next I know, the man was helping me. He wouldn't let them get me. He told me to get to the car. They were going to shoot him but he didn't back down. I knew I was dead." She took several deep breaths, "He dragged Ian by his shirt to the car and Summer and I - I don't know where she came from - got him inside . . . and we left . . . He's hurt, you know?"

"We'll take care of him." Jonah comforted her. "Fucking pigs!" He shouted. "They won't get away with this. I promise! Did you see any of them?"

She nodded.

"Can you identify them?"

Lana frowned, "Yes."

"Enough." Petra said to Jonah. "Out of the tent. Close the flap." Petra pushed him out with both hands against his chest. "Now."

Outside, Carter was waiting. "Ian's in bad shape, man. Seriously."

The two men rushed to the first aid van. "He's history, man," Carter whispered. "Like seriously. What are we going to do?"

Jonah ignored the question and when they got there a crowd was waiting.

Ian was unconscious and Jonah knelt next to him.

"His blood pressure is low and his breathing is shallow," Chris, the medic, nervously told him. "I think his brain is swelling! He needs a doctor!"

Without taking his eyes from Ian, Jonah told him, "Do what you can, Chris. We need to sort this out."

Nearby, McVey shouted, "I'm for killing somebody's fucking ass!"

Jonah told the gathering, "I know what you're thinking, but now is the time for cool heads." His voice was filled with anger. "I'm just as fucking pissed as the rest of you but we can't be weirding out!" His eyes were wild and he stood in front of McVey. "We need focus. We need time to think. It's imperative not to forget to do the work. We need to stay focused. The last thing we need is to go weirding out!"

"Are you okay?" McVey asked calmly but looked frightened. He held his assault rifle across his chest. "You alright, Jonah?"

"It depends on your definition of okay," Jonah uttered sarcastically. "From where I stand, everything is totally fucked! We need to put our heads together."

"Agreed," McVey barked, in his paramilitary voice. "The area is secure. No one followed them in - I made sure of that. I sent out scouts and lookouts and guards. I'm in radio contact - every few minutes."

"Good man! Excellent," Jonah said, relieved. He grasped McVey by the upper arm and squeezed. "Good move."

CHAPTER EIGHT

Garrett and Ateen descended their perch and by noon were back in the town of Escalante. Ateen wanted to pay a visit to Alex Benay, a Dineh who owned The Sunrise Trading Post with his wife Carol on the outskirts of the Mormon town. They found Benay sitting astride his pottery wheel, leaning forward at the waist and focusing on the clay his hands formed into a tall Anasazi-like bowl.

Alex acknowledged his guests with a nod then went back to work, not looking up again until he was finished. Garrett dropped into the sunshine on the sidewalk and Ateen leaned against a work shed. In the yard, a mother magpie taught her chicks to pick maggots from dog shit. Ateen watched the potter's wheel spin as Benay's fat, swollen fingers worked the clay expertly upward. Benay wore sandals, cut off Levi's and an Atlanta Braves tee-shirt.

Benay and his wife, Carol, were Mormon Navajos. They had taken up the ways of the Latter-Day Saints, especially their ardent pursuit of material blessings and cherished worldly ignorance.

The Sunrise Trading Post was filled with Mexican made knockoffs of Native American art. "If you can't beat em," Alex once told Ateen, "join 'em. It's the American way." Now he owned a house, a new truck and some fancy furniture from a store in Salt Lake City. European tourists took one look at the natives, Alex and Carol, and were convinced to buy. Benay was short, stocky and his hands were huge. It seemed impossible that such clumsy looking hands could produce such intricate work.

"I've been waiting for you," Benay said in Dineh.

"Yutahey," Ateen answered. "You knew we were coming?" he asked in English.

"The wind told me."

"Did the wind tell you anything else?"

"It is not for the Anglo," he said in Dineh.

66

The men turned to Garrett who clearly understood. He got to his feet, tipped the bill of his cap and left. Garrett was never offended by Dineh abrupt behavior, in fact, he respected their straightforward honest manner, especially compared to his peoples' proclivity for lying and never saying what they truly meant. He walked the few blocks back into town, meandering along Main Street to Gleason's Market. He wondered what was going on with Ateen, he had been unusually quiet and seemed uneasy.

After buying water he stood out front of Gleason's watching the locals come and go on Main Street and taking short quick swigs of water as if it were whiskey. Years ago, he rented a room nearby, escaping the city while writing a book. He half-hoped to run into someone he knew. When he returned to the trading post, Ateen and Alex were gone. Carol pointed to the sweat lodge in a small grove of willows next to the creek at the far end of the property and told him they were inside.

Garrett drove to the new convenience store, picked up a six-pack and went to the cemetery a few blocks from Main Street. He parked in the shade of a one-hundred-year-old cottonwood tree and sprawled out on the grass. He awoke half-drunk hours later at sunset, bought another six pack, and rented a cheap room at the Ranger Motel. Later, he stumbled down Main Street into a bar where he got into a fight with an angry husband after he tried to pick up his wife. The last thing he remembered was leaving.

He woke up back at the motel the next morning. He couldn't remember a thing. After showering he drove to the trading post where Ateen was sitting in some high weeds near the highway.

"We have a witness," Ateen announced proudly, climbing in.

"To what?"

"The cows - Doo Doo! The shooters." Ateen did a double take. "You look like shit."

"Thank you, I'm sure. What happened?"

During the sweat lodge, Alex admitted to Ateen that there was a secret witness to the killing of the cows. "No one knows about him," Ateen told Garrett, "he's Dineh and doesn't want to come forward. You will like him, Doo Doo, he is like you - cuckoo. He is a half-breed who has trouble on the reservation."

"What kind of trouble?"

"He got drunk and tried to stab his brother and chased his sister down with the truck - nearly killed her."

Garrett's face contorted, raising one eyebrow and squinting the other.

"What does he know?"

"He works out on the range for a sheepherder. He was tracking strays up a narrow canyon when he heard shots. He got a good look at the shooters."

"He'll talk?"

"Alex is talking to him for us."

Later, they meet Alex on a side road outside of town. He told them that the witness, Leon Nemelka, had disappeared. Apparently, two white men driving an SUV with tinted windows, showed up at his place yesterday and tried to kill him. He escaped by crossing into Navajo country in a row boat on Lake Powell.

Alex was shaken and frightened. He went to Nemelka's trailer to find it burned and his three dogs shot. He then went to Nemelka's boss's house, an Anglo sheepherder, who told him Leon showed up in the middle of the night, claiming someone tried to kill him. Alex told Ateen, "I have washed my hands of it, I can't get involved. I will not speak to you anymore about it."

Ateen knew Alex had more information but was not telling. Garrett drove to Nemelka's trailer and it was just as Alex described it. The house was still smoldering and Nemelka's dogs were lying in pools of blood in the front yard. Ateen dug a bullet from one of the dogs and holding it side by side to the slug taken from one of the cows, he could see they were the same - both rounds were restricted military issue.

CHAPTER NINE

Twelve hours after Ian, Lana and Summer arrived, just after dusk, the EarthIsland camp was packed up and ready to leave. It was a feverish day, everyone rushing about, packing, cleaning, burying the latrines and making certain not a single trace of their stay was visible. The mood was tense and defiant; everyone was afraid to stay but even more afraid to leave. Jonah and his lieutenants spent the day pouring over maps, satellite images, monitoring police radio bands, pondering exit routes and devising a security plan to keep them safe.

Minutes before their caravan was scheduled to depart, four trucks filled with heavily armed men went out ahead. Their job was to secure the road and make certain no one was waiting for them. They were equipped with powerful spot lights and two-way radios. Jonah made certain that neither McVey nor any of his men were among them.

Shortly after Ian arrived, he fell into a coma. Terri and Mick, the medics, were convinced his brain was swelling and it was imperative to get him to a hospital. At the same time, Shon in the communications van, received e-mails from operatives on the outside, warning them of roving bands of vigilantes and police roadblocks. There were new reports of acts of vandalism, arson and assaults.

It was clear they needed to get out quickly and do it without being seen. The problem was they were 40 miles down a dead-end road. They were at the center of a million acres of wild outback, catacombed with old mining roads and cow trails - all leading nowhere.

Jonah was known for keeping a cool head and for his ability to articulate issues, positions and rebuttals. He moved easily in many arenas - government, politics, the environmental community; it was only recently he deserted conventional tactics to become a proponent of confrontation and civil disobedience. But out here, commanding a band of armed eco-warriors against murdering local cowboys, he felt inadequate and overwhelmed.

From his communications van, packed with every high tech computer hacker tool available, Shon bent over his keyboard generating code which he then used to instruct military and weather satellites in geosynchronous orbit to redirect their powerful cameras on the Grand Staircase. He directed them to photograph possible escape routes and download the images onto his hard drive. He, Jonah and others analyzed them, searching for road blocks, groups of vigilantes or cowboys hiding or searching for them. A number of suspicious groups of cars were located but most, they concluded, were likely backpackers parked at trailheads. There were clusters of vehicles that worried them including one strange grouping, only five vehicles, hidden in a roadless area just a few miles away from them off the Hole In The Rock road near the turn off to Egypt.

"Did you get that cell number?" Jonah asked Shon.

"Yep. It took a while, but here it is."

Jonah dialed. Fifty miles away, Garrett and Ateen sat in their pickup when from his old leather rucksack, Garrett's cell phone rang.

"Your cell phone?" Ateen asked.

"Can't be," Garrett answered. "Not out here."

"Sounds like it to me."

"There's no service out here!" Garrett countered, opening his pack and searching for the phone. "Hello?"

"Garrett Lyons?"

"Who is this?"

"Is this Garrett Lyons?"

"Who wants to know?"

"Garrett, this is Jonah Sandborn. Remember me? Jonah and Petra, remember? EarthIsland?"

"Jonah. Right." Garrett was perplexed. "How did you get my number?"

"The phone company."

"No way. I have an unlisted number."

"Listen Garrett, does it matter? This is important. I will explain everything later. We need your help."

"Explain it now."

"Look, Garrett, I called because I felt I could trust you. You and Ateen. We are in a sticky situation and need your help. I may be wrong about you but I suspect not."

"How did you do it?" Garrett interrupted.

"What?"

"There's no service out here. Is this some kind of trick?"

"No tricks. We just did it," he said, impatiently, "Listen . . . Will you help us?"

"One question."

"Name it."

Garrett was quiet for a moment before asking, "Did you shoot the cows?"

"No way."

"Any of your people?"

"That's two questions! Look, I can't vouch for everyone," he said, hesitantly. "So, you can believe me or not but as far as I know no one involved with EarthIsland had anything to do with it."

"There are a lot of people who . . . "

"Look, what?" Jonah interrupted, desperately, "Your signal is breaking up. We are in bad shape out here and need help."

"Yeah. . . "

Garrett was quiet as Jonah explained the situation. Ateen watched his friend for a clue but Garrett's face was expressionless.

"Got a pen and paper?" Jonah finally asked.

Pulling his notebook out, Garrett responded, "Shoot."

Once on the road, Jonah drove the lead vehicle with McVey sitting shotgun. Guards were strategically placed throughout the caravan and Jonah gave explicit orders that no one brandish a weapon unless it was a matter of life and death. The situation was disintegrating and if they didn't make an escape the chances were likely that more blood would be shed. The last thing he wanted was a confrontation out on the road, one he knew would turn deadly, but he had no choice.

Many were in a state of shock, the brutal attack against their comrades made them timid one minute and reckless with anger the next. Jonah was puzzled by McVey. Instead of using the incident as a platform to foment hatred and push for retaliation, McVey went quiet and seemed withdrawn. He moved at the periphery, stroking his thin long beard and whispering privately to his men.

Was McVey waiting for Jonah to stand and fight? If Jonah didn't fight, would McVey implement some secret contingency plan he and his men formulated? Like Jonah, McVey was a leader, accustomed to giving orders. Could there be another reason for McVey's strange behavior? Could it be that after McVey saw what happened to Ian, he lost his blood lust? Was he afraid? This was no longer a hypothetical, blood had been spilled. This was not some Rambo movie-land theme park, where he could huff and puff and strut back and forth like a little Napoleon, without any real consequences.

When Jonah asked if he was okay, McVey blew him off, saying nothing was going down. McVey bent over at the waist, held himself around the middle, and rocked back and forth. He contorted his face into a mask and he rubbed his hands back and forth, "I understand the situation," he told Jonah nervously. "Like you, I just want to get outta this crazy . . . desert. It is too big and quiet . . . there's something out here . . . it's getting to me. . . I don't know."

The road out was slow going. At every hill or blind turn, they braced to find a roadblock or have someone jump out and shoot at them from the trees. They were sitting ducks. The full moon added layers of false, untrustworthy light onto the scene. The moonlight was magic and cast the trees, rocks, bushes and deadwood with shadowy intent. Ghosts and apparitions darted from tree to tree. Nothing looked familiar; the ruts in the road seemed deeper, the hills seemed higher, and the cedar forest crowded in from both sides of the road and created a hypnotic and spectral effect as they passed through it.

When the advance team arrived at the Collett Top road, a dangerous trail climbing the east side of the Kaiparowits, they found Ateen and Garrett waiting in the moonlight at the appointed place. Even though they recognized the two men as those who hiked out with Jonah and Petra, they were still suspicious and trigger-happy. They searched the surrounding hills with spotlights, making sure no one was with them.

"Waiting for Jonah?" one asked, from the back of a truck.

Garrett nodded, "Who else?"

Ateen leaned against the truck with his arms folded.

"Any time now," the man replied, talking into a two-way radio. "They're . . . behind us . . . five minutes."

When the convoy arrived Jonah jumped from the VW and approached Garrett and Ateen. Petra, McVey and some others rushed to the second vehicle and began transferring Ian, Lana and Summer to Ateen's truck.

Jonah held out his hand, "I can't tell you how much we appreciate this," he started.

"In the back," Ateen said, as the men approached carrying Ian on a stretcher.

"He needs a hospital immediately." Jonah added, "A good hospital, if possible. He's really bad."

Petra, walking arm in arm with Lana and Summer, approached slowly. The two women were frightened and pleaded with her not to make them leave with the strangers.

"In front," Ateen told her, "I'll ride in the back with the injured." Petra helped the women into the cab while Ateen closed the back gate and jumped into the bed.

After making certain Ian was safe, McVey approached Jonah and Garrett, "You can tell them from me," he said in a threatening and disgusted voice, "If Ian dies there's going to be some dead cowboy dudes down here!"

"That's enough McVey," Jonah demanded, "We don't need any more of that talk . . . "

"I ain't talking to hear myself," he said looking at Garrett. "You tell them what I said. I mean it."

"Tell them yourself," Garrett answered dryly as McVey walked off.

"The women need special help," Petra interrupted softly. "They have been through hell." She reached out to touch Lana's arm, tears filling her eyes.

"These are good men," she told Lana. "They will take care of you, sweetie. You can trust them. They won't let anyone hurt you." She looked to Garrett, giving him an imploring look.

"You can count on us." Garrett answered, and turned to Lana, "We'll make sure you are safe."

"We'll get you home." Ateen added in his deep medicine man voice. "You'll be safe with us."

"What's next?" Garrett said, squaring himself with Jonah.

"We've got to go. We have a lot of territory to cover before light."

"Going over Collett Top?" Ateen asked.

Jonah paused, "You think it's open?"

"It'll be slow going."

"It's open," Garrett added, "you'll make it easy."

The Collett Top Road was a little used ranch trail blazed generations ago and hardly used or known about until the new monument's designation. Local ranchers used the canyon road to move cattle to higher grazing in the summer then return them in late fall.

"We've looked at the maps," Jonah said and paused, "it links up to the Smokey Mountain road, right?"

"Once you climb out of the canyon, it's not more than a mile or two." Garrett confirmed what Jonah already knew.

"Going south toward Big Water?" Ateen asked.

"Better you didn't know," Jonah added, respectfully.

It's the only way," Ateen said, flatly. "Unless you want trouble in Escalante."

By taking the Smokey Mountain road they accomplished two goals. They avoided the authorities and those who might be laying in wait for them; and secondly, the road would drop them off just a few miles north of the Arizona border, the sooner they were out of Utah the better.

Jonah felt relieved. He studied the maps and the satellite images and was testing Garrett and Ateen, to see if they would be straight with him. He was now convinced they were trying to help. He patted Garrett on the shoulder, "It's my responsibility to get these people out safely."

Garrett and Ateen searched his eyes.

"Ian can't wait," He explained and turned to leave.

"Watch for the Kelley Grade, down the back side of Kaiparowits," Garrett cautioned. "It's dangerous. Go slow."

"Wait until sun up," Ateen added, "You won't get there until then any-way."

"Will do." Jonah shook the men's hands, started off, but stopped and turned back, "Just so you two know, we had nothing to do with the cows or the arson."

"Was it environmentalists?" Ateen asked.

"Don't know, Ateen. Could have been. I can only vouch for us."

After crossing the plateau, stopping for flat tires and rest, the EarthIsland caravan cautiously descended Kelley Grade at dawn. By mid-morning they entered Monument Valley. The escape had gone off without a hitch, except one thing. At the top of Collett Top, McVey and his men opened fired on an old road grader and destroyed it.

The next morning, one hundred miles to the west, Garrett and Ateen delivered Ian, Lana and Summer to St. George Regional Hospital. They also alerted the authorities.

CHAPTER TEN

The week of the "Coyotes on a Stick" incident brought one crisis after another for Garfield County Commissioner Lonnie Bullock. On Monday, it was Sheriff Anderson who went too far with his Marshall law mentality, stopping and questioning anyone who looked like an environmentalist. He and his deputies unlawfully raided camps of well-known hermits living out on Tanner's Flat and Butler Mesa. He had long suspected some were hiding from authorities elsewhere and this gave him an opportunity to pull them in and do background checks.

From her office in the century old Garfield County Courthouse on Panguitch's Main Street, Commissioner Bullock spent ten hour days fielding calls from pushy, big city news reporters. They wanted answers about the coyotes or to inquire about the ongoing investigation into the arsons, cow killings, the series of vandalistic attacks, and the growing number of confrontations between residents, tourists and hikers.

Built in 1902, the courthouse and its expansive lawns and gardens was the city's most beautiful building and served as the gathering place for holidays. Every Fourth of July, red, white and blue streamers and a giant American flag festooned the face of the building, and a parade that started at the edge of town ended on the courthouse lawn where everyone gathered for a barbecue. Only the Mormon church rivaled the courthouse for beauty and importance.

Bullock's second floor corner office was paneled in golden oak and carpeted with the same deep blue carpet that adorned the governor's office in Salt Lake City. The large office had floor to ceiling windows on two sides and a commanding view north on Main Street and west up First South Street to the mountains. From her desk, Bullock could see the boarded-up store fronts on Main Street. She was hopeful that after years of economic decline the new monument and her fellow Americans new interest in the national parks might bring an upturn in business on Main Street.

Lonnie never felt comfortable in her office, it was Mack's office and she never forgot it. Before Mack was elected county commissioner, the office belong to Mack's father, the honorable Randolph Woods Bullock who, for nearly four decades, directed the county with the imperious style of a dictator and a homegrown grittiness - a willingness to roll up his sleeves and get down into the trenches - that was still admired and talked about today. Old man Bullock ran the county with a tight- fisted autocratic rule as if he owned the place. He was, in fact, the richest man in the county and owner of the largest ranch in the state, grazing thousands of head of cattle and raising award winning horses. Old timers still compared the old man to his son Mack, who only reluctantly ran for office after his father died and after the county endured a series of lesser commissioners whose only downside was their last name wasn't Bullock. Mack was his own man and a strong leader, but instead of making decisions without consulting community leaders, Mack was a coalition builder and a far better manager than his father.

Not only was the office too big for Lonnie's liking, but it was too masculine. Many viewed the office of county commissioner as a man's job and they felt uncomfortable letting a woman make decisions. In her first few months, Lonnie alienated almost everyone; she refused to consult with the Mormon elders, the real power in the community; and, she failed to bond with the women who ran the county offices. She didn't befriend or socialize with them so they treated her as an interloper, an outsider who didn't belong there. Lonnie was too beautiful, she wasn't a Mormon, her mother deserted her, leaving her father for another man, and her father was an alcoholic. Worst of all, the women clucked endlessly about Lonnie marrying Mack for his money. Mack was a good man but couldn't tell a slut if one were right in front of him.

For Lonnie, the worst thing about her office and job was that it kept her away from the ranch, her horses and from her beloved Cody. Something was up with Cody and she was worried. He was moody and distant and seemed troubled. It must be the burning of the line shack and the current upheaval, she concluded. If the crisis and the potential economic backlash was not enough, Bullock received calls from angry motorists and their attorneys threatening lawsuits claiming Sheriff Anderson and his men were conducting illegal road blocks on Highway 89. The sheriff stopped everyone in the dragnet, checking identifications, conducting illegal searches and treating outsiders as if they were guilty of a crime. When motorists demanded to know why they were stopped, he refused to answer and even threatened some with jail.

She appealed to his sense of community and impressed upon him that no matter what his personal feelings were about the tourist economy it was extremely important to the county's coffers, bringing in fifty percent of the county revenue, and even paying his check. When this didn't work she mentioned the potential of costly lawsuits against him personally.

With his hands clasped behind his back, Anderson stood at ease in front of her desk pretending to listen. He nodded affirmatively at the appropriate times but tuned the commissioner out in the way a battle hardened marine ignores an inexperienced second lieutenant. The truth was Anderson never felt comfortable taking orders from a woman. Until Lonnie became a politician, he admired her and even held her on a pedestal as a true American beauty. He had worked for her husband, Mack, who was also his best friend, but now that he was gone, she was just another woman doing a man's job. He did his best to follow her orders but didn't take her seriously.

After Mack died and Lonnie replaced him, taking over his seat as county commissioner without being elected, Anderson decided it was his duty to help her, to show her the ropes and to do some on the job training. Bullock saw through him and resented it. "Don't patronize me," she chided him. "I'm not some silly little schoolgirl, I'm your boss." That was two years ago and since then he steered clear, refusing to give her regular police reports or informing her of his plans or decisions about police matters.

When she discovered he was operating independently, she threatened to fire him. To show how serious she was, she placed him on a seven day suspension. As usual, he stood at attention, hands clasped behind his back and did not say a word. Afterwards, he turned smartly, marched down the hallway to his office, typed out a one line resignation, returned to her office and dropped it on her desk.

She narrowed her almond-shaped green eyes and pushed back in her chair, "You've done a good job here over the years, Andy," she started, "and Mack respected you. But, you have forgotten who is in command here. Good soldiers and good policemen follow orders - they do not disobey them. Until you sit in the commissioner's chair, you take orders from me and make sure they are carried out." For the first time, she could see he was listening. "It will be difficult to replace you" she said slowly, swiveling in her chair, "but with all due respect, I think its a good move -

for both of us. I'll start the search for your replacement immediately."

Anderson was shocked, "Yes Ma'am, I agree."

"Any suggestions for your replacement?" she asked, searching for her pen. "What about Franklin or Trueaxe?'"

"Respectfully, neither is qualified." He couldn't believe it, after all he had done for the county and for Mack and then for her. He worked his jaw so hard it betrayed him.

"Some people will be happy to see you go, others will miss you. I will do both."

Two days later, Anderson showed up at her office and asked to be reinstated. "I was wrong," he told her, "and besides, this is my home town. We both know," he pleaded, "that it's no time to be looking for a new chief." That was months ago and not only was the sheriff still operating independently but now, with the current crisis, he was becoming part of the problem and making matters worse.

She had more to worry about. Bradshaw and his group of Circle Jerk outlaw ranchers were organizing meetings, talking vigilante justice, parading around town with American flags waving from their trucks, and shooting off their guns inside town limits. They hung out over at Taber's gas station a few miles south of town at the turnoff to Bryce Canyon National Park. They parked near the road, sat on their trucks, played patriotic Western music, made crude remarks and hand gestures to passersby. They listed the license plate numbers of every out of state vehicle. She received reports from park rangers of scuffles and shoving matches between ranchers and hikers and tourists inside park boundaries. It wasn't just Bradshaw and his Panguitch cohorts; they were getting support from Escalante and Boulder and Kanab and the fanatic anti-United Nations hamlet of La Verkin.

Bradshaw and his followers were adamant: nobody was going to come into their country, kill their livestock, burn down their historic buildings and terrify their families without a fight. They had had enough, years of battling the environmentalists and the federal government. The current situation was but the most recent in a long history of blatant abuses. The environmentalists opposed mining, so they closed the mines and lost hundreds of high paying jobs. The environmentalists opposed logging so a one-hundred-year-old industry died at the mill. The environmentalists opposed grazing so the federal land managers were locking the land up and evicting the descendants of the men who tamed it.

On Thursday, Lonnie received a surprise visit from two FBI men and two military police officers investigating what they called "a breach in national security." They showed up at the courthouse wearing business suits, dark glasses and driving government cars. Everyone in the courthouse was abuzz and knew something important was up. Someone in the area, they told her, a computer expert, using a remote satellite uplink dish, hacked into the command program of several military and meteorological satellites in geosynchronous orbit and instructed them to photograph remote areas and then feed a download to them. As closely as they could calculate, the break-in originated south of Escalante near the Hole in the Rock road. They told her one computer made the uplink but two computers at different locations received the downloads.

Late Friday afternoon she received a call from the Associated Press asking her to comment on the investigation. She stated no arrests in the cow shootings and arson had been made but they were working hard to solve the case and did have a number of possible suspects. The writer interrupted and told her he was not referring to that investigation but the near fatal beating of one man and the brutal rapes of two young women on the Hole in the Rock road outside of Escalante the day before. The victims were in a hospital in St. George and reportedly, the crimes were committed by group of truck-driving cowboys.

She was shocked and told him she'd get back to him, then called the chief of police in St. George. Indeed, three people were in the hospital there. They were admitted into the hospital just eight hours earlier. The man was unconscious and in critical condition, he had been beaten and suffered a serious brain injury. The two women were being treated for trauma and injuries resulting from a brutal beating and rape. The women claimed cowboys stopped them in Garfield County, held them overnight, beating the man unconscious, and repeatedly gang raping them.

An hour later, Sheriff Anderson, members of the Utah Highway Patrol, all Garfield County department heads and a representative of the Grand Staircase National Monument found seats in the turn-of-the-century commission chambers.

By the time the meeting adjourned Lonnie was exhausted and driving home, she broke into tears. What would Mack do in this situation, she thought? She felt lost without him. What would her father advise her to do? She was a fighter and tried to take solace in that fact but it was no use. She felt weak and incompetent. She needed someone to trust, someone she could let down all the false airs with and just be herself.

From the winding dirt road driveway, she could see the house was dark. Cody was gone again. Before going into the house she went to the horse barn. The horses stepped to the front of their stalls and looked with wide eyes at her surprise visit. She went to each stall, talking sweetly to each one, caressing them and giving each a bucket of oats and grain. In the last stall, Eloise waited for her. She was the mare her daddy gave her just weeks before he died. Eloise was old now, spending her days in the pasture and nights in the barn. Picking up a curry comb, Lonnie opened her stall and stepped inside.

Like Eloise, her one-time mustang - once wild and free - Lonnie was now locked in and corralled too, but it wasn't always that way. As a girl, when the bishop forced her into the Mormon church, out the window she'd go. They tried to catch her but never could. She ran off to Las Vegas a few times and always came back a week or two later. Her father was an alcoholic and her mother took her baby brother, Lark, with a traveling salesman and built a new life in Los Angeles. Lonnie stayed with her father out of loyalty and out of love. Her father had a deep love for horses and Lonnie loved them even more.

On Saturdays, they loaded the saddled horses onto the trailer, hitched to the Chevy four-wheeler and pulled it up to Timber Mountain where they grazed a few cows and had a small trailer house nestled in some purple oxide hills. They spent the days riding the ridge top, searching for strays and enjoying themselves. Lonnie liked to find perfect lunch spots, places with spectacular views. She would spread out the checkered tablecloth her mother left and they would sit in the cool shade and picnic. Lonnie did the best she could to take her mother's place, but she could never cook - her mother left before teaching her. Lonnie usually brought tuna fish sandwiches and potato chips and green Jell-O with whip cream.

Like her mother, she grew tall, rangy and shapely. By seventeen she was the best looking girl in Kanab. She wore tight, faded work jeans and manly shirts tucked in snugly at the waist. At nineteen, despite her stubborn independent streak, she was voted Kane County Rodeo Queen. As royalty, she rode her horse around the rodeo arena, carrying an American flag all decked out with streamers waving in the wind behind her. Her beauty was innocent yet sexual and the boys and men wouldn't leave her alone. At first, she was pleasantly surprised and felt lucky at all the attention, but as time past, after countless attempts to charm, cajole, and even bully her, she became angry and mean. She asked her daddy what to do, but he was no good, telling her simply, "that's the way men are." When the bishop of the Mormon Church tried to kiss her in the parking lot of Food Town, a man with eight children and old enough to be her father, she had had enough and threatened to call his wife. Lonnie admired men but why couldn't they just leave her alone? Why did they take it so far? Men aren't all that bad, how could they be, with a dad like mine, she thought.

Sometimes, her father coughed so hard at night she was afraid he'd die. She sat for hours at a time watching him breathe after he'd pass out from whiskey. His chest would rise with a reassuring sucking force but his exhales were weak and tapered off to a whisper. It was the time in-between the exhales and inhales that were the worst. She watched him die a thousand times. After exhaling his flattened chest did not move for the longest time, until suddenly he would gasp air and his chest would inflate and the process began again. If he dies, she wondered, what will I do? Should I give him mouth to mouth resuscitation or let him go so he can be with grandma? Sometimes, when he failed to return from the liquor store she stayed up all night waiting for him. She rode her bike around town searching, occasionally finding his truck parked at one of this drinking buddy's houses or at one of the two bars in town.

Lonnie could have had any man in the county but instead she chose Ronnie Lee Johnson. No one could believe she would make such a bad mistake and many who were jealous saw her choice as a personality flaw. Ronnie Lee was raised in Los Angeles by his father but lived in Kanab with his grandparents. He got into some kind of trouble in LA and used Kanab as a hideout. He was handsome and blonde and funny and unlike anyone else in town. He never worked and spent his time shooting pool at Roscoe's or drinking beer from the back of his pick up out in the desert. Everything about him fascinated her.

Ronnie Lee often disappeared without telling Lonnie. They might spend weeks together then suddenly without a word he was gone and she was left alone. A week or a month later he'd return, acting as if everything were normal and telling her he had business in California. She knew something was up, that he probably had another girlfriend, but she took him at his word and somehow, it made her want him more. She dedicated herself to waiting for him, watching the days and then weeks come and go, trying her best to be patient and at peace, and many times not doing a very good job of it. If he really cared for me, he wouldn't do this, why doesn't he just call me, she wondered.

One day, sad and tired of waiting, she decided to have a beer with her father. Within a few months, she was knocking them back like an old pro. It started with a couple of beers the first night but quickly evolved into her main preoccupation. She and dad would start drinking Friday afternoon and call it quits late Sunday night. Like her old man, Lonnie was a natural.

With Ronnie Lee gone most of the time and Lonnie drinking, the men in town got the idea she was easy and started to hit on her, making crude remarks or propositioning her; others hung around trying to get her shit-faced, hoping she might pass out or put out. The town's righteous men treated her with disgust, but secretly wanted her. Not only had she not given them the time of day, she picked a well-known drug dealing loser.

At twenty-two, Lonnie was considered a slut in her hometown of Kanab. She was belligerent and didn't take it sitting down. She paraded around in tight clothes openly flirting and when men took the bait she humiliated them in public, saying they were ugly or short or fat or stupid. She threatened to call the wives of several upstanding citizens if they didn't leave her alone. The talk soon stopped but she had burned her bridges.

She began spending more and more time at the trailer on the bench above Timber Mountain. She packed up her dad and the Chevy with food and beer and whiskey and they spent weeks riding and drinking and sitting around a campfire in fold-out chairs. One morning Lonnie woke early, got dressed and went outside the trailer to find her father dead. He was sitting in his fold-out chair, head tilted down, a cigarette between his lips, and a week's worth of shaggy beard on his face. She leaned over and hugged his neck - but he was cold and stiff and smelled of alcohol-tinted perspiration and death. She pulled back and as she did, he fell forward and off the chair into the cold white ashes of the previous night's fire. It was a forty mile drive to anywhere, so she lifted him back into his seat and stayed another couple of days before wrapping him in a tarp and driving him back into town.

At twenty-five, she was living with Tom Levitt, a man thirty-five-years her senior and feared by everyone. Levitt had a mean streak and reputation for violence, once breaking a man's leg with a baseball bat after beating him unconscious. They worked cattle up on the Kaiparowits and seldom came into town. Tom wasn't what he used to be, but he was still strong and a man to be reckoned with. Sober, he was sweet and sentimental, drunk he was nasty and mean. She and Tom ended up living along with his horses and dogs out on the land, sixty miles from anyone.

It didn't take long before Tom started beating Lonnie. They drank, argued and then he'd hit her, often knocking her down or blackening her eye. "Your nothin' more than a worthless whore, like your mother," he told her. He often threatened her with his guns, and finally one night, in a last desperate attempt to bring him to his senses, she hauled off and hit him with a piece of fire wood. He took one step back, drew his pistol and shot her on the spot. She fell forward face down on the kitchen floor. Thinking she was dead, Tom put the pistol in his mouth and pulled the trigger.

Two days later, ranchers looking for some cows found them lying there. Tom was dead but Lonnie was still alive. Six months later, she was as good as new - but changed. The story of Tom and Lonnie was told and retold and she became a legend in redrock country.

She stopped drinking and ran into a professional rodeo bull rider named Mack Walker Bullock. They knew one another from school, he was a football player for Panguitch High and she was a cheerleader from Kanab. Mack came from the wealthiest, most prominent ranching family in the state. He left for college and ended up spending seven years as a professional rodeo man, winning a national championship, before coming home to take control of the family's extensive ranch holdings.

Chapter Eleven

A week after Ateen and Garrett delivered Ian, Lana and Summer to the St. George Regional Hospital, Garrett was still holed up at the Twilight Motel. Ateen left for Page and Navajo Mountain after giving a statement to the authorities. He was anxious to talk to the elders about Nemelka and get back on his trail. "We need to find him," he told Garrett. "He will lead us to who did this."

Garrett couldn't be blamed for wanting to hang around St. George. Journalists from Salt Lake City, Las Vegas, Denver and Phoenix wanted to interview him. Events were cranking up towards an explosion and people were talking about a Western land war. Not since the 1890s when sheep and cattle men battled over grazing on the windy Wyoming plains had the potential for bloodshed been so high. A New York Times writer called on Wednesday and CNN and the BBC requested interviews. It had been two years since Garrett disappeared, losing contact with his agent and the editors who depended on him for years.

Friday afternoon a sexy television journalist, Randy Lawrence, of ASB News, showed up at his motel wearing a short skirt and high heels, accompanied by a camera and sound man. She insisted on an interview.

"As if I give a shit who you are," he slurred after her introduction. "I was writing about the land when you were suckling your mother's bosom and wearing swaddling clothes - more than you're wearing now.

"Is that suppose to impress me?" she shot back.

"Obviously, you really don't know anything about news gathering or story telling - but I'll give you some advice. Read the police reports, talk to people who know more than you - in that case, that would mean anyone - and then listen to what they tell you."

"You're just like they said," she put her hand on her hip, disinterested.

"Yeah, fuck 'em."

"An alcoholic loser. A has been."

"Tell you what," he laughed, "read my story when it comes out. Learn something. This is my story. Tell your boss to send somebody who knows what they're doing next time."

It was all true enough, for anyone who read Garrett's books, essays and articles about the West and the sandstone deserts he could be considered an expert - or even a reluctant sage. Editors on both coasts called when they needed a writer who understood the West. After his disappearance, most wrote him off as a good writer who ended up a melancholy and ugly alcoholic.

Garrett got his start in the writing business in the mid 1970s. He built a reputation for clean copy and compelling prose; he never missed a deadline. He broke into the national markets taking dangerous undercover stories or covering war zones. He infiltrated racist organizations and investigated paramilitary religious groups. Working for an infamous paraplegic pornographer, he assumed a new identity and penetrated the inner circle of Louisiana's most famous television evangelist. His expose brought the self-proclaimed man of God to his knees.

Garrett's success came after a decade of wandering. He dropped in and out of schools, worked for antiwar organizations, lived as a gypsy, rode freight trains, smuggled hashish from Amsterdam, wrote childish poetry and always followed the insatiable compass of his divining rod. He tried on many identities - a salesman, underground miner, nude model, logger, university instructor, truck driver, backpacker, business owner, smuggler. He looked in the mirror and was always surprised. He asked his reflection, Do you know me? His pathetic quest for self was perhaps his most endearing quality. Women loved him for his manliness and his overabundant tragic qualities. He loved them back but seldom for long. "It's your own fault," he told them. "If you fall for a worthless sack-of-shit like me you get what you get." Or, "Now that it's over, you can marry an accountant or dentist or a business man, someone rock solid, someone you can depend on." Besides, he insisted, "Isn't everyone responsible for his or her own happiness?"

By the time he married, his lost and lustful years were over - or so he thought. He was a sought after journalist and publisher of a small art magazine. Lexi was a beautiful computer scientist with a sharp eye for wonder and experience, but neither found time for the other, and one morning while on assignment for a New York men's magazine covering the Hopi - Navajo land dispute, he found himself in bed with a beautiful Jewish journalist from People Magazine. Like a good soldier he marched home and told Lexi and broke off the marriage, saying he couldn't deny this flaw in the fabric of his character. He loved Lexi and their parting left him empty and melancholy.

That night at Cory's, a favorite local bar and grill in St. George, Garrett already had too many drinks when the TV journalist Randy Lawrence and her crew showed up. He stumbled over and asked her to have a drink, saying he might consider giving her an interview. She didn't bite. "Sorry," she said, "I know what you want and I never fuck anyone older than my father." She flashed a venomous smile and turned away.

Next, he tried an overweight waitress, but she was busy and married and would have none of it so he left and walked back to the Twilight.

On the sidewalk ahead of him he spotted a petite woman. From behind, she was thin and had thick long black hair. It's still early, he thought checking his watch, maybe she's the one. At the intersection, the woman half-turned and smiled in his direction before disappearing down a neighborhood street. I know her, he thought, glimpsing her face. Where have I seen her before? She wants me to follow her. She's leading me . . . to her place. At the corner, he saw the woman's silhouette fade into the darkness. The faster he walked to catch her, the faster she seemed to move away. He called out but she kept moving, staying the same distance ahead of him. She's toying with me, why won't she stop?

A desert sirocco blew up from the south and caught in the treetops, swirling around them and making the sound of a river rushing down a canyon. The rush of air was so strong it forced the thick tree trunks to sway back and forth. The faster he walked, the faster she retreated. Soon, he was jogging and when she disappeared around another corner he broke into a full run. At the corner he expected to find her just a few feet down the sidewalk but she was gone. He scanned the sidewalk and then the road and then the opposite side of the street. Nothing.

The streetlights caught the wind blown treetops and created eerie, moving shadows on the asphalt below. They expanded and contracted and contorted and Garrett stood in the middle of the street searching for the woman who was no longer there. He ran to the next corner, crossed the street and came back again. She had simply vanished.

On his way back to the Twilight, he found himself walking along the Virgin River parkway. It was late and the alcohol made him woozy so he dropped into the deep grass on a hillside overlooking the river. Gazing up at the stars, a cloud soon obscured the stars and darkened the night. Against the night sky, the cloud was shaped like a woman's silhouette.

"Nancy!" Garrett called out to it without thinking, "Is it you?" He leaned up on his elbows and rubbed his eyes.

"Yes," A voice came from above. "It is me."

Garrett tried to sit up but could not, as if gravity held him in place. The cloud undulated and transformed in an ever moving dance. It floated and ascended and began to dissipate.

"Oh Nancy," he cried out, "please don't leave me, not again!"

For a moment, Nancy's face appeared in minute detail then morphed away. One by one the many faces of the people Garrett loved and lost appeared. Mick, who shot himself in the heart at a busy restaurant as a shocked lunch crowd watched. Then his father who died in his arms. As a child, Garrett feared and even hated his father. He learned later that his father's cruelty was jealousy over his closeness with his mother. Next came Randall and Sylvia and Leslie and then Nancy again, the petite, pig-tailed girl from the neighborhood who grew into a stunning, raven-haired beauty. They discovered many secrets together. At thirty-eight she developed liver cancer and right before his eyes, she shriveled up and died. The last face to appear was his mother's.

The next morning he awoke at the Twilight. His head throbbed and he had no idea how he got there. Garrett felt at home at the Twilight Motel. In his twenties, he used the Twilight as a jumping off point for LSD trips in Zion National Park, and then years later, it became a safe house, a place he could hide from bad relationships or use as a sanctuary for writing. This time around, he asked the motel owner, a man named Russell Godfrey, for a small table and with his laptop computer he re-connected with publishers and editors.

One hundred fifty miles east, on the morning of August 8th, a group of University of Colorado students and a few archaeology and anthropology professors hiked a serene half mile route across Cedar Mesa from a remote back country parking area to the Ghost Panel of the Ancients. They moved through cedar and juniper forests, around hills, up and down a series of orange and pink ridges to the hidden canyon where the panel was located.

The group made the hike five days a week for nearly a month, living in a nearby campsite and studying the panel by day. The area was the richest among the archaeological sites of Anasazi Indians and the Ghost Panel had fascinated scientists since its discovery at the turn of the last century. Its importance was measured in artistic and religious significance.

Located in a wraparound cathedral setting with perfect acoustics and containing more than seventy-five pictographs, the panel was impressive. Every sound echoed with purity. Visitors were sometimes overcome with spiritual or soulful feelings. The panel was dominated by six twenty-five-foot high ghostlike figures in long robes. They had wide square shoulders, frightening face-masks and bizarre looking head dresses. It appeared as if they were hovering or in flight. The bottom of their robes tapered and swept away like wisps of smoke. One small pictograph below resembled a man smoking a pipe and caused some experts to theorize the ghosts were incarnations of the gods, called by medicine men smoking pipes.

Below the ghosts were scores of smaller pictographs and among them was one that interested the scientific community more than any other. It was called the Green Mask and was provocative because its design and color were unlike any other. It was oval-shaped, resembling a Zulu shield and possessed a striking green background with a yellow arcing horizontal slash running though its middle, resembling a frown. Only three other Green Masks were known to exist and they resided at places of special religious significance. One was located on the sacred Second Mesa in Hopi land. The second was near the great Pueblo Bonito at the ancient Anasazi city of Chaco. And the third graced the entrance to a subterranean cavern where in 1920 archeologists discovered the remains of nearly a thousand people. Skulls were stacked in one place, femurs in an other and hips in another - the hip bones were interlaced together like nesting spoons.

The Panel of the Ghosts remained largely unknown and unvisited until the 1970s. It was a sacred place of rejoicing and renewal, and while only a few thousand people visited every year, it was not uncommon to find people camping nearby.

On the morning of August 8, when the group arrived at the amphitheater, they found the panel obliterated. It lay in thousands of pieces stacked atop each other at the base of the wall. It appeared the giant slab sheered off and crashed down leaving nothing but debris. The students and teachers were shocked and devastated. At first, they believed it was a natural occurrence - when the eroding outer sheath had worn and collapsed under its own weight - but under closer examination, they found pockmarks where bullets had struck the panel. One professor theorized the sound of the guns going off in the acoustically perfect amphitheater amplified the vibration and brought the entire wall down. They were hesitant to approach, fearful more rock was yet to fall, but when one graduate student climbed the rock pile, he discovered a message in fresh spray paint. It read, "ENVIRONMENTAL FUCKERS GET OUT - OR DIE."

A few days later, a famous Hollywood old-West film set outside of Kanab, Utah, frequented by bus loads of German and Japanese tourists, was burned to the ground. John Wayne, Frank Sinatra, Montgomery Cliff, Clint Eastwood and an entire generation of actors starred in Hollywood's most famous westerns filmed at the site in the 1940s and 1950s. Again, the perpetrators left a similar message, spray painted on a garbage can and directed at tourists.

Within days, a caller identifying himself as a radical environmentalist, called in a bomb threat to the managers of the Glen Canyon Dam. If the dam were taken out, the water of Lake Powell would create a wall of water two-hundred-feet high in the Grand Canyon. Park officials ordered boaters off the lake above the dam and alerted river runners below in the Grand Canyon to get to higher ground. The caller warned if the gates to the dam were not opened within 72 hours, it would be demolished. The bomber's intention was to set the land straight by draining Lake Powell and return-ing the Colorado and San Juan rivers back into their original river beds.

CHAPTER TWELVE
Boulder, Colorado

At its home base, EarthIsland, released a series of press releases and sent mass volume e-mails denying any involvement with the acts of vandalism and arson in the redrock country. From its sprawling mountain home headquarters in the foothills overlooking Pearl Street and the University of Colorado they networked with other national and international environmental organizations, attempting to build a united "Save the Redrock" coalition. By implementing a media campaign to first deny involvement in the violence, and educate people about the issues of the fragile redrock desert ecosystem they hoped to deflect the growing impression they were at the center of the controversy.

EarthIsland admitted to being in the area at the time the original crimes took place, even going so far as to say that it might appear they were involved, but they unequivocally denied any part in it. They theorized the crimes were staged to make them look responsible but had no real evidence to back the claim up. They denounced the cow killings as barbaric and emphatically stated if other environmental organizations or individuals associated with the movement were guilty, it would work with law enforcement to bring them to justice. At the same time, it blasted traditional land users, claiming that the fragile desert ecosystem, with little water or feed, was no place to raise red meat for people who will eventually develop heart disease from it.

EarthIsland leveled its harshest criticism at Garfield County for its inability to arrest the people who attacked Ian and raped and beat Lana and Summer. It outlined several cases of assault and minor crimes against tourists and innocent nature lovers by locals. At the same time it was pointing the finger of blame at Utah authorities, EarthIsland was being attacked by conservatives, pro-business newspapers, Western politicians and local officials who called them "radical environmentalists."

After leaving Utah, Jonah divided his days between his dark room developing images for his new book of naturalist photographs, and gearing up for the new campaign. He rose early, before the other fifteen staffers who lived at the house, meditated for an hour, took a five-mile run then sat on his private patio where he planned the new campaign, or what he liked to call a "comprehensive environmental offense" for the redrocks. The centerpiece of the plan was to return to the land with an overwhelming force of people. He considered setting up a regional headquarters in Escalante, Utah and moving a thousand people there. Since Escalante had a population of 800, the plan was to take over all local governmental offices and impose its agenda.

Jonah met daily with the organization's managers from ten until noon. These roundtable discussions dealt with all manner of not-for-profit business issues such as budgets, fundraising, staffing and the status of pending law suits against various businesses, municipalities, and state and federal governmental agencies, requiring them to enforce current environmental regulations or laws. But with Ian in a coma and a new battle engaged, Jonah was intense and uneasy. He paced around the room as if in his own world, sometimes not responding to questions directed at him. He possessed a sense of urgency few had ever seen in him. He barked orders, gestured wildly as he made important points and, in general, frightened everyone - except for Petra. Most had never seen him this way and when it got the best of him, Petra intervened to plead with him to settle down.

On his private patio, he and Petra ate lunch away from the fast pace of the house. Although Jonah served as EarthIsland's inspirational leader, a man whose clarity of purpose, energy and personal charisma moved the organization, he could also be difficult, distant and often confrontational. When in one of his moods, people knew to keep away, fearful he might turn on them with little or no provocation. Petra made certain everything worked as planned. She understood detail and diplomacy and worked behind the scene to make sure every objective was accomplished and that everyone understood his or her own importance. She saw to it that each staffer's ideas and contributions were acknowledged by Jonah and many were convinced that without her charm and enthusiasm, the organization would implode.

In the afternoons, she and Jonah hiked to a ridge with a spectacular view where he could be rejuvenated and reconnected with the purpose of his life. Raised in Denver, he first visited the back country of the Rockies as a boy with his family. His father, Howard, a sometimes distant and other times warm and charming man, was a mining geologist and liked to camp with the family near places he worked. Howard took them to places few knew about, but it wasn't until Jonah was twenty that he started making solo trips into the wild. Nature possessed a powerful gravitational pull over him and without much intervention on his own, he found himself pulled out onto the land, spending more and more time alone.

His life took a dramatic turn one rainy weekend as he hiked the saddle trail from Mt. Massive to Mt. Elbert, two of Colorado's biggest mountains. On the morning of the second day, as a storm rolled in and fog and mist shrouded the two great mountain peaks, a brilliant ray of sunlight emerged through a slip in the clouds and sent a luminous shaft of clear light deep into the valley's floor below, illuminating a grove of trees as if it were the hand of God. The grove radiated from within and without. Suddenly, in that one perfect moment, he was transformed and more alive than he'd ever been before. He was truly awake for the first time, as if he spent his entire life in some foggy daze and only now, at this exact moment, astride these two great mountains, he was reborn.

He spent the next two years hiking and camping and trekking the lost and lonely places. The further he went the closer he came to the truth about himself; and in a way, it was as if he were chasing himself, the true Jonah waiting around the next corner and if he hurried he might catch him. The beauty and the solace was intoxicating; it nurtured in him a respect he could not have fathomed before.

The more time he spent in the wild, the less connected to people and to the world he became. He gave up his job as a commercial photographer, sold his possessions and bought a truck and camper and moved into the mountains. He traveled from place to place, spending a week or a month, hiking the mountains, exploring the deserts and living off the land, before moving on to the next place. When his mother discovered he foraged for berries and fished the mountain brooks for food, she begged him to come to his senses. Once, in Glacier National Park, after two months elapsed without him contacting her, she alerted park authorities who mounted a search and found him happy and healthy living at a remote base camp in a rugged section of the park. He was unaware of just how much time passed.

Jonah's life took its next pivotal turn when he revisited one of his favorite places, a ponderosa forest in the Rio Grande Mountains just outside of Luna, New Mexico. After setting up camp and spending an hour musing next to the wide but shallow river, he decided to hike the four miles to a pristine forested valley he discovered the summer before. The valley was one of those special places that somehow escaped man's enterprise. The pathway was populated by majestic ponderosas, some standing in families and others in stark solemnity. He rested at a small clear lake with an adjoining bog of lush flowers before meandering to a rock fall where the trail climbed a ridge line. Everywhere he looked, he was home. He was a part of this place, of this natural world, of a cosmos in perfect tune. Cresting the ridge, the pathway entered a deep forest that welcomed him in peace and wonder. Suddenly, he stumbled out of the cool dark green tunnel of trees into the blazing hot sun. For a moment, he was blinded and disoriented. After shading his eyes with his hands, he discovered he was standing at the edge of an enormous clear-cut area. The devastation was of unimaginable proportion. Nothing was left standing, the loggers had taken it all.

Behind him was a perfect natural paradise with old growth trees, a hundred of types of flowers and undergrowth; a place with a thousand varieties of wildlife - birds and deer and foxes and elk and bears and fish and spiders and insects. In front of him, a hot blaring desolation and utter destruction. The trees were replaced by stumps and deep ruts where logging equipment swept through the forest, cutting, destroying, clearing and leaving piles of discarded tree tops and limbs behind. From his vantage point, he could see the destruction reach down into the magical valley that was his destination. Not a tree was left standing, the destruction was complete, the valley was decimated. The devastation spread out on either side and continued up onto the facing mountains, an area of many square miles.

The buzz of chain saws and the rumble of heavy equipment came from somewhere in the distance. Immobilized for a long time, he stood flatfooted trying to understand what he was witnessing. He turned and rushed back into the protective forest where his legs came out from underneath him and he sprawled out onto the rich forest carpet. For the next hour he sat in the dirt unable to move. Finally, he ventured back into the desolation. A deep primal rage grew within him as he surveyed the scene. As the days and months past his rage matured into a deep conviction that sent him off on a new mission, the one he was on today.

That was twelve years ago and in the intervening years he moved back to the city and worked tirelessly, at first as a volunteer, then as a leader in the environmental arena. He was respected for his command of the issues and for his articulate and impassioned speeches. He had the ability to reach inside even cold hearts, and convince people to do his bidding. He tired quickly of the petty disputes and ego problems in the established environmental community and revolted, starting his own organization.

At first, EarthIsland was a shaky coalition of fringe groups - anarchists, idealists, diehards. Some people were not fully formed, others were over baked - but everyone hated the establishment. They were young and brash and all works in progress - Jonah, Ian, Petra, Shon and a handful of others. They lusted to know and to command, they ached for a place to belong. After several attempts, EarthIsland coalesced or evolved. From a budget that amounted to the balance of Jonah's personal checking account five-years-ago, to a 3.5 million dollar a year budget today. EarthIsland's new ideas and edgy approach attracted attention, money and young people - thousands of worldwide supporters sent money.

Three weeks after escaping redrock country, as Jonah and Petra returned from a ridgeline hike, Shon ran to meet them. He had bad news. It couldn't wait. Ian was dead. A part of their dream died with him.

CHAPTER THIRTEEN
Navajo Mountain

A brazen purplish dawn displaced the night, expanding north and south along the line of the eastern horizon until a pinprick of brilliant sunlight broke at the center, spilling out the new day. Shadows and eddies of darkness took temporary sanctuary in the misty canyons and sleepy cedar and ponderosa forests as light illuminated the broad shoulders of Navajo Mountain.

Somewhere in the distance a dog barked and deer grazing in the foothills moved silently, instinctually higher on the mountain shoals. The forests were cool and the darkness was reluctant to give way to the light. At the same time, Betty Jane Ateen, the matriarch of the Ateen clan, at ninety-eight-years-old, knelt next to her outdoor stove, lighting a match to the twigs and tinder she gathered. Her family numbered 5,000 and many lived in places with names like New York City and Tuba City and Montreal, but Betty Jane never ventured off the mountain in her entire life. Getting down on all fours, she softly blew the tinder to give the fire a head start and as she did, the flames illuminated her wizened and incredibly wrinkled face.

Every day for ninety-two-years, since Betty was six years old, she rose before dawn to make fry bread. It all started one day when her grandmother wrenched her from bed and took her out back to the fire pit to help. Her grandmother told her, "My grandmother taught me and now I will teach you." Through the vast and incalculable cycle of living and dying, of seasons coming and going, of revolutions and circles of the earth and moon and sun and all the distant stars and universes rolling through space, Betty Jane now known simply as Granny, and many grandmothers before her, cooked fry bread in this very place. In winter Betty dressed in boots and threw a heavy blanket over her shoulders but other than that every day was much the same.

Granny paid no attention to the new day, her black-oiled pan was hot to cook, she'd finished her first cigarette, and the dough was ready to drop into the hot oil. The chickens and ducks scratched and jostled restlessly, letting her know it was feeding time but she ignored them, too. Next door at her daughter Alice's house, Brigham Joseph Ateen, who arrived from St. George the night before, awoke to his mother making coffee at the stove. Alice scooped three handfuls of coffee from the can and dropped them into the roiling water.

"Good to be home," Brigham said softly, sitting on the edge of the couch, pulling his socks and trousers on. The room was dark and filled with night shadows.

Turning from the stove, she handed him a cup of black coffee, "Go kiss your grandmother hello. She asks about you every day. You are her favorite. She tells everyone that you are special."

Brigham walked from the one room house through the grove of giant ponderosa pines to Grandma Betty's hogan. It was indeed good to be home and Ateen felt at peace, the crisp air carried the scent of pine and decay and nature's preparations for winter.

Granny looked up from her pan and smiled a toothless grin at her grandson, "Is the war over yet?"

"Yes, Grandma, the war is over."

"Who won?" she asked snapping a small branch and adding it to the fire under her pan.

"We won, Grandma."

"Oh good," she said, slowly standing and looking confused. "Who did we fight?"

"The Vietnamese, Grandma," her grandson answered; he could see a tear in her eye.

"Oh, yes. The Gooks. That is the way it is supposed to be."

Placing his coffee cup down, Ateen took his tiny grandmother into his arms and hugged her tenderly. His enormous hands and arms surrounded her and held her against his massive chest.

Pulling back, she told him, "I knew you would come back to me. You are a great warrior." Then, wagging a finger, she scolded him, "I lost your father to the Koreans and I will not lose you!"

"Yes, Grandma. The war has been over for a long time. I am safe and home."

"Put me down," she said, and their eyes met. "It is time for fry bread."

Ateen loved his Granny but he would rather eat dirt than eat fry bread.

When he went away into the army, he swore he'd never eat it again. He sat in an old wooden chair as Grandma cooked bread, spreading it out on some paper napkins to dry. His mother showed up with more coffee, carrying the heavy metal pot from her house. The three sat in the sun, ate Granny's fry bread, and talked of family and the mountain.

The Ateen clan lived at the foothills of the mountain. Of all the Dineh clans or chapters, the Ateen family considered itself the most wild, the most pure and the most religious. They were the protectors of the mountain, Tassumia, hallowed place of the gods. For hundreds of years they kept outsiders out and took their orders directly from the gods. Once, they were even separated from the rest of their tribal brothers for more than sixty years. It happened when the U.S. General Kit Carson and his army rounded up all the Dineh, more than 9,000 people, and marched them to Fort Bosco Redondo, where they remained for two years. The Ateen warriors met Carson's army on the high plains near the mountain and fought the invaders with such ferocity the army turned back after heavy losses. For sixty years no one left the mountain and their tribesmen were afraid to visit, fearful the gods were angry and spiteful after the Anglo invasion.

Brigham spent the day with his mother and grandmother, hauling firewood and fixing the water line that runs up a hill from the house to the holding tank. Several cousins stopped by and the women sat under the canopy of trees and worked weavings while talking incessantly. Granny smoked cigarettes and kept them laughing and slapping their sides.

Later, when Lena Tsosie showed up, Brigham wanted to get in his truck and leave. Lena was young, in her early thirties and still beautiful. She had two young children by her first husband who died in a car accident three years ago and Alice had been trying to line her son up with Lena for months, but he was a hard man to pin down. Brigham never married and since returning home from the war, refused to even date. When his mother begged him, saying the family needed more children, he told her, "My heart is not mine to give."

The next day, Ateen drove the eighty miles of dirt road to Page, Arizona and Joey Nez's Bonanza Cafe. The elders were anxious to find out what happened with he and Doo Doo in his Pants. Ateen stood at the end of the red leather tuck-and-roll booth and reported the incident with the coyote killers on Kaiparowits, the scene where the cows were shot, the mysterious shell casings; about meeting up with EarthIsland, how close the cowboys and environmentalist were to fighting, the rapes and beatings;

and, about the witness, Leon Nemelka.

The elders seemed unimpressed and when he finished, Natani asked, "Nothing else happened?"

Ateen thought for a moment, "I saw my great-great grandfather along the way - three times."

The elders sat straight up, shifted from bun to bun and rattled their coffee cups and plates. "Why didn't you say so?" Crank spoke up.

"The first time was at dusk where the cows were shot, then in the morning on the old Anasazi trail below Egypt, and finally at dusk again on the perch above the Escalante drainage."

"What was Doo Doo doing this whole time?"

"Looking the other way," he said. "It always happened the same way." He pointed with one finger to the corner of his eye. "It happened right here in my peripheral vision. When I caught sight of him, he moved off quickly or vanished."

"Was it to your left or right?" one asked.

"My left."

"What did it look like, did he glow?" another asked.

"I don't think so."

Each asked a question.

"Was he human?"

"Did he have four legs?"

"Was he floating?"

"Did he want you to see him?"

"Was there a light?"

Ateen couldn't answer the questions and the elders acted as if they were miffed, like he had the answers but was playing stupid. They talked among themselves and decided it was important for Ateen to follow this spirit. Joey Nez told him, "We want to show you a place on the mountain."

The elders piled into Nez's Cadillac and Ateen followed in his truck back to Navajo Mountain. Instead going east to the town of Navajo Mountain, they turned west to Endeshe Springs. No one lived on the west side of the mountain and by the time they arrived, Joey Nez's shiny red Cadillac was caked with a thick coat of chocolate colored dust. The dust coagulated into mud on the wiper blades and gave the windshield the appearance of crying.

A mile or two past the springs, they parked and hiked onto the mountain with Nez leading the way. The path was steep and narrow and at one point it cut across a dangerous exposed hillside just a few feet above a high cliff. None were dressed for hiking and all of them, except for Ateen, were men in their seventies. The old men moved slowly but with surprising strength and endurance and an hour later, at the base of a towering rock pinnacle of Kayenta sandstone, they stopped at a secret Anasazi cliff dwelling.

Ateen was the last to arrive at the ruin and moved past the others to take a closer look. His eyes were drawn to an unusual pictograph above the structure. It was oval-shaped with a bright green background and yellow slash frowning through the middle. He studied it intently.

"Is this what you wanted me to see?" Ateen asked, after noticing the men were not looking at the pictograph but at him.

"We thought you would like it," Nez replied, smiling widely and showing his mouth filled with 14 caret gold. The elders were all smiling or laughing.

"Inside," Natani ordered him, pointing to the remarkably well pre-served ruin.

Because the entryway was low, only three feet high, Ateen got down on his hands and knees and stuck his head inside. Sitting upright and cross-legged against the walls were four mummies dressed in elaborate ceremo-nial leather gowns. At first, Ateen thought the mummies were mannequins and the whole thing was some preposterous joke. Sitting next to them and all around the room were priceless religious dolls and ceremonial icons.

"Are any of these men your great grandfather?" Natani called out.

Ateen was surprised by the question and flustered at his inability to focus on their faces. "I don't know, I can't tell," he shouted back.

"Look closely. Get inside. Closer." Crank demanded, "Look at their faces!"

Ateen squeezed further inside and sat where the light was best. He felt disrespectful, like he was intruding on a final resting place, a place to be honored and left alone. Two of the faces were nothing more than skulls but strangely the two others possessed leather-like skin and one looked slight-ly familiar - perhaps it did look little like his great-great grandfather - a man he never met. He had seen this face before, but how could he be sure? He moved in closer. Yes. He had definitely seen this face but he wasn't sure if it was the apparition who visited him.

Outside, he asked the elders what it meant.

"We do not know," Nez replied, shaking his head.

"It is strange," Natani added, smiling at the others.

Nez told him, "We have decided that you are staying here until we come back for you." He and the others spent an hour collecting firewood and building a fire ring directly in front of the ruin and below the frowning green and yellow pictograph. From their pockets they brought an apple, a can of beans and a Snickers bar.

"These will do you," Natani assured him and they left.

CHAPTER FOURTEEN

The image of the "Coyotes on a Stick" hit the front page of newspapers across America and Europe. The gruesome image and story caught the public's imagination, airing on national television and was a subject in countless blogs and internet chat rooms. A stream of journalists, media personalities and documentary filmmakers arrived in southern Utah; Robert Redford was rumored to have flown in by private jet to gauge the situation. The long simmering hostilities between environmentalists and traditional land users was about to boil over. It was a battle pitting two armed groups of American patriots against each other out on a biblical landscape of beauty and majesty.

There was something for every market. The story offered the threat of real violence with a world-class view. A modern-day, flag-waving confrontation at high noon. The lines were crossed and now it was time to kick somebody's ass - American style. Panguitch was ill-prepared to handle the media outsiders and in characteristic Western rural form, it refused to accommodate the rush of self important phonies. They knew no matter how gracious, charming and complimentary the media stars were, ultimately they would get the shaft on the tube, portrayed as small-minded backwoods morons, and in this case, animal abusers.

Some motel owners on the verge of bankruptcy refused to rent rooms and local eateries that could always use the business, let the outsiders wait without taking their orders. A few new entrepreneurs who arrived after the Grand Staircase Monument was established, and who built new motels, gift shops and gas station convenience stores, and who counted on monument visitors that never materialized, welcomed the expense account using, SUV driving media types, catering to them as though they were latter-day gods.

The media talked with anyone who would speak to them: townsfolk, law enforcement, victims of the vandalism, hotheaded cowboys, gas station attendants, local and national environmentalists who arrived for their slice of the action. They set up cameras at Fifty Mile Ridge with the burned line shack in the foreground and the panoramic vistas surrounding it in the background. They filed reports shot at sunset when the sandstone cliffs were golden and magic.

High on everyone's interview list was Garfield County Commissioner, Lonnie Bullock. She was everything a good story ever wanted: a true Western woman, beautiful on camera, resourceful, spirited, sassy and always a lady. She did her best to field their questions, portraying her neighbors as honest, responsible, animal loving people. To one she said, "We're just like city folk, we pay our taxes, read the newspaper, have the same values, but we choose to live in the country." To another, "We got our share of hotheads and fools, just like you in the city. They don't represent the majority of us." And to another, she quipped, "Face it, everyone in America is just a generation or two away from their roots on the farm." And, "We've got nothing against responsible environmental minded Americans. It's the radical environmentalist fringe terror groups we want to eradicate."

With the media came the gatherers. They arrive without hoopla, drawn to places of conflict or turmoil or history for entirely personal reasons. They were young, old and middle aged; among them was naturalist writer, Carrie T. King. But King had a real reason to be there. She would serve as mediator. She passed out press releases claiming she knew both sides and could skillfully speak for both groups. She was uniquely qualified to serve as a dispute mediator, or at least, as a media facilitator. A native of the West, her lineage went back to the first Mormon pioneers. She could speak for the locals and their concerns. She was one of them. At the same time, she was a well-connected environmentalist, a mover who knew the issues and mindset of tree huggers worldwide. She was one of them, too.

As it stood, the potential confrontation, was not unlike many other recent battles in the West between environmentalists and long time local residents. But it was the ghastly image of the coyotes that focused attention. There was plenty to feed on, from locals the list included claims of arsons, the poisoning of important water wells, the vandalism of ranch equipment, the killing of cows destined for market and the destruction of important historic private property on one hand. From environmentalists there were reports of assaults against tourists, the turning back of tour buses filled with Germans and Japanese as they neared the area's national parks, the mysterious bulldozing of a new road into pristine wilderness, the destruction of the Ghost Panel, and the fatal beating of one man and the brutal rapes of two women - reportedly at the hands of drunken cowboys looking to even the score.

Later that night when Lonnie returned to the ranch after a long day dealing with the chamber of commerce, taking calls from the media and Sheriff Anderson, who couldn't stop running his mouth to journalists, she spotted a light in the tack room as she came up the drive. She was relieved Cody was home but felt anxious because she had sensed trouble for a week. It was nothing Cody had said or done - and that was the problem. He hadn't done anything, he had hardly spoken to her since the trouble began.

"You in here?" she said, coming through the doorway and finding him putting a second coat of saddle soap on his father's saddle. Empty beer cans littered the floor around him.

"Just me and the barn flies," he answered, without turning to face her.

"Since when you take up drinking by yourself?" she asked, looking at the pile of cans.

"I'm a Bullock, aren't I?"

"Stop it."

"I come from a long line of hard drinkers on both sides of the family." He spun around and grinned.

"You okay?"

Cody smirked and moved to hug her. "Yeah. Okay. Great. Wonderful!" he said, cynically.

"Haven't seen much of you lately."

"Pretty much keepin' to myself," he answered. "I noticed you're not around much either."

She took a deep breath, "I shouldn't have let them talk me into finishing your dad's term," she lamented. "I need to be here with you and the horses."

The truth was Cody was avoiding his mother and everyone else. He rose every morning before she did, packed his saddle bags and left on horseback, taking the dogs and disappearing like his father when he needed to think or work through some problem. He'd return late or not at all; once he was gone for three days.

"Everything okay in town?" he asked.

"Couldn't be worse. But let's not talk about it. Let's talk about you."

She nodded to the saddle. "I've been meaning to talk to you about . . ."

"Finishing the saddle?" he quickly interrupted.

"Not exactly, but it's time you started using it, don't you think?"

Cody unfolded the cleaning cloth and refolded it. The idea pleased him.

"Your father would like it."

He picked up the can of saddle soap, worked the cloth in a circular motion and applied the soap. "Beautiful isn't it?" His voice carried a deep satisfaction.

"It truly is."

The two admired the saddle. It was classic and its simplicity was the source of its elegance. The two gazed at it for a long time until it became uncomfortable; it was impossible not to look at the saddle without thinking of Mack sitting atop it. Oh Mack, how we could use you now, Lonnie thought.

"You alright, son?" she asked, trying to look into his eyes but he looked away, avoiding her. "What is it?"

"Well . . ." he started but couldn't finish. He shook his head slowly back and forth as emotion swelled his chest.

"What is it, Dolly?" she asked desperately, using the name she called him as a boy.

"I need to deal with it on my own."

"Can't you tell your mother?" she said incredulously. "I'm your mother - whatever it is, I need to know. . ."

He turned to the saddle so she could not see his struggle to control his tears. "It's one of those things a man can't tell his mother about."

Lonnie was frightened. Since he was a little boy, she and Cody always talked and divulged every secret. Neither could remember a day of discord. "What is it, Cody?" she pleaded, "Please! Is it Michelle, are you two fighting?"

"Mother," he said sternly, "Remember? Michelle left for college a month ago."

"Oh. Yes. How foolish of me. I'm sorry. I forgot." She felt stupid. "Are you in some kind of trouble?"

"Troubles all around us these days. . . " he said, outstretching his arms as if to say something, but instead fell silent.

"Please, give me a hint? What is it?"

"Mother, stop! I told you, I don't want to talk about . . . " He turned back to her, his red face flush with rage, alcohol and hurt. "I wish I hadn't brought it up."

"Won't you tell me?" she begged. "I can't stand to see you this way. What can I do? I can help. We can work it out, if you'll just tell me."

"Mother!" he screamed, "Leave me alone!" He rushed to the door as if trying to escape but stopped before leaving. Instead, he turned and hit the wall with his fist so hard it broke a wall plank.

"Okay, okay. Don't go! Please . . . " she pleaded and backed off, frightened. She rarely saw him like this. "I'm sorry. I'm sorry," she repeated, her mind racing. She felt helpless and didn't know what to do or say.

"Have you eaten?" she finally blurted out.

Something about her question broke the tension and they both burst into laughter and ran to the other and hugged.

"Haven't eaten all day," he told her.

"What would you like, Dolly?"

"You decide."

She squeezed his middle tightly, then left for the house. She was worried. She'd only seen him act this way once before - when his father died. When Mack died Cody broke down and sobbed in front of everyone at the hospital. At first he tried to be strong for his mother, but his own devastation was too much and it immobilized him. He was humiliated and his inability to rise above his anguish to care for his mother still haunted him. The day of the funeral, he mysteriously disappeared in the morning, only making it back just before the service. He spent a day at the old line shack at Fifty Mile Ridge, pacing back and forth, carrying his Colt six-shooter, trying to get the nerve to blow his brains out for disgracing the family.

From the day of this birth until he was nine or ten Cody and his mother were inseparable. He followed her around wherever she went and Mack liked to tease him about being her puppy dog. The two took weekend trips to Las Vegas and Salt Lake and even to L A where Lonnie tanned on the beach with friends while he played in the surf. But by his early teens Cody started going out onto the range with his father to round up cattle and help the men dig fence posts, build water catchments and troughs. By nature, Mack possessed a strength others found comforting and irresistible. Always in control, polite and a gentleman, his father's easygoing but take charge nature allowed him to never waiver in the face of problems or obstacles and earned the respect of everyone. Even in the most troubling circumstances, like the death of his mother, Mack thought of others first, making certain everyone was taken care of. Cody wondered if he were truly like his father as some people said or if he was secretly a momma's boy.

Out on the range together, usually after a long day in the saddle and around the campfire, he heard the stories of his famous forefathers - how his great granddad was the first man to live in the valley and fought off Indians to build a homestead on the mountain. One old-time ranch hand told Cody how his grandfather, Mack's dad, showed up one day at a local widow's house with a crew of workers and spent a week digging a four-foot-deep ditch from the reservoir to her fields, more than a quarter mile away, so she could irrigate her crops. Granddad built the ranch into the largest and finest in the state, with more than six-thousand acres, thousands of beef cows and the best horses in the West.

By the time Mack died, when he was seventeen, Cody could out ride and out rope his dad and was a national champion rodeo rider. He knew when to stand his ground and when to stand down - and if pushed, he'd fight. At the same time, Cody saw beauty in everything, he was gentle and an advocate for the underdog. He was a combination of his father's strength and determination and his mother's compassion. Only years of seasoning, of successes and mistakes, would forge this young man into what he was destined to become.

A half hour later, Lonnie returned with a platter of sandwiches and potato salad. She changed out of her business pant suit and into an old pair of faded Levi's and one of Mack's favorite work shirts. When Cody saw her coming, he cleared a place on the work table and pulled up another chair. He could see she was tired by the way she walked and the lines in her face.

"Boy, I'm hungry!" he said, taking the platter and kissing her on the forehead. "Don't worry about me - everything will work out."

"I just can't be at peace when you're . . . "

He interrupted, "What's the news on the investigation?"

"Which one?"

"Andy arrested the god-damned radicals who shot the cows yet? Son-of-bitches!"

"Who said it was environmentalists?"

"Who else? Who ever killed the cows - and all the rest - should be shot." The alcohol was speaking again. "I'll do it myself if I run into 'em." He was getting hotter, "I'll blow 'em away."

"Cody!" she demanded. "You will do nothing of the kind! Is that what's bothering you?" she said, taking half a sandwich in both hands and avoiding his eyes. "I understand how you feel and I'm damned angry myself," she continued, "but the law will take care of it. Everybody needs to cool down, especially now."

"We gotta band together."

"Not you, too?" She saw an opening, "I don't want you to go off half-cocked but Maureen Jacobson tells me she saw you hanging with the Circle Cliff crew . . . "

"Don't you go worrying about me." he said, waving her off. "I can handle myself. Nobody's going to be telling me what to do." He paused and asked nervously, "What about the other investigation?"

"Please Cody," she went on, "you're going to get yourself into trouble if you . . ."

"Trouble!" he repeated. "There's gonna be trouble all right! Especially when we find the low down dirty rats who've been takin advantage of us."

"I know but we've got to do it the right way. It's not going to help any of us to go make trouble for ourselves."

"If I run into them, there's going to be some hell to pay."

"I can't tell you what to do," she said, resolutely. "You know the difference between right and wrong."

He nodded and ate some potato salad.

"What investigation are you talking about?" She asked, "We've got more than we can handle."

"You know," he said in between bites, "the rapes and . . . "

"Oh, I feel so sorry for them. Who would do such a thing? Poor innocent girls brutally raped like that. It must have been a nightmare."

"Serves them right." he said coldly. "They shouldn't have been out there doing what they were doing!"

"I can't believe you'd say such a thing!" she interrupted and slapped his arm. "What is wrong with you? They weren't breaking any laws. They didn't do anything wrong and even if they did, those two girls were raped and tortured!"

"EarthIsland people, I hear."

"So? That's right, they were," she told him. "When does that give some horse's ass the right to . . . "

"They probably had something to do with the line shack and the cows."

"Well, they didn't! And even if they did, one stupid act doesn't justify a horrible crime. A worse crime!" She was angry and disappointed in her son's callousness. "They just got in from Colorado the day it happened. They weren't involved with the cows. The sheriff told me. They had nothing to do with it."

"That's not what I heard. If they didn't do it, some of their friends did. I guarantee."

"I don't know. That does not give anyone a right to do what they did!" She paused to control her anger and wipe her mouth with a napkin. "I'll tell you something else, the boy's probably going to die. And if he does, we're going to have a murder investigation on our hands!"

Cody tensed and swallowed without looking up. "Die? How do you know?"

"That's what I hear."

"He was beat up that bad?"

"Bad enough for his brain to swell."

"Did he tell them who did it?"

"He's never regained consciousness. Most likely never will but the girls gave the sheriff over in St. George a description."

"Got any suspects?"

"I think so, but I don't know. We're having a meeting."

"Outsiders, I suspect," he said pursing his lips. "Nobody here abouts would pull that kind of . . ." he stuttered.

"I suspect it was . . ." she paused, "We've got some pretty bad apples around here these days. There's no telling who did it. I'm just hoping he will pull out of it. I talked to his mother on the phone the other day."

"What if it's someone we know?" Cody asked.

"They'll have to pay the price like anyone else. They need to be behind bars. I promised his mother I'd help!"

Chapter Fifteen

Park officials at Zion National Park realized something was up when the line of cars at the two main entrances began piling up and stretching back for blocks. The day shift supervisor got on the horn and called the superintendent who arrived at the south entrance in his big green SUV to gauge what was happening. Throughout the day the back-up continued and by night, two thousand extra visitors had streamed into the park. At one point, automobiles were backed up through the adjacent town of Springdale.

Zion was accustomed to hosting millions of visitors annually, but the unexpected guests didn't fit the profile of the normal autumn visitors: the mostly graying, Winnebago-driving retirees who arrive after school is back in session so they don't have to put up with mom, dad and the kids. The unexpected guests were young, edgy and arrived by the carload, four or more people packed in each car. Their vehicles displayed tags from many states and bumper stickers like, "Save Our Planet," "Outlaw Logging," "EarthFirst!," "Save the Whales," "Mining Sucks," "Free Leonard Peltier," "Cheyenne Power," and "EarthIsland." They all asked the same question, "Which way to Watchman Campground?"

"The campground is filled," they were told, but once in the park they crowded into the huge campground, named after the Watchman monolith towering one-thousand-feet above. They parked wherever they could, along the road, at the Visitor's Center or lodge, at the trailheads and rest-rooms. Many parked in Springdale and walked into the park and by after-noon, the road was so filled with cars and pedestrians, it looked like a scene reminiscent of 1969's Woodstock. Many visitors who were already there, overwhelmed by the onrush of outsiders, packed up and tried to leave but were caught for hours in the traffic jam.

Like the Roshneshis when they arrived in Antelope, Oregon, awaiting their spiritual leader, the Bagwan, the new arrivals were polite and respect-ful, paying the park's fees without complaint, and remarking about the "awesomeness" of the place. They stopped at the Visitor's Center to talk with rangers about hikes and history and wildlife. When staffers enquired what was going on, the new guests were friendly but offered little information. By afternoon, hundreds of mountain bikers worked up the beautiful Zion's canyon, as hikers packed the steep trail to Angel's Landing. The trams shuttling people up and down the canyon were filled to capacity and every parking place in the park and adjacent town was filled; park employees rushed to open overflow camp grounds and within minutes they were maxed out. Singing echoed down through the canyon when hundreds of people atop Angel's Landing broke out in an impromptu sing along. At dusk, the Great White Throne was cast aglow and the yellow leaves of the cottonwood trees lining the Virgin River wafted in the breeze and created an unreal light show. The energy of the natural wonders and that of the new arrivals filled the canyon.

In town, the coffee shops, gift shops and restaurants were packed. Every available room was rented and lines of hungry people stood outside trendy eateries along Main Street. Some never made it inside when the restaurants ran out of food.

Watchman Campground, once a beautiful meadow and now a sprawling camp area able to accommodate thousands of nature lovers, was transformed into what appeared to be a counterculture refugee camp with wall to wall tents and thousands of people milling around. At the amphitheater, a single solitary drummer pounded out a single note and within an hour twenty or more joined in; the drums sounded out a welcome that could be heard up and down the canyon. Congas, Eastern Indian, African and Native American drums brought the newcomers in like a homing beacon.

When rangers arrived to inform the drummers of the park noise ordinance, the musicians apologized but did not stop. "I'm going to have to ask you to stop playing," one ranger told them, but he was ignored.

"We're the welcoming committee," a drummer said, without missing a beat.

"Welcoming what?" he asked.

"Sorry," one said, "we can't say. We have our instructions."

When the ranger asked who gave the instructions, the drummer just smiled and told him, "You'll see soon enough."

The rangers were outnumbered five-hundred-to-one and without wanting to cause a confrontation, they tipped their smokey bear hats and backed away. "I think we might have a situation here," one radioed the superintendent, who was on the horn to the National Parks headquarters in Washington, D.C..

As night fell, the newcomers built a bonfire near the cliffs at the amphitheater and shadows were illuminated a hundred feet high on the cliff walls. When twenty or more rangers arrived, some carrying side arms, they were blocked from entering. Hundreds of people met them at the gates and refused to budge. "What do you want?" they asked.

"We have a 10 p.m. noise and lights out policy. You need to hold it down," the head ranger informed them angrily.

"You need twenty armed men to tell us to be quiet?" one man enquired and shouts of support went out from the crowd behind him.

When the rangers informed them they were disturbing the peace and quiet of the other park visitors, the drums were silenced and everyone sat around the camp fire and talked in hushed tones. "We're not here to ruin anyone's experience," a man told them. The rangers were relieved and surprised at just how quickly and completely the crowd quieted down.

Since its establishment in 1901, Zion National Park has hosted many unexpected guests, like in 1974 when the Oakland Chapter of Hell's Angeles invited five-thousand outlaw bikers from around the country to meet at the park for a weekend of endless beer drinking, wet tee shirt contests, rock music and all night parties. They arrived prepared with a semi-truck loaded with kegs of Coors beer. Visitors scrambled for the exits and park officials called for reinforcements. Hundreds of law enforcement personnel from jurisdictions throughout the West rushed to the park. Outlaw bikers, armed with rifles and hand guns, set up road blocks and faced off with the lawmen, telling them it was a private party and they weren't welcome. More recently, the much smaller but more distasteful Aryan Nations prayer group arrived at Zion from its Northern Idaho compound. The group was so taken by the spiritual essence of the park they decided it should become the capitol of its White Homeland and conducted a sunrise prayer ceremony, consecrating the park as such. Fighting and scuffling broke out when they ordered brown, black and red people to leave. Ultimately, the supremacists were forced to leave but not before the national press showed up and gave them what it wanted, a soapbox to espouse their particular variety of hatred.

Zion Canyon has long been a spiritual magnet, casting its spell on millions who visit it. The native American Indians who populated the area for hundreds of years before the Mormons wiped them out refused to visit there. It was a place of such great magic and power not even the most honored wise man was worthy of a visit.

Jonah and his entourage arrived in Utah on the second day leading more than two hundred vehicles from Colorado. Before entering the park they paraded slowly through Panguitch fifty miles north displaying their colors, flying EarthIsland banners and holding up signs saying, "Justice for Ian - Justice for the Land." They blew horns, waved American flags from the windows and shouted greetings or obscenities to everyone on the street. Commissioner Bullock, Sheriff Anderson and everyone at the Garfield County Courthouse lined up outside to watch the disgusting parade.

When Jonah's caravan arrived at the East entrance of the park, they were greeted by forty park rangers and a dozen Utah Highway Patrol officers. The superintendent asked what their intentions were. "We are here to enjoy the park," Jonah told them. The superintendent was friendly but skeptical. "We will do everything possible to abide by all the rules," Jonah told them.

Some rangers were secretly pleased to see the environmentalists and had been waiting for a long time for someone to make a stand. Others didn't like it one bit, one telling a highway patrolman, I'll bet there are drugs in every car. The trooper responded by saying he wished he could bust some chops. By the end of the second day, nearly five thousand EarthIsland members and supporters were there.

While the implementation of Jonah's "Save the Redrocks" campaign was now in full swing, it started many days earlier when he received word of Ian's death. An hour later, EarthIsland pulled its internet newsletter web page and replaced it. The masthead was draped in a black ribbon and below it was a half page photograph of Ian standing alone in the tropical forest of Hawaii with his handsome and boyish "hey-can-you-dig-it" smile. Below the picture, it read, In Memorial, Ian McCarthey July 31, 1968 - Aug. 1. 2003. In smaller text was Ian's favorite poem from the famed Spanish poet, Antonio Machado:

The wind one brilliant day
Called to my soul with the odor of
Jasmine and said,
"In return for the odor of my jasmine
I'd like the odor of your roses."

"But I have no roses," I answered,
"All the flowers in my garden are dead."
The wind then said,
"I'll take all the withered petals and
Yellow leaves," and the wind left -
And I wept. And I asked myself,
"What have you done with the garden that
Has been entrusted to you?"

At the bottom of the page, a small red-and-black box flashed on-and-off. It read: Members Only. Alert Priority. Password required. Inside, was a general call to mobilization and instructions of what to do, where to go and what to say.

The EarthIsland website was flooded with responses, getting over two thousand solid hits a day. They posted articles about Ian's murder and the circumstances including demands for the authorities to make arrests. It called authorities in Utah incompetent and requested everyone flood Washington D. C. with calls demanding an immediate investigation. From around the world including Holland, England and Germany, e-mails and faxes flooded into the EarthIsland system with offers of help and money.

Since the incident at Fifty Mile Ridge, EarthIsland and especially Jonah came under intense scrutiny and criticism. Conservative columnists excoriated and vilified him, Western politicians used EarthIsland as an example of the worst kind of out of control extremist element. Even Western environmental groups, especially the Sandstone Wilderness Alliance, attacked Jonah and his group. SWA chairman, Alan von Bank, was furious and demanded to know what EarthIslanders were doing at Egypt in the new monument in the first place. He called Jonah by tele-phone, "This is our turf," he said, "what do you think you were doing here?" He chastised Jonah for destroying the delicate balance between opposing factions in the area.

"What balance are you referring too?" Jonah quipped angrily. "You mean the balance where you lock yourself in an intractable legal dance, where you never really do anything? Or the balance where ranchers con-tinue to let their cows eat all the natural forage and shit in the only water sources available? Or are you referring to the balance where local yokels blade new roads into wilderness?"

"The truth is," he told von Bank in a calm voice, "when we first arrived at Egypt we were just checking the area out, taking a sabbatical, doing what nature lovers do, visiting a place of peace and solitude." He paused, "Unfortunately, we got caught up in a senseless crime against the cows."

"Don't shit me, Jonah!" the chairman challenged. "Are you trying to tell me it was just a coincidence that after years of no violence you just happened to show up on the scene at the exact same time and place where the cows were killed?" von Bank was incredulous, "Come now, don't play games with me. We know who you run with and if it wasn't you it was someone flying your banner!"

"Believe what you will," Jonah countered, "I told you what happened. We had nothing to do with it. What seems obvious to us is that you and your cronies aren't really up to the challenge of protecting the land so we've decided it's time to change that and get things done."

Before von Bank hung up on him, Jonah held out an olive branch, "You can join us or you can become even more irrelevant than you already are."

Many within the community of environmentalists were ready for a change. One of their cadre was now dead - he gave his life for the cause - and now it was time for the rest to ante up. A cold wind was sweeping through the environmental hallways across the country and even the oldest and most stodgy organizations reconsidered their tactics. They could change or be left behind - a new movement was afoot. Many leaders in the community were so alarmed by the shooting of the cows, by Ian's death and the beatings and rapes that they set aside long standing disputes and power struggles to discuss forming new alliances and coalitions. It was a new millennium, a time to unlatch the shutters and open the doors.

That night at Watchman Campground, the group went silent when Jonah stood next to the bonfire and spoke. "The death of our comrade Ian has forced us to refocus our ideals and renew our commitment," he began. "In times such as these, we need to band together and close ranks. We need to stand shoulder to shoulder and speak with one voice. Each of us, each person here, has a voice and while many here are articulate and have found willing audiences, it is only when we speak together, as one united voice does the resonance of what we say really get heard. Ian's voice is silent now - but listen," he stopped and they listened to the silence of nature, "He is here alive among us. I can feel him. His energy and spirit surround us - right now. But now, we must do his talking. If we do not speak for him,

Ian's voice will have truly been silenced. And that, is exactly what the people who killed him want, to silence people like Ian and like you and you and you," he pointed out into the crowd. "But, I for one, I will not stand for it. No one wants to die, and no one wants to be forgotten, so let's live and have Ian's legacy live in a new united voice."

A thunderous wild cheer went up and echoed off the Watchman Tower and back to them.

"Make no mistake," Jonah hollered, "Ian did not intend to die. Ian intended to live and work for something he believed deeply in. He lived and died doing what he was supposed to be doing." Jonah stopped and turned to face the canyon entrance. "The wind is blowing, do you feel it? It is coming up through this canyon right now as I speak. Can you feel it against your skin? Can you hear it? This same wind has come up this canyon for millions of years . . . and the sun set right over there an hour ago," he pointed to the west, "and it will continue to set every night until the end of time. But we are here now, for this one glorious instant, and tonight we share this time and space, and let it be said to all that would listen, that our moment here was spent doing good work, taking care of the people we love and making certain that nothing we do changes the cycle of the wind or the sun or the waves of the ocean or the trees growing in the woods or the silence and peace of this great redrock country. There are many paths of honor to follow in this life . . . and this one is ours."

The next morning Jonah paid a courtesy call to the park superintendent. "Essentially, we have taken over the park," he told the silver-gray haired man. "We intend to use our time here - which will be short - to bring attention to the murder of our friend, Ian McCarthey, and to tell everyone about this remarkable land and the threats to it."

The superintendent, a man of many environmental battles himself, did not argue or protest, he just sat back in his chair and smiled.

"Tomorrow morning," Jonah told him, "I'll have one thousand men and women at your disposal. We are ready to go to work. We know your budget has been slashed so we are here to pick up the trash, to build or repair trails, to do whatever you have on your list of jobs needing to be done."

Before leaving he handed the superintendent a check for $5,000 as Shon captured a digital image of them shaking hands.

One of Jonah's lieutenants took him aside and told him they had a visitor. Surrounded by a seas of campers, the lieutenant told him they spotted her the night before setting up her tent and taking pictures. At the center of the campground he pointed out a rainbow colored dome tent and a woman with long, thick straight salt and pepper hair sitting on a backpacking chair. She talked to several people who sat in the dirt listening.

"Well, Ms. King," Jonah said, interrupting, "you always seem to show up where the action is." His tone was friendly but condescending.

"Something wrong with that, Mr. Sandborn?"

"Could be. I don't know yet." Turning to Carrie T. King's audience, he asked, "I wonder if I might speak to our distinguished guest alone." They smiled meekly, got up and left.

She smiled too and waited.

"I just wanted to ask what you think you are doing here?"

"I go where I feel I belong - and I feel I belong here."

"Come now. Your antennae is off," he responded coolly. "Look around, how many people here do you recognize?"

"What does that have to do with anything?"

"Look around, tell me."

"What's your point?"

"These people are members or supporters of EarthIsland. They believe in our goals and movement. You don't know any of them because you are not one of us. You are an outsider. You spend your time in Aspen or Park City sucking up to fat cats - and trying to avoid the little people like these."

"What do you want?" she asked, impatiently.

"I told you. I want to know what you are doing here."

"Why?"

"Ultimately," he said, stroking his chin, "for your safety. This is an EarthIsland gathering. Need I remind you of the unflattering things you have said about us?"

"Are you threatening me?"

"Of course not. I'm attempting to educate you."

"I'm here because this is a free country and last I heard this is a national park," she snapped, paused and checked herself. "I feel as if I belong here," she said slowly, acting as if the spirits were speaking through her.

"No. You are really here to push your own agenda - which means to promote yourself. These people are the vanguard of a new movement. You don't belong here."

"I was just hoping I could help," she said, deferentially.

"Help?" he burst out laughing. "That's a good one. Help with what?"

"With what you are trying to accomplish here."

"I see."

"No. I don't think you do. I can help. I really can. I am so impressed with what you are doing here. The energy here is . . . is infectious."

"And you've become infected?"

"In my heart, I'm with you!"

Jonah laughed loudly again, "Come now, Carrie. The only person you are infected with is your own image in the mirror. Your reputation as a shameless self-promoter is well known."

"My books have . . ." she started.

"Your books have used the environment as a springboard to build your own self-centered reputation and nothing else."

"I'll have you know my last book won national acclaim."

"None of that so-called acclaim, which I don't believe, came from anyone here. I suspect you manufactured it yourself."

"You can't see into my heart!"

"I do not profess to see into your heart. But I do know history and your reputation is well documented."

"Look who's talking," she protested. "At least hear me out. I am a native of Utah. I know these people. My roots are here. I know how they think. I can help you . . . We can accomplish . . ."

"No!" Jonah interrupted, "We cannot accomplish anything."

"Listen," she insisted, "You need help talking to the other side. You may question my sincerity, but give me a chance. I can help you avoid . . . violence and misunderstanding . . . and I . . ."

"No! Stop! You sit back, schmooze with rich folks and politicians and then try to interject yourself as a leader when someone else has done all the work. It's not going to fly here."

"I resent that! You're a liar!" she shouted.

"Resent it all you want. The only people who don't know it are the morons who buy your claptrap."

"I have worked for years . . . I sit on the board of ten organizations. . . I have connections."

Jonah crossed his arms and tilted his head back. She could see she was getting no where so she changed approaches, "I don't like you either, but I truly believe in what you are doing."

"Don't patronize me. Look," he said, watching Shon approaching with some papers in his hand, "I'm busy so let's cut the crap. We don't want you here. We don't need your "spirit" or energy here. We don't trust you."

"You truly offend me," she said, scrunching up her face like she'd just stepped in a dog turd. "My books have introduced thousands of people to the power and spirit of this great land. Without people like me, you would have no following at all. This is my land, too! It is in my soul and I love it."

"We've all heard it before. You have one objective: to promote yourself at everyone's expense!"

"Look who's talking," she interrupted. "You are an outcast, an outsider. No one will have anything to do with you, Jonah!"

He smiled, "That's quite a compliment, Carrie. I hope you are right. I'd rather be alone than be a part of your self righteous group of friends who profess to be environmentalists as they drive gas guzzling $50,000 SUVs and build ten-thousand square foot houses in the mountains and post no trespassing signs. You make us sick - you are worse than the ranchers. At least they aren't duplicitous and they know how to work!"

"Please believe me," she implored, almost begging. "I applaud your move here. It's about time someone has done something! Let me stay. I can help."

"I'll tell you what. You can stay as long as you keep your mouth shut and don't peddle your books."

"I knew you weren't a fool," she replied, satisfied.

Before he left, he instructed a lieutenant to post a 24 hour a day watch on her.

Chapter Sixteen

Commissioner Bullock arrived early and after tying an apron on she took her turn frying bacon and sausage, scrambling eggs and welcoming the line of hungry folks with a big plate of homemade buttermilk flap jacks. Even in an apron, she was beautiful. She wore a tight fitting pair of wranglers with a turquoise and silver belt cinched snugly around her tiny waist, a double breasted leather jacket, red leather boots and a white silk scarf tied around her neck. She recognized most of her constituents as they filtered through the line but every year new faces appeared, usually family members of ex-residents who have returned, bringing their families back for the Founder's Day celebration.

Founder's Day was held at the Panguitch City Park, next to the rodeo grounds, the new Mormon church and the historic courthouse on Main Street. Festivities started with a sunrise pancake breakfast and continued throughout the day ending up with a fireworks display at ten. At dinner time they feasted on a four-hundred-pound steer barbecued on a rotating spit over an open fire. Visitors stopped at the pit to marvel at the meat turning round and round on the heavy duty industrial spit.

After sunset, Ms. Spackman, the elementary school music teacher, staged a pageant of local talent. The park was flooded with stage lights, casting long shadows across the lawn from the century-old cottonwood trees and creating a dreamlike atmosphere. Blankets were spread out everywhere and partiers ate steak and potatoes and corn on the cob as they watched the show. For dessert, it was cake, ice cream and fireworks.

The celebration was getting so large a few years back they decided to start wearing name tags. Many were descendants of the first Mormon settlers and their family names were synonymous with the town, the Redds and Kimballs and Jensens. They numbered in the hundreds and while most had gone off to Salt Lake or elsewhere for work, they returned every year for the celebration. Even the kids raised up north in the city, consider Panguitch their hometown.

The celebration was the only opportunity, excluding high school grad-uations and the 4th and 24th of July, that people set aside their chores and isolation to come together. Most saw each other at church but even though the Sabbath is a day of rest, they had wood to chop, cows to feed and repairs on equipment to make. When Sunday service was over they high-tailed it home, changed out of their Sunday clothes and went to work. The first celebration of Founder's Day was held in 1875 after two years of failed crops, bad weather and a series of tragedies, including the death of the town's first leader. Back then, life in the town of Panguitch resembled a prison. Some wondered what they had done for their church to exile them to such a godforsaken place to start a town. At the first celebration, they ate elk and bear and loaves of wheat bread. For dessert they had mountain blueberries in whipping cream.

The women congregated under the old cottonwood trees on the lawn connecting the park to the Mormon church house. Tables were set up for the county's best quilters and nearby the women prepared plates of cheese and fruit and vegetables and enormous bowls of potato salad and Jell-O. Everyone brought either a family specialty dish or some homemade pies or cookies. For the most part, the women were free of the kids for the day, most of them fending for themselves, competing in sack races, baseball games and rodeo events.

After breakfast, Lonnie moved from one table to the next, visiting with the quilters, sampling the food and small talking with the women. She was admired by every woman there - but she would never be truly accept-ed by any of them. She had far too many strikes against her. She was not from Panguitch but from Kanab. She didn't belong to the Mormon church. She wore tight clothes showing her shapely figure. She was doing a man's job that she didn't deserve. And, worst of all, she married Mack Bullock, the most handsome and eligible bachelor in the county. A dozen Panguitch girls, now women, and their mothers, would never forgive her. It didn't help that her father was a notorious drunk and she was a wild drunken hussy herself until settling into the comfort and respectability of the Bullock money.

She chatted with Mrs. Wells, the oldest person in the city, who at 98, sat with perfect posture at a picnic table surrounded by her many daugh-ters, granddaughters and an army of great grandkids. Mrs. Wells weighed less than one hundred pounds but her daughters, who cared for their moth-er with great tenderness, were big women with lard-hips and cream cheese thighs. Mrs. Wells wanted to tell Lonnie something privately and motioned her to come closer so she could whisper. Unlike the others, Mrs. Wells liked Lonnie from the very start. "I need to talk to you alone," she said ever so softly. Lonnie held her arm and rubbed it, "I'll come by later, dearie," she whispered.

Crossing the lawn to inspect the barbecue, a fortyish-looking woman wearing a beautiful flowered summer dress and floppy garden party hat with gray and black streaked hair approached Lonnie and thrust out her hand. "Commissioner Bullock?" the woman asked.

"Yes, that's me," she answered, taking the stranger's hand.

"My name is Carrie T. King. I just wanted to introduce myself and tell you how much I'm enjoying your town and this wonderful get-together. It's really nice!"

"Thank you. It's very nice to meet you," Lonnie replied, wondering why the woman's name sounded familiar. "We like it."

"Isn't it just wonderful," King gushed, looking around at the festivities and pleased to be part of it. "I just love it here. I'm really envious."

They smiled politely and watched some boys putting on a show by throwing a Frisbee to a fast small dog out on the far lawn.

"I remember as a child," King started, "in Holladay where I was raised," she pointed up north. "We had something we called Fun Days. It reminds me of this - the kids, the pancakes, the people. My house was not far from the park. I'd go out my back door, across the lawn, jump an old barb wire fence into the orchard and then cross the field next to Little Cottonwood Creek and jump another fence and be at Fun Days. . . It was wonderful - back then."

She paused theatrically, gazing out at the festivities as if moving back in time to some carefree yesteryear. Her eyes filled with tears, "It's all gone now," she said, turning to Lonnie. "The orchard and farm is now a subdivision with hundreds of houses, two gas stations, and a brand new strip mall."

"That's too bad," Lonnie remarked sincerely. She was surprised at the woman's candor. "I guess I don't realize how lucky we are here."

"Oh yes, you are so lucky," King beamed. "People in the city would love to live in a place like this."

Lonnie took a real look at King. "I guess we all see it greener . . ." she started to say but stopped. "Why don't they, then?" she asked. "Why don't more city people move here?"

King hadn't expected the question and thought about it. "Oh, I guess there are many reasons. Jobs, opportunities, money. It's gotten away from us. . . time passing so quickly. Everyone dreams, though."

"Yes. We all have dreams . . . " she said and stopped. "I'm glad you are enjoying yourself. It's a lot of work but we think it's worth it." Then, it finally came to her, "I talked to you last week, on the phone, right?"

"Yes!" King said, excited and embarrassed. "We talked. I asked if I couldn't talk to you for a new book I'm working on."

"Oh yes," Lonnie stepped back and looked into her eyes. "You are the one working on a new book."

"You've read my work?" she asked, enthusiastically.

"No. No. I haven't. Sorry. It's just I'm receiving calls from writers every day and can't keep it all straight."

"Oh, I was only hoping you had because . . . because then you'd know what I write about so you would trust me . . ."

The commissioner didn't know what this woman was getting at and searched her face for clues. They stood and looked at the crowd without speaking until it became uncomfortable.

"Are you here with friends or family?" the commissioner asked.

"Actually, no. I'm here to see you, actually. I was wondering if you might have some time to talk?"

"About what?"

"What's happening! The arsons, the cows and coyotes, the vandalism, murder, rapes. You know, EarthIsland breathing down your neck over in Zion."

King had gone too far. "Sorry, but it's my day off. I'm not interested in an interview."

"No. Sorry. You misunderstand me," King apologized. "I don't want an interview. I want to help you."

The men folk gravitated to the other side of the park where for a hundred years men on this day stood around bragging, joking and back slapping - the only difference today was they were angry and frightened.

"It was those son-of-a-bitchin' radical environmentalists," one said.

"You see them parading through town!" another exclaimed.

"If I'da had my 30.06 I'da cycled a few rounds their way."

"It's those EarthIslander pricks from over in Colorado," another added.

"How would they like it if we went over in Colorado and paraded through their towns?"

"Or told them how to run their range or manage their land?"

"Sons-of-bitches."

"They could use a good ass kickin'."

"They killed Drew's cows and I damned well know it."

The men stood in a large circle, looking at the ground, hands tucked in their back pockets.

"Doesn't look too good," another huffed. "We're in for it now, I can tell."

"Cocksuckers."

"I hear there's ten thousand of them over in Zion."

"I'd like to send them all back to New-fucking-England or wherever they came from."

Some faces engorged with blood while others puffed their chests out above their folded arms. They shifted from one foot to the other, kicked at the grass in front of them.

"That's nearly as many as we got in the county."

"I ain't afraid, I'm goin' to bag me a few of them."

"Lost four cows," one said. "Took out a section of fence running next to the highway. I spent two days out rounding them up. Four of them still out there. Gonna have to go out again tomorrow."

"Count me in."

"I'll be by before half-past six."

"I'm in," another piped up.

"It'll take two days maybe, none of us has two days."

They grumbled.

Another added, "We look like pretty inviting targets. We got everything to lose." Turning to Sheriff Anderson who was wearing worn ranch clothes and had been drinking vodka and coke in a paper cup all day and by now was all tanked up, he added, "I don't care what Andy here does to me, I'm not waiting for them to come pick me off! I'm going to do something . . ."

"Yeah, like what?" Anderson slurred.

"Hell, I don't know! Nobody's coming in here and destroying everything I spent my life building!"

"Don't tell me what you're planning then," Anderson insisted, saluting the table top. "I don't want to know about it. I know nuth - think," he said in a Colonel Klink voice.

Everyone laughed, a few slapped their legs.

"The wife's afraid and spends the whole day on the damned phone talking to the other women."

"If I wanted this kind of life I'd move up north to Salt Lake where I'd lock my front door and carry a gun so nobody could come inside and murder me and the misses. She's so afraid she ain't getting her milking done on time."

"Whoever killed that stupid kid didn't do us any favor," one said, scratching his forehead.

"And the girls! Who in the hell would pull a stunt like that?"

"Don't believe it!" Cody jumped in. He listened to the older men silently but had to speak up. "I don't know how they pulled it off, but I don't believe it!"

"Wait just a minute, Cody," Sheriff Anderson said, from his seat at a picnic table. "They're telling the truth all right. I talked to the girls myself, and seen the hospital report. " He looked into his cup and swirled its contents. "It happened all right. One won't be having any kids. . . her insides are all messed up . . . pretty little thing."

"Who did it?"

Anderson swirled his drink again, "We got some pretty good leads and a suspect or two. We're working it."

By the hottest part of the day, the older men retired to the shade and the younger men including the Circle Cliff gang stood out in the parking lot in the unmerciful heat, getting more and more steamed up. They fueled the fire with beer and straight whiskey from brown paper sacks. They drank behind the trucks which were lined up like horses waiting to gallop off. They hid their alcohol not out of fear of getting caught or out of respect for the town's values but because the Mormon girls wouldn't have anything to do with them if they were labeled a drinker.

Cody had had his share and then a little more. He hugged everyone and embarrassed himself by telling them, "Hey man, I love ya, man." He challenged everyone, "Hell, I can out drink any man here - under the table." He fell to the ground, tripped over the curb, smoked cigarettes and laughed until tears streamed down his face and he cried like a baby.

The other men paid no attention to him, except to help him stand up so he could get beer and to watch out for his mother. After passing out in the gravel between two trucks he woke up angry. He wanted to kick someone's ass, preferably the muther-fuckers who burned down his great grand-pa's line shack but anyone else would do, if they got in his way. They were all drunk now, talking about catching some radicals by the short hairs and showing off their guns.

One man knew where a bunch of yuppies were camping so they all piled into their trucks, revved their engines and popped the clutches, spraying gravel fifty feet away and setting up a cloud of dust that hung over the park. Watching from the shade, the older men folded their arms and glared. They knew something was up and one told Sheriff Anderson, "You better get after them, Sheriff, they're up to no good." Anderson laughed and smiled, "Hey, I'm on their side. They just need to blow some steam off."

Outside Bryce Canyon, in beautiful Red Canyon, they found the campsite where the yuppies had been, but it was empty. Cody rolled out of his truck with his six shooter blazing, firing three shots into a nearby tree, turning and firing another three into the outhouse in rapid succession. The blasts echoed and reverberated off the surrounding sandstone canyon walls. They took aim at everything, the forest service tables and chairs, the parking signs, the garbage cans and the sign-in box; they didn't quit until they ran out of shells. Collapsing on a picnic table some took pulls from a Texas fifth of whiskey, others drove their trucks through the surrounding trees and sagebrush, destroying the campground signs and knocking over the metal barbecue stands.

Cody took the firewood the yuppies collected and stacked for the next campers and piled it around the outhouse. Someone doused it with gasoline and put a match to it. Cody barely escaped the explosion of flames by leaping backward and falling back over a tree stump and landing on his rear-end. They fed the fire and talked of retribution and guns and heroic scenarios. They would beat the invaders back, and settle the score - they would let everyone know they meant business.

CHAPTER SEVENTEEN

After the elders left, Ateen sat by the fire outside the Anasazi ruin until he became restless and searched the surrounding area looking for something familiar. He was raised on the other side of the mountain and until the elders brought him to this place, he believed he knew everything about the mountain. He spent his childhood summers exploring and aimlessly wandering from morning to night here. He listened to the stories about the spirits living there and knew each by heart. He even witnessed the magic of the strange faraway lights himself. Still, he couldn't fathom how he missed this place - especially the pinnacle rock. It's so obvious, he thought to himself, I would have been drawn here.

Working up a steep hill onto a ridge east of the pinnacle, he discovered a secret plateau and a heart-shaped pond at the center of a beautiful meadow. Long mountain grasses and wildflowers filled the meadow and a deep but narrow brook fed a steam of cold water into the pond. He rested in the grass and watched dragonflies in the reflection of the water. The sun dappled and cool air wafted with the scent of pine and he fell asleep. He slept deeply, as if he had never slept before and hours passed before he was suddenly awakened. Someone was watching him. Sitting up, he glimpsed something - an apparition - moving away to his left. It was oblong-shaped and stopped in a archway between two groves of fir trees. For a moment, Ateen saw it clearly. It was a floating oval-shaped ball of light and at its center was a strange figure. The ball moved into some trees and before Ateen knew it, he was following. Like a great mechanical device acting independently, his body pulled him forward. His arms swept forward and back like some clockwork, his hands grabbing the underbrush and pulling him upward. Further and further they went, up over rocks, through stands of fir trees, along narrow ridge lines - always moving higher and higher on the mountain. Ateen tried to keep sight of it, but time and again it disappeared over a ridge, around a corner or into the dense forest.

Finally, at the base of another ridge, Ateen could go no further and leaned against a giant granite boulder, heaving for air. His chest rose and fell and his lungs pulled but he was getting little air. Sweat poured off his face and his legs burned with fatigue. Above him, the ball of light crested one last ridge and disappeared behind it. I have lost it, he anguished, there it goes. I have failed.

But a moment later, the apparition reappeared, floating at the edge of the ridge, allowing Ateen to see it, hovering motionless as if waiting. "It wants me to see it!" he cried out loud, wiping the sweat from his eyes and trying to focus. Getting to his feet, he cupped his hands and shouted, "I'm coming!"

He moved slowly up the rock and debris strewn ridge. Each footfall felt like ten. When he finally crested the ridge, coming over the top slowly, he was blinded by the light. It was so powerful he reeled back, nearly losing his balance. He dropped onto all fours. He looked at the oval but it was like looking into the sun, yet it strangely possessed no heat. He curled into the fetal position, covering his head with his arms and hands as the light, hovering fifty feet away, pulsed like a heart beat with greater and greater intensity. Emotion swept him away. He wept fitfully and then laughed, rocking back and forth in some strange conjunction of joy and anguish. He shivered and the mountain turned cold, leaving him feverish and delirious. Unaware, the spirit vanished leaving him there alone in the growing darkness.

After a long time Ateen got to his feet but his legs could barely hold him. He stumbled to the place the apparition had been and when he reached the spot, the ground gave way and he fell into a swampy bog. He submerged and then wallowed, desperately flailing and fighting to save himself before pulling himself up onto some firm ground. He was soaked in a heavy black viscous tar-like substance.

The sun is going down, he thought, realizing his predicament. Down the mountain he went, fear pushing him forward. He had no idea where he was. In his headlong rush to follow the apparition he had not taken note of where he was going. All he knew was that he climbed higher and higher and now he needed to get down before it was too late.

Sunset gave way to dusk and night followed quickly. With help from the half moon he staggered down the mountainside, everything looking unreal and laced with overlapping shadows in the flat moonlight. He fell again and again, once tumbling head first through scrub oak and stopping just feet from a fifty-foot drop off. Despite his exhaustion, he continued until dawn's first light and he stopped on a level clearing. He discovered he was standing on the road just a few feet away from his truck. He couldn't believe his good luck, and at first, thought it was the apparition playing another joke on him. It made no sense! By his reckoning - even conceding he didn't know where he'd been - there was no way he could be there on the road.

After resting in the bed of his truck he started back to the secret Anasazi ruin. Within a short distance he realized he was off the trail and somehow going in the wrong direction, so he backtracked, found the trail again and start off but soon was lost again. Every time he found the trail it lead to a dead-end or a deadly cliff edge. He labored up a ridge where he could spot the pinnacle rock but once there, the pinnacle rock was no where to be found.

He remembered what Nez said the day before. "You do not know this place because it has not shown itself to you. We are introducing you to it. You are in the world of the Spirits here." Defeated, he returned to the road, resigned he would never find the pathway. To his surprise, Nez, Tahonnie, Natani, Crank and the others were waiting for him, sitting in Nez's dirty Cadillac.

"What happened to you, tar baby?" Nez teased, laughing.

"We told you to stay put until we came to get you," Natani added, getting out of the Cadillac.

"Let me sit down," he began, opening his truck's back gate and collapsing onto it. He was decorated from head to toe with pine cones, pebbles, twigs, broken branches, leaves and a layer of dirt. The only skin visible was the pink around his eyes, making him look like an owl or a coal miner. The elders were amused and acted as if something of great importance was about to play out.

"Well, what happened?" Nez demanded.

"What are you covered with?" Tahonnie asked. "Is it tar?"

"Don't ask me. What does it look like to you?" Ateen asked.

"Hell if I know," Natani offered, smearing a bit of the black matter on his finger and tasting it.

"What happened?" Nez demanded. "Did you see something?"

"A spirit," Ateen answered, picking a twig stuck to his forehead off and flipping it away.

"You were frightened," Crank mocked, "so you ran away?"

"I followed the spirit and got lost."

"What did it look like?"

"It was a ball of light, - oval-shaped!" he said excitedly.

The elders looked at one another, laughed and then congratulated themselves by slapping each other on the back as if they just won the lottery or someone told a great joke.

"What's so funny?" Ateen barked. "Don't fuck with me!"

"Ooh!" they said, jumping back in unison, mocking him.

"You tell us you saw a ball of light," Crank explained, smiling, "but all we see here in front of us is a big ball of black tar!"

The old men could not contain themselves any longer and staggered around laughing, holding their sides and hiding their faces in their hands.

"Tell us," Natani finally demanded, "what happened?"

Ateen told them the story and while everyone tried, none could keep a straight face.

"So you ended up here?" one asked.

"At dawn," he admitted, embarrassed. "I couldn't believe it. How could that happen? Then, I went back up the trail and . . . "

"You couldn't find the way," Nez finished for him.

Ateen shook his head, "What's going on?"

"Isn't it obvious?" Crank jibed. "You are a full blown lunatic."

They all laughed again, exhausted but complimenting Crank on his jokes.

Ateen stared past them.

"The Spirit tested you," Tahonnie told him, sweetly. "It is the way."

"Did I pass?" Ateen asked, looking down at the little old man.

"You are not dead," Tahonnie answered, raising his eyebrows and shoulders and then dropping them quickly.

Tapping a finger to his own temple, Natani added, "Think Ateen!"

Each elder told the story of his first visit to the place. They marveled that Ateen was returned to his truck. No one had seen the Apparition as closely or as clearly as Ateen. They did not know of the plateau or the meadow with the heart-shaped pond. "You have been touched with a great gift," Natani told him.

When Ateen arrived at his mother's house, she, Granny and Lena Tsosie were sitting on the front porch swing. When Lena Tsosie saw him covered in black she did not look at him, instead she gazed into a shadow laying in the yard fifty feet away.

His mother rushed to him, "What happened, son? Are you okay?"

"I think so," he answered.

"You have been on the mountain," Granny announced, holding up one finger.

"How did you know?"

"I know the look. I have seen it in the eyes of many men." Her eyes grew large. "What is the stuff all over you?"

"I had an accident."

"Who were you with?" his mother asked.

"Nez. Natani. Tahonnie. Crank. The rest."

"Ooh . . . " His mother gasped, understanding some unspoken importance.

"He's okay," Granny said, assuring her. "He made it back, didn't he?"

"I'm lucky. I was nearly killed!" he retorted.

"Don't talk back to me!" Granny said, leaning forward and taking a swipe at the air.

His mother and Tsosie boiled water and all afternoon they kept filling the tub while Granny scrubbed Brigham, first with a stiff brush and gasoline, then with soap and water. After napping, he sat with the three women on the porch.

"Go get my tobacco," Granny ordered him. "It's at my place. I need a smoke."

Brigham started off for his grandmother's hogan and Lena Tsosie jumped up and following after him.

"Stay here," he said, stopping to face her. He made certain to not look directly at her.

"Take her with you," Granny hollered. "She knows where I left it."

He turned and walked away and Tsosie ran to catch up.

"What happened," she asked, catching up, "on the mountain?"

He made a sweeping gesture with his arm as if to say, nothing - "I can't talk about it. The elders told me to keep quiet."

"It must be of great importance. Tell me please."

"No," he said in a friendly tone and kept walking.

When the two reached Granny's hogan, Ateen waited for Tsosie to retrieve the bag of tobacco, but she went from one place to the next looking.

"I thought you knew where it was?"

"I don't."

After finding the bag of loose shag tobacco next to her bed they returned without a word. She walked a step or two behind the giant.

When Ateen handed her the tobacco, Granny asked, "Were you alone on the mountain?"

"They left me. I was alone," he put his hands in his back pockets. "I was there all night."

She loaded a cigarette rolling paper with the shag, rolled it tightly and drew it across her tongue. "Did you shit your pants?" she asked.

"Mother!" Alice said, protesting. Tsosie covered her face with both hands . . . "don't . . .don't. . . " Alice kept saying.

"Did you?"

"I was too scared to."

She pointed at him, "Never go onto the mountain at night, you might end up dead." She laughed, cackled and then told them a story they had heard a hundred times. "When I was a child one man got lost on the mountain so two men, one brother and his best friend, went looking for him and they never came back. Everyone was pretty worried so four men went looking for the three men and they never came back." She paused to light the smoke and took a long drag.

"What happened, Grandma?" Tsosie asked, politely.

"They stopped sending men. No one would go. We stopped going onto the mountain for many seasons until Takoe lost some sheep up there and he was the cheapest man in the family and he wasn't going to lose no sheep to no mountain, so he went looking for them. Everyone thought to themselves, well that's the last we'll see of Takoe, but when he showed up with all his sheep and a few others he found, we were all surprised. After that, we went back on the mountain . . ." She paused for effect, "But never ever after dark! No way!"

No one spoke for a long time. Grandma sat Indian style on the swing, rocking back and forth smoking her cigarette. Alice disappeared into the house with Tsosie to make dinner. Ateen sat outside with grandmother before he went to check on the wood pile at her hogan.

CHAPTER EIGHTEEN

The road out to the Utah/Arizona Strip from Navajo Mountain headed northeast over long deserted stretches of desolate tabletop sandstone where only the faint telltale discoloring of tire-tracks marked the way. It skirted a colony of sand dunes marching across a wide windswept valley. The wind was taking the bright pink colored dunes southwest and on a good year they advanced ten feet. The colony started its migration a million years ago and nothing would stop it until it reached its destination. When the dirt road was first blazed, the forty or fifty giant dunes, some more than six stories high, were two hundred feet away but now their advance crossed the road in places and in another twenty years the road would be closed.

The dunes captured vehicles who tested its resolve and would not set them free without considerable effort. Some were simply deserted there and from a distance, they looked like insects trapped on orange fly paper. The only safe way to cross the dunes was to not cross them, so Ateen cut a path down through a dry creek bed and around.

"What have you done to you face?" Garrett finally asked. "You've taken up using moisturizing cream?"

"I had an accident."

"Yeah. What's in your hair, grease?"

Ateen was quiet.

"Well?"

"Well, what?"

"What happened?"

"I had an accident."

"Oh, I see. Leaving it to my imagination? Okay then, you decided to give little-ole Tsosie a roll in the sack and afterwards she was so thankful she gave you a complete oil treatment by dunking you in a fifty gallon vat of chicken fat."

Ateen was insulted that Garrett would bring up such an intimate issue but his anger gave way and he smiled widely. "You Anglo are too disrespectful! No wonder you can't stop killing each other."

"Or," Garrett said, "you ate so much fry bread you've turned into a grease bomb."

"That's why I like you, Doo Doo. You are so full of shit."

"It's easy when you have clowns for friends."

"You have friends?" he asked. "Don't go stretching things too far. Remember, I was in Vietnam."

"The only thing you ever did in Nam was hold-up in some Mama San's shack in Saigon to play with all the little girls."

Ateen pounded the steering wheel, "I remember going into town for the first time after weeks in the jungle and rice paddies. I asked the sergeant how much money I should take and he hollered, "Ateen, you Indian wonder child, don't take twenty! Take plenty!"

They laughed and Ateen started sniffing the air.

"Something smells - bad."

"Must be your breath blowing back into your face."

"The elders wanted to know, too."

"What? If I shit my pants?"

"Yes."

Garrett was surprised, "I'm glad they like me."

"They don't like you," Ateen paused. "To them, Doo Doo, you are like a whimpering lost dog. They know you are lost and want to help you find your way back home. But they do not like you enough to want to take you home themselves."

"At least they care - so few people do today, wouldn't you agree?"

Ateen did not answer and the two fell silent, hypnotized by the road as it wound up and down over hills, around wide corners, down through dry washes and across sagebrush plains. In his head, Ateen was back on Navajo Mountain, searching for the pinnacle rock and wondering what his encounter with the apparition meant. It was his test, to unravel its secret so he went over every detail searching for clues.

Only the most powerful medicine men had grand visions and visitations, but few of them could boast of such an experience. It is said in Navajo country that a baby can be born up north in the morning and by night everyone in the south will know. When the elders recounted Ateen's experience to others - leaving out the secret details - it spread throughout the tribe and made him an even bigger man. Many had waited a generation for such a warrior to surface.

Garrett was lost in thought about his stay in St. George. He landed an assignment with Pacific Monthly Magazine to write about the growing crisis, but mostly he thought about his encounter with Nancy. He longed to be with her again and to experience his tight-knit group of ill-fated friends whose lives played out before they were forty years old and who were now long gone. Every close friend he ever had was dead. He longed for the time when he could drive through his childhood neighborhood and go to his mother's house and walk right in without knocking and find her there in the kitchen. She would throw her arms around his neck and call him her Doonerkins. He searched the landscape for some sign of her; for some sign of any of them. He felt anger at his estranged siblings who rushed to sell the family home after she was gone. In his mind, he strolled the flower garden his mother so tenderly cared for, past the peonies and delphiniums and walnut trees to the fragrant memories of all the love he and she once shared. What's wrong with you, he questioned himself. Inside his abdomen, hunger pangs churned and roiled and he needed to be home once again.

Suddenly, as they neared the box canyon where Leonard Nemelka was said to be laying low in his dead grandfather's hogan, a thunderous whirling sound frightened the men and brought them from their inner worlds. At the same time, a helicopter rose above the cedars, churning the trees and sagebrush then turning north and swiftly moving off.

"What's that?"

"A Huey," Ateen answered. "They're trespassing. Sons-of-bitches. They can't fly here. This is reservation land. . ."

"Maybe they had engine trouble . . ."

"This is a no overflight area - restricted."

Ateen grabbed the binoculars but the helicopter disappeared over the horizon. "Did you see any numbers?" he asked.

"No."

"It was coming from Nemelka's!"

Five minutes later at Nemelka's, they found his fire still burning but when they called out no one answered. The empty five gallon paint bucket he used as a chair was overturned and his tobacco and matches were scattered about. Ateen spotted Nemelka's footprints as well as the prints of two other men, wearing sharp edged boots. "This way!" he called to Garrett, pulling his pony tails behind his ears. With one arm stretched out toward the ground, he pointed at each footprint as he followed them up the hill behind the house and down the other side into the dry creek bed before climbing another hill and then into the sage and cedars.

"Here!" Ateen announced as Garrett caught up. "Look!" He pointed to a shiny object in the sand. "Shell casing! Like the others!" He retrieved it and ordered, "Get down!" Both men hunkered at the base of a hill and Ateen listened.

"What is it?" Garrett enquired.

"Shhh. Quiet!" Ateen put his finger to his lips. Turning his head from one side to the other, he stood up for a moment then crouched down quickly. "Stay here," he demanded and disappeared into the sage.

Garrett did as he was told, Ateen was never wrong when it came to danger. Five minutes later, Garrett heard the sound of Levi on sagebrush and turned quickly to find Ateen standing next to him.

"Hey, don't do that man! You scared the shit outta me!"

"They're gone."

"Who was it?"

"They killed Nemelka. I found him. He is dead."

"What? Killed him!"

"Over there," he pointed. "They hunted him down and shot him. Finished him off with a round to the head."

For an instant, Garrett thought Ateen was joking, it was all so absurd, but he could see in his face that he spoke the truth. "Dead?"

"It doesn't make sense," Ateen answered, bewildered. Following the tracks back to the ransacked shack and then to the place the helicopter landed Ateen searched for clues.

After digging a shallow grave in the orange oxide-colored soil, they wrapped Leon in his grandmother's beautiful hand woven rug and buried him. Ateen covered the grave with large stones from a nearby pile and he built a fire. He harvested fresh, pungent sagebrush fawns, tied them together like fans and draped them over the fire. At first, the sage choked the fire, sending up a deep blue-white smoke. Then the fawns ignited and a column of thick smoke rose into the air. Garrett kept his distance, sitting atop Nemelka's paint can, drinking shots of whiskey and losing himself in the flames.

On the way back to Navajo Mountain, Garrett was nervous and scanned the sky constantly, waiting for the chopper to swoop down. Don't worry, Ateen told him, they didn't see us. We wouldn't be here now if they did.

They decided not to go to the authorities - not yet anyway. Ateen had to first report what happened to the elders. And, if they reported it to the authorities now, they might become targets themselves.

"No one cares about Nemelka," Ateen told his friend. "He was only an Indian and Indians do not count."

"We need to find out who was behind the murder." Garrett replied.

Ateen remembered something important about the helicopter, "It was a Huey 168. A rare bird. They are all phased out."

"You know helicopters?"

"I flew on many '68s and '72s in the Ashua Valley."

"If we had its registration number it would be easy."

"But we don't."

"If it's a rare enough bird, we can trace it," Garrett added, confidently. "There can't be too many around."

"No more than a few thousand." Ateen added.

Garrett slapped his hands over his face.

"This one could be easy to find though."

"Yeah."

"It was an older '68 with a the newer '72 engine fairings."

"You could see that?"

"It's obvious, if you know."

"Well, it's a start," Garrett mused, shaking his head. "What about the shell casing?"

Ateen took it from his shirt pocket and rolled it round in the palm of his hand. "The same as killed the cows. Same caliber. Same military jacket, Special Forces, armor piercing. Same."

"Military chopper. Military ammunitions. If it weren't totally crazy and bizarre, I'd say military."

"Military wouldn't use 168s."

"Why not?"

"They wouldn't. There is no reason to think the military had anything to do with this."

"Who, then?" Garrett wondered. "Who owns a helicopter like this. Ranchers? The state? The feds? Business?"

"Someone who would commit murder to cover the shooting of a few mangy cows."

"Sounds desperate to me."

"It happens all the time. Robbers kill store clerks after stealing twenty dollars. No witnesses. Besides," he said slowly, "they assumed no one would see them. Taking Nemelka out was not risky for them. It's not like killing a white man."

"What about Ian?" Garrett asked, "Last time I looked Ian was a white man. These folks are equal opportunity killers - with a helicopter and restricted rounds."

"Right."

"Whoever killed the cows and burned the line shack also killed Nemelka. But how did they know where to find him?"

"Everyone knew he was hiding out here."

"They did? Can't the Dineh keep their mouths shut?"

"I don't think so," Ateen admitted. "It is just not in us."

Lena Tsosie was sitting on Ateen's mother's front porch swing when they reached home. "Your mother has gone into Page for groceries," she told Ateen. "She will be back later."

Garrett sat on the porch swing next to Tsosie while Ateen went inside and packed. They did not speak or look at one another, each stared out across the yard and into the sage and cedar beyond it. Tsosie's hands were folded in her lap and her face was placid. When Ateen reappeared he carried his Winchester 30-30 model 94 rifle and two boxes of shells.

"Just in case," he said to Garrett. Turning to Tsosie, he told her, "You didn't see this. Not a word to Granny either."

She nodded and looked past him.

In Page, Garrett rented his favorite room and wasted little time getting online. He discovered that only a handful of Huey 168s were still currently registered and operated by companies or individuals in the area. A sizeable number were still in the hands of the national guard but many were cannibalized for parts and the rest were either mothballed or on the docket to be destroyed. A half dozen were owned by utility and energy companies, used for exploration and to ferry crews to remote locations. Three were owned by individuals: one a Phoenix car dealer who owned a ranch near Flagstaff; the next, an ex-military man who owned a successful tourist guide business in Moab, Utah; and the third, a famous billionaire publishing giant who lived on 6,000 acres outside of Yellowstone National Park.

Ateen reported to the elders at the Bonanza Cafe. When he finished the story of Leonard Nemelka the elders' faces were long and dark. Nez stroked his hair again and again. Jack Crank rocked gently back and forth and looked into his cup of coffee. Natani closed his eyes and let his skinny and fragile frame lilt slightly back and forth. The women who ran the restaurant sensed the darkness and moved about gingerly, trying not to make a sound and talking in whispers.

The elders agreed it was a good idea to keep Nemelka's death quiet. They would leave tomorrow for Nemelka's and give him a proper burial. The entire incident was Indian business and should be kept within the tribe. But how will that be possible, Crank wondered. Someone here at the table will shoot his mouth off and then everyone will know. They agreed he was right. But what then? They would try their best to keep the secret.

"What of Doo Doo?" someone asked.

"He is using his computer to find out who owns the helicopter."

"Good. Let him do what Anglos do so well," Crank added, "pick through other people's shit."

"Can he keep his mouth shut?" Nez asked.

"Yes."

"We've been thinking," Natani said, changing the subject. "We want you to go back out to Endeshi Springs and take a hike."

Ateen was surprised but tried not to show it. "When?"

"Now."

"What about Nemelka?"

"That will wait. We have packed everything you will need."

"We want you to return to the pinnacle rock."

"What if I can't find it?"

"You will find it," Nez assured him.

"Build a sweat lodge," Crank instructed him. "Figure it out."

Pressing a finger to his temple, Natani admonished him, "Think!"

At the motel, Garrett was astonished when Ateen informed him he was on his way to the mountain.

"Maybe the spirits up there will tell you who did it!" Garrett said sarcastically.

"While you are at it, ask them about who owns the Huey."

"I told the elders about Nemelka," Ateen admitted.

Without looking up from his computer screen, Garrett shook his head, "I thought we were keeping this to ourselves!"

"We are."

"You told everyone!"

"So?"

Garrett looked perplexed, "Did I miss something?"

"I convinced the elders you were not only harmless but trustworthy. They asked if you could keep your mouth shut. I gave them my word. They were worried about you, Doo Doo."

"About what?"

"About you."

"Let me get this straight. When you and I decided it is between us, what you really mean is it's between us and the entire Navajo nation, right?"

"I am pleased at your progress."

CHAPTER NINETEEN

Ten days into the EarthIsland occupation of Zion National Park, the ageless rhythm of work broke the stillness before dawn. Breakfast was served for thousands in a meadow called The Mess Hall in the Cathedrals. Lines formed at the showers and restrooms; crews were dispatched for general park pickup and to help rebuild remote trails. Newly arrived members of the media congregated at the park entrance where they harnessed up with cameras and started the anxious search for today's story. Nearby in Springdale, a tired workforce - just getting accustomed to the autumn pace - arrived to prepare food, sell, hawk and service the unexpected visitors.

Park facilities were overwhelmed. Toilets clogged, the roads were impassable and the Visitor's Center ran out of maps and supplies. The peace and solitude of the park evaporated, escaping out a back canyon. Park personnel were exhausted and the hundreds of extra security people, brought in from around the West during the first few days, were sent home. The question on everyone's lips, "What next?"

Jonah met every morning with park officials. "When are you leaving?" they asked. It was not that they weren't sympathetic or appreciative of the peaceful way EarthIsland members handled themselves, but as the superintendent told Jonah, "We are not happy about handing the park over to anyone."

"We won't be here much longer. I promise," Jonah told him. "Be patient."

Jonah walked into Springdale every morning for coffee with the press and to meet other dignitaries. The tall lean leader wore hiking shorts, boots and an EarthIsland tee-shirt, and a crowd followed wherever he went. Strolling in the sublime morning light he felt guilty expropriating the solemnity of the park to accomplish his objectives.

At the communications tent, Shon was stressed. Everything had gone wrong since their arrival. It was impossible to send or receive satellite transmissions in the narrow canyon, so he and his team worked around the clock setting up relay systems atop mesas outside park boundaries.

"Listen to this," Shon told Jonah, puffing away nervously on a clove cigarette. "It's live! The BBC. In London." He fed the report through some loud speakers.

"Here, surrounded in the natural splendor of Zion, one of America's premiere National Parks, located in the West," the BBC World News reporter, Ronald Riggel, began, "an American environmental group calling itself EarthIsland has taken over the park. But make no mistake, you won't find hundreds of riot police squaring off with thousands of rowdy demonstrators. More likely, you'll find the two groups sharing the work of cleaning the portable water closets or picking up rubbish at the side of the spectacular redrock highway.

"Literally thousands of environmental protesters from America and Europe, including members of Great Britain's EarthFirst!, have arrived by by car and lorry to protest the death of one of their leaders at the hands of unknown assailants. The environmentalists claim locals are responsible for the death, but residents in surrounding communities will have none of it. Locals scoff at the allegation and accuse EarthIsland of starting the current trouble when it slaughtered a herd of grazing cattle with assault rifles and burning a famous ranching line shack.

"While the mood inside the park is peaceable and even down right chummy, outside in the surrounding ranching communities the acrimony borders on bloody hatred and everyone is deadly serious about getting the environmentalists out."

As the two listened, a commotion outside the tent interrupted. A man burst in, pleading with Jonah to come outside. "I have a group of senior citizens who are hopping mad. They want to speak with you."

Outside, Jonah was met by a group of American retirees. They were in no mood for pleasantries and launched into Jonah for EarthIsland's occupation of their RV pads. "We reserved them a year ago. . . You've got a lot of damn nerve. . . Your mother didn't raise you to be disrespectful. . . Play by the rules, young man. . . Stand in line like the rest of us. . . We didn't get nothin' for nothin'. . . We fought in WWII. . . We didn't take anything over in our day. . . Get off the government gravy train. . ."

Jonah assured them they would get their reserved parking spaces. He would only be a minute longer and then would personally help them. Ducking back into the tent, he whispered, "Whew! Boy, I wish they were on our side!"

"Shhh!" Shon whispered, pointing to the speakers.

"And so," BBC reporter, Ronald Riggel, concluded, "all in all, it appears to be shaping up to be a jolly-good old West showdown at high noon. On one side, the Marlboro man riding his trusty steed into the blazing sunset and wearing a six shooter strapped to his hip. On the other side, a new breed of enviro-patriot - confrontational, determined, and savvy in the ways of technology and public relations. Each has drawn a line out in the red sand, and now they face off to see who will cross the other's line first."

The occupation of Zion was a success but not a complete one. It fulfilled their objective of publicizing Ian's murder and applying pressure on local and state authorities to make arrests. Still, arrests had not been forthcoming. They also brought attention to important environmental issues and put a positive spin on EarthIsland nationally and internationally. Supportive e-mail outnumbered hate e-mail five to one. National networks aired favorable stories. NPR did an extended interview with Jonah and millions heard the story and saw the pictures. Locals did not fair as well. A single, shocking image stood out, the dead coyotes impaled on the road markers. The incident made it appear they were blood-thirsty and cruel.

Jonah made it clear EarthIsland's intentions were peaceful and designed to bring maximum pressure on Utah authorities, especially in Garfield County. Privately, he was impatient and angry. Local authorities were dragging their feet and he needed results now. His surprising decision to occupy Zion was a bold move and while many in the shallow-breathing environmental movement applauded it, he was aware that occupying the park could easily backfire; one minute he might be hailed a visionary, the next minute made a goat. Jonah was no fool and had little taste for leading a movement if he didn't get results.

He was concerned about the extreme element in his own ranks. McVey found allies in the new arrivals and while they remained in the shadows Jonah knew they would not stay there forever. After the humiliating and frightening departure from Egypt, McVey and his men returned to Seattle to regroup. Since returning to Utah he spoke little, kept to himself and stayed out of the limelight. Jonah's informants and security kept track of him and reports came back that he was criticizing Jonah's handling of the takeover. Without arrests in Ian's murder case, Jonah would have a hard time keeping McVey and others from taking justice into their own hands. They were ready to fight and Jonah couldn't blame them.

He exuded confidence but privately worried about an exit strategy. I will not be another Jimmy Carter holed up in the White House, he thought to himself. I need to move, be creative and stay fluid. 'Stay fluid. . . stay fluid,' he repeated. He knew EarthIsland's shelf life in Zion was reaching its expiration date, but hadn't decided what they should do next. Outside the park boundaries, it was dangerous. The chance of confrontation and bloodshed were high. Unfortunately, his attempts to manufacture a confrontation with the rednecks while within the safety of the park failed.

While some in the environmental arena wore the blush of true infatuation with Jonah, the pallor of others darkened considerably. Alan von Bank of the Sandstone Wilderness Alliance called via satellite phone from his organization's secret hideaway, somewhere in the Escalante where he was wooing big money donors at an invitations-only catered affair.

"Provocative!" von Bank chided Jonah about the occupation. "How dare you, without informing me?"

Von Bank had an instinct for survival and a talent for knowing which way the wind was blowing. Later that day, he arrived at Zion in his new Lincoln Navigator - to pay a begrudging homage to his adversary. "I can't believe how many people are here!" von Bank exclaimed, shocked. "Your move might prove to be a real winner," he told Jonah, "but I'm not convinced yet."

"Which would you prefer?" Jonah asked, smiling.

Von Bank was accompanied by two lawyers from New York wearing North Face fleece vests in the eighty degree heat, and two young actresses from California wearing almost nothing. They tagged along just to meet Jonah.

"I'm telling you," von Bank insisted, pressing his point, "there aren't enough fundraising dollars for one major organization, let alone two."

"This is not about money!" Jonah countered.

"Well, of course not!" von Bank added, putting his hands on his hips, "It's never about the money, only the principle. Right? Look, we need to talk, when all of this is over. Promise me."

In the week since talking with Jonah, naturalist writer, Carrie T. King broke her promise and did four interviews, two with newspaper writers and two with TV stations in Salt Lake City. In a move reminiscent of Secretary of State Alexander Haig, when then President Reagan was shot, she told the cameras, "Everything is under control here. I have the confidence of all involved and I'm sure we'll put our heads together and work everything out to an amicable solution."

When Jonah heard she had talked to reporters he sent security to evict her. They found King sitting on a camp chair next to a small fold-out table stacked with her books. She was reading a poem from her latest work and five or six people lounged on the ground.

"You are outta here," a security man told her. "Get your stuff. You're leaving."

King was defiant and protested, threatening a lawsuit and screaming obscenities. Security disassembled her tent, loaded her books into boxes and placed her camping gear into the bed of a truck. When she refused to get in, dropping to the ground and folding her arms, four men picked her up and placed her in the bed of the truck. With a man on each side, they drove her out of the park to the town of St. George.

A few hours later, she showed up in Springdale at Flannigan's Inn looking for a room. She was confronted by EarthIslanders who heckled her so badly the Inn's manager pleaded with her to leave. Jonah spoke with members of the press, convincing them not to cover her. "She'll say or do anything to get in front of a camera," he told them.

CHAPTER TWENTY

Garrett drove south out of Page in the late morning, crossing the Painted Desert in the day's best light and climbing the long slope toward San Francisco Peaks and Flagstaff. The commercial drag entering Flagstaff was still lined with 1960s vintage motels and restaurants. It was tawdry and run-down now, but years earlier Garrett set up shop along the stretch while covering the Hopi-Navajo land dispute. Life was good back then, he thought to himself, everyone was alive, my career was skyrocketing and the demon was at bay.

Garrett was working through the list of model 168 Hughie helicopters he compiled starting with the individual owners. He stopped at the BLM office to search the topographical maps for a Phoenix auto dealer's ranch site southwest of town. He didn't want to approach any out-of-the-way ranch without first knowing its geography. As an investigative journalist he learned the best source of free, accurate information was found at BLM map offices. Staffers were like scientists whose only serious infatuations or loves were maps and information. The truth was, they were unappreciated and under utilized. This angered them and they were desperate to have an audience so they could parade their knowledge. When he asked directions to the Phoenix auto dealer's ranch, three experts offered contradictory routes, none willing to give an inch. When he left they were still debating.

At the Flagstaff Airport, he struck up a conversation with a middle-aged office worker manning the counter. She hadn't seen a 168 and wouldn't know one if she saw it. She didn't know anything about the flamboyant rancher either. She walked Garrett from one hangar to another, talking and looking for helicopters. She was divorced, raising two teenaged sons, alone. He inquired at Sunrise Flight School about helicopter lessons and was informed they trained exclusively on fixed wing aircraft. They didn't know of any helicopter pilots with their own bird.

He drove west through an old ponderosa pine forest populated with

145

towering trees and surrounded by the corpses of family members in various states of decay. The deadwood lay haphazardly like pickup sticks. At the ranch road turnoff he pulled over and hiked up a low ridge that ran parallel to the road. A quarter mile away, he spotted the sprawling ranch house, barns and corrals - all possessed the look of real work.

More than a dozen dirty trucks, front-end loaders and tractor-trailers were parked adjacent to a large corrugated metal garage whose doors were closed. It was easily big enough to house a helicopter and Garrett concluded he needed to get a look inside. But how? Moving further along the ridge and using binoculars he spotted something at the other end of the garage. It was the Huey 168. One side of the chopper was wrecked, the windshield was shattered and one rotor was bent and the other broken off and missing. Weeds grew around its landing gear. This machine hadn't seen air in some time, he concluded, and left.

Back on the highway, he drove two hundred miles north to Moab, Utah. Garrett no longer cared for Moab, not since the mountain bikers and Espresso bars and brew pubs arrived. It was hard to reconcile his memories of the town with the reality of its recent development. He longed for the drunken nights in the late 1960s at the Poplar Place and after hours at the Town and Country. Back then, he camped along the River Road and after hiking the outback during the day, drove to town to drink and party. I remember camping at Dead Horse Point for days at a time, he reminded himself, and never seeing a soul. After they built the Visitor Center, Garrett ended up forty miles farther west in Canyonlands at Grand View. What a wild time, he reminisced, back then the great spirits lived there. Mick and Nancy and Randall and Leslie - we all hiked together. But the spirits are gone now, he ruminated, they left to find the last remaining vestiges of silence and power. He felt sad and resentful. Nothing stays the same, he thought, driving past the two-hundred-million-year-old sandstone formations. Everyone who shared this place with me is dead - and I am the last survivor. A deep loneliness overcame him.

The second Huey owner on his list was the ex-marine, Michael Hoskins. Hoskins was one of the first entrepreneurs to arrive in Moab in 1970 opening Canyonlands Tours Company. He started with day float trips down the Colorado River, then added a RV park with a gas station and convenience store. He bought the old airport concession and now operated Scenic Flight Tours, purchasing a Huey 168 in 1980.

Garrett found the second Huey perched atop the gift shop, painted in

Desert Storm camouflage. Across its length was a neon sign announcing, "Desert Tours - Open." Back in town he ate dinner at Pasta Johns a new-aged, funky Italian restaurant housed in the same building that housed the Canyonland's Cafe for fifty years. At his table he figured he was sitting in the exact place where in 1969 he ate breakfast with Ed Abbey.

Two days later in Gardiner, Montana, he learned from the Clark County Clerk that the billionaire rancher who owned the third Huey 168 sold out several years earlier to the Church Universal and Triumphant, a free love cult from southern California. The skinny clerk told him everyone in town was excited and happy at the time, hoping the God fearing church goers would save their ailing economy but they were soon surprised to learn the church members were all sex maniacs - and worse - they planned to take over the county by moving thousands of sex-crazed baby-boom devotees into the valley. "Things got dicey," the clerk told him, "when they got paranoid and one of the leaders was caught transporting 200 machine guns to the ranch."

"Since then," the skinny, chinless man told him, "the cult has been quiet, except for that god-damned helicopter." Apparently, the sale of the ranch included the helicopter and when relations between the church and the town soured, church leaders harassed towns folk with low level over flights. "They hovered for twenty minutes over my house. I never heard such a racket. "

"What did you do?"

"We got a court order and the helicopter has been grounded ever since. Why in the sam hill do they need a helicopter anyway? I'll never know."

Garrett nodded as if he understood and asked if there was any way they could have used it recently without anyone knowing.

The clerk shook his head, "Hell no! This is a deep valley, we all know the minute they fire that god-damned engine up."

From Gardiner, Montana Garrett drove south to Denver. The Anaxalrad Corporation, the huge multinational energy development company, headquartered in Amsterdam, Holland, owned two Huey 168s. Garrett knew about Anaxalrad. Until the lame duck President proclaimed The Grand Staircase, Canyons of the Escalante National Monument and stopped all development, Anaxalrad owned the oil and mineral development rights to a million acres of redrock country and were just about to develop an enormous open pit coal mine atop the remote Kaiparowits. It was bad enough that American oil companies attempted to develop the last remaining section of wilderness, but to have the Europeans here and doing it too, struck him as despicable.

Arriving in Denver late, he drove to the American headquarters of Anaxalrad, located in a prestigious business park in East Aurora. It was housed in a spectacular eight-story black glass building with a futuristic German design. Garrett parked and walked to the front doors. It was late, no one was around; he pulled on the locked doors, cupped his hands and looking inside the smoked glass entryway.

After renting a room, the next morning he called Anaxalrad and asked to speak to the vehicle fleet manager.

"We have no such position," the receptionist told him in a crisp English accent laced with Dutch.

"Perhaps you might direct my call to the appropriate person." He started, "My name is Randall Burton and I represent Heli-International, the world's largest dealer in rotor blade aircraft. I'm wondering if I might speak with the person responsible for purchasing such equipment?"

"One moment," she replied and put him on hold.

"Hello, my name is Ben Possett, how can I help you?" Possett also possessed a Dutch accent but his English was impeccable. Garrett told him the same story he told the receptionist.

"Well, Mr. Burton, you must be new to this work," Possett postulated, but did not seem put off. "We closed our operation at this location nearly two years ago and have no need at present to consider purchase of helicopters."

Garrett apologized and said, "I see from my information sheet that you own two Huey 168 helicopters . . . "

There was a long silence.

"Yes. We own many pieces of equipment, Mr. Burton, including a worldwide fleet of aircraft and helicopters. I'm sure if you contact our international office in Amsterdam Holland . . ."

Garrett interrupted, "I'm sorry again, Mr. Possett, perhaps I should have been more specific. We Americans can be so direct at times, I did not want to be impolite."

"Yes," Possett said, understanding. "And how might I assist you?"

"Thank you. I am in charge of purchasing used equipment here at Heli-International and we are wondering, since your operation has been inactive for sometime, would you consider selling your Hughes Aircraft 168s?"

"I don't handle these matters. Please wait," Possett excused himself and put Garrett on hold. A few minutes later, he came back and instructed Garrett to meet him at the office the next day at eleven.

As an investigative journalist, Garrett was forced to assume false identities occasionally, and while he was good at it, he disliked doing it. He became so adept at lying and being someone else it began to frighten him; after one particularly long assignment, he didn't know who he really was. Over the years, he had been a white supremacist sympathizer, an Evangelical devotee, a Mormon polygamist, and a right-wing antiabortion activist. He nearly lost his life covering the Contra Rebel war in Nicaragua.

The next morning he bought a beautiful European suit, shirt, tie and shoes - all on discount. Standing in the mirror, the sales woman told him how handsome and wonderful he looked dressed up. "You like older men?" he asked. "I hadn't thought about it," she replied.

At Anaxalrad's glass tower, Ben Possett was waiting in the spotless lobby. He was tall, six-foot-six, handsome and very distinguished. He had blazing blue eyes with long white hair combed straight back and pulled tightly into a pony tail. He wore a long, elegant white goatee.

Shaking Garrett's hand, he bowed, "Your card, please?"

"My card," Garrett answered, distressed. He hadn't counted on this. He searched the sewn-shut pockets of his new suit. "Oh, I am so sorry," he said. "I feel foolish. I'm wearing a new suit and I left my wallet with my cards at my room. Please accept my apology."

Possett stepped back and took a more thorough look. "Well, Mr. Burton," he said, slowly, "it does not matter. This will not take long. Please, this way," he stepped out of the way like a matador and made a sweeping gesture forward.

He led Garrett to a blue leather couch located in a glass enclosed alcove. "I have contacted our facility in Colorado Springs where the Hughes helicopters you are interested in are stored," Possett explained. "This is the name of the man you should ask for," he handed Garrett a business card. "I'm sure he can help." Possett then stood abruptly, "I apologize but I am very busy."

"Thank you," Garrett offered, standing and smiling. "This is exactly what I need. Thank you very much."

Possett extended his hand and the two men shook but instead of releasing Garrett's hand Possett held on and did not let go. His grip was remarkably strong and as the two men stood there, face to face, Possett smiled as if acknowledging some shared secret between them. Garrett was confused and wondered if Possett was being overly polite or if he derived some perverse satisfaction or amusement from holding his visitor's hand.

"Well," Garrett said politely, trying to pull away. "I'll go then, it has been a pleasure."

The handsome Dutchman stood at attention, smiled but did not release his hand. Looking directly into Garrett's eyes he nodded several times, again acting as if acknowledging some shared secret or communication.

"Thank you again," Garrett repeated, "It's been good . . . to meet you."

Finally, Possett bent at the waist in a noble fashion and released Garrett's hand, "I hope you find what you are looking for Mr. . . Mr. . . you did you say, Burton, right? Ah, yes. Mr. Burton. I certainly hope you find what you are looking for but I strongly doubt you will find it - not at Anaxalrad anyway."

On his way out, Garrett wanted to turn back and confront Possett. But confront him with what? That he was lying about Heli-International? That he was not Mr. Burton? That he was really searching for a Hughes helicopter used in a mysterious murder of a Navajo outcast? He hadn't expected this, what did Possett really know? How could he know anything? Was Anaxalrad involved in all this?

Hours later in Colorado Springs, Anaxalrad's operations manager took him to the giant hanger where the two Hughes 168s were stored along side a dozen other mothballed aircraft. The manager told him that while the helicopters were old they were in excellent condition and, after checking his chart, said they had just ten hours flying time logged since they were last serviced two years ago, prior to being decommissioned and stored. Garrett circled the birds, examining them closely. They were caked with a thick even layer of dust; he ran his finger against the cockpit glass.

He left disappointed and rented a room near the Interstate, took a long nap, then went out to eat and plan his next move. He hadn't known what to expect at the hangar, but after his morning meeting with Possett he felt he was onto something very important and hoped to get something - anything - more to go on.

Picking a restaurant at random he went into the bar where he drank two doubles of scotch and water at a small table. With three more 168s still on his list, he was convinced Ben Possett held some important information. Sitting across the room, he spotted a man who looked like his dead friend Mick. The man was sitting at a table with his family. Garrett couldn't decide if Mick was a brave man or a coward for shooting himself in the heart. It was an argument that started for him the moment after he learned Mick shot himself, and continued to this day, fifteen years later.

"Mr. Burton. Excuse me. May I intrude?"

Garrett brought himself from his muse to find a man standing next to his table. He hadn't seen the man approach and had no idea how long he had been there.

"Mr. Burton?" the man said again.

"No," Garrett finally blurted out. "I think you have the wrong . . . " then he stopped, realizing the man standing there was Ben Possett, from Anaxalrad. "I mean . . . I didn't expect . . . oh, yes. I mean . . . No. Mr. Possett, you are not interrupting." Garrett was confused and paused to collect his thoughts for a moment.

"How coincidental," Possett said casually, rubbing his large hands together as if they were cold, "to find you here."

"Why yes, yes indeed. I guess it is a coincidence . . . How are you, Mr. Possett?"

"Quite well, Mr. Burton. Thank you." he nodded politely and looked at the vacant seat opposite Garrett. "Are you waiting for someone?"

"No, I'm not."

"Did you find the helicopter you were looking for?"

"They are fine machines," Garrett said, giving Possett a sly glance. "I do appreciate your help. Won't you join me?" Garrett stood slightly, and shook Possett's hand. "Please, have a seat. I must say that both helicopters appear to be in perfect condition."

Possett nodded and sat down.

" And you, Mr. Possett, how are you? I'm surprised to see you."

"I am fine - doing quite well." He paused and looked into Garrett's eyes, "Ah yes, it is a coincidence that we are here. Yes? Tell me, Mr. Burton, you do believe in coincidence, don't you?"

"You might say I do. Sometimes certainly." He looked into his empty scotch glass, "I'm wondering if you might agree that true coincidence rarely occurs. . . That most of what we believe is coincidental is truly not."

"Exactly. I agree."

They smiled and looked at each other, wondering what was next.

"Look," Possett finally said, glancing around the room and then at his wristwatch nervously, "I don't know who you are, but I will very soon . . ."

"What?" Garrett interrupted. "I don't know what your talking about."

"While I do not know your true identity yet," Possett continued, "I believe I do know what you are looking for. . . "

"I assure you, Mr. Possett . . . "

"No, please!" Possett interrupted, "No more pretense. There is no Heli-International. There is no Mr. Burton. Right? Or, is it Mr. Smith or Mr. Johnson?"

Garrett started to protest but stopped. He kicked back in his chair. "Yes, Mr. Possett, how clever of you. You are right, I am not who I said I was. I am sorry I misrepresented myself. My name is Garrett Lyons and I am an investigative journalist working on a story about helicopter safety, specifically Vietnam era Huey 168s. As you can imagine, many people are reluctant to talk with me so . . . so I have reluctantly learned that sometimes I must tell a little white lie so I can get information . . ."

"Please, please, please, Mr. Lyons!" Possett said, getting more excited with each word. "It is Mr. Lyons? Correct?" He narrowed his eyes, "I think you are not researching safety of helicopters at all, I believe you are searching for something else entirely. Correct me if I am wrong, right?"

"Like what?"

"I believe you are searching for a particular Huey 168. A helicopter that has been in use recently, perhaps in Utah or Arizona?" Possett sat back and smiled wryly.

Garrett's eyes betrayed him. He was still a click or two behind, he had never been caught red-handed. Possett cornered him and he was not prepared for it. He suddenly felt weak and he swayed in his seat, his equilibrium slipping away. How could Possett possibly know what I am doing, he wondered. It's impossible! The murder had not even been reported.

"Look," Possett said impatiently, "this is very dangerous. I honestly do not care to know who you are, but I am very vulnerable just being here. Understand?" He looked around the room quickly. "I will make a deal with you. You tell me who you are and exactly what you are doing, and in return, I will tell you what you want to know. What is fair is fair."

Possett waited and when Garrett did not respond immediately, he became impatient and grew disgusted. At the same time, he spotted someone coming in the restaurant that he did not want to see.

"Okay. I see." Possett said standing up. "I must have everything wrong. You obviously do not know what I am talking about. I will be leaving now. Thank you." He abruptly got up and shook Garrett's hand.

"No! Wait!" Garrett finally answered, "It's a deal. I'll tell you, you tell me."

Possett glanced around, gave him a snide look and then passed him a business card. He quickly strode away and left the restaurant, never looking back.

Back at his room, Garrett googled Possett and Anaxalrad on the internet. Possett held degrees in political science and geology. He began working for Anaxalrad in 1976 at its Venezuela office. From there, he transferred to Malaysia, then onto America and Denver. He was a high level executive and troubleshooter who often closed down unprofitable operations, laying off people and selling resources. In an online annual Anaxalrad report, Garrett found a picture of Possett sitting next to the CEO at an important meeting in Paris. As for Anaxelrad, it was a quiet giant, one of Europe's best kept business secrets. It was created when six multinational energy development companies, the biggest individual corporations in Europe, banded together to form an alliance large enough to rival any in America or Asia. It had holdings on five continents and was worth billions.

The next day Garrett called the number on Possett's card but no one answered. He left his name and cell number. He checked out of the hotel and drove the one hundred miles back to Denver. When Possett did not returned his call by four in the afternoon, Garrett called Anaxalrad's main number and the beautiful Dutch receptionist told him Possett was out of the office. When pressed, she told him Mr. Possett was called back to international headquarters in Amsterdam for a meeting.

CHAPTER TWENTY-ONE

Two weeks from the day they arrived at Zion National Park, EarthIsland broke camp and left. In the wake of their departure, dust devils swirled and churned up and down the narrow canyon. At a Watchman campfire rally the night before, Jonah warned they should be ready to return on short notice. "This battle will neither be won quickly nor without significant commitments of time, resources and help from all of you. I am deeply moved by what has happened here, it has been nothing short of unbelievable.

"We arrived here with the idea of justice, we now leave with a hope and a sense of new community - a community each of us now belongs to. Ian would be very proud and I want to thank each one of you for his sake. Keep this new spirit and power alive. Take it home with you and tell people about it. Make it grow in your heart and in your community. Protect this spirit we have kindled because the truth is we will need it. This is not the end, it is the beginning."

EarthIsland's general call to action was a success. For the first time environmentalists of many persuasions crossed organizational lines and international borders to rally for a single cause. Some arrived with significant resources and expertise; others brought nothing but idealistic longings and dreams. Some arrived dragging their disillusionment with them, desperate to vanquish their cynicism from years of participation in do-nothing organizations. The hardcore activists made the pilgrimage: Greens from Germany, EarthFirst! from England, Green Peace from Holland, PETA from the East coast, Vegans from Canada. It was a magical mystery tour carried aloft on the hot air dream of actually making a difference. Streaming out of the park, each left buoyed by the idea that once in a person's lifetime they were at the right place, with the right people, for the right purpose, at exactly the right time.

Those who stayed behind, the "core" as they referred to themselves, more than six hundred strong, caravanned east out of the park with a Utah

Highway Patrol escort. At the junction of Highway 89, they left the escort behind and headed north toward Bryce Canyon National Park and then east to Escalante, Utah. In Escalante, they paraded slowly through town, the line of vehicles stretching from one end of town to the other. They honked horns and shouted greetings. They were convinced Ian's killers lived in Escalante and they wanted to let them know who their new neighbors were.

Down the Hole in the Rock Road they churned up twenty-five miles of dirt, creating a plume of dust so dense and large that satellites could easily pick it up. Fifteen miles out, near Harris Wash, they crossed into the Grand Stair Case National Monument and a few miles further they took the left turn to Egypt.

No one liked the way they left last time, frightened and escaping in the middle of the night, especially Jonah. It was important that they return - and within a few days Jonah and his lieutenants realized it made an excellent back country headquarters. From Egypt, they could continue to pressure Garfield County to make arrests, and at the same time, they could continue to push their media offensive from the monument.

They set up a tent community at the trailhead where it would do the least environmental damage. They bought a water tanker truck and set up showers and a communal kitchen. Every day convoys of trucks arrived and departed, bringing in food and supplies and people and taking out garbage and those leaving. They were all well guarded and traveled nonstop to St. George in Washington County, a hundred miles away.

Halfway between the Hole in the Rock road and Egypt, McVey set up a security check point. No one came or went without passing inspection. Manning the checkpoint were unarmed security people but riflemen were stationed on hills a few hundred feet away. Jonah made a special effort to visit McVey and the security detail daily. Since moving from Zion to Egypt, McVey stopped criticizing him and Jonah knew this meant trouble. He learned that as long as McVey was running his mouth he was harmless, but when he clammed up, it was time to watch him closely.

Shon set up the communications tent so people could make satellite calls or use one of a dozen generator-powered Apple computers for e-mail and internet access. He created a high quality remote live-cam internet linkup and EarthIsland broadcast live Monument webcam vistas and ambient sounds of the desert. He also produced a five minute public service weekly, showcasing destruction to the fragile desert ecosystem by cows and traditional land users and focusing on ways the land could be rehabilitated.

After the road maintenance crew called it a day, locking the gate to the Garfield County Vehicle Maintenance facility on Highway 12 near Calf Creek campground, three men emerged from the cedar forest and moved to the back of the yard. Using wire cutters they cut a hole in the chain link fence, broke a window to the office and climbed in. Going from one office to another they turned over desks, pulled files from the cabinets, destroyed computers and everything else they found.

Two men wired explosives from the three dump trucks in the buildings repair bays to the road graders and utility trucks outside. They taped four sticks of dynamite to each gas tank and then rolled the detonation cord to the hole in the fence just outside the property. A third man spray painted "The Burr Trail Forever!" on an office wall. They won't be using these machines to pave any more new roads into the wilderness, one joked.

It had long been the contention of Garfield County that it owned all the roads within its jurisdiction including the right to maintain them. Since the county was catacombed with hundreds of cow paths, mining exploration roads, and seldom used ranch roads, they believed none of Garfield County qualified as wilderness. In an effort to drive home their jurisdictional claims and without permits from the federal land managers, they paved the once famous Burr Trail. The road equipment at the maintenance facility was used to pave the Burr Trail and had already been the target of vandalism and attempts to destroy it.

Out of harm's way, the men ignited the detonation cord but it malfunctioned and extinguished. "I told you," one said, "I knew the cord wouldn't work! It was too old when we took it!" They nervously lighted it again and again, each time the old cord burned a few feet before going out. Each attempt took them closer to the potential blast area.

Finally, at the back wall of the building, just feet away from the first explosives charge, two of the men refused to go any further, arguing it was too dangerous. The third man, the leader, sent the others back where it was safe. On his second attempt, the fast-burning cord did not fail and before he could hit the ground, the first sticks of dynamite detonated, ripping into a truck gas tank and exploding its contents in a tremendous blast, sending him sprawling backwards. Rocketing flames and shrapnel shot in every direction. The next four detonations exploded simultaneously, one after another, and a series of fireballs rolled high into the night air. On his feet, the man sprinted for safety as explosions and fireballs rocked the facility. Just as he reached his companions and safety a piece of shrapnel hit him from behind and sent him to the ground.

The sound of the explosions rolled back and forth off the sandstone cliffs, thundering and reverberating down the canyons as flames engulfed the structure and a series of secondary, smaller blasts ignited. The two men dragged the third to safety just as a two-thousand gallon gas tank under the building's foundation ignited. The concussion obliterated the building and catapulted its burning roof hundreds of feet into the air. Debris rained down everywhere. A single column of fire curled up into the air and mush-roomed, illuminating the surrounding forest and cliffs. Parts of the burning roof landed on the hillside five-hundred-feet away where it ignited the dense cedar forest. By the time the three men raced away in their vehicle, the tinder dry cedar forest exploded and flames began working over a ridge.

Word quickly made it to Jonah that McVey was injured and needed emergency medical help. Apparently, a car tire jack slipped when he was changing a flat and somehow the jack was dislodged and flipped into the air hitting him in the lower back. When Jonah arrived with Natalie the nurse and five of his top lieutenants, they found McVey under a shaded lean-to, laying on his side on a cot, surrounded by his men. He was naked from his waist up and a large bloody bandage was wrapped around his lower back.

"You okay?" Jonah asked, rushing up.

"I'm really fucked up!" McVey answered as Natalie went to work examining him.

"When?" Jonah asked, moving closer to take a look.

"A few days ago - Tuesday or Wednesday."

"You didn't tell anyone?" Jonah asked, shaking his head.

"Shit happens," he replied, obviously in pain.

"Jesus, that bandage - it needs to be changed."

Natalie cut away the old bandage and exposed a deep L-shaped wound on McVey's lower back. "Three days ago?" She asked, shocked.

"Something like that."

She touched the wound and McVey whined.

"Looks like it just happened," she said, raising her eyebrows to

Jonah. "It needs cleaning. A few days, huh?"

"God damn it," McVey shouted. "Does it fucking matter? Just fix it!"

"You need a doctor, right away!"

"No!" he cried out, in pain. "No doctors! Got any Oxicoden? I need heavy-duty, bad-ass, pain pills. Pericodine? Just bandaged me up. I'll be fine." He tried to sit up but could not. Sweat beaded on his forehead and neck. "You've got pain pills, don't you? Demerol?"

Natalie turned to Jonah, "He needs a doctor." She searched her medical kit, adding, "It's very serious."

"No doctor - I said."

From the looks of it, Jonah could not understand how a crow bar could have caused a wound like that. He watched quietly as Natalie cleaned the wound and applied a new bandage. Without antibiotics and a visit to a doctor, Natalie told him, there is a strong chance of infection.

Jonah followed her to the truck where she informed him there was no way the wound was three-days-old. It is more likely, she estimated, less than a day old.

Jonah wanted to speak to McVey alone and asked everyone to leave but McVey's men stood their ground until McVey nodded for them to go. The two groups of men, Jonah's lieutenants and McVey's security men moved into an open area twenty or thirty feet away.

"Alright,"" Jonah said, in a low voice, "what happened?"

"God damn it Jonah, I told you what . . . "

"Don't fuck with me," he hissed and pointed a finger in McVey's face, "that wound didn't come from a fucking tire jack. You take me for some kind of idiot?"

"I told you . . ."

"Play it your way." Turning to his men, Jonah ordered, "Okay, looks like we're taking him into St. George. Come get him. He needs a doctor." As Jonah's men moved toward the lean-to, McVey shouted to his men, "Stop them!" His men quickly stepped in front of Jonah's lieutenants blocking them and the two groups pushed and shoved each other back and forth.

"Outta the way!" Jonah demand, moving toward the melee, ordering McVey's men to step away.

"You don't tell us what to do," one man shouted.

"The hell I don't!" Jonah answered, rushing forward and pushing the man in the chest with both hands, sending him backwards to the ground.

"I'll kick your fucking ass," he shouted, standing over the man. "I'm leader of this group! You all take orders from me!" Jonah was furious. "Back off, Jonah!" McVey shouted. "They're just doing what I told them."

Nearby, a nervous McVey follower, started raising his rifle as if to point it at Jonah but two of Jonah's lieutenants were on him, grabbing the gun and knocking him down.

"Don't!" McVey screamed at his men, "No more! Back off."

For a few tense moments no one moved or spoke. Finally, Jonah motioned with his hands for everyone to back away and McVey nodded at his men to obey.

"Looks like we got a little anarchy going here, huh?"

"It's not like that!" McVey said, clutching his side. "We're all in this together. Don't blame them, they're loyal to me."

"You going to tell me," Jonah demanded. "This has something to do with the bombing of the maintenance yard and the forest fire, right?"

Sitting heavily on the edge of the cot now, elbows resting on his knees, his head in his hands, McVey said weakly, "Maybe you have forgotten about Ian, but we haven't. The law isn't going to do anything until we put some real pressure on them. They've got to know they can't fuck with us."

"Damn it McVey, we've put real pressure on them! "Jonah cried out, pacing back and forth, "I asked you to be patient. Now, you've ruined everything! All the good work - shot in the ass!" Jonah continued to get more distraught, "You son-of-a-bitch. I should rip your head off!"

"Here it is, muther fucker," McVey whispered, rocking back and forth. "Go for it if it'll make you feel any better."

"How could you?" Jonah shouted, shaking his head back and forth, as if speaking to himself.

McVey stared at the ground between his feet.

"We've made real progress. Can't you see that, man? We've built credibility - a coalition."

"This is not about some fucking coalition, man," McVey began. "It's about making somebody pay. Ian was murdered right here, by some shit-kicking cowboys. Wake up Jonah! If you haven't noticed the pigs haven't done a goddamned thing! And they are not going to either. They probably did it themselves! There aren't going to be any arrests, my man. Wake up!"

159

Jonah stood with his back to McVey looking out at the sandstone landscape unable to fathom the damage he'd done.

"Look," McVey went on, "you and I are alike. Over the years we have been on the same side many times . . ."

"I should turn your fucking ass in," Jonah said, turning back to face him.

"Yeah, but you won't. It's too late for that now. No one's going to believe you weren't in on it."

"We've put so much positive energy into this then you go out and unilaterally fuck everything up?"

"It's a done deal, my friend," McVey said, laughing. "Time to start dealing with it. We can't go back, not now."

"What about the god damned fire?"

McVey grimaced, "That was an accident, we didn't know . . . "

"You call yourself an environmentalist," Jonah interrupted, "What happens when they come looking for you?"

"They won't find me. Nobody will ever know. You won't loose your precious credibility. It will be just another one of the mysterious crimes."

"Where are you going to hide?"

"Plenty of places - in plain sight." He motioned to the landscape.

"If push comes to shove, I'm turning you over to them."

"Do what you've got to do."

Jonah turned to leave but turned back, "What else, man? What else have you and your bad-assed, trigger-happy patriots done? You shot the cows and burned the line shack, right? Admit it! What about the fences and water troughs?"

"If anyone shot those cows it was you!" McVey countered, angrily. "We've thought it was you all along! It's time you admitted it Jonah! You and Petra were the only ones down there. You shot those god - damned cows and started this whole thing!"

"Fuck off!"

"I bet in your uppity mind you could just see those bovine shit machines eating up all the grazing and shitting in the only drinkable water! Didn't that just piss you off, Jonah? Didn't it make you want to blow their fucking heads off? To you, those fucking cows were just Big Macs rollin' down the assembly line." McVey tried to stand but couldn't. "Admit it! Didn't you just get so pissed off about it you just shot them! Wasn't that the way it was, Jonah? Don't be a hypocrite, man, I stood up for what I did. You shot those cows and I know it! We all do! You orchestrated this whole scenario. Don't think I don't know it. You have always wanted the spotlight - by any means necessary!"

"Take your men and clear out!" Jonah shouted.

"What did you bring us out here for in the first place, Jonah - not for Espresso and bran muffins? We're fighters! It's time to take a stand and fight. I, for one, ain't going anywhere!"

Jonah pointed down at McVey, "I hate these small-minded, backwards idiots just as much as you. I want Ian's killers found and castrated, but I won't let you or anyone else turn this into some kind of personal blood bath."

"And my advice to you," McVey said slowly, trying pathetically to grab Jonah's finger, "better get ready to defend yourself, my man. There is a bull's eye tattooed on your back, man. They'll be coming soon. Looking for you. I guarantee it."

CHAPTER TWENTY-TWO

The last of the Founder's Day revelers departed around midnight when the part-time courthouse maintenance man, Dan Harrie, switched off the floodlights and went home. The park was left as it was, festooned with balloons and streamers and hundreds of folding chairs standing empty next to long tables covered with butcher paper, plastic plates, utensils and empty soft drink cans. The cottonwood trees were wrapped in candy cane crepe paper and the pavilion was decorated with patriotic red, white and blue flags. The glorious mess would have to wait to be cleaned up until morning.

Alley cats worked the trash barrels filled with turkey and ham and steak bones. The darkness brought a strange soft, dreamlike quality to the park. The IGA at the intersection of Main and Highway 89 closed early, and the owner of the all night gas station and convenience store at the edge of town took the day off. The only lights still burning were three flood-lights mounted in the lawn at the base of the flagpole in front of the court-house. They illuminated the buildings strong brick lines, the stately rooftop cornice corners, the fancy scroll work.

Four blocks away at the Pink Cliffs Motel two men dressed in black, wearing ski masks and 40 caliber Glock autoloader pistols with silencers, slipped out of their room and moved from one shadow to the next to the courthouse. They carried a long black duffle bag between them. Sticking to an alley, they avoided Main Street. At the south side of the courthouse, they used a diamond cutting tool cut a hole in a window and climbed in.

Inside, they checked to make certain they were alone then one pulled a two-way radio from a pocket. "All clear," he told someone at the other end. "The building's secure. The operation is a go. Yes, sir. Implementing the plan now."

They carried the duffle bag to the courtroom chambers on the first floor, just a few feet from the sheriff's office. Inside the chambers, they placed the bag against a load bearing outer wall, set the remote detonator switch to the "on" position and then checked the wiring to the twenty pounds of military quality Semtex plastic explosives. Taped to the explosives were four containers of airplane fuel. Back at the window, they made sure it was clear before climbing out and returning to their motel room. The entire operation took less than thirty minutes. In their room, they placed everything out exactly as instructed, climbed into their vehicle and at exactly 3:45 a.m. they activated the remote detonation device and drove north out of town. "Mission accomplished," one radioed as they departed.

By the time Sheriff Deputy Franklin dressed and ran out the door toward the courthouse a block away, he could see flames leaping high above and thick black smoke billowing from shattered windows on the first floor. The thundering blast shook everyone in the valley awake; some thinking it must be an earthquake. The north wall of the courthouse was gone, leaving a gaping hole from the ground floor to the roof. Flames leapt from the east and west side of the building. Deputy Franklin frantically radioed Sheriff Anderson who was already on his way. Within minutes the chief of the volunteer fire department activated the siren mounted atop the Mormon church, calling the faithful to come running. Ten minutes later most of the town was rushing to the horrific scene.

Townspeople attacked the flames in a desperate battle to save the building. Two fire trucks poured thousands of gallons of water onto the flames. Every available resource was pressed into service. People covered their faces with towels or shirts and worked their way to the basement where historic archives and important documents were stored. They formed a bucket brigade but instead of hauling water they passed boxes of important papers up the stairs and out the back door. The heat and flames were out of control on the north side of the building and soon the dense, deadly smoke reached the brigade and drove them out.

Racing to town with Cody, who arrived home drunk just minutes before Sheriff Anderson's call, Lonnie pulled up to the scene where a crowd of women and children stood. They watched in anguished disbelief as the north side of the building collapsed. From the edge of town, Lonnie and Cody could see flames leaping from the courthouse spire. One hundred years of history and legal documents and photographs and records and irreplaceable community objects fueled the fire.

Every able-bodied person fought the flames, throwing themselves into the melee, having neither the right equipment nor a coherent plan. Fire crews from Richfield to the north and Escalante and Kanab from the east and south arrived bringing fresh men. They laid hose five hundred feet to a irrigation ditch and shot thousands of gallons of water onto the fire. Cody moved in and out of the building, saving what he could get his hands on. He made it to his mother's office on the second floor in a desperate attempt to save his father's prized Indian blanket before he was pushed back. It was no use, the heat and smoke were too much. He got close enough to get a look at the office, it was fully engulfed in flames.

As the sun rose over the eastern horizon, the valley was submerged in a dirty smoke cloud and the courthouse lay in ruins. Firefighters moved through the rubble, dousing pockets of smoldering lumber and searching for clues. Most of the town's people huddled together in the park, many in shock and still in their nightclothes. They sat on the fold-out chairs or sprawled on the grass. The Panguitch Volunteer Fire crew was exhausted and defeated - just twelve hours earlier they used their water cannons to spray the children at the Founder's Day celebration; all of that was now forgotten, replaced by a deep sense of defeat. Even Mrs. Wells, at ninety-eight-years-old, the oldest person in town, sobbed like a child. Her father placed the cornerstone for the building the year she was born.

Lonnie sat in the gutter with Cody, his arm around her shoulder. They were caked with soot and ash and perspiration. Cody was so angry he could not speak. If the lowlife radical environmentalists who did this were standing before him he would kill them with his bare hands. Lonnie sobbed softly and seemed small and fragile, as if something inside had collapsed.

Two days later, Garfield County government reopened in the old elementary school two blocks west of Main Street. No act of terrorism would stop the work of the county. Commissioner Bullock spent the first day moving in, meeting with department heads, and working out logistical problems. One of the first priorities was getting communications up and working, an emergency crew from Denver worked around the clock to get the county wired for telephone and internet service.

Bullock, who slept little since the bombing, fielded calls from the media, worried constituents and law enforcement officials. Sheriff Anderson led the investigation with assistance from state and federal agencies including investigators from the FBI. They supplied resources and expertise and helped coordinate with other agencies. Federal agents offered technical and scientific experts and the State of Utah's Attorney

General's office would help with the prosecution. Sheriff Anderson appreciated the assistance, but this was his investigation and he was not about to let outsiders start calling the shots. Within days, his turfy behavior alienated most of the outside help. Some were openly critical, saying the bombing was a direct result of the sheriff's inability to make arrests in the murder of Ian McCarthey. If they were in control of the investigation, the foot-dragging would end and suspects in the murder, the arson at the maintenance facility, and now courthouse bombing, would be brought to justice.

Privately, Anderson told Bullock he didn't trust any of the outsiders. Commissioner Bullock wanted results and believed the feds could help but as her late father-in-law would say, "The people of Garfield County have done well for ourselves. We don't need outsiders coming in and telling us what to do." Still, she had taken considerable heat for the delays in Ian McCarthey murder investigation and called Sheriff Anderson into her office twice to get updated reports. "Andy," she asked apologetically, "you any closer to making any arrests?"

He believed outsiders did the killing and spent two critical weeks checking national crime spree suspects who might have been in the area but without developing any real leads or suspects. In truth, Anderson cared little for who killed the environmentalist and spent his time outside the county snooping around Zion National Park taking pictures of EarthIslanders coming and going.

Because of the suspect descriptions, offered by the rape victims, Anderson did tell the Commissioner his investigation was looking at some of the men out on the Circle Cliffs and some other well-known hotheads in town. The ranchers who worked the Circle Cliffs and called themselves the "outlaws" were holdovers from another time. They were born a hundred years too late and didn't abide with outsiders. They had their own ideas about justice and weren't beholding to anyone. Anderson believed any one of them could have easily beaten a man to death for killing the cows but when it came to raping two young women, probably not.

Anderson angrily informed Bullock he wasn't about to charge someone with murder unless he was convinced the prosecutor's office could get a conviction. "We need proof," he told her, "not just the eyewitness account of two sluts."

"How do you know they're sluts?" she angrily demanded, once having many in town bestow that title on her.

"I don't have proof," he said, "but I'll bet. . . "

165

"If you have no proof, keep your myopic opinions to yourself, Sheriff." Bullock was furious, "Besides, what does their personal life have to do with the crime?" she demanded.

"It could have a lot to do with it when it comes before a jury," he snapped back. "The truth is, I don't trust the state or the federal government. Do you? Did Mack? Or Mack's daddy? What have they done for us, except come in here and strut around like they own the place. They treat us like country bumpkins. This is my investigation and I will run it as I see fit."

"We are country bumpkins, Andy!"

Bullock had no choice but to wait, even when Utah State Assistant Attorney General Julie Bryant called, accusing Anderson of withholding important evidence and telling Bullock that Anderson was obstructing the investigation by his unwillingness to be a team-player.

The Garfield County Prosecutor, a man named Joel Zitting, at first seemed impatient with Anderson as well; he was anxious to move forward with the murder case once charges were filed. Zitting, an aggressive, local athletic hero, left Panguitch to perform a two year Mormon mission, then went on to Brigham Young University on a football scholarship and obtained law degree before returning. He was smart, ambitious and politically correct. He saw himself as having a bright future in politics, perhaps even a governorship. It was no secret he wanted Bullock's job, which he viewed as a steppingstone to much larger prizes.

Zitting relished the spotlight and wanted to ride the successful prosecution of the murder case into the state legislature. So, it was surprising when he suddenly lost all interest in the crime, the most controversial in county history. Quietly, he reassigned staff onto other court cases. He left only two low level legal assistants to assist Sheriff Anderson. Privately, Zitting told staffers he believed the death of Ian McCarthey was nothing more than a common assault, probably instigated by the victim. It was, in all likelihood, a case of self defense. The rape charges, according to him, were much stronger because of the DNA evidence but it would be difficult to impossible to get a conviction because of the victims' history of promiscuity and especially since they were members of a radical environmentalist organization, one currently involved in a dirty tricks campaign against the county.

As far as the courthouse bombing investigation, Anderson openly courted outside help and shared information. He needed the FBI crime scene investigators. The bureau had two primary suspects, two men who several days before Founder's Day rented a room at the Pink Cliff's Motel and told the office manager they were sightseers visiting Bryce Canyon National Park. They drove a new, four wheel drive Subaru with Colorado plates.

The motel clerk told authorities he heard the two men leave just before the blast at the courthouse. In their room, investigators found considerable evidence including architectural renderings of the courthouse floor plan, a recent issue of BackPack magazine with a cover story about an arson at a Vail, Colorado ski resort, a new copy of Edward Abbey's, *The Monkey Wrench Gang*, and scrawled on a pad of paper was the website address of EarthIsland. They cordoned off the room and conducted a thorough search and analysis. Surprisingly, they didn't find a single fingerprint on any surface in the room, not on the architectural plans, the magazines, books, nothing.

Everyone in town was edgy and suspicious of strangers. They worried another sneak terrorist attack was in the offing. For the first time, people removed the keys from their cars and locked their houses at night. In just a few short weeks radical environmentalists shot the cows, burned the famous line shack, destroyed the Garfield County maintenance yard and brought the venerable courthouse down into a heap of ash. One resident quipped, "I guess this is what living in the city is like."

The most galling insult was that the people assumed to be responsible were just a few miles away. For more than a month, locals were forced to endure five thousand radical environmentalists just forty miles away at Zion National Park. Locals heard stories of passing through the park and witnessing hundreds of angry-looking environmentalists blocking the steep narrow canyon road and choking off traffic just below the tunnel. Now that EarthIsland left the park, moving seventy-five miles further east down the Hole in the Rock Road, residents of Panguitch hoped the worst was over, but now with the courthouse gone, many feared it was just the beginning.

The destruction of the Garfield County Courthouse struck a nerve and became the instant rallying cry for every disenfranchised rancher, miner and logger throughout the West. If it can happen in Panguitch, Utah it can happen anywhere. Within days of the crime, help from other Western communities started pouring in: truckloads of building materials, food and donations of money.

The courthouse ruins became a symbol of the threat to western culture and tradition. People came from hundreds of miles away to pay their respects and leave miniature American flags. Some brought cowboy hats and tossed them onto the blackened rubble. Assailed for decades by outsiders coming in and telling them what to do, it was time to unite. It was time for true Westerners - those who believed in historic traditional ways - to close ranks and take a stand. No matter how they sliced it, it was time to fight back.

The federal government was no help, in fact, they were part of the problem. Eastern liberals pushed the government to establish national parks and wilderness areas out west. Everyone loved a good steak but they no longer wanted cows to graze on public land. Everyone wanted to be safe and protected but they wanted to take the guns away from law abiding citizens. Everyone wanted cheap power but didn't want the waste in their backyard. Truck the radioactive waste out west where no one lives. The feds were nothing more than lackeys for the environmental extremists.

One of those who arrived to pay his respects was Thomas Westley, a rancher and sometimes finish carpenter who was also a one-time leader of the defunct Sagebrush Rebellion. Westley pulled into town, parked his rig at the courthouse and spent the afternoon circling the symbol of American freedom. He walked with his hands in the pockets of his faded levis, head bent down, eyes shaded by his cowboy hat. He carried a styrofoam cup he used to spit his tobacco juice into.

He parked his truck and flatbed trailer, carrying a D-9 bulldozer, on Main Street where everyone could see it. Plastered across the bulldozer's side were American flags and a tall red, white and blue banner that read, "Take Back Our Land!" He talked to everyone who would listen, meeting with Sheriff Anderson and attempting to find out what he could do to help.

Twelve years earlier, Westley was a hero to traditional land-users for blading a new road into a proposed wilderness area in eastern Nevada. He was filmed by the international media sitting a top his bull- dozer and aiming it into pristine sage and cedar desert. The son of five generations of ranchers, Westley lost the family spread to federal officials after they caught him rounding up wild mustangs owned by the federal government. According to him, they were eating the forage belonging to his cows. The fact was they weren't indigenous mustangs at all, they came from domesticated stock abandoned fifty years earlier. After Westley repeatedly failed to show up for court proceedings, he was found in contempt of court and jailed. Ultimately, he lost the ranch and spent a year in jail for assaulting officials who served him with the eviction notice. After his release, he became an outspoken critic of federal intrusion on western land.

Westley hated the federal government, the U.S. court system, the United Nations and its New World Order, the abortion rights activists and he especially hated environmentalists and the Federal Interior Department. He believed every American had the right to carry a side arm and he openly paraded a cowboy type holster and .45 caliber six shooter on his hip. He lived in his truck and traveled from one outpost to another, talking cessation and civil war at gun shows with angry Westerners who felt the same way.

Two days after the courthouse bombing, six cars filled with local, state and federal investigators lead by Sheriff Anderson showed up for a surprise visit at EarthIsland's encampment at Egypt. Instead of catching the group off guard as they expected, they were the ones who were surprised. Halfway to Egypt, at a place where the road crests a small hill then quickly drops into a narrow dry wash, the road was blocked by trucks and vans.

Lookouts stationed five miles away at the Egypt turnoff from the Hole in the Rock spotted the police and alerted Jonah by two-way radio. By the time the police arrived at the road block, 200 men from the main camp arrived to reinforce the checkpoint. Anderson and the other law enforcement personnel exited their vehicles, some cranking shells into riot shotguns. They were immediately surrounded by Jonah and his unarmed men. McVey's armed security men held positions above the convoy on either side of the steep sandstone wash, creating a perfect crossfire situation. They openly displayed assault weapons but McVey was no where to be found.

Jonah and his men confronted and heckled them, "Go home!" "Pigs!" "Gestapo!" "You are not welcome here! Get out!"

The investigators hadn't expected to be caught by surprise and the sheer numbers and militancy frightened them. Some environmentalists pushed forward, moving so close that two state troopers lifted their shotguns to the firing position before deciding against it, and lowering their weapons.

Sheriff Anderson stepped forward, "We are not going anywhere until we speak to your leader, Jonah Sandborn."

"I'm Jonah Sandborn. What can I do for you?" He stepped forward and folded his arms in a flamboyant, swaggering gesture. "I hope you are here to tell us you have made arrests in the murder of our compatriot, Ian McCarthey." Jonah made a sweeping arm gesture, pointing to his companions.

No," Anderson answered. "We are conducting an investigation into the bombing of the Garfield County Courthouse." Anderson was not impressed or frightened by the confrontation force. He had been on the beach at Wake Island in World War II against the entire Japanese Pacific fleet and this scruffy bunch of kids didn't scare him.

"That was a tragedy," Jonah said matter-of-factly, "but we are not interested in that investigation. We are only interested in hearing that you have finally made arrests in Ian's murder case." The crowd hollered and jeered its approval. Shon moved back and forth between the two men, pointing a digital camcorder at them.

"We're not here to answer your damned questions," Anderson shouted. "We're here to get answers to our questions!" He looked around at the crowd, "The terror bombing of the courthouse is a serious offense, punishable by a term of life in prison!"

"Is that supposed to frighten us, Sheriff?" Jonah asked.

He continued, "We are also looking for suspects in the bombing of the maintenance yard. We have an idea who is responsible." He and his men scanned the crowd as if looking for someone in particular.

"I see," Jonah said, stroking his chin. "By the way, Sheriff Anderson, it would be impolite of me if I didn't inform you that we are live on the internet." He motioned to Shon's camera.

"The what?"

"The internet. You know, computers." Jonah ran his fingers over an imaginary keyboard. "We are on a live satellite hookup, right now. Thousands of people are watching worldwide."

Shon moved in for a close up of Sheriff Anderson. His face had a blank, stupid expression as he processed the information. "Get that goddamned thing out of my face!" He demanded, putting up the palm of his hand.

"Smile, Sheriff," Jonah said, laughing. "You're on candid camera!"

"Turn that godamned thing off!"

Shon moved back quickly as Anderson took a step forward as if to grab the camera.

"No way!" Jonah retorted, stepping in front of Anderson. "This is America. Remember? We are documenting this meeting." Before Anderson could say anything, Jonah quickly went on, "Look, Sheriff, we have nothing to hide. We are happy to answer any questions you might have, but first I have two questions of my own that I'd like you to answer."

Anderson didn't respond, so Jonah continued, "Tell us, Sheriff Anderson, when are you going to make arrests in Ian McCarthey's murder?"

"That's police business and none of your concern."

Shon moved in closer again as Anderson tried to contain his anger and stay professional. "When arrests are made you'll be the first to know about it."

"So, that means you are planning arrests?"

"We have suspects."

Jonah turned to the crowd, "The Sheriff has suspects!" A cheer went out. "Good work, Sheriff, some of us have thought you've been stonewalling. We now have hope arrests will happen soon. Right? No one wants trouble but things can't drag on too much longer."

"Is that a threat?" Anderson shot back.

"Just an observation."

Anderson attempted to take control, "We're here investigating the bombing of the Garfield County Courthouse and . . . "

Jonah interrupted, "I have two questions, remember? My second question has two parts, first, do you suspect someone here, and secondly, do you have a warrant to arrest me or anyone else?"

Anderson wanted to tell the smart-mouthed outsider to shut his trap or have it smashed in. "When I have warrants, I will make arrests," he looked around with hatred in his eyes, "And, I'm looking forward to it."

The crowd jeered and pushed forward. Privately, Jonah was relieved the sheriff had no warrants, fearing they were there to arrest McVey and that he'd be forced to give him up. "We won't hold our breath, Sheriff. We know how you work."

"Can you vouch for all the members of your group?" Anderson demanded, turning in a circle and looking at the crowd.

"Can you vouch for all of yours?" Jonah shot back, "Obviously, you have some cowardly rapists and chicken-shit murderers among you."

"Look," Anderson shouted, getting into Jonah's face, "I've had enough of you."

"What I'm wondering is," Jonah hollered, "if you aren't here to make arrests, what is the purpose of coming here with an army? Why risk what could end up as an ugly confrontation - broadcast to the outside world?"

Anderson ignored Jonah and spoke to everyone, "I'd like to run the whole bunch of you out of here, send you back to wherever you belong."

"We belong here," Jonah stood toe to toe with the sheriff. "This is public land, Sheriff."

"And I'd like to get you alone . . . I'd teach you a lesson . . ."

"Until then, old man, eat me!"

The two men stood face to face, nose to nose. Shon moved in for another close up.

"If you have warrants or solid evidence someone from this group was involved in this crime or any other crime, I will turn them over to you myself. If not then - fuck off."

"I could arrest you right now for interfering with a peace officer!"

"Knock yourself out!" Jonah clasped his hands together in front of him as if waiting for the handcuffs.

Anderson had an urge to hit Jonah but held back.

"If you are not going to arrest anyone," Jonah said, "I suggest you leave. We have nothing more to say to you."

Anderson glared and started to move away, "I'll be back. Then we'll see who has the upper hand." He and his men climbed into their vehicles and the crowd reluctantly allowed them to turn around and drive away.

CHAPTER TWENTY-THREE

Denver's Stapleton Airport was packed and Garrett was forced to wait, first at the ticket counter then again at security while they fixed the x-ray machine. He went directly to his gate then positioned himself in the lounge where he could drink and look for Ateen among the onslaught of people coming down the long concourse. Garrett and Ateen agreed that Ben Possett was their best lead and decided to follow him to Amsterdam.

What did Possett mean when he said, 'This is bigger than you think?' Garrett wondered. How did he know I was looking for a specific helicopter? There was no way he could know anything about Nemelka. It didn't make sense. Why would someone at Anaxalrad have information? The companies mining leases were terminated when the President established the monument two years earlier. If they could just get Possett to open up, Garrett felt certain they would find the answers they needed.

After three double-martinis Garrett spotted Ateen coming down the concourse. Normally, because of his size and the fact he was Native American, Ateen received plenty of attention but today, wearing an expensive, beautifully tailored off-black business suit and a ceremonial Navajo blanket draped over his shoulders, he was a real stand out. The blanket was a muted blue-gold weave with bold horizontal and vertical strips of black, brown and gold. He wore no ponytails and his rich shiny black hair fell loose over his shoulders and down over the blanket. Even jaded travelers noticed him.

"Fry Bread!" Garrett called out, slightly drunk and moving toward his friend. "When I told you to bring city clothes, I didn't think you'd arrive as a foreign dignitary!"

Ateen was happy to see his friend and opened his arms out to embrace him and as he did the blanket folded out like wings. "You have a way with words, Doo Doo," Ateen replied, greeting him. "You are right. That's exactly what I am, a foreign dignitary."

Ateen looked exceptionally handsome, as if he were a younger man.

He continued, "I represent the sovereign nation of the Dineh. I am on my way to the United Nations. Like the Arab peoples from the Middle East, we too, are surrounded by a dangerous and dominating enemy."

Garrett laughed wildly, "That's rich! And the blanket?"

"For protection," Ateen shook his head, showing his winning smile and perfect white teeth.

"Are we going to need it?"

"Granny made it. It's for the airplane. She said I'd end up dead without it."

"Can I get in there too?" Garrett asked grinning, happily. "Anything for Granny."

"I will do what I can, but do not expect much, He Who has Doo Doo in his Pants. You are too far gone for redemption or protection for that matter."

Standing in the boarding line, a Japanese family stopped and politely introduced themselves to Ateen, while several Germans crossed the busy concourse to ask if he was an American Sioux. They wanted pictures. At the gate, a young beautiful flight attendant who at first seemed irritated and distant, lit up when Ateen handed her his ticket.

Besides his choice of attire, Garrett considered, something else was changed about Ateen. He was particularly charming and gracious and his countenance and posture seemed almost royal. I wonder what happened on his vision-quest to the mountain? Garrett knew that sojourns onto the mountain were spiritual and not for Anglos to know about. But he sensed something powerful occurred and didn't know what. Ateen possessed the presence of someone of tremendous confidence and peace. He was simultaneously part of the world around him, easily able to access it and be accessed, but at the same time, apart from the world, somehow separate and invisibly removed. It was as if Ateen's six-foot-seven height was now ten feet tall.

Once on board and in their cramped economy class seats, the flight attendant asked to see Ateen's boarding pass and then instructed them to follow her forward to first class. "We have some cancellation seating," she offered, smiling at Ateen, "I hope you will be more comfortable here."

It was the same in New York's Kennedy Airport. People stopped Ateen to shake his hand and introduce themselves. One passerby gave him the peace sign and said, "Free Leonard Peltier." In Reykjavik, Iceland the flight crew including four beautiful Icelandic blondes wanted to pose with him and handed Garrett their cameras. One Icelandic shopkeeper handed Ateen a rare and expensive bottle of Icelandic liquor.

At Heathrow in London, Ateen caused quite a stir when the paparazzi, waiting for a brutal African dictator to arrive with his leggy British showgirl paramour, thought Ateen must be someone of great importance and deserted their encirclement and descended on the two men. A high ranking airport official saved them from the crowd and offered to let Ateen use his apartment in the city; all they had to do was accept. "Are you Cheyenne?" he inquired.

"Well, Fry Bread," Garrett said during the short flight to Schipol in Amsterdam, "You are quite the star. Personally, I can't understand what these people find so interesting."

"Yes, I agree, Doo Doo," Ateen answered, with humility. "I do not exactly understand it myself. I must remember in the future that not all Anglos are like you. Some are truly awake in the purest sense."

As the plane circled Amsterdam, Garrett looked down at the city he loved and thought of Ushi Binder, the beautiful, intense German dancer he fell in love with years earlier. Like many American students of the 1970s, Garrett lived in Holland and traveled Europe as a gypsy. He lived in a commune in the center of city where the energy was self-induced and he could float on a dream cloud of hashish.

Garrett met Ushi Binder at the Milky Wez Club and she introduced him to the Window Pane commune on Baarjezweg Street where she lived. They slept off many wild nights at the Milky Wez and the Paradisal clubs smoking hash and drinking heavy Dutch and German beer at the commune. After partying, they made love until dawn, spent the day sleeping then did it all over again. She introduced him to the city and took him to many private houses where artists and writers argued and collaborated. Ushi could have any man but chose Garrett, not because he was intense or passionate or smart, but because he was an American. She had had many German and Dutch boyfriends and she wanted an American.

In an airborne holding pattern, Garrett wondered if he should try to find Ushi, just to say hello. Perhaps, he fantasized, there would be something else as well. Who knows? So much time had passed but where passion was concerned, there still might be a chance.

Garrett ended up living with Ushi at the famous Window Pane commune - its name coming from the LSD tablet call Window Pane that they smuggled from San Francisco in the late sixties. The commune turned on

Holland and then all of Europe to LSD. It imported millions of the micro-dot acid trips and soon it made its way through the continent. Germans, Dutch, French, English, Indonesians, Austrians, Americans and an endless parade of people made the commune their home, including hundreds who crashed at its sleep-in every night.

The commune's leader was a handsome Dutchman named Corr. He was fair and honest, had a lantern jaw and was perpetually sad; he'd lost his wife to a drunk driver. He and his two children occupied a charming apartment on the top floor facing the street and the canal. The commune was a family of unrelated people brought together by the love they shared for Corr's wife. They were young and hip and smart and supported the house with the sale of LSD and hashish.

Ushi Binder was a founding member and occupied a large room on the fourth floor. She was the on-again, off-again lover of Corr and saw to it that Garrett had the best bedroom where she visited him often. She was tall and willowy, had a perfect dancer's body and studied ballet for years until she turned to modern and jazz. She wore black leather, colorful boas wrapped around her neck and passionate red fingernails and lipstick. She was theatric and every gesture, even the way she held a cigarette. Ushi studied Martha Graham technique from an expatriated New York choreographer who owned a studio in the city. Garrett often visited her there, sitting at the doorway on the floor quietly, watching as she rehearsed.

It was more than twenty years since they had seen each another. The last time didn't go well. Ushi was traveling in the states and on her way to San Francisco had a layover in Salt Lake City. She was drunk yet edgy from cocaine but still as beautiful and intense as ever. After a tour of the city and the surrounding mountains, she scolded him, "How can you live here! It's horrible!"

"We can't choose our homeland," he told her sternly. "My family is here."

"Your family can be here but you need to live somewhere else - or you will die." She went on, sarcastically, "I envisioned you in some exciting, vibrant place, but this! For christ-sake, the city is named after a lake of salt!"

"What about the Amstel River?" he countered.

"I was born in Hamburg!" she squealed, "I'm not Dutch!"

"When you come back," he begged, "I'll take you into the sandstone desert. You'll discover what keeps me here."

That was the last time he heard from her.

After their flight landed, Ateen and Garrett took a tram to the train station where they checked their bags and walked a few blocks to the Damm Square, a picturesque section of the old city where many respectable bed and breakfast hotels were located. They decided on a large sunny room off the Westermarkt Plaza next to the Keizersgracht, the largest canal in the city - just around the corner from the Anne Frank House.

Later, they walked to the Newmarket and the red light district. Garrett remembered the beautiful tall blonde Russian sixteen-year-old prostitute he visited when Ushi was busy with rehearsals. At the time, he felt no guilt because he and Ushi never spoke of commitment or a future or anything other than drinking, hashish and talking about America.

The red light district was filled with young rowdy Englishmen in Amsterdam for a national football match. They scrounged up enough money for sex or just milled around gawking outside the store fronts where the women danced, primped in lingerie and waited for customers. As drunk as they were, the English football fans were respectful to Ateen, knowing he was some important personage. As they strolled the canal street, admiring the women in their window stalls and watching the spectacle of Europe's most free wheeling sex and drug trade, one exotic bird with beautiful breasts hardly concealed in a see-through top, opened her glass door, "I want you," she cooed in broken English and pointed at Ateen. "Free to you. No pay," she said.

Ateen looked to Garrett for direction.

"Well, Mr. Visiting Dignitary, what do you say?"

"No condom," the woman said. "I have been waiting for you for a long long time."

Ateen nodded and motioned no with his hand, "Another time."

The woman smiled, never taking her eyes from him, "Come back later," she whispered, "I'll buy you dinner."

Later, they ate a twenty-one course Indonesian meal at a famous restaurant but when it came to pay the bill, the owner told Ateen it was on the house. He wondered if Ateen minded a photograph with him and his staff, so they could put it on the wall with other images of noteworthy people. The staff of Indonesians came out of the kitchen and gathered around Ateen who stood in the middle as Garrett snapped several shots.

The next morning they awakened to the bells of the Westcourker Church and after a continental breakfast, hit the streets with thousands of working Dutch. They found Anaxalrad's international headquarters in the government section of the city, a place diplomats and law firms and corporations had offices for four hundred years. They sat across from the headquarters at a coffee shop and watched, hoping to spot Ben Possett as he entered or departed.

They rode Tram 17 to Vondel Park and strolled around its tree-lined promenade. It was Ateen's first time in Europe and after the silence and solitude of Navajo Mountain he was glad to be in the expansive park.

"I feel as if none of it is real," he told Garrett.

"I know what you mean. It is so different than what we know."

"It reminds me of San Francisco. I would wake up somewhere - in the park, under an overpass, in an alleyway - not knowing where I was. Sometimes I would be lost for days, searching for something familiar. There is too much happening in cities. One cannot connect to the spirit of the Creator." He was quiet for a few minutes, then looking around said, "In this place, this Vondel Park, I feel at peace."

Garrett told him how in 1940 the Nazi occupiers of Holland sent letters to all the Jews living in Amsterdam demanding that they show up at the park to be registered. "It happened right here," he said, pointing to a nearby amphitheater. "When the Jews arrived, hundreds were jailed and deported; everyone was fingerprinted and given new identity cards. The intellectuals, leaders, writers and college professors, were summarily shot on the spot. When the Dutch citizens of the city heard what the Nazis did, they went into the streets to protest and the Nazis opened fired with machine guns."

"I see. This is sacred ground."

"Many times over."

"I knew it. I feel spirits here."

Garrett left Ateen sitting on a park bench with hundreds of pigeons surrounding him and spent the rest of the day searching for Ushi Binder. He located Corr, the commune's leader, at his government office. After police cracked down on the commune, Corr became Holland's most successful concert promoter and now worked for the Dutch government as its official poetry festival organizer. He traveled the world seeking talent, bringing them to Holland and staging free poetry readings.

Corr was happy to see Garrett and since they hadn't spoken in years they went to a nearby espresso stand, then sat near a canal.

"I read your book," Corr told Garrett. "Many Dutch and Germans know your work. You have an audience here in Amsterdam." Garrett did not know how to respond, the idea of an audience seemed obscure and even ridiculous. "No one gives a shit about me in America."

"Let me organize a reading for you. I can get hundreds of people. You can read from your new work."

"What new work?"

"You are not writing?" Corr asked, incredulously.

"Does it matter?"

"Of course! Your work is of significance." Corr sensed Garrett's defeat and enquired. "What has happened, my friend? You have changed."

"What do you want to know?"

Corr thought for awhile, "If you were writing these days, what would you write about?"

"Emptiness. Death. Grieving."

"Good!" Corr responded, enthusiastically. "These are big subjects. Very important now. There is a lot of heartache in this world. . . you'll have a big audience. Take them on your journey."

Garrett did not respond. Instead, he changed the subject and they talked of the old days, and Garrett asked about Ushi, saying he wanted to look her up.

"That was then and this is now," Corr said slowly in his deep Dutch voice, "I would not suggest it, my friend. Too many years have come and gone. We have all changed. I can't speak for her, but don't think she wants to see you."

"How can you say that?" Garrett asked.

Corr looked pained and diplomatically offered, "It is not for me to say. You two were once so close."

Corr's comments fueled Garrett's interest, "Do you know where I can find her?"

Corr jutted out his lantern jaw and stroked his mustache. "Try the Belarus Coffee House at the Newmarket. Be warned old friend, we seldom find what we seek."

After promising to come by again before leaving, Garrett left his old friend and walked toward the NewMarket many blocks away. He knew the streets and even though many years passed since his last visit he felt as if he never really left. He remembered details about shops and cafes and even the curtains in windows. He remembered how once he and Ushi were deported from France. On arriving in Paris by train, carrying nothing but a pillow case stuffed with clothes and little money, French officials detained them for eight hours before deporting them back to Amsterdam, labeling them as undesirables.

At the Belarus, he asked for Ushi and the bartender, a middle-aged Dutch woman, told him she knew Ushi but hadn't seen her. Garrett nursed a Heineken and waited. He ordered from the hashish menu and bought four grams of black Afghani and decided to try again later As he was leaving, he passed a group of handicapped people in the entryway. They reminded him of the American homeless, dirty and wrapped in many layers of old clothing. The group included a woman in a wheelchair, her legs amputated below the knees and three people using a canes or crutches. One man shuffled along behind them, pulling himself haphazardly forward with a walker.

That night, Garrett and Ateen stayed in the room and ate bread and cheese on a small window patio overlooking the Damm Square and the canal below before sleeping. Garrett drank two liters of wine and sat in the window gazing out at the city he loved so long ago. In the morning, they dressed in suits and took the tram to the offices of Anaxalrad.

"We'd like to speak with Ben Possett, please." Garrett requested to the haughty, high fashion model-like receptionist. She couldn't take her eyes off Ateen, wearing the chieftain's blanket across his shoulders. "You have an appointment?" she asked him.

"Please tell Mr. Possett that a representative of the American Indian Tribal Council, Mr. Brigham Joseph Ateen, requests to speak with him."

"May I tell him for what purpose?"

"A courtesy call."

"Please, if you would, follow me." She led them to a partitioned glass room adjacent the reception area. "I will see if he is in. . . And who should I tell him you are, sir?"

"My name is Garrett Lyons. He knows me."

She tipped from the waist and backed away.

Ateen watched as a garbage barge negotiated past a small fishing vessel in the canal outside the window. Five hundred feet away, a draw bridge opened slowly, allowing the barge to pass. Ateen clasped his hands behind his back, "This is an amazing place," he said more to himself than his friend. Garrett thumbed through magazines nervously and watched the receptionist talking on the telephone.

A few minutes later two men, dressed in blue suits - what Garrett called universal security uniforms - appeared at the receptionist's desk. They spoke with her in a whisper, occasionally glancing up to look at Ateen and Garrett. One of the men used a two-way radio, then approached.

"Mr. Ateen?" one asked in a beautiful Dutch laden English accent.

Ateen heard him but did not move, he remained with his back to the men.

"Mr. Ateen," the man repeated, "Mr. Possett will see you now."

Again, Ateen did not move and Garrett wondered what was happening. After an uncomfortable period, Ateen turned to face them. He folded his arms and looked down impassively.

"If you are ready," one inquired, stepping out of the way.

Ateen turned to Garrett.

"Oh yes." The security man inquired, "You must be Mr. Lyons?"

"At your service."

"Mr. Possett requested that we tell you that he cannot speak with you at the moment. Here is his card and you may call and schedule an interview."

"How kind of you," Garrett waved off the card. "I already have one, thank you. Please give Mr. Possett my best regards and please inform him I will call later today."

"Mr. Ateen?" the man asked, and bowed slightly.

"We came together."

"It's okay. You go," Garrett acquiesced, hesitantly.

Ateen nodded and strode off.

Garrett left and went back to the Belarus, hoping to find Ushi. When he entered, the waitress who just arrived for her shift, recognized him.

"You found Ushi yet?" she asked.

Garrett indicated he hadn't.

"She came in right after you left," the waitress said.

"Good!"

"You must have missed her by just a few seconds. I told her a man was looking for her."

"I need to . . . " he started to say, but the waitress interrupted, excited.

"If you hurry you can catch her. I just passed her not five minutes ago on my way here. She was at the corner of Sliykstraat and Rokin with some people. If you hurry you might catch her."

He thanked her and rushed out. He was excited and frightened at the prospect of finally seeing his old lover. He knew this area well and as he moved forward he scanned both sides of the street, not wanting to miss her.

He could just see the tall beautiful German striding along the cobbled streets. It will be good to see her, he thought. Then, for a moment, he worried she might not remember or recognize him. He was older for sure, his long dark brown hair was now short and gray. He no longer wore a beard, and his goatee was salt and pepper colored. But, all-in-all, he considered, over the many years, I haven't gained a single pound.

Approaching the corner of Sliykstraat and Rokin, he slowed down, trying to spot her. A group of six or seven people stood around smoking cigarettes and talking. The tall and beautiful Ushi was not among them. Desperate, he rushed past the group and went up and down the intersecting streets searching the throng for her. When that failed, he returned to the corner to ask if anyone knew her. As he approached he realized that some of the people at the corner were the same street people he passed when leaving the Belarus the day before.

Just as he was about to interrupt and ask if anyone knew Ushi Binder, the old amputee in the wheelchair caught his attention. She lifted a cigarette to her lips in such a unique way it immediately reminded him of something or someone he knew. Her hand gesture was elegant, even theatrical and her fingernails and lips were painted passionate red. In a blaze of white realization, he knew it was Ushi's hand. He had seen her smoke a thousand cigarettes and could never have forgotten it. He looked at the woman's face, hoping to disprove what his heart and mind already knew. It was her! Ushi Binder! Her face was bloated and dark circles marked her under eyes. With her unaware he was standing there, he just stood flatfooted and stared at the old homeless amputee in total horror and disbelief - trying to take it all in. How could it be? It was impossible! How could the tall, beautiful dancer be transformed into this pathetic street throwaway?

He stood transfixed, staring at her in the wheelchair, trying desperately to make it all work inside his head when Ushi noticed him. She was about to ask the stranger what he wanted when she, too, realized there was something familiar about him. A few seconds elapsed then she realized it was her old lover and traveling companion, Garrett Lyons. But before she could say a word, he turned on his heels and quickly walked away without saying a word.

"Garrett," she called out, as he moved off. "Garrett! It's me - Ushi! Garrett! I read your book! Please! Come back!"

He heard her calls and he recognized her voice but he kept going, never once turning around to look.

Instead of going to the room, he lost himself in the streets of the ancient city. What had happened to her, he wondered? I can't believe it was really her. He now understood Corr's reluctance. Garrett was humiliated and hated himself for denying Ushi. What is wrong with me? Everyone I have love is dead and now that I find Ushi, I turn my back on her.

Back at the hotel, he bathed and stood naked in front of the full length mirror. He turned sideways and held his stomach in. I am the same man I have always been, aren't I? From his many internal dialogues, a voice spoke to him: You are crippled and handicapped, too. You are no longer the man you once were.

Chapter Twenty-Four

After the courthouse bombing in Panguitch, Thomas Westley visited Boulder, La Verkin, Escalante and Hurricane. He paraded his banner covered bulldozer up and down Main Street, stopping to talk to the frightened and angry people. Westley was considered a hero for his stand on traditional rural values. He was admired as a true leader; a man who lost his beloved ranch and went to prison for standing up for principles of freedom.

At the Kanab City Park, a wheelchair bound rancher told him how the BLM impounded his herd when he failed to get the cows off the range on time. "It didn't matter, I was recovering from a stroke and Millie, my wife of fifty years, just died of cancer. They broke my back," the proud rancher said, holding back his tears. "It defeats a man, ya' know?" A mechanic told him of closing down his truck repair shop after most of his customers lost their jobs at the logging mill. "I spent twenty years building that business. . . what am I supposed to do now?" Mothers worried about their children, "They're all leaving," one complained. "Look around, there is nobody between the age of twenty to thirty. They are all up in Salt Lake or down in Vegas. There's no work here."

Kanab was a hotbed of hatred for the ex-President and his proclamation establishing the Grand Staircase National Monument. According to them it cost hundreds of high paying jobs at the proposed Anaxalrad coal mine atop Kaiparowits. "The mine would have given us jobs and benefits for a generation," one told Westley. Another admitted, "All I can find now is maybe minimum wage at the Quickie convenience store." "All we want," a grandmother said, "is to be left alone to raise our children in peace and teach them the value of work and family." Not only did the last President lock up all the coal on Kaiparowits, but he added two million acres surrounding it, a move that doomed the economies of Kane and Garfield counties. Around a campfire in the city park they signed a petition to decommission the monument then hung an effigy of the President and torched it.

In Boulder, Utah Westley heard the heartbreaking stories of a town torn apart because people couldn't afford to live in their own hometown anymore. "The yuppies came in," a farmer explained, "bought everybody out and built those damned trophy homes and left. No one even lives in them! They fenced off the land, posted no trespassing signs and now the property values are so high our kids can't afford to live here, and most of us can't afford to pay the property taxes!"

Over in La Verkin, Westley met with the town council and the Citizens for the USA, a group opposed to the United Nations. They believed the New World Order was a conspiracy by enemies of America. The town council voted to give him their full support for any action against the federal government and gifted him a fully automatic assault rifle to show they meant business. "Every home owner in La Verkin," the mayor told him, "is required to have a gun. We're ready to stand and fight with you - just give us the word!" And in Escalante, he was embraced by ranchers who called themselves "the outlaws" and lived out on the remote Circle Cliffs. "We need to teach the damned environmentalists a lesson," one told him. "They're down there on the Hole in the Rock right now laughing at us." "We oughta string 'em up!" another said. "Tell us what you need - we can round up at least thirty good men."

The last ten years in the West proved devastating. Newcomers from the city brought money and squeezed out locals; generations-old grazing leases were systematically eliminated, cows were impounded by the federal government, and the loss of jobs in logging and mining had a ripple effect on Main Street forcing the closure of thousands of small tax paying businesses. The next generation was quickly disappearing, forced to leave to find work in the cities, and those who stayed lived in poverty. The assault on the traditional Western heritage threatened to end their beloved way of life.

"It's the same story throughout the West," Westley told them. "Since Utah has more national and state parks than any state in the union and the federal government controls seventy percent of the land, it's a perfect place to make a stand. We can use it as the tinder box for an uprising. We'll burn it down, before giving it over to them!"

Everyone blamed EarthIsland for the current violence. "It was tough enough before," one told Westley, "now we're afraid to leave the house." Most locals were disgusted and infuriated that a bunch of ragtag, tattooed, espresso-drinking, drug-using, just-do-it outsiders had taken over Zion

National Park, and then moved to the hated Grand Staircase National Monument. "They are sticking it in our faces," Westley told them.

Thomas Westley spoke with eloquence wherever people would listen, in parks and on street corners, at courthouse steps and even once at a Mormon ward house. "The time is coming when people are going to have to stand up for what they believe in. We can't wait for the law or anyone else to help us, we have to help ourselves. Our forefathers didn't have anyone they could call to come bail them out and neither do we. Like them, the hard work had to be done." He talked about organizing, pooling resources, speaking with one voice. "If we don't organize," he warned, "you can go ahead and kiss your lives here goodbye." At every stop the crowds grew larger. And it wasn't just natives of Utah, hundreds of supporters from around the West made the pilgrimage to southern Utah to stand alongside their Western brother.

It was no surprise then when on the sunny morning of September 21, Thomas Westley and two hundred followers including off duty Sheriff Anderson and Cody Bullock paraded from Panguitch out to the Grand Staircase outside Escalante. Westley led the way, pulling his bull dozer to Carcass Canyon on the Kaiparowits Plateau. When they arrived Westley posed for pictures as he unloaded his D-9 bulldozer. One man documented the event with a video camera. They would distribute the edited tapes to the media later calling it, "Road to Freedom."

Westley led them in prayer, "Let this Road to Freedom signal a new day in the American West, amen." Afterwards, festooned with American flags, he lowered the bulldozer's blade and pushed forward across the land, toppling ancient cedars, ripping through colonies of sagebrush and over white tabletop sandstone, gouging out the soft rock. Westley decided on Carcass Canyon because a year earlier, the monument manager, a woman from the East Coast, impounded 80 cows from a grazing allotment there after the lease holder, a bedridden eighty-five-year-old, didn't round them up on time.

Garfield County fought many battles with the federal government, BLM and park service over some of the hundreds of dirt roads within its borders. The county maintained that the existing roads, most cut for uranium mining exploration in the early 1950s and used only once, belonged to the county. They also maintained the right to make new roads and because of this, according to Thomas Westley and his followers, including Sheriff Anderson, the new road in the monument was perfectly legal. They pointed to the Wilderness Act of 1963 which stipulated that any section of land being considered for a park or monument would be disqualified if it possessed roadways. Because there were scores of old roads when the monument was established, many believed including state's right activists, it was illegal. The federal government saw it differently, maintaining it had jurisdiction over federal land and since it controlled most the land within the counties, it alone, and not the county, had jurisdiction.

The issue boiled over in the 1980s when Mack Bullock, then Garfield County Commissioner, ordered his road crews to pave the famous Burr Trail, the remote back country road between Boulder and Lake Powell. His grandfather financed the cow trail years earlier in 1912 when John Burr needed money. Without informing the federal government or the National Park Service, Mack Bullock and his crews moved quickly to grade and widen the forty-mile long dirt road, and laid a sub-roadbed. It was all accomplished over one long holiday weekend. Environmentalists and federal land managers were outraged and sought relief in the federal court. The result was a protracted legal battle, but Bullock defied courts and the Burr was paved. Since his untimely death, riding his favorite horse, no one emerged to carry on the fight.

Behind Westley's bulldozer came a parade of vehicles honking their horns and shooting off guns. In a flat bed truck, the Kanab High School Chorus, sang "God Bless America." At some free standing rocks a half mile from where they began, Westley cut a circular shaped turnaround and the group stopped for a picnic. Women brought out coolers filled with homemade fried chicken and potato salad, men cut firewood with chain saws and children chiseled their initials into nearby sandstone formations.

Thomas Westley spoke to a camera. "We have struck a blow for all the honest, hardworking and ruined Americans in the West. We will not allow outsiders to dictate to us any longer." About EarthIsland, he shook his head and warned, "Every American has the right to believe what they want but EarthIsland needs to go home where they belong - and stay there. We won't come into their city neighborhoods and tell them what to do and we will not have them coming here and destroying our proud culture and communities." He added, "Members of EarthIsland and other groups think they are patriots but they are traitors. Soon, everyone will see who they really are - arsonists, bombers, drug addicts, liars and terrorists! Mark my words, one way or another, they are leaving. They can go peaceably or they can go another way. I have my preference - but it is their decision."

When Grand Staircase Monument manager, Leslie Majors, got word she and her top monument officials, escorted by four park rangers, arrived but it was too late, they could do nothing but watch.

Dressed smartly in a dark designer suit with a short skirt, Garfield County commissioner, Lonnie Bullock climbed the two hundred white granite steps to the Utah State Capitol Building. She was furious. She planned to come to Salt Lake City to meet with Julie Bryant, one of fifty attorneys working at the Attorney General's office, about the AG taking over the stalled murder and rape investigation, but the day before the appointment she received a message from Bryant's secretary saying the meeting was off. She left Panguitch at half-past three in the morning anyway, driving the two hundred miles into Salt Lake City, determined to find out what was going on.

When Bryant called weeks earlier, complaining about Sheriff Anderson's refusal to share information and her fear he was holding up the investigation, Bullock liked Bryant immediately and they exchanged several friendly calls about the matter. If Anderson wouldn't move the investigation forward, Bryant was anxious to get her investigators working on the case. She made her name prosecuting rapists and sex offenders and wanted to sink her teeth into this rape and the murder case. She pegged Sheriff Anderson as a chauvinist and wanted him out.

According to Bryant, the AG's office was convinced Anderson was incompetent or worse; and she invited Bullock to the state capitol to discuss removing him and taking over the case. At first, Bullock was reluctant and defended her deceased husband's right hand man. But Bryant was aggressive, pushing her case against Anderson vigorously and ultimately convinced Bullock to discuss it. Then strangely, almost overnight, Bryant stopped taking Bullock's calls. At first, Bullock thought nothing of it, thinking she was just busy, but when Bryant failed to return her calls she knew something was wrong. Despite the cancellation, Bullock decided to drive to Salt Lake City and get to the bottom of it.

In the richly appointed anteroom of the Attorney General's office, Bullock informed the receptionist she was there for her eleven o'clock meeting.

The receptionist called Bryant's office. "There must be some mistake, Commissioner Bullock," the receptionist told her, "Ms. Bryant informed me your appointment was canceled. I'm so sorry if you didn't receive the message."

"Please tell her I need to see her!" Bullock demanded, defiantly, "I just drove 200 miles. I need five minutes."

The receptionist demurred, bowed graciously and called again. "Please have a seat, commissioner," She told Bullock afterwards, "She'll be with you in a few minutes."

Twenty minutes later, Assistant Attorney General Julie Bryant appeared from a hallway, her hand outstretched when she came into view.

"So good to finally meet you," she said. "I've been looking forward to it."

"It's my pleasure as well."

"I'm so sorry for the mix-up. I'm afraid you didn't get my message. It is unfortunate I had to cancel at such a late date, but another pressing matter needed to be addressed." Privately, Bryant was surprised and glad that Bullock was there.

"What could be more important than a high profile murder and rape in Garfield County?"

Bryant liked Bullock's candor and smiled nervously, "Yes. I'm sorry. I agree wholeheartedly. You're right, of course. A murder case is the highest priority. Please forgive me. Let's discuss this where we can talk, in my office or a conference room."

Bryant led Bullock through a labyrinth of finely appointed hallways with works of art on the walls and western bronze sculptures at intersecting hallways. At the entrance to an ostentatious conference room with a huge table and oversized leather chairs that created the appearance of money and power, they passed a tall, handsome, distinguished, gray haired man in his mid-fifties. Bryant stiffened, then introduced the two.

"Garfield County Commissioner, Lonnie Bullock, I would like to introduce you to the Utah Attorney General, Robert Orkman, my boss." Turning to him, "Robert, I would like to introduce you to Lonnie Bullock."

He narrowed his eyes at Bryant and turned to Bullock, smiling and taking her hand. "Welcome, Commissioner. It is my pleasure to meet you."

"Thank you, the pleasure is mine." Lonnie said, embarrassed but pleased by the formality; she lowered her eyes, showing her long dark eye lashes.

"May I ask, are you here on official business or is this a courtesy call?" Orkman asked, flashing Bryant a look of puzzlement.

"Business."

Without responding, Orkman lowered one eyebrow and raised the other. He nervously checked his wristwatch, "Very nice to meet you. My apology, but I'm late." Orkman started off, then stopped abruptly, "I hope you don't take offense to this Commissioner Bullock, but you are much more beautiful in person than you are on television."

"How kind of you," she said, blushing.

"Come with me," Bryant said, flashing a look of utter hatred to her boss and leading Bullock away by the elbow. "We'll use the small conference room." Orkman smiled impishly and delayed leaving, watching the two women's behinds as they walked away.

In the conference room, Bryant closed the door and offered Bullock a seat. She dropped heavily into a chair across from her.

"I wish that hadn't happened," she said.

"I wasn't offended."

"No, not that. He is a famous womanizing pig, but off-the-record I was hoping we wouldn't run into him."

"Why?"

"Let me just say, as we all know, things are never what they appear to be. They always look different from the outside."

"I'm not following."

"Look," Bryant leaned forward across the table, her eyes darting back and forth. "I am in a difficult position, Lonnie. A very difficult position. " She paused, sat back and brought her hands together in her lap, intertwining her fingers. "Okay. Here it is, something has happened and I am not at liberty, in my capacity as an assistant AG, to divulge to you what it is."

Bullock looked into Bryant's eyes. "Why haven't you returned my calls? I've needed to speak with you . . . As I have said, I am under tremendous pressure . . . don't you understand? This issue needs to be dealt with!"

"Please, let me finish," Bryant interrupted, "I'm sorry but what I'm saying is simple: I am no longer able to work with you on your case, nor can I answer any questions."

"What are you talking about? What is going on?"

"All I can say is that the Attorney General's office has many very important cases currently in process and I have been instructed to let you and Garfield County conduct your own investigation. We are unable to assist you."

"What about Sheriff Anderson? You pushed this. . . You told me you had resources . . . you were excited, remember?"

"I spoke out of turn," she said earnestly. "I am very sorry but there is nothing I can do. I wish I had talked to you before you drove all the way up here."

"You can't help us?" Bullock was a click or two behind.

"I'm sorry. My hands are tied."

"You have to help . . . "

"No, Commissioner, I do not. Nor does the Attorney General's office." Bryant was now agitated, "Garfield County has a fine attorney . . . what is his name, Zitting? I suggest you take this matter up with him."

As the women talked, Robert Orkman, pretending to read a legal brief passed the windowed conference room slowly.

Brian was nervous, "This has nothing to do with you, personally. If it were up to me, I would help but . . ." She paused, shifted in her seat and added, "I need to go . . . What I just told you is off-the-record, you must honor that. I'm sorry we can't be of further assistance. I'm running late."

"You haven't told me anything."

"I'm trying to offer an explanation - of sorts - when I have been instructed not to. "

Bullock sat stunned and then blurted out, "Why not?"

"Look, I can't speak freely! Don't you understand?"

Bullock looked down as if thinking and did not say a word.

"Okay," Bryant said, anxiously scanning the hallway, "Look, you have to promise me you will not divulge what I am gong to tell you. I must have your total confidence before I speak."

"I promise."

"I don't know what's going down but word came from the top that this case is strictly hands off. "

"But why?"

"Politics. I don't know. I'm only an assistant but word has it, it's big. Somebody doesn't want us nosing around."

"Orkman?"

"He's just following orders. Someone higher up on the food chain."

"I don't understand."

"Neither do I. Orkman is running scared. I've never seen him like this."

"What now?"

"I am not your council, but I'd try the feds. The crime happened on federal land, right? They have a jurisdictional claim." Just as Bryant finished, Orkman came back down the hallway.

"As I was telling you, Commissioner Bullock," Bryant said loudly, getting up and opening the door, "I hope you understand, if we can free up our overloaded case load, I'll give you a call, but until then, unfortunately you are on your own."

Bullock nodded and quickly left.

Later in her hotel room, Bullock turned on CNN new only to see Sheriff Anderson, dressed in his chief of police uniform, and her son, Cody, riding atop Thomas Westley's bulldozer cutting an illegal road in the Grand Staircase. She sat stunned, then furious. She dialed home but no one answered. She watched the story again an hour later and listened as Westley declared war on environmentalists and said people in Utah were ready to fight.

Sheriff Anderson betrayed her - they all had! She had no advance knowledge of the blading! Why wasn't I informed, she wondered? No one told me anything; but it's obvious everyone knew. She dialed room service and ordered a stiff cocktail. She drank it down quickly and called for another. She dialed Anderson's house and when no one answered she phoned the police station. Deputy Trueaxe told her Anderson was off duty and didn't know how to reach him. "You wouldn't tell me if the chief were standing right there," she scolded and hung up.

Driving home the next day she was lost. She cried about Cody, wondering what was happening, and she was furious with Anderson and fantasized firing him. In her heart she knew she couldn't fire the sheriff, Mack would not have wanted it. Andy was devoted to Mack and until recently, she considered, he was trying to help me. What would Mack do, she wondered? She knew what Mack would do, he would fire Anderson for insubordination, no questions asked. Mack would have agreed with the new road, but the sheriff's betrayal would not have been tolerated.

In Panguitch, she went to her temporary office. No one in the office dared look at her, fearful she considered their silence about the blading a betrayal. After all, she was their boss. When Sheriff Anderson pulled in the parking she was waiting for him at the door.

"In my office," she directed sternly, "we need to talk." She marched him in and closed the door behind them. Anderson stood military style, legs spread apart, hands clasped behind his back. Bullock left him standing there while she went out into the office and told everyone to take the afternoon off. She stood in the foyer as one by one the six employees filed past her.

Back at her desk, she looked at Anderson from top to bottom. "I want you out of that uniform. You are a disgrace to it."

Anderson stared passed her and did not say a word.

"Nothing to say after your little television escapade?"

"With all due respect Commissioner Bullock, I suggest you resign or get with the program. This office needs someone who . . . "

She interrupted, yelling, "What this office needs are people who understand they represent the county. It needs people who leave their personal opinions at home and never confuse them or let them reflect negatively on the county. Your little stunt has not only embarrassed the county but made it appear we condone breaking the law."

"Are you asking for my badge?"

"I don't want to see you in front of any television cameras again. Period. I want you to keep your moronic mouth shut. I want you to represent Garfield County with integrity and without compromise. I want arrests made in the Ian McCarthey murder investigation. You have been dragging your feet, Sheriff!"

"It's not true. If you knew anything about law enforcement, you'd understand." He looked past her out the window. "Too bad Mack isn't here right now, he knew how to lead people . . . "

"It is too bad," she countered. "He'd have you outta here in a second. He wouldn't stand for your insubordination. But he isn't here, Mack is gone. I am your boss and I want you to give me a report on the status of our murder investigation right now!"

"When I'm finished . . ." he began.

"No! Now!" she demanded, pounding her fist on the cheap desk. "I want to see the file on the Ian McCarthey murder and the rapes of those girls on my desk right now. I want a progress report!"

"I can't do that."

"This is not a request. It is a direct order."

"You run the commissioner's office," Anderson shot back angrily, pointing a finger at her, "and I run the Sheriff's office!"

"For now perhaps, but that may change very soon," Bullock shouted. "Do you know where I've been while you and your patriotic friends pulled your little publicity stunt?" She did not wait for his answer, "I was in Salt Lake City at the request of the AG's office. Do you want to know what I was doing there?" Again, she did not wait for an answer, "They want you removed from the investigation."

Anderson stiffened and looked ashen.

"Right now, Sheriff Anderson, you are very close to being the subject of an investigation yourself - for impeding a murder investigation." She wheeled back in her chair.

Anderson's chest pounded and the veins in his neck hardened. "They can't . . . it's not true!"

"Believe it! Right now Attorney General Orkman wants to have you and your men investigated. You are stonewalling and everyone knows it!"

"You don't understans . . ." he pleaded.

"I can't protect you much longer. I felt like a fool defending you to them," she said, lowering her voice, "then later I see you on the television. You betrayed me, Sheriff!" She felt uneasy with her gambit, "Look, it might not be too late . . . but if you want my help I need to know what is going on."

"All right," he said, in a cocky voice. "Okay. I see. You're right." He stepped forward and put his hands on the edge of commissioner's desk. "Okay, you wanted it, here it is. I admit it. I've been taking my time. Is that what you wanted to hear?"

"Why?" She looked into his steel gray eyes.

"I have strong suspects," he said, wiping his face from top to bottom with the palm of his hand. "You just won't let good-enough alone, will you?" he shook his head back and forth. "No, I don't think so . . . Okay then, I do have something to show you." He motioned with his hand toward his office and then walked out, returning a minute later with a thick file folder.

"Take a look at this." He opened the file and handed her a bunch of pages. "Page seven, the victim's statement with a description of one of the people involved in the attack."

Lonnie read the description in horror. When finished, she swiveled her chair around with her back to the Sheriff and gazed out the window.

"Perfect match." Anderson confirmed, his head down.

"I want you to leave!" she screamed. "Right now!"

Anderson dropped the entire investigation file on her desk and marched out. As soon as he was gone Lonnie grabbed her coat and purse and raced home.

CHAPTER TWENTY-FIVE

W hen Ateen returned to the hotel from meeting with Possett, Garrett was sitting in the dark, an empty bottle of Amstel next to him. Ateen turned on a lamp and handed his friend a manila envelope.

"What is it?" Garrett demanded, opening it.

"What does it say?" Ateen asked.

The envelope contained a twenty-five page technical document containing tables and graphs and maps and text. It appeared to be some kind a geological analysis conducted by Anaxalrad.

"What is it?" Garrett exclaimed, looking at it with disgust.

"You read German, right?" Ateen asked, sincerely.

"Yeah, about as well as I speak Navajo!"

"It is important."

"Of course it's important, they always say that. We need an interpreter. Did he tell you what it was?" Garrett stood, walked across the room and dropped the report on the table as if it were a copy of the Republican platform.

"He said it would answer our questions."

"A holy grail of insight? I can't wait. I might never sleep again."

"Isn't this the reason we came?"

"What else did he say?"

"Possett talked about vision quests and spirituality. He knows about the Healing Way ceremonies."

"That's helpful," Garrett said, cynically.

"He hiked the narrows in Paria and the table top of the Aquarius. His heart is in the right place, I sense it."

"Come on, Ateen! An oil man with a good heart? His heart has a tattoo of a dollar bill on it."

Ateen laughed and lowered his voice, "Contradictions are part of us. Take you for an example, Doo Doo."

Garrett stood at the window with his back to the room. He was thinking about Ushi and his disgust with himself.

"Possett loves Holland," Ateen went on, "it is his homeland, but something important happened one morning as he hiked alone in Paria."

"Yeah, he had an epiphany, right?"

"It was a spiritual experience." Ateen was amused, "You Anglo always have religious or spiritual experiences in the desert."

"Be glad it happens."

"He asked me what it meant."

"What?"

"His experience."

"What did you tell him, that he was full of shit?"

"I told him these experiences can't be interpreted by someone else."

Outside the room, the busy Dutch street was filled with trams and cars and bicycles and Dutchmen rushing home from work.

"I told him these experiences are part of everyday life."

"Why doesn't it happen in the city then?" Garrett asked, earnestly.

"It never happened when I lived in San Francisco," Ateen admitted. "I thought it was the booze and the spirits of the men I killed."

"It doesn't happen in cities?"

"I do not know. It probably does but we can't pick it out."

"When I have spiritual feelings I try to figure them out and . . ."

"That's is the problem with you, Doo Doo, "Ateen interrupted. "You dissect everything. It's not for your brain, it's for your heart and spirit. You destroy it with your analytical bullshit."

Garrett turned back to the window. "Did Possett tell you anything of value?"

"He asked about you."

"Yeah."

"I told him you were harmless."

"Well . . . not entirely," Garrett answered, sighing deeply.

"You found your friend?"

"What is left of her."

Ateen's posture begged for an explanation but it was not his place to ask.

"Did he say anything about helicopters?" Garrett asked.

"You are slipping my friend." Ateen picked up the envelope and threw it to him. "Top right hand side, it says Las Vegas Air Tours."

Back in the states at Denver's Stapleton airport, Ateen and Garrett separated. Garrett went north to Boulder, taking the geological paper to a German interpreter, Lessel Opel, at the University of Colorado. Ateen went south first to Navajo Mountain for a short visit with his mother and grandmother then onto the Bonanza Cafe in Page to give the elders a report.

In the busy college town of Boulder, Garrett sat on a bench on Pearl Street, drank coffee and read The New York Times. He learned of the bombing of the Garfield County Utah courthouse. The headline read, "New Millennium Violence - Old West Land War Imminent. Extremist groups may clash, tension rises as powerful bomb destroys an old West icon." The story profiled EarthIsland's Jonah Sandborn whose bold move of taking over Zion National Park brought national attention, and the traditional land-users champion, one-time Sagebrush Rebellion leader, Thomas Westley, and his bulldozer. With two leaders sharing a confrontational style and ardent followers brandishing guns, the story concluded the battle for the land was out of the court system and back on the land where the two groups of American patriots seemed destined to fight it out.

Garrett found Lessel Opel on campus in her Communications Department office. Because she was not tenured, Lessel occupied a storage room made into an office at the end of a hallway near the men's lavatory. He stood at her door but she didn't look up. She was aware someone was there but was intentionally ignoring them. Her office was stacked with books and papers and computers and the walls were sticky with nicotine from the Samson shag tobacco she rolled into cigarettes and smoked incessantly. Finally, she swiveled around quickly, throwing herself back in the chair and sweeping the thick mop-top of auburn hair away from her face with her fingers.

Lessel Opel was once a student of Garrett's after becoming infatuated with a collection of his desert essays. She was a German national who before reunification in 1990 lived in Berlin and worked for the East German government propaganda apparatus. After seeing a John Wayne western filmed in Monument Valley as a child, Lessel fell in love with the American West and dreamed of visiting Monument Valley. She immigrated to Colorado in 1991 to teach public relations at the University of Colorado and became an ardent sandstone devotee.

The last time he'd seen her, Lessel was considering returning to Germany, disappointed with the lack of intellectual curiosity in America and disenchanted with her idea of the America dream. Lessel was disappointed with Garrett as well. American men, she concluded, even good writers, are weak and defeated; they want sex continually and weren't very good at it.

Lessel didn't like being caught unaware and every time it happened she was furious. At first, she didn't recognize Garrett, assuming he was just another in the long line of students wanting a favor or wanting to flirt. Either way it was the same, they wanted to steal time. It was finals week and Lessel's famous short fuse was easily ignited.

She's even more beautiful than I remember, Garrett thought to himself, checking her out. He felt alive and the knawing anxiety that never left him suddenly evaporated. I feel good, he thought, it must be Lessel. How can beautiful women do this to me?

"What a surprise," she said, but did not look happy. She reached for a half-burned cigarette in the ashtray and tapped it against the glass. "What do you want?"

"As articulate and diplomatic as ever, I see," Garrett observed. "Good to see you too, Lessel." He smiled nervously, wondering if he hadn't forgotten something.

"Yes," she said dryly, "you too, Garrett."

"I'm glad to find you," he paused, "last time you were sick of America."

"Sick of Americans," she corrected and took a theatrical drag from her cigarette and tilting her head back, opened her throat and exhaled smoke straight up, like an industrial chimney.

"They let you smoke those skanky things in here?"

"Let them try and stop me."

He shot a glance into her eyes but she was ready for him and tried to hold his gaze. Even her undeserved scorn was beautiful and at thirty-five her icy Aryan exterior and innate sexuality was breathtaking. She's a horny bitch, he thought, a truly modern self-reliant European intellectual. Unlike American women, she wasn't trying to own anyone. They enjoyed each others' company for a while, and when it ended they parted and he hadn't thought of her again.

"Obviously," he said, taking two mock-steps back, bowing as he went, "I see this is not the right time. . . I should have called first, of course."

"It's finals week," she added, sharply.

"Right. How foolish of me."

She knew he was not going to leave, that this was part of his performance. Her German confidence was supreme. She checked him out, he was still handsome and looked good in a suit. He smiled sheepishly and did not speak.

"You are interesting," she finally said, breaking the silence. Her voice was deep and masculine. "You disappear for what is it, two years now, then without a word - Voila! - here you are. How do you expect me to act?"

"That's me," he started, deferentially, "perennially at the wrong time and the wrong place. I can see you are busy so . . ."

"Of course I'm busy," she snapped. "I have papers to grade. I told you. I really don't have time for this. I didn't expect anyone, especially not you."

Taking another mock step back, "I wanted to talk to you. I have a favor to ask."

"What?" she demanded, angrily.

Her anger was a good sign, he thought. Garrett appreciated Dutch and German directness. It was brutal and without pretense. He told her about the document but his quixotic explanation was a lie and she knew it. Could she translate it, he asked. He tried to hand the document to her but she wouldn't accept it, never once taking her eyes from him. As he spoke, her stern unfriendliness began to soften around her almond-shaped green eyes then around her lovely mouth.

"So," she said, "you need my help?"

"It's important."

"Don't make me laugh, that's what they all say." Pointing to the report, she asked, "Is this what you are working on?"

"It's related."

Lessel had heard enough, she told him to leave it with her, she would take a look and be finished at 10 p.m. "Meet me at Ricco's, remember, near my apartment?"

Garrett was surprised and thanked her profusely.

"Get out! Don't make me sick with your phony gratitude." She turned away. "I'll make you pay."

Arriving early at Ricco's, he figured out why Lessel was angry. The last time he saw her, he invited her to join him on Cedar Mesa to explore some Anasazi burial mounds, but when he needed to cancel out he called late and offered a lame excuse. That was two years ago and he had completely forgotten the incident. It was not like Lessel to not confront him about it immediately.

She arrived late, after eleven and without apology announced she had-n't read the report. It was at her office. He decided not to bring up the Cedar Mesa mess unless she did but when she didn't and then after dinner and drinks she took him home for sex, he concluded everything was all right.

In the morning, she was angry and disgusted, "I make myself sick," she told him, arms crossed in her bathrobe, sobbing. "I have been in this country too long. I act like American women - letting men shit on me and taking it."

Garrett apologized, dressed and left. Lessel promised to read the report soon and give him a call. She could have a translation by the week-end, no sooner. Garrett was anxious but after his sweet reunion with this German beauty he didn't say a word.

When Ateen arrived at the Bonanza, Nez, Natani, Tahonnie, Crank and the rest were waiting for him. He was surprised to find "an outsider" sitting with the elders. He was not a Dineh but a Hopi. His name was Alan Sakiqua and he needed no introduction. Sakiqua was a Hopi holy man who interpreted prophesy. He was a small thin man in his mid-seventies with a big smile and an easygoing way. They climbed into Nez's Cadillac and drove twenty miles east out of Page and turned onto the reservation. Out across endless dirt roads that embroidered the land like some intricately woven fabric they went, stopping at the hogans of other important elders. At each stop, they piled out of the car and talked for a while then piled back in and left. They went from place to place all day long until sunset found them at the foot of No Man's Mesa.

Now on foot, Natani led the group single file through sage and cedars to a broken pile of standing boulders some distance away. The wind blew up and made the rushing sound of eternity in the cedar tops. A dark bank of clouds moved to control the new night as they sat in a circle, Indian style.

Natani opened his shirt and drew out a medicine bag. Sitting next to him, Nez covered his face with his hands quickly when he saw the bag. The group began chanting softly and the rain started to fall gently. Great drops of rain spattered on the sand and sagebrush. Within a few minutes they were soaked. The chant grew louder but never rising above the singsong rhythmic way a Dineh medicine man calls on his Gods. Natani swayed slowly back and forth, lifting his shoulders and dropped them again and again. Dipping into the sacred buckskin medicine bag, Natani drew out a pinch of dust and sprinkled it over Nez.

Nez uncovered his face, which was wild and fleshy, and bent forward letting his fingers run through the deep bronze colored sand. Twice he threw "earth" over his chest and then getting on all fours he built a mound of sand. It was the mountain, Navajo Mountain. With a finger, he drew two crooked lines intersecting above it, they were the Colorado and San Juan Rivers. He then pushed a hill of sand into a long, low flat-top mound next to the mountain, it was Kaiparowits Plateau. He took extra time to add detail to the plateau, making the three separate appendages or fingers that make up the Kaiparowits.

When Nez finished, he sat up and rocked back and forth. The elders chanted and called to the Gods. A few minutes later, Natani took another pinch of dust and sprinkled it over the sand creation. Natani chanted quietly, moving his thin shoulders slightly with the rhythm of his song, his voice fine and resonant, beautiful in every tone. The rain grew colder and fell harder.

The chanting ended abruptly. Natani sat with head fallen, breathing deeply, as if very tired. The rain stopped and the cloud bank broke above, showing a brilliant starry sky. Natani looked up and pointed to the sand sculpture - to the south end of the Kaiparowits, to the Straight Cliff's finger and sang out, "Do you see it? It is here." The elders all leaned forward, searching the sand plateau closely. No one spoke but one by one they all sat back and started the chanting again. The song went from slow and melodious to discordant and nasal.

Natani was not finished, "I do not see clearly. There is something blocking my view. I see a white man. There is a shadow, it is unlike any shadow I have ever seen. I see more white men, two or three of them. They are floating around and up to no good."

Nez slowly turned to Ateen, "We want you to go look see. It is not good Anglos are there."

Ateen nodded.

"The white man is too close," Natani added.

A sensation of fear gripped Ateen. He knew this sensation well, he felt it before a fire fight or dangerous mission in Viet Nam.

"Ateen," Crank spoke up, "forget your fear. The Gods are with you." He paused, "You, Ateen, are our greatest warrior."

201

Alan Sekiqua, who remained quiet, told him, "I have seen it all in prophesy, my son. You are a chosen one."

Natani patted Ateen's forearm, "See? We need you to go have a look see for us. To be our eyes and ears."

"What do I look for?"

"You will know," Sekiqua answered softly.

Crank added, speaking to everyone, "We thought we were safe after the monument was established but the threat remains."

"What threat?" Ateen asked.

Natani scanned the stars, "We are sending you to check out The Place of Emergence for the Fifth World."

"It exists?" Ateen couldn't contain his excitement.

Nez and Natani nodded simultaneously and turned to the Hopi holy man, Alan Sekiqua.

"The Place of Emergence must remain secret," Sekiqua declared and lowered his eyes.

"On Kaiparowits?"

No one moved or said a word. Ateen sat stunned, his heart raced. In a tribe famous for not being able to keep a secret, the acknowledgment of the existence of the next Place of Emergence was extraordinary.

"We and our brothers the Hopi have made secret pilgrimages there for a thousand years. It started when The People emerged out into this, The Fourth World," Natani told him. "When the Creator destroys the Fourth World, the world of today, we will be saved and emerge again onto this land at The Place of the Fifth Emergence."

Ateen was speechless, he just received the greatest gift and greatest responsibility of his life. He knew of the prophesy but never imagined it was true. The Place of the Fifth Emergence!

Natani looked into Ateen's eyes. "Never speak of this."

He nodded and his chest and heart filled with honor.

Chapter Twenty-Six

When Cameron Longmire's body was found near the Burr Trail lying face-up, spread-eagle in a large colony of cryptogrammic soil, his friends and colleagues at the University of Colorado were shocked and couldn't believe it. Who in the world would want to harm him? Longmire reputedly didn't have an enemy in the world. He was the most loved professor of geology in Boulder, Colorado. People concluded it must have been a despicable random killing. Utah locals claimed since he was a geologist it was radical environmentalists; EarthIsland countercharged that Longmire was a longtime environmental advocate so he probably died at the hands of rednecks.

The circumstances surrounding Longmire's death were mysterious. He was last seen a week before his body was found by two of his students who caravanned with him from Colorado to Kaiparowits Plateau. They camped together on the lonely plateau for two days before the students left for the North Rim of the Grand Canyon to meet friends. The plan was to meet back up in Page, Arizona five days later, but when Longmire didn't show they contacted authorities. But, when his body was found some seventy-five miles away from Kaiparowits near the Burr Trail, Garfield County authorities, already overwhelmed, were at a loss to understand it.

According to the students, on the morning of Sept. 1, they left Longmire ten miles from the nearest road out in the wilderness. He was on his way to Harvey's Fear, fifteen miles away, at the extreme south end of the Straight Cliff's finger of the plateau. He was in excellent physical shape, in good spirits and excited for the adventure. There was nothing out of the ordinary and in the previous days they hadn't seen a soul.

Friends told authorities Longmire talked for years about going back to the Kaiparowits Plateau and exploring Harvey's Fear, an extremely remote half-moon shaped region of cliffs and canyons. It was so remote it could only be accessed by foot or by horseback. Years earlier, while working for an energy company doing seismic testing, he spent several weeks in the area. Since it was first explored in the 1880s only a handful of white men have visited the area; and to this day, years come and go without a single white visitor.

Longmire told his closest associates that he discovered an "undisturbed Anasazi settlement" there. He spoke of priceless religious icons and fabulous pottery, and of finding a leather medicine bag filled with individually wrapped powders and seeds. In one cliff dwelling, he discovered six mummies. Longmire theorized the outpost was a religious shrine whose devotees isolated themselves on the lonely escarpment and then, one by one, died out.

The students told authorities that Longmire enlisted them to help ferry water out into the cedar and juniper country. That way, he told them, he wouldn't have to carry heavy loads both ways. For two days, they transported 100 pounds of water over endless white tabletop sandstone and cedar covered sandy hills. They deposited the water under an overhang near some tall freestanding turrets. That was the last place they saw him. According to them, his plan was to work his way to Harvey's Fear, find the Anasazi shrine and spend a few days exploring. He was very secretive, they said, and it was of the utmost importance that no one know the location of his destination. The shrine's only protection, he told them, was its isolation. He theorized, it was possibly the last and most important undiscovered Anasazi settlement left.

On his way to meet Ateen and then on to Las Vegas to investigate Las Vegas Air Tours, Garrett heard of Longmire's mysterious fate and decided to detour to Panguitch and check it out. He stopped at the burned out courthouse and walked its cordoned-off perimeter. At the middle school temporarily converted into the county seat, he read the police report. Longmire was found by two campers, a married couple, as they meandered the Burr Trail. The body was fully clothed and no sign of foul play was found. His injuries were extensive and consistent with a long fall, yet the highest point around was a squat juniper tree.

Garrett talked to the couple at their motel as they prepared to leave. They were still shaken and told him it was eerie because Longmire was implanted five inches deep at the center of a large colony of undisturbed cryptogrammic soil. He had a strange smirk on his face. There were no footprints or tire marks anywhere. Cryptogamic soil, a dark fungus which grows in colonies on top of sand, holds footprints or tire tracks for years, ultimately conforming to them. How could he have gotten there, the man asked. A colleague of Longmire's who traveled from Colorado to claim his body, told Garrett by phone that his hands were discolored with a dark viscous substance and his boots appeared to have tar on them.

The police report said the victim's truck was found where he parked it on Kaiparowits - more than seventy-five miles away. After leaving a message for Ateen at the Bonanza Cafe to meet him at the Kaiparowits location, Garrett spent the day driving across the lonely plateau. When he arrived he was surprised to find Ateen already there. After filling Ateen in about Lessel Opel and the translation of the document, they hiked several miles out, following the footprints left by Longmire and his students. It was exactly how the students said it happened - three sets of tracks went out and two sets returned.

They camped near the road and built a fire. It was good to be free again, to be out of the city where silence reigned. The night was dark but the Milky Way pulsated with light and energy, and the cosmic peace swirled around them. Shooting stars and satellites floated across an inky canvas saturated with billions of points of light set against a beckoning, black void. The next morning, Ateen loaded his backpack and carrying his Winchester set off to follow Longmire's tracks. He insisted on going it alone, asking Garrett not to question his judgment.

"Have it your way, my friend," Garrett simply replied.

Ateen was many miles out when he encountered a valley populated with checkerboard domes of eroded Navajo sandstone, the size and shape of the great pyramids at Giza. Hugging the base of these monuments and growing high onto their shoals were tall strong looking ponderosa pines. The scene was real, but somehow unreal at the same time. He stopped to take a long look. Perspectives and forms tilted forward, as if some energy source within was pressing out against line and form. At the base of one pyramid he thought he saw his great grandfather standing on a lower shelf but when he looked again he was gone. He moved into the country of steamy vistas and evaporating horizons; to the place heat and silence trick the senses.

By early afternoon the land was ugly, inhospitable and especially unforgiving, yet it pulled him forward, offering the answer to the great mystery of man - perhaps of destiny itself - lying just over the next horizon. He continued on through the heat, resting often and drinking plenty of water. It was easy to follow Longmire's tracks, even when he crossed long sections of tabletop sandstone. Ateen's primary objective was to find the Place of Emergence but he knew Longmire played some part in the perplexing puzzle. It was as Natani had told them while in trance, white men were "too close" to the Place of Emergence. Somewhere out in this last bit of wilderness, Longmire met up with someone or something and Ateen was determined to find out what it was. He rested at a place where the rocks were so old and porous he could crush them in his bare hands; they were made of tiny fossils and sand from an ancient ocean.

He located Longmire's water safely stashed under an overhanging rock to keep it cool. Longmire had camped there and Ateen found the tell-tale clues - pieces of paper from food wrapping, two paper clips and several short pieces of rope he used to tie his tent to the ground. Ateen was tired and decided to camp for the night.

The next day he worked through an ancient forest of cedars. There were actually two forests, one that was alive and one that was dead. They intermingled in the secret canyons, on the hillsides and across the wide and varied plateau. It was difficult to tell which was which, the living from the dead; both were austere and both lifted their boughs to the heavens, swirling and dancing like flames. Many of the trees had been dead for centuries and Ateen honored them as members of his family.

By afternoon with the forest behind him he crossed a high wide mead-ow-like valley with commanding views in all directions. At the far end of the valley in a dense stand of cedars and junipers, he found Longmire's second camp. It looked as if its owner walked out into the trees and simply never returned. His tent sat next to a cedar and inside was a sleeping bag, clothing and some camera equipment. A few feet away Longmire's backpack leaned against a rock and sitting on a flat stone were cans of tuna fish, a bag of dried fruit, utensils, a coffee cup, paper towels and a light-weight cook stove. Three containers of water sat in the shade of a tree. A fine layer of vermillion colored sand frosted everything.

Among the items was a leather journal. The last entry read, Sept. 1. - Will spend this morning searching south for the settlement, then in the afternoon investigate the source of the smell that permeates this place.

The dead man's footprints crisscrossed the campsite going in every direction and it took a few minutes before Ateen found his last prints leaving the camp. Longmire went east, moving through a series of low brushy hills and then onto a high open flat area. At a small shaded canyon entrance Ateen discovered a nasty smelling pool of what appeared to be tar or heavy viscous oil. The smell was putrid and he had never seen anything like it - or had he? The pond was a foot or two deep and twenty feet in diameter. He probed it with a piece of deadwood and noticed it was bubbling up like an artesian spring. He touched the pole with his finger and tasted it. Oil.

After Longmire circled the pond, his footprints disappeared over a ridge. At the top of a low hill, Longmire stopped abruptly, then ran towards some free standing rocks. Ateen was excited, knowing this was the place where whatever happened to the geologist occurred. Ateen moved quickly but cautiously when suddenly - out of the sagebrush from the left and inter- mingling with Longmire's - were a new set of tracks! They were follow- ing or chasing. The new tracks were made by Army issue boots, the same as found at Nemelka's hogan. Ateen ran now, head down following the chase - over a hill, down into a dry wash, along the wash bottom before crossing a stretch of white tabletop before disappearing into some sage- brush. Another set of tracks entered from the right! There were two peo- ple now chasing Longmire.

Ateen spotted something ahead, it was the place the men caught him. The pink sand told the story. There had been a violent and intense strug- gle. The impressions of knees and hands were clearly visible in the sand. A deep furrow where someone had been dragged trailed off over a slight hill. At a nearby clearing, the trail of the two men dragging someone sud- denly vanished. Left behind in the sand was the distinctive landing struts of a 168 Huey helicopter.

Ateen left quickly. The spirits can decide about the camp of a dead man, he concluded. He was uneasy and wanted to put some distance between him and this place. An hour later, at the bottom of some strung- out ridges, near a stand of lonely box elders, the path seemed to have a hypnotic effect and he was quite satisfied to watch the land come and go as he wound into it.

He worked for hours through twists and turns, up and down hills, around deep canyons, through sagebrush flats and across desolate plateaus where he could see a hundred miles in all directions. To the south, forty miles away the great Navajo Mountain climbed into the sky. From his van- tage point, he could clearly see a pinnacle rock halfway up the mountain - the same pinnacle rock that eluded him - and home to the secret ruin and its Green Mask pictograph. The spirits are probably there right now, he thought, watching over me.

He wandered aimlessly south into the cedar forest and towards a circle of freestanding boulders about an hour away. The boulders formed a Stonehenge-like enclosure but on a much grander scale. When he reached the massive stones and passed between the perfectly matched boulders, a strange realization swept over him. He no longer felt anxiety or fear; a deep soulful peace replaced it.

He moved quickly forward, letting his legs and body carry him around trees, bushes, rocks and obstacles. His body seemed to know where it was going but he could only acknowledge things mentally a moment or two later. His arms swept back and forth mechanically, reminding him of the arms of some great timepiece from another world. Tick-tock, tick-tock. Waves of euphoria rushed in on him from all directions. I feel very good, he said to himself. I like this. There is nothing to fear. He moved forward into a dissolution of his individual self and a merging with the serenity of time and place.

Cresting a small hill he was astonished to find a hidden side canyon situated in such a way as to be impossible to find unless stumbling into it. Under a high overhang sat fifteen architecturally perfect Anasazi dwellings. He threw his arms into the air, turned in a tight circle and corkscrewed himself deep into the sand. He dropped to his knees and cried out. He prayed for forgiveness - for disturbing the solitude and silence of this sacred place.

It was the Place of Emergence to the Fifth World - the world of tomorrow - just as Natani and Nez described to him. The prophesy went like this. When the Fourth World, the world of today, is destroyed by Taiwa, the Godhead, the pure and uncorrupted people will go underground here to live with the Ant People. When Taiwa builds the new world from the ashes, The Fifth World, He will call the good people out again. They will emerge at this Place to discover a new world. He sat for a long time in the sand letting his eyes and heart soak up the images.

The sound of crows "kaa-ing" brought him to his senses. He sat back and looked into the deepening dusk. Two crows sailed and circled above. According to Hopi legend, crows protect the burial mounds of the Ancient Ones for eternity. Instead of proceeding to the sacred site, he went back the way he came, camping in a circle of cedars. He would wait until morning before trespassing the sacred site.

Ateen made a big fire and huddled next to it. The world was still and quiet, witness to the days and seasons of thousands of years. A blue haze floated above some sagebrush and the night's eyes went from tree to bush.

Like the wind, spirits moved through the trees and up into the starry skies. He sat Indian-style, his ceremonial blanket over his head and shoulders and he chanted, asking the spirits to bless him and his passage. He circled the fire all night long, digging a deep pathway into the sandy earth. At the moment the sun rose over the eastern horizon, he threw off his blanket, climbed the hill and went down to the Sacred Place.

He went from one building to the next. Inside each structure were pots and baskets, storage bins filled with dried corn, water jugs hanging from leather straps, and woven reed sandals awaiting their owners return. Stone and leather tools and bows and arrowheads and feathers and turquoise sat on benches and shelves. It was as if time stood still and a thousand years elapsed - but it could have been just a day or an hour or a moment. Sand was piled high in some doorways, the only sign of passing time.

At the center of the complex was a great subterranean kiva with an ancient wooden ladder protruding out the top. He sat Indian-style next to the entrance for a long time. He tried to see down into the kiva but the shaft of sun light cast down into it only illuminated a small circle of floor and little else. He laid on his stomach and put his head over the edge, attempting to see more. He tested the ladder, half hoping it was in bad shape but it was strong. Retrieving a candle from his pack he started down, knowing if the ladder collapsed he'd not be able to climb out. One rung at a time, the thousand year old leather straps binding the steps, stretched and creaked and cracked but held under his weight.

At the bottom, Ateen lit the candle and let his eyes acclimate. His heart pounded in his chest as he made out the silhouettes of twelve people - six men and six women - sitting upright on a stone bench encircling the circumference of the room. The people were dead and mummified. They sat upright, arms resting in their laps. Ateen moved from one to the next, nodding to each and asking for their blessing. Attired in leather, their faces were perfectly preserved, as if at any moment they could open their eyes and speak to him. The women's fingernails and toenails were painted red and some of the men's faces were lime green. Each wore elaborate religious medallions made of silver and turquoise and held priceless religious icons in their laps. Tall ornate bowls and pottery sat next to them.

He was about to leave when he noticed the circular shaped room wasn't circular at all. The kiva was actually the center of a spiral pathway that wrapped around and led down to an unknown destination. The Place of Emergence. A breeze blew from the hallway and a cold chill ran down his spine. "I honor you," he said, and climbed out.

CHAPTER TWENTY-SEVEN

Garrett collected firewood and discovered several beautiful amber balls of frankincense at the base of a wide cedar tree. After Ateen departed he wrote in his journal, then threaded a needle from his mother's sewing kit and fixed a nagging hole in his old sleeping bag that deposited tufts of goose down everywhere he slept. He nibbled on figs and read Robert Persig's book, *Lila*, about patterns of quality. After reading the same paragraph three times, he put the book down.

He couldn't avoid it any longer, it was time to follow the silence of the sandstone desert, out past the blue horizon. He headed out for a lonely butte on the western horizon. The butte looked to be several hours away, but as he hiked toward it, it seemed to back off, moving farther away. The ground was carved by erosion and warped by pressure, taking him on side trips through intricate mazes of glens, grottoes, fissures and hidden passageways. He let his feet carry him, honoring the path as it presented itself, taking shapes and directions and detours he could not have predicted.

He continued on, catching glimpses of the butte occasionally when he crested a hill or skirted around a vermillion-colored canyon system. It is much farther than I thought, he admitted, and in the middle of the midday heat and the tumultuous burning rock, his optimism collapsed into the self-loathing and defeat he knew so well. One footfall at a time, he went down into the labyrinth of his defeats. Down into the place of dead-ends, twisting canyons of pain and foolish self-centered narcissism. Down where the textures of the land are paradox: dried mud flats and countersunk potholes, overhangs and interlocking sediments, siltstone and stone sand dunes.

He slipped by degrees into the lunacy that so characterizes the modern odyssey. The place was hot, at least one hundred and ten degrees, and in the heat the two sons he sired but never fathered suddenly appeared defiantly before him, standing next to the pathway. He brushed by them, pretending not to have noticed. The lovers he retreated from were there too, each crouched next to an alligator juniper, each waiting to jump out and thrust a middle finger into his face.

"I am guilty!" he yelled into the vacuous silence. "I am guilty. I lied to you. I lied to all of you. - Oh, the lies - forgive me." He sobbed and gesticulated wildly, speaking incoherently to each and every one of his victims as they wafted down on the hot wings of Artemis, the Goddess of Solitude.

He kept walking through the tears until the wonder and magic of his own mysterious life returned. The pathway stretched out before him and afforded a vision of an unblemished idealism. He picked his way out of a canyon and spotted the lonely butte on the western horizon. I am no closer to it than when I began, he puzzled. I will not make it to the butte today, perhaps I will never make it that far.

After a long rest on some hog-back domes, Garrett turned back and descended into the shadowy canyon. He thought he saw his mother standing in an alcove below but when he quickly looked again she was gone.

Back in camp, an orange sunset opened the gate to eternity and he rushed to the top of a petrified sand dune. He loved being on the plateau alone - but the truth was, he was not alone. Out in the solitude he was reunited with his beloved and ill-fated companions. They resided there now and frequented the secret canyons where the silence connected them to him. It is the silence, he concluded, that bonds us together. It is the only substance that connects all things, the past, the present, and the future; silence stretching from his desert campground to the furthest point of light in the distant cosmos. It is eternity.

He built a small Dineh fire and sat next to it, venturing out occasionally to pee and search the night sky. He stretched out on his sleeping bag, hands behind his head and gazed into the swirling night. "I can feel you," he said softly. "This is as close as we get," he said a little louder, "without me joining you." Emotion rushed up his gullet and getting to his knees, he cupped his mouth and shouted all their names, "Mick! Nancy! Randall! Bask! Scout! Sylvia! Leslie! Tsar! Pop! Mother! . . . " When he finished it did it again. He retrieved the 9.mm Beretta handgun he kept under his seat in the truck for occasions like this. His longing to join them; his commitment to join them pressed in from all sides.

Two days later, exhausted and hungry, Ateen arrived back in camp to find it deserted. After drinking water, he followed Garrett's footprints out to a circle of cedars. He found his friend lying in the pink sand, an empty whiskey bottle next to his head and his Beretta still gripped in his hand.

Ateen was silent standing over him, "Hey, Doo Doo, wake up. I gotta take a piss." He spoke in his most beautiful and clear elder's voice. Garrett did not move. "I'm going to piss on your head."

"Don't try it, Fry Bread!" Garrett croaked and looked up; his face greasy and imbedded with tiny pebbles of sand.

"The desert will kill you one day soon, my friend." Ateen said, non-chalantly.

"You got that right."

Garrett drove to Las Vegas to investigate Las Vegas Air Tours and Ateen went to the Bonanza Cafe to report to the elders. Before leaving Ateen told his friend about Longmire's camp, the pool of oil, his assailants and the helicopter tracks; he said nothing about The Place of Emergence.

At the Bonanza, after listening to every detail, Nez asked, "Are you sure no one discovered the Place of Emergence?"

Ateen was certain. "Longmire's killers could have flown over it, but I don't think so. It is impossible to spot from above."

The elders were agitated. "The time has come," Crank asserted, force-fully, "to protect our destiny."

Alan Sekiqua added prophetically, "The Gods will deal with those who trespass the Place of Emergence."

In the end, Natani waved a hand in front of his face as if to say, Enough! I have made my decision. Turning to Ateen, "Meet us tomorrow at dusk over at Endeshi Springs. Bring your rifle."

When Ateen arrived, trucks were parked along the road and out into the high chaparral. Some were familiar but most had license plates from New Mexico and Colorado and Wyoming and California. On a large flat piece of white tabletop sandstone, hundreds of Dineh braves - some in war paint - danced to the insistent beat of drums.

Nez and Natani ran out to meet Ateen. "We have been waiting for you," Nez said, excitedly.

"Who are these men?" Ateen asked.

"Braves from every family and every chapter in the nation," Natani answered and bowed from the waist. The fire light danced in his eyes. "They are the best warriors of the Dineh."

"You must join the dance!" Nez demanded, taking Ateen by the arm and leading him to the center of the action. Natani sat in a lawn chair near the drummers and watched for hours until Ateen and the braves were exhausted and saturated in sweat.

Natani stood atop his chair, raised his arms and the drummers stopped. He called out for Ateen, who came forward and stood near him. Facing Ateen, but speaking to the entire gathering, Natani lifted both arms over his head and came down hard with his hands on Ateen's shoulders, "Ateen!" he shouted, "these warriors are yours! Look at them. They are here for you to lead!"

The dancing put Ateen into a trancelike state and he did not truly understand what Natani was saying. To the braves, Natani continued, "This is Brigham Joseph Ateen, our greatest warrior. He is your leader. You will do what he says! If he says fight, you will fight! If he tells you to kill, you will kill! If he tells you to die, you will die!"

A tremendous chorus of war whoops rose up in the throats and hearts of the braves. Coming down again on the giant Ateen's shoulders, he went on, "You, Ateen, will take these warriors to the Kaiparowits and to the Place of Emergence. You will protect it with your life."

A hush came over the crowd - most had heard of the Place of Emergence but few believed it truly existed. Some cried out in joy, others dropped to one knee and bowed their heads, gently sobbing.

Without thinking, Ateen raised his rifle over his head and let out a powerful war whoop. It came from the center of his being. The braves followed his lead, cutting loose with war cries of their own. The drummers started again. They danced all night, arm in arm around a huge fire, chanting and moving clockwise.

Lonnie arrived home in a sunset fading into dusk, the desert hills submerged in an ethereal pinkness. Above, a royal blue sky darkened quickly and a deeper pink throbbed and pulsated at the horizon. The shadows of the hills smoked in the oncoming dusk. Her thoughts skipped from one thing to another, caught in a loop of ideas and visions that came and went; Mack taking her into his arms and asking her to marry him; Cody coming home from the hospital as a newborn; the ranch house festooned with lights and newly fallen snow at Christmas time; her father's loving smile as he waved goodbye; kissing Mack then closing the casket; watching Cody blacksmithing in the tack room. The visions morphed from one into another, ever transforming, growing, dissipating. She felt hollow and her breathing was shallow; below her rib cage at the center of her chest a deep primal pain radiated outward.

The house was cold and empty, Cody was out on the range, moving cattle from the higher Paunsaugunt where the grazing was now sparse, to a lower elevation on Fosters Dome. She went from room to room, standing at the threshold and searching it before moving to the next until there were no more. She opened a can of chicken noodle soup and ate at the counter, floating saltine crackers on top, as she loved to do as a child. This old log house has seen so much life, she thought, glancing around. We were so happy here before you died, Mack. Now it's just me and Cody - soon it will be just me. She cried and looked around for something to give her comfort. She longed to have her father back, to look at his grizzled face and to hear him tell her, "Everything will work out, my little darlin'." She could see the milky substance at the corners of his eyes and mouth. He was gone now for twenty years but her vision was clear and pure, as if she had just seen him that morning.

Outside on the hardwood porch she sat in the chair Mack made from old saddle parts and a saw horse. At the bottom of the porch steps, the paths leading away were worn deep by years of use and now troughs of darkness settled in them. She heard Mack's voice, 'When all hell breaks loose its time to hunker down, put your back to it and let the hot winds blow over you.' She saw his dancing eyes and heard the timbre of his voice. 'After the wind dies away,' he would say, 'pick yourself up, brush yourself off and go about your business.'

"Thank you, my darling," she muttered to the darkness.

The evening was liquid and warm and a sagebrush scented breeze carried from east to west. The mere idea that Cody could hurt a woman, let alone be involved in a gang rape and murder was incomprehensible. It has to be a case of mistaken identity. There are a thousand people who fit his description. But it was the truck, too. There's no way he could ever do such a thing. It's just not in him, she pleaded with herself. He was such a tender child, she remembered. When Mack had to shoot Jacob the family dog, after he and some other dogs killed some sheep, Cody cried for a week. She tried to be objective, to think clearly, but it was no use.

Cody had been quiet and distant for the last month now - ever since about the time of the . . . rape and murder. When she asked about his sullen behavior, he avoided answering then screamed, "Leave me alone!" It must be those Circle Cliff men, the "outlaws" he's been chasing with, she thought. They got him into this. Thank God Mack is dead, she shook her head, this would kill him.

A gust blew up from the south bringing a faint scent of leather and without thinking, she went to the kitchen and retrieved the key to the tack room. Walking around the porch to the other side of the house she suddenly saw a light coming from the tack room across the yard. Cody's truck was parked half behind it. There were two other cars she didn't recognize.

Her feet hardly touched the ground crossing the long yard toward the door. Her heart pounded and she felt outside herself - as if floating. She heard laughing and the popping sound of a welder. At the tack room's threshold, she saw Cody and two other men, standing at the center of the room, with their backs to her. They appeared to be examining a spot weld one had just made.

She calmed herself, trying to maintain composure. "Cody?"

"Yes, ma'am," he acknowledged, turning and coming towards her, arms outstretched, a smile on his face. They embraced and she surrendered into the strength of her son's arms. The emptiness she felt evaporated. No matter what happened, no matter what he did, no matter where this would take them, she loved him and would stay by his side. She pulled back and looked into his eyes. "I'm so glad to find you here," she finally said, still clinging to him.

He sensed something was terribly wrong and wrapped his arms around her.

"Are you all right, Cody?' she asked, suddenly terrified, "Something wrong, son?"

"Everything is okay, mother," he answered, letting her go and trying to understand what was going on. Embarrassed, he glanced back to the two men.

"I thought you were on the mountain."

"I was but," he gestured to the men, "Me, Rob and Jim here - you remember them - got a great idea."

She was so pleased he was there and so relieved to see he was all right, she hadn't noticed her overt display of emotion was so public. She cocked her head back, the way the commissioner might, folded her arms, and sized them up.

"Evenin', Ms. Bullock," the men said politely, in unison. They shuffled uncomfortably. She nodded and wondered if these were two of the men who raped the girls and killed Ian McCarthey.

"Check this out," Cody said, "We're welding a heavy duty, industrial strength bumper," he motioned to it.

"It's our version of a Mad Max battering ram," Tom added.

"Mad Max?" she asked, squinting.

"The Road Warrior, ma'am," Ron answered.

"You know, the movie," Tom said, looking at his feet.

She ignored both and looked at her son.

"It's going on the front of Tom's two ton," Cody told her.

"You two men live out on the Circle Cliffs?" she asked, craning her neck out.

"No, ma'am," Tom said, "we live over in Tropic."

"My daddy went to school with Cody's dad," Ron commented, smiling.

"Oh, I remember now. Good to see you, Tom. I see," she said, turning to Cody, "Can we talk, it's important."

"Everything all right?"

"It can't wait." Turning to Tom, she held her hand out and when Tom took it, she started backing up, leading him toward the doorway. "Good to see you again, Tom. I hope you and Rob don't mind but Cody and I have family business to discuss. In private."

"Yes, ma'am," they said, tipping their hats and walking out. Cody followed them to their trucks. They would meet later to finish the job.

"What is it?" he asked alarmed.

She searched his eyes wildly. "Promise me," she said, holding his arm tightly, "Promise me Cody that no matter what happens, you and I will always be together."

He knew what was coming. "I promise." He wanted to go to her since the morning after it happened. They both broke down and sobbed, clinging to each other. He tried to stop but could not, he had been carrying this burden for far too long, and she was his mother.

Lonnie never saw her father cry, but she did see his eyes cloud over once or twice. She witnessed Mack cry two times, once when he was drunk and professing his love to her, and at his father's bedside when he died. Mack cupped his hands over his face and broke out in loud wailing agony. He stumbled around and nearly fell over before slouching in a chair. Not knowing what to do, she cradled his head into her midsection.

"I was there, Mother, but I didn't do anything. I promise." He started, "Eight of us went out drinking whiskey that night - straight whiskey. We picked up a few more people and were out looking to find the cow killers.

We got the idea to stop people driving out on the Hole in the Rock, to check them out. Everyone was partying pretty hard and we ran out of whiskey so I decided to go back into town to buy some beer before the convenience store closed. When I got back, an hour later, it was pretty much over. They were going to kill the girls!"

Sitting in Mack's old office chair, she was speechless and just looked at the ground.

"They beat the guy up so bad, they pretty much knew he was a goner. It was crazy. He didn't have a chance. I've never seen any of them act like that. They didn't want to get caught so they decided they'd better kill the girls, too - so no one could identify them."

He paused, embarrassed, then continued. "Becker decided to have some fun first, since they had to kill them anyway. When I got there and saw what was going on . . . you couldn't have believed the look in those girl's eyes. They knew they were going to die. I wasn't going to have anything to do with it and started arguing. It got ugly for a few minutes."

"Who's Becker?"

"Becker and his buddy, Billy, over at Circle Cliffs. Next to Bradshaw's place. They started it. When I showed up, I tried to settle 'em down but they'd already gone too far and would have none of it. I told 'em flat out, I wasn't going to be a party to it . . . I nearly had to shoot my way out."

"You didn't touch either of them?"

"Mother! I told you . . ."

"Did the women get a look at you?"

"Yeah! I helped them. They got a good look at me."

"And you didn't . . . ?"

"Mother!" he shouted. "I took 'em to their truck and told them to get the hell outta there - while they still could!"

"Okay, okay," she interrupted. "I just knew you couldn't be involved. We've got to find a way out of this."

"How did you find out?" he asked.

"Andy Anderson."

"Yeah, he talked to me, too. I denied everything."

"Why didn't you tell him?"

"And end up dead? I'm not ratting anybody off."

"Cody! We're talking murder and rape!"

"Becker and his boys came and threatened me. Said I'd be dead if any of them got fingered. He said they'd all swear on a stack of bibles I was in on it."

Lonnie sat numb and shook her head. "If you weren't part of it, and the women know it . . . there's a way out of this."

"You should have seen them," he told her looking down at his feet. "They were beaten up bad and crazy with fear. They knew they were going to die."

"I'm proud of you, son. You did the right thing." She hugged him "We'll get through this. Somehow, it will all work out."

"We can't go messing with Becker and his friends. They mean business."

We'll get through this," she said, resolutely, brushing her hair back.

By the time Ateen finally made it to Las Vegas days later, Garrett already rented an office in an empty building once used to manufacture airplane parts across the street from the Las Vegas Air Tour's private airport, abutting Nellis Air Force Base. He found the Huey 168 parked in an open hangar and made digital images of it and everyone who came and went for the last three days.

"Something's definitely fishy, Fry Bread. They advertise they carry sightseers and transport freight but in three days they haven't had a customer."

"What happened to you, Doo Doo?"

"What do you mean?"

"You look like shit!"

"I've been working, Fry Bread."

"What about the translation . . . ?"

"It's coming. It's late."

"You made a copy. . . "

"She can be trusted."

"No copy, Doo?"

"I told you, Fry!"

"When?"

"Tonight." Garrett was worried about Lessel Opel. He left messages at both her apartment and office but she had not responded. He hadn't understood her outburst the morning he left and wondered if it had something to do with it. She screwed me and now she's screwing me over, he thought. Did she ever intend to translate the report or had she dumped it into the trash can, believing that was what I did to her? Was this her way of getting back at me?

"They have seven employees," he went on, "two eight-seater Cessnas, a used but very nice corporate jet and two helicopters, the 168 and a fancy new Cobra. That's a lot of overhead for not doing any business. They aren't even listed in the yellow pages."

Garrett tracked the ownership of the company to an off shore holding company in the Cayman Islands. It had recently been sold by a Houston, Texas oil company to a shady holding company there. The new principal partners were two ex-Air Force officers, one the brother of a current member of the Inrom Board of Directors, a mid-sized Texas-based oil exploration company and chairman of the Texas Republican Party. Before its sale, the air-taxi business flew Inrom executives and ferried oil exploration engineers between Texas and its worldwide holdings, especially to South America. After the sale, it moved its headquarters to Las Vegas and took the new name, Las Vegas Air Tours. It began offering scenic flights to the Grand Canyon and the area's national parks.

With assistance from an underground hacker program guaranteed to crack into any business or university computer system, Garrett accessed the company's computer files. He found employee information, accounts receivable and payable, invoices and records of inventory, memos, flight logs and maintenance reports. "Looks legit on paper," he told Ateen, "but check this out." He pointed to his laptop screen, "The 168 was used for unspecified flights to unknown locations on the dates Nemelka was killed and Longmire disappeared."

Garrett did look bad, he had been drinking and stewing again. He spent three days without a break, hunched over his computer and keeping surveillance. He hadn't showered, his hair was a mess and he looked ten years older than he was.

"You smell like you look, like shit," Ateen told him. "You need a break."

"I can't figure it out," Garrett explained, ignoring him. "I've checked all the employees names, social security numbers, addresses, credit reports and everything comes up the same. Zippo! Nothing! No one who works for them has a history - it's like they were just born yesterday or never existed. It can't be right, I should be finding something."

Among the electronic documents was an e-mailed letter of resignation from someone named, Robert Laramie, a flight navigator. The tersely writ-

219

ten resignation said he was leaving because of highly suspicious and perhaps illegal activities of staffers on flights over Utah.

"We need to contact this guy," Garrett said, "disgruntled ex-employees are always the best source of information." There was also a record on Robert Laramie. "He's legitimate," Garrett went on, "from Texas, a veteran of Desert Storm. A tough guy. A patriot."

"Take a break, Doo Doo," Ateen ordered.

"Since when you started giving orders?"

"Since now, my friend."

Garrett was wired from coffee and nerves so he drove aimlessly through the streets of the new Las Vegas until dawn. He ended up in the parking lot of the Modern Dance Department at the University of Nevada at Las Vegas. At the receptionist's desk, he asked to speak with Debra Stone. Stone was a longtime friend and one-time lover who taught modern dance there and now lived with her Tai Chi Master husband, Ronald. Stone taught by day and choreographed Zeigfeld-type extravaganzas for casinos on the strip at night. They met years earlier in Boulder, Colorado when mutual friends invited them to a pot luck dinner for down and out hardcore artist types.

The receptionist was frightened, thinking from his appearance he might be unbalanced or even dangerous. He looked like a transient and she didn't recognize the name Debra Stone. She apologized, telling him she was new to the department and left to get the department chair, whose office was nearby. When she returned the department head was with her. The chairman politely informed Garrett that Debra Stone left the department six years ago.

"What! Six years ago?" he exclaimed, exasperated and truly surprised. "It's been that long?"

Later, he stopped at a coffee shop for eggs and coffee and picked up a copy of the Las Vegas Times. On the front page were two interesting stories. In a reprint of a guest editorial published two days earlier in The New York Times, Utah's senior ultraconservative Republican Senator, Hatch Kimball, called for the temporary closing or even a decommissioning of the Grand Staircase National Monument. He cited several reasons, the killing of the livestock, the violent rapes and beating death, the mysterious death of a well-known geologist, the takeover of Zion National Park by radical environmentalists, and the terrorist attack on the Garfield County Courthouse. He wrote, "The ongoing campaign of vandalism and property crimes is worsening, and the extensive media coverage adds little clarity, but fuels the caldron of hatred and divisiveness." Kimball went on, "With two radical and militant groups facing off, the potential for an old-fashioned Western land war is higher than it has been since the 1890s."

Kimball went on to claim that no one had been pleased since the monument was establishment, and America would be better served if it were decommissioned all together. "We in the West didn't want it in the first place. Hard working men and women of Western America, the people who built this country from the ground up, deserve better."

The Eastern liberal establishment scoffed at the idea, no one had ever floated such a ridiculous proposal and they discounted it out of hand. It was just another bad idea from the far right that would drop into the vast ocean of ideas without a ripple. But the next morning, these same politicians were shocked and astounded when the President of the United States reportedly commented to a group of oil executives, at a White House luncheon, that he liked Kimball's proposal; and that he had instructed his Secretary of the Interior to study the idea. In the meantime, he was firing the existing Grand Staircase Monument manager for not being more receptive to local needs and replacing her with an ex-mining corporate executive.

Garrett had a bitter taste in his mouth. The second headline read: Area Pilot Intentionally Run Down in Mirage parking lot. The victim's name happened to be none other than Robert Laramie. Garrett recognized the name immediately, the man who sent the letter of resignation to Las Vegas Air Tours. Witnesses were adamant that the crime was intentional. Several reported watching a late model navy colored SUV accelerating across the parking lot and running Laramie over as he tried to flee. One witness was quoted: "Whoever did it, wanted him dead." Another added the vehicle had a satellite dish installed on its roof.

After Garrett showered, he and Ateen rushed to the hospital where Laramie was in a private room in the intensive care ward in critical condition. Garrett pretended to be a concerned friend and the charge nurse confided that Laramie would most likely not regain consciousness. He has a severe head injury, she told him. As they were about to leave, she added, "Are you with the two other men who were just here? They are friends, too."

"Two men?" Garrett asked as Ateen scanned the ward entrance and hallway.

"They were just here." The nurse came around the desk and looked up and down the hall, "You just missed them."

Both men searched the waiting room and hallway. She pointed up the hallway, "There they are!"

Standing at the end of the hallway were two tall men wearing suits and sun glasses. They were watching Ateen and Garrett and as soon as they realized they had been spotted, they turned and disappeared down a hallway. Garrett and Ateen started after them but a few feet down the hall, Ateen shot down the emergency stairs, planning to head them off in the main lobby. Exiting the stairwell into the lobby, they spotted the two men crossing the spacious, sunny lobby and going for the entrance. They were cool and outwardly at ease but, at the same time, their heads darted back and forth as if nervously expecting something.

Ateen followed them into the parking lot and watched them drive off in a navy, late model van, equipped with a communications array. He got the license number. Back at the rented office, Garrett confirmed the vehicle was registered to Las Vegas Air Tours and he had digital images of it parked at the flight school two days earlier.

"This is big time," Garrett told his friend. "It's a well financed, well planned out, secret operation. I can smell it."

"Laramie knew too much." Ateen added.

"What now? Go to the authorities?"

"With what? Suspicions? Speculations? We don't have anything. We need proof."

"We can put the police onto the SUV!"

"I don't know," Ateen hesitated.

"How about murder then? We can put the chopper at the scene of Nemelka's murder!"

"It's our word against theirs. We don't have enough to go on yet."

Garrett was incredulous, "What are we going to do, nothing?"

"We need indisputable proof before doing anything. We need to find out what this is all about. Without putting it all together first we have nothing."

"What are you worried about?"

"Wake up, Doo Doo!" Ateen said harshly, "For all we know the authorities are involved. Think about it. For all we know, we could become targets too! Just like Ian and Nemelka and Longmire. Remember, they got a look at us, too."

From Vegas they caravanned north to St. George, Utah then east through Zion Park and into Kanab where they rented the John Wayne room in the famous Peery Inn. After a good night's sleep Garrett would start off for Boulder, Colorado to get the translated report from Lessel Opel. Ateen told his friend he would return to Page and wait to hear from him, but he was really headed back to the Kaiparowits to check on the Dineh braves he left guarding the Place of Emergence.

Outside the John Wayne room, they sat on the porch in the cool night air on white plastic chairs. Ateen turned to Garrett, "You ever heard the story of Willow, Utah?"

"Willow, Utah?" Garrett snapped. "There's no god-damned Willow in Utah."

"You're sitting in Willow right now." Ateen informed him gently. "The word Kanab is the Paiute word for Willow."

"Smart ass!" Garrett said, raising an eyebrow. "Never heard of it."

"Since the beginning of the Fourth World, more than seven hundred years ago, the Paiutes lived here in Willow where the river cuts down through the Vermillion Cliffs and the willows grow along its length. It was the Paiutes' home and countless generations of them lived and died here. They hunted the ridgetop and grew corn right here where we are sitting. Travelers and nomads stopped by for water and food and to rest and the Paiutes welcomed them, always giving them what they needed.

"One day a Mormon wagon train sent by Brigham Young came down the canyon looking for a place to build a new town. The Paiute welcomed the white men, telling him the best place to camp was above the river on the flats. The Mormons said they would forage their teams of horses and mules then be on their way.

"But the Mormons got to talking and decided this spot was a pretty good place and they wanted to build their town right here. So the Mormons told the Paiute of their plan and told them there wasn't room enough for both groups and ordered the Paiute to leave.

"The Mormons gave the Paiutes a deadline and after much talk the Paiutes decided the women and children and old people should leave and they did, going south toward Pipe Springs. The Paiute braves refused to go. It was their village - their home. Their ancestors were buried here and their spirits remained. It was not white man's land, they told the Mormon leader, the creator made it for all men to use.

"When the Mormons attacked they killed all the braves. It wasn't much of a fight, since they had repeating rifles and outnumbered them. Afterwards, the Mormons got scared. They feared word would get out about what they had done, and the new federal army who didn't like the Mormons would arrest them. So, not wanting to have any witnesses they tracked down the rest of the Paiutes - the women and children and old people - and killed them, too. They caught up with them south of here in the Kaibab Forest."

Garrett listened in disbelief, "You can't be serious! I can do without the pious brethren myself but I've never heard or read anything that comes vaguely close to what you are saying."

Ateen sat back, "Of course you haven't, Doo, Doo. You are an Anglo." Then, measuring the words, he continued, "It's part of the real story - the untold story - of the American West."

Before dawn the next morning, Ateen walked a few blocks to the all night gas station for coffee. As he paid the clerk, he noticed a late model, navy SUV with dark tinted windows and a nearly hidden communication array, rolling through town.

Outside, he ducked into a driveway next to the gas station and knelt beside a broken truck. The van cruised back by, going slowly down Main towards the Peery Inn. Shit! Ateen thought, we've got big trouble. He watched as the van's brake lights illuminated and turned into the Peery Inn's parking lot. "Here we go!" he blurted out loud, and took off in an all out sprint for the Peery. Suddenly, headlights appeared and the vehicle pulled out of the motel parking lot. It was coming his way. He dropped into the black shadow of a tree next to the road and did not move. The SUV went by and turned left into a neighborhood.

CHAPTER TWENTY-EIGHT

When Allan von Bank arrived at EarthIsland's Egypt headquarters with two representatives from a national San Francisco based environmental organization they found the camp in chaos - the exodus was underway. A stiff wind howled from the south and last year's tumbleweeds rolled through the camp on their way over the cliff and down into the mixed-up Escalante drainage.

Word of the redeployment came at dawn when Jonah rousted everyone from bed and gave them marching orders. "We have until sunset to be at our new destinations." He made no apology. "I waited to tell you until now so the information could not be leaked. We should be safe."

Behind the wheel of his Lincoln Excursion, von Bank was frightened, wondering what it all meant. Everywhere around him, people fought against the wind to disassemble tents, roll and pack sleeping bags and load their belongings. The kitchen was packed away and sanitation crews hurriedly buried communal toilets and put the filled-to-overflowing port-a-pottys on a flatbed truck next to the makeshift showers.

Camp residents were confused and emotional. Yesterday, they were a community, today they were being torn apart. They were entering a new, more dangerous operational phase, Jonah told them. Goodbyes were quick, strained and tearful. Gallows humor carried across the camp. Couples were being separated, friends and compatriots found themselves going in opposite directions, and groups who arrived together were being absorbed into other groups. The loose arrangements for reuniting seemed weak and hollow.

Allan von Bank and his two guests found Jonah lounging on a petrified sand dune, overseeing the camp break down.

"What's happening?" von Bank asked, without introducing his associates.

"My name is Jonah Sandborn," he said, offering his hand to the two attractive women with von Bank. One was elegant and in her fifties, the other was intense-looking and in her mid-thirties. They were from the national headquarters of the Conservancy Club.

Turning to von Bank, Jonah went on, "Yes. We are redeploying our resources. All noncombatants are returning to Zion's for security reasons. The Confrontation Force is on the move."

"How militaristic of you," von Bank, quipped. "You expect trouble?"

"Don't you?" he shot back. "Isn't that why you are here? Wanting to get an update. Afraid of what we might do?"

"It does worry people, Jonah."

"I'll try not to shake your little money tree."

"You son-of-a-bitch!" von Bank said, stepping back. "You don't know when to quit!"

"You're right. No. My apology. You know me, I've never been much of a diplomat." Jonah bowed from the waist. He needed to know why they were there, until then it was best not to alienate them. Turning to the women, he smiled, "And, what do I owe this visit to?"

The younger woman, dressed smartly in a Madison Avenue business suit and high heels, stepped forward. "We want to know what your intentions are." She was the group's legal advisor. She pulled the hair away from her face and narrowed her eyes.

"To protect the land."

"Against Westley and his Sagebrushers?"

"Against anyone who would damage it," he paused. "Let me say this, no more roads will be bladed in the monument."

"We're not the press, Mr. Sandborn," the younger woman said sarcastically. "Your charm offensive doesn't impress me."

"Perhaps it's something you might try," Jonah folded his arms, smiled and nodded politely.

"We have it from reliable sources that you and your people were involved in the bombing of the Garfield County Courthouse,"

"Check your sources," Jonah looked away, matter-of-factly. "If you've come all this way to make baseless accusations, you are wasting my time. I see no further need to . . ." He took a step away but stopped.

"We are trying to help . . . can't you see that?" von Bank added. "This is serious. Why else would we be here?"

"Go on."

"Were you aware that EarthIsland literature was found in the motel room rented by the suspects?"

"That's news to me," Jonah said, genuinely surprised. Turning to the intense young woman, "You look smart enough, councilor. Does that make sense to you?" He raised his eyebrows theatrically.

She glared at him and didn't answer.

"Come on," Jonah continued, "what we know about the bombers is that he or they are consummate professionals, highly trained and experienced in explosives - most likely ex-military. Does it make sense that such professionals would pull off a perfect crime, then leave their calling card laying behind?"

"How do you explain it?"

"I don't. It's not my job. How do you explain it?" he started, defensively. "If EarthIsland's literature was found in the motel then it was a plant. Let me ask you a question. Do you believe we burned down the courthouse?"

"It doesn't matter what I think."

"Why am I talking to you then?"

"Are you telling us," von Bank broke in, "none of your people have been involved in any of the crimes or tit-for-tat vandalism going on down here?"

"I'm not saying that, either. Get real. You asked about the courthouse and I can categorically and emphatically tell you we had nothing to do with it."

"I'm satisfied!" von Bank concluded, as if his questions were satisfied and he was ready to leave.

"According to Thomas Westley," the young woman interjected, "they claim to have proof you . . . "

"According to Thomas Westley," Jonah interrupted, angrily, "there are enough trees in America to supply the world's needs for a hundred years without threatening the survival of the forests! According to Thomas Westley, global warming is a figment of everyone's imagination! What are you doing here?" he demanded, staring at von Bank. "Why have you come? I'm busy."

"Don't expect any help from us if you continue this bellicose approach," the attorney chided.

"How's this for bellicose?" he taunted moving toward her aggressively. "You better climb back into that yuppie mobile and go back where you came from before something happens to you."

The woman stepped back, nearly tripping over a barrel cactus.

"Jonah, she's just trying to tell you that you are on you own," the older woman offered in a conciliatory tone. "What you are doing is very important to all of us. You must be careful and consider the larger ramifications of your actions. Please be prudent. Everything rides on you."

He raised his eyebrows and exhaled, "Really? Everything rides on me."

She went on, "Word has it Jonah, that someone very powerful, perhaps at the very top, is pulling the strings here."

"No one's pulling my strings."

"Not that you are aware of anyway," the young attorney interjected, defiantly.

"Your point is?" he insisted, looking to the horizon.

"We don't know yet," the elegant woman admitted. "We just know that something is going on and it's coming from the top down. Influential political forces are at work. People close to the center believe some in the highest echelon want this confrontation - and not for ideological reasons."

Jonah was taken aback; he didn't understand.

She paused and looked directly into his eyes, "You know, Jonah, you can't expect help from law enforcement. They will not be there when you call. You are truly on your own."

"With all due respect," he responded with characteristic confidence, "we are capable of taking care of ourselves." Privately, he was very worried. After seeing Sheriff Anderson on CNN in his uniform atop Westley's bulldozer during the blading episode, he knew where they stood. Despite the tremendous outside pressure from the media and the powerful environmental politicians, the investigation into Ian's murder had gone nowhere. Were they right? Was someone pulling his strings?

He asked, "If not for ideological reasons, what then?"

"We do not know."

"Locals tell me," the attorney confided, "Westley and his men are expecting a confrontation. They are nearly ready to move. They have stockpiled guns and are preparing for casualties."

"Hence our departure," Jonah replied, now pacing back and forth. "Our sources say the same thing. I'm glad we're on the same page about that anyway."

"We do support you and most of what you are doing," the older woman added. "But you must understand we cannot openly support any kind of violence or criminal behavior. You scare us. This entire scenario scares us. At the same time, we are painfully aware that sometimes change is inevitable and painful. We are willing to see what this brings. If, in the end, as I believe it will, this strategy benefits the movement, we will applaud you."

"We just don't want some martyr situation, Jonah."

"That's refreshing," Jonah laughed. "Me neither!"

"If you fail," the young attorney added, "and I'm convinced you will, you will have set the movement back a generation."

"Where did you get her from anyway?" Jonah pointed, and looked at von Bank. Turning to her, "But just think of all the dead bodies you'll be able to climb over if it happens! It will be a good career opportunity!"

CHAPTER TWENTY-NINE

"Doo Doo!" Ateen shook his friend who was still in bed. "Let's go! We need to get out of here - now!" As Garrett pulled on his clothes Ateen scanned the parking lot from the window of the John Wayne room and told Garrett what just happened. Garrett had never seen his friend frightened like this.

"Listen," Ateen told him, "you go North on 89 and I will go east to Page. They can't follow both of us."

"We need to stick together!" Garrett insisted.

Ateen shook his head, adamantly. "No. Don't worry, Doo Doo. I'll make sure they follow me." He cracked the door open to see if anyone was there, "Clear. Let's go!"

They rushed to their cars in the dawn light. "What are you going to do?" Garrett asked.

"I'll take care of it."

"Hey, let's do this together," Garrett insisted, bear-hugging his giant friend. "You and me!"

"No. No! You'll just slow me down. Believe me." He moved away to his own truck. "Your job is to get to Denver and get the report, it is the proof we need." He looked at his friend, "Promise me, you won't stop for anything!"

"I promise."

Garrett barreled out of the Perry parking lot onto the empty Kanab Main Street and accelerated north through town. Checking his rearview mirror he was shocked to see Ateen following him. He panicked and wondered if he heard wrong. "You're supposed to be going the other way, Fry Bread!" he shouted. "What are you doing?" He was just about to pull over to check the instructions when suddenly, from a side street, the navy SUV pulled out behind Ateen.

"Holy shit!" Garrett said, hitting the accelerator again, racing through town with Ateen and the SUV behind him. At the edge of town, the road entered the mouth of a narrow canyon and he noticed Ateen slowing down, as if he were pulling over. "Come on, Ateen!" he frantically shouted, pounding the steering wheel. "Let's go, Fry Bread!" Garrett pulled his foot from the accelerator, deciding he would stand with his brother - then he remembered Ateen's last words, "Promise me, you won't stop for anything!" He reluctantly gunned his engine up the canyon, soon passing out of sight around a long curve.

At the place where Kanab Creek cuts through the Vermillion Cliffs and the road narrows dangerously, Ateen made a U-turn, stopping in the middle of the road and blocking it. The SUV slowed and came to a stop five hundred feet away. Swiveling in the driver's seat and rolling down his window, Ateen wanted to look his enemy in the eye. He reached under the seat and retrieved his Winchester .94. Racking a shell into the chamber, he waited for them to make a move. He needed to give Garrett a good head start and every moment he held them off would better his friend's chances.

When it became obvious they weren't going to make the next move and Garrett was halfway up the canyon, Ateen completed the turn and punched it, accelerating straight at them. In his right hand, he held the steering wheel and with his left hand, he held the Winchester out the window and aimed it at the SUV. The speedometer read 50 then 60, and by the time he reached the SUV he was going 75 miles per hour. At the last possible moment he cranked the steering wheel to the right, narrowly missing the SUV but coming so close he took its outside mirror off. Two men sitting in the front seats dove for the back.

Back through Kanab Ateen went, slowing a little to making certain the SUV was behind him. They won't make their move here, he thought, not in town where they can be seen. They have already made too many mistakes, they won't make another one here. East out of town, Ateen hit the accelerator again and the SUV stayed safely behind, seemingly satisfied to follow a half mile back. It was sixty desolate miles to the next down of Page and they could pick the time and place.

For the next half hour, the SUV stayed safely back until Telegraph Flats, a lonely straight-out section of road, where they made their move, trying to come alongside. Ateen sped up, accelerating to more than ninety miles an hour but he couldn't outrun the newer SUV. When they attempted to come along side again, Ateen moved to the left and blocked them. Just past the old Pariah ghost town turnoff at a place where the highway crosses the south section of the Cockscomb ridge and winds through a series of sharp curves, a crashing explosion shattered his back window, sending glass and debris everywhere. He felt a terrible stinging pain above his ear. They were shooting at him. He struggled to control the truck, going off the road one way then steering back on again and off the other side. He hit the brakes and fought to keep the truck from rolling. Blood gushed down the side of his head, running down his neck and covering his arm. The bullet grazed his head, cutting into his scalp and taking off the top of his right ear.

When he finally regained control, he saw a man in the rear view mirror leaning out the passenger's side window firing. Instinctively, he hit the brakes just as another bullet whizzed by, exploding the front windshield and spraying glass everywhere. The SUV slammed into the rear-end of his truck, sending it swerving back and forth onto two wheels and nearly rolling. It went off the road to the right, over corrected, came back across the highway and off again to the left before finally regaining control. The shooter struggled not to be thrown out but dropped his rifle before pulling himself back inside. Ateen sped up, getting a good lead, but soon they were back on his tail again. He slammed on his brakes again, but this time the SUV tried to come around on the left. He cranked his wheel to the left, trying to run them off the road.

Behind him again, he brought his Winchester across the back seat, fired and hit the SUV's windshield, directly where the driver sat - but nothing happened. The bullet made a small indentation and nothing more. Bullet proof glass. The SUV dropped back, then came up fast again. Ateen pumped several shots into the engine compartment, hoping to damage the motor. With each shot, the SUV slowed before accelerating again.

On the straight-away before the polygamist outpost of Big Water, the SUV tried again to come alongside but Ateen rammed his heavy truck into them, trying to force them off the road and into a deadly embankment. At the last moment, he swerved onto the Big Water turnoff and raced through the deserted town and onto the dusty Smokey Mountain Road. The SUV was right behind him but as soon as they hit the dirt road, with its deep ruts and washes and narrow curves, it was impossible to come alongside. With the dust cloud Ateen's truck threw up, they couldn't get a clear shot.

Nearing the towering Kaiparowits Plateau, Ateen smiled when he saw the dangerous Kelly Grade climbing the three-thousand-feet to the plateau's top. At the base of the grade, he slowed and shifted into four wheel drive. He wanted his adversary to catch up and when they were a few hundred feet back, he gunned it up the dangerous road as a hail of bullets pounded his truck.

The SUV followed closely up the first section of the grade as it snaked up the improbable route, following seams and cracks. By the time his pursuers crested the first section, Ateen was climbing the treacherous second section as it serpentined through a series of steep switchbacks and exposed rock faces to its top. On the inside, block-shaped boulders were stacked haphazardly atop one another, and on the outside, the aging roadbed crumbled away where water and wind had weakened it. The narrow roadbed consisted of millions of marble-sized rocks making traction difficult, and the drop-offs plummeted more than fifteen hundred feet.

Ateen kept to the inside track, climbing the precarious section expertly while the SUV and his pursuers struggled forward below. The SUV took the first several hundred feet in stride before losing traction and fishtailing back and forth across the narrow road. The driver raced the engine, churning and spitting rocks and gravel as it desperately scrambled for traction. Back and forth it went, lurching forward a few feet before squirreling around; finding traction and losing it again. The driver fought for control and after nearly losing it on a corner, the SUV turned dangerously sideways. The rear-end churned up the roadbed on the inside as the front end swung out closer and closer to the eroded edge. Suddenly, the roadbed collapsed under the weight of the front-end and it fell away. The SUV's front-end dropped to its frame and rocks and debris sloughed away and plummeted a thousand-feet to the bottom. The rear-end was safely on the road but the front end and wheels dangled in midair off the edge.

Watching from above, Ateen exited his truck and saw three men climb out. He had seen two of them before at the hospital in Las Vegas, the third he didn't know. They stood at the edge of the road, surveying the situation. When one reached for a satellite phone, Ateen cranked a shell into his rifle, brought it to his shoulder, took aim and fired, dropping the man instantly. The other two dove for cover and Ateen kept them pinned down, working from one place to another to get a better shot. He would end this chase here. From behind some rocks, they fired aimlessly back at him, unable to spot him. After Ateen emptied his rifle of ammunition he returned to the truck and sped away.

Several hours later and now on foot, he moved through the silent cedar forest toward the Place of Emergence many miles away. He went from one landmark to the next - a freestanding boulder, a family of ancient cedars, a group of hogback domes, a clearing on a far-off slanting ridge, a forested hillside. To the south, Navajo Mountain anchored the spirit of the sky to the Mother Earth. He pushed forward relentlessly, his breathing was deep and rhythmic, his powerful legs carrying his huge frame effortlessly up and down hills, around canyon systems, over tabletop sandstone and through stretches of sage and cedar. He practiced the Dineh Gait of Power, a running technique little known to the outside world where a trained warrior lifted his legs high as he ran and came down on his toes. At the same time, the warrior crossed his eyes and ran while unfocusing. Once a warrior mastered this difficult technique, he could run great distances without tiring and easily negotiate any surface, even on moonless nights, without faltering.

His mind was clear with purpose. He instructed the braves to protect the Place of Emergence and told them he would return in a week - it was now ten days later. He would make certain everything was quiet with the braves, then return to the Bonanza Cafe and report to the elders.

In the middle of a large flat expanse of flesh-colored tabletop sandstone, stretching more than a mile across, and populated by huge petrified sand dunes shaped like giant breasts, Ateen felt a series of deep concussions carrying from some distance away. He turned in the direction of the sound, stopped, then suddenly took off running, searching for cover across the open expanse. He needed to find an alcove or overhang or fracture line in the sandstone where he could find sanctuary. Looking over his shoulder continuously, he had no idea how much time he had to escape. The deep vibrations came back, then trailed off like drums carried in the wind from miles away.

The concussions grew heavier and louder and closer, sweeping one way then another, like a desert locust restlessly searching the chaparral for insects to devour. Ateen was still a thousand feet away from safety in a drainage system covered by a thick canopy of cedar and junipers. From behind some hills, the Huey 168 model with the 172 model fairings, the machine they traced to Las Vegas Air Tours, the bringer of death for Longmire and Nemelka, appeared at the far edge of the tabletop and hovered slowly forward. The sound of its engine and rotor vibration bounced off the petrified dunes and loose tabletop rock and hit him from all directions at the same time. The concussive, blasting-vibration was a sensation he once loved as a ranger in Vietnam on dangerous missions or long patrols. It meant his guys were coming to kill the enemies or to take him home. This time it meant the enemies were closing in on him!

This helicopter, with its deafening noise and its tumultuous fury, did not belong on this sacred mesa - home to eternal silence and The Place of Emergence to the Fifth World. Its mere presence here was a crime, a sacrilege and an intrusion whose mockery filled Ateen's heart with disgust and rage. This machine and the men inside were evil. He and the gods must find a way to fight and defeat it. But first, he had to escape.

He ran for all he was worth, for all the Dineh were worth; for all the prophecies of the elders; for all the ancestors whose lives played out a thousand years earlier; and for all the people yet to be born, the people of the Fifth World. Navajo Mountain towered above the hills to the south and the Gods were watching. "Help me," he called out to them. "Give me the strength and power to defeat this enemy!" He sprinted from sand dune to sand dune, gazing at the mountain occasionally, and searching for a hiding place. His lungs filled with inspiration, his heart beat with the driving force of his people.

The chopper moved slowly, inexorably forward towards him, scanning back and forth across the wide tabletop, searching. The two survivors from the SUV were now strapped into harnesses and stationed in the chopper's open doors, leaning out and searching the tabletop, looking for Ateen, machine guns at the ready. After Ateen left them stranded on the Kelley Grade, they summoned help with the satellite phone. A pilot and another man picked them up and they followed the Smokey Mountain Road across the Kaiparowits until they found Ateen's truck parked in some trees.

There was little chance Ateen could make it to the forest before they spotted him. Looking over his shoulder, the 168 was moving slowly towards him, perhaps only three hundred yards away. He made out the silhouette of the pilot and a spotter sitting next to him. It would be impossible for them not to detect him running across the flesh-colored tabletop.

Ateen's time ran out when he was less than one hundred feet from the forest. The pilot spotted him, alerted the door gunners and swung the chopper around a quarter turn, allowing the left gunner a clear shot. Bullets pocked the soft sandstone with deep divots and sprayed chips and debris as Ateen ran through it. He changed directions to the right, moving with tremendous agility, employing the Gait of Power to jump from one place to another, then after zigzagging he rolled down a small decline, got to his feet and with superhuman speed, made for the trees. The pilot came around the other way to give the opposite gunner a shot when Ateen did something they didn't expect - he suddenly stopped, spun around, brought his rifle to his shoulder, aimed and fired one shot at the pilot before diving headlong into a wide crack at the table top edge. The bullet hit its mark, piercing the old helicopter's windshield and grazing the pilot's head, half ripping off his helmet and earphones. The chopper listed heavily to one side as the pilot nearly lost control, then struggled to regain it.

As the chopper lurched up and away, Ateen darted into a small ravine where floodwaters channeled off the tabletop. The ravine quickly turned into a deep section of narrows, maybe four feet across and fifty feet deep. From above, the narrows were only a slit, a mere crack in the broken landscape. It reminded him of the famous Antelope Canyon narrows on the reservation where two years earlier twelve German tourists were washed away in a flash flood. He was comfortable in the deep narrows. It was his homeland. As a child, he explored many narrows like it on the shoals of the mountain.

Ateen worked quickly down the secret narrows. After the pilot regained control, he touched down at the edge of the tabletop and the two gunners disembarked and followed Ateen into the narrows. Just as they had done with Longmire and Nemelka, the assassins would track their prey on foot while the chopper circled above. Ateen moved quickly but cautiously forward as the narrows began to close off, forcing him to walk sideways for a long time before widening again and he was able to move more quickly. After a long straightway where he could see hundreds of feet ahead, he rounded a corner and discovered a deep drop-off. At its bottom was a pool of stinking, stagnate water. Rather than working down, knowing there were probably more drop-offs ahead, he decided to friction climb up and out. Wedging his back against one wall and using his hands, knees and feet to apply pressure on the opposite wall, he worked up and out.

Once at the surface, he found himself in a wide gully, near the center of a family of cedar trees. It was a difficult climb and as he sat at the top resting, he could hear the chopper's concussive clatter somewhere in the near distance. He was safe there and rested in the protective canopy, considering his next move. As the chopper moved further away, Ateen thought he heard something in the narrows below. He strained to listen but concluded it was nothing. Just as he was about to move, he heard it again. It was a man's voice echoing up from below. The assassins had followed him and he had only a few minutes head start. He made tracks out of the trees and over a hill.

When the first assassin emerged out of the narrows, he scanned every direction before dropping back down below the surface. He was very cautious, this quarry could be dangerous, not like the others whose only thought was of escape. This was a hunter and a worthy opponent. He listened for Ateen until he was satisfied he was gone, then slowly climbed out, crouching next to a huge dead cedar tree, its trunk and branches twisting up into the sky. His finger was on the trigger of his rifle, ready to fire at any provocation when he spotted Ateen's footprints disappearing over a sandy hill. He couldn't be too far ahead now.

The second assassin climbed out of the narrows and using a head-mounted two-way radio set, contacted the helicopter. At the same time, the first assassin stood and nodded to his comrade, pointing out the footprints leading away. As the first man turned toward the tracks, Ateen, hiding behind the knarled cedar, stepped out and grabbed him from behind by the chin, pulled his head back and brought his razor sharp hunting knife across the man's throat, nearly decapitating him. The man's legs dropped out from under him. Seeing what was happening, the second assassin brought his rifle around to fire, as Ateen cocked his arm and threw his knife - hitting his target squarely in the chest and burying the knife to its hilt. The man stood up, dropped his rifle, grabbed the knife handle with both hands, stared at Ateen - eyes bugging out - and tried to pull it out. Then he fell face forward, dead before hitting the ground.

Ateen stood over the two dead men. He had not killed since Viet Nam. It was never something a man wanted to do, and for the Dineh, a man's life was everything he possessed and everything he would ever be. But this was different, these men needed to die. They were without the root of humanity. To trick his pursuers, Ateen intentionally made tracks over the hill then doubled back around.

The helicopter moved toward his location, alerted by the assassin's call, scanning from one place to another. This is my chance, he thought, I cannot let it get away. If the helicopter were to escape it would only return with more men and the Place of Emergence would be compromised. It was time to end this charade, but he had to act quickly. Retrieving his rifle, he lifted one of the dead assassins up and draped him over his back so the man's front faced out, the knife still protruding from his chest; his face still filled with horror.

Leaning over like the hunchback of Notradam, Ateen carried the man from beneath the canopy of cedars into the open and up a small hill. He carried the man in such a way that from the air it appeared the man was standing on his own and backing up the hill. The Viet Cong used this tactic many times to draw American helicopters down into ambushes. Ateen hoped to confuse the pilot just long enough for him to make the mistake of moving in for a closer look. As the helicopter searched, hovering above, Ateen took the man's sleeves and lifted his arms up and down, making it appear the dead man was waving to the pilot. Just as he hoped, the pilot saw the man and took the bait, moving in closer. Ateen waited patiently, counting on the element of surprise and the pilot's curiosity to overwhelm his suspicion.

When the chopper hovered only fifty feet above, Ateen shrugged off the dead man's body, stood straight up, brought his rifle to his shoulder, aimed and fired in quick succession. The surprised pilot backed the aircraft away quickly as Ateen pumped one shell after another into the cockpit. Undeterred, the chopper turned forty-five degrees, lining up the spotter who now sat in the open side door with a .60 caliber machine gun in his hands.

Ateen continued firing until he had no more shells. He had nowhere to hide. Still unfazed, the chopper hovered and positioned itself for the spotter to open fire. Ateen now made an easy target and just as the spotter was about to open fire, he suddenly slumped like a rag doll and dropped the machine gun. The chopper was taking flack! Someone was shooting at it! Ateen heard volley after volley of shots above the roaring rotor wash. The gunfire was coming from several separate places in the forest simultaneously. The pilot desperately tried to pull away but as he turned to leave, his left fuel tank was hit by gunfire and exploded, creating a huge fireball, tearing the top rotor and tail completely off and sending the body rolling away end over end into a canyon behind a hill. Ateen dove for cover, heard an explosion and saw a ball of flames rising over the hill.

Before he could get to his feet, he was surrounded by his Dineh warrior brothers, the braves from The Place of Emergence. He was incredulous and hugged each man as they excitedly recounted what had just taken place. Later, around a campfire near the crash site, the braves talked of downing the helicopter and of the strange occurrences that brought them to Ateen's rescue.

"When we got up this morning," one told him, "the spirits instructed us to leave the Place of Emergence and head out north across the plateau."

"How did the spirit manifest itself?" Ateen asked.

"We kept spotting something, an oval light moving in the trees," another added. "It moved ahead of us so we followed it. It was enticing us forward."

"I know you gave us orders not to leave," one said bluntly, "but we couldn't stop, a yearning overwhelmed us."

"You did right," Ateen assured him.

"We followed the orb north," one told him, "when we heard the helicopter and the shooting. From the top of a petrified sand dune, we spotted you and the chopper."

"We ran for all we were worth," another interjected, shaking his head in disbelief. "My feet had wings! I have never moved so fast."

They were convinced the Creator brought them to help. They spoke in hushed and reverent tones. They gazed into the fire and looked at each other with amazement, as if unable to truly comprehend all that happened. They had been instruments of the Creator.

No one slept that night, they talked and chanted and danced around the fire. In the morning, they buried the dead men and worked back to The Place of Emergence.

CHAPTER THIRTY

Ten days after their first road project into the national monument, Westley and his latter-day Sagebrushers congregated at the Panguitch City Park, adjacent to the bombed out courthouse before dawn. By half-past nine more than four hundred and fifty men milled around quietly. The Fourth of July atmosphere surrounding the earlier Carcass Canyon road building event was absent, replaced by a solemn - time to take care of business - mood.

Westley greeted each man personally, shaking his hand and searching his eyes, "Are you ready for this?" Most just nodded resolutely or simply replied, "Yes." One man smiled widely and said, "Bring 'em on. When do we get started?" Another added, "This is going to be remembered for a long time." Most of the men stayed close to their outfits, making adjustments to loads, checking trailers and caring for their horses.

They came from the surrounding towns but contingents from Wyoming, Nevada, Arizona and New Mexico were present as well. To a man, each was devoted to the cause of ridding the West of outside influences. One family from Nevada arrived with three generations. They were ranchers north of Battle Mountain: a grandfather, father and six grown sons. They hoped to finally make a stand against the forces they blamed for destroying the West. The ex-Garfield County Sheriff, Andy Anderson, who resigned a day before, drove the first truck behind Westley. Anderson arrived early wearing army fatigues and packing his pearl-handled .45 caliber Smith and Wesson pistol on his hip and an AR 15 assault rifle slung over his shoulder. The Circle Cliff "outlaws" arrived early, Bradshaw and Becker and Billy - all brandishing high powered rifles and openly talking of using them. Tom and Rob, Cody's friends were there sporting the new Mad Max bumper they built for the occasion, but Cody Bullock, was noticeable because of his absence.

Westley worked the crowd, telling everyone, "We didn't start this and no matter what happens we can't be seen starting a shooting war. They

240

have to start it. We'll give 'em a fight all right but unless they start shooting, we'll have to take 'em on hand to hand."

The assemblage burned on the inside with a deep patriotic love and they burned on the outside with an all-consuming hatred of environmentalists. They were a determined lot, most had broken their backs on the rocks of hard work and knew how to hunker down and get a job done.

At ten-thirty Tom Westley climbed behind the wheel of his truck and started east down Main Street, a hundred vehicles behind him. Heading east out of town, hundreds of townsfolk lined the sidewalks, cheering and waving American Flags. "Go get 'em," they hollered, and "God Bless America!" The time had come to protect their threatened way of life and to take a stand for traditional culture. Westley's eyes filled with tears when he saw the well wishers. Pride filled every heart. He laid on his diesel air horn and everyone in the procession hung out the windows shouting, waving and honking.

At Canonville, the column turned left off Highway 12 and onto the wild and dangerous Cottonwood Canyon Road, a sixty-mile dirt double track, famous for its remoteness and remarkable scenery. For three generations the road was largely unknown except for a few ranchers grazing cows until the 1980s when a new breed of backcountry travelers discovered its magic.

The column moved slowly south towards The Gut, a wild section where the road descends a long steep grade. On one side was the Cockscomb, a monumental break in the earth's crust creating a double row of blue and red oxide colored upthrusts, resembling sharks' teeth and appearing as if ready to rip an angry hole in the sky. On the other side were the badlands, an impenetrable and confused plateau that looked like a giant gray tidal wave, frothing and crashing and colliding but frozen in stone.

The Cottonwood was rutted and populated with washboard sections that went for miles. As Westley and his column worked slowly south, a cloud of dusty haze floated high above and could be seen for miles around. After they passed Kodachrome Basin State Park and Grosvenor Arch about sixteen miles in, they would have to cross the deep and narrow Tyler Wash before reaching their destination, Four Mile Bench. Once on the other side of Tyler Wash and just before The Gut, they would cut a new road east across the barren Four Mile Bench to Paradise Valley. The area was a desolate, hot and inhospitable territory of sagebrush flats, rolling cedar hills and endless secret canyons. Paradise Valley sat at the center of

241

the largest roadless section in the entire 1.3 million acre Grand Staircase Monument. They planned to cut a road into the heart of this empty godforsaken nothingness and, in doing so, inflict the greatest damage to the despised monument.

At the top of Tyler Wash, Westley stopped and got out. He wanted to take a look at the road before starting down. He was worried it might collapse under the weight of his truck and bulldozer. The steep, downhill grade cut across a sandy hillside, strewn with boulders. Over the eons, rare storms gouged out the deep and narrow wash through a plateau of soft and unstable soil. Tyler Wash was famous for sloughing off sections of hillside and taking out the road with it.

Andy Anderson joined him at the edge of the wash to take a look while the phalanx of trucks idled behind them. The road looked like it would hold but from their vantage point, they spotted vehicles blocking the narrowest section of the wash, at the place where the road crossed the empty drainage between two towering sandstone walls. They couldn't get a good look because the cottonwood and tamarisk trees blocked the view.

Westley, Anderson and a few of the outlaws walked down the road to have a look see.

"Here we go," Westley muttered.

"I don't like the looks of it, " Anderson warned, scanning the rocks above. "It's a trap. . . I can tell." They moved cautiously down the hill then along the narrow, arcing road to the bottleneck where the eroded canyon walls climb two hundred feet above on either side. Giant boulders stood on edges, tilting at impossible angles.

"We don't want to get caught down here," Westley said.

From five-hundred-feet away, they could plainly see two rows of vehicles wedged tightly into the bottleneck.

"It's a roadblock all right!" Anderson announced.

"Where are the chicken shits?" an outlaw asked. "They afraid to come out and fight?"

"Don't underestimate them," Westley cautioned. "Never underestimate your enemy."

"I've seen enough," Anderson added, backing up. "We better get back."

Westley eyeballed the situation a minute longer. "Okay," he finally said, half-laughing. "Okay. Better get back. Doesn't look so bad. This is going to be fun."

Word of the roadblock traveled back from one truck to the next. At Westley's bulldozer, the men stood in a circle and talked nervously about their next move.

"Well," Westley finally told them, "it's time to fish, not cut bait. It's gotta be done. "

"Let's roll!" Anderson declared.

"Pull out the runners," Westley pointed to the trailer, and he unhitched the chains securing the bulldozer. Climbing aboard, he started the earth mover and it rumbled to life. The engine raced and the sound was unnerving. Backing it down, the giant machine screeched and belched and clanged; the ground quaked and surrendered under its weight.

"No piss ants are stopping us!" Westley shouted over the engine. He flashed a big smile and raised a thumbs-up.

"I'm ridin' shotgun," Anderson hollered and climbed aboard, holding his assault rifle over his head defiantly. Becker and Bobby, the outlaws, climbed aboard, too. A crowd stood at the edge and watched the bulldozer descend into the wash. "Stay put and watch for trouble," Westley shouted to the men. He tipped his cowboy hat gallantly and everyone shouted approval.

The bulldozer rumbled down the hill without incident. Once in the wash bottom, it slowly rounded the slight arc and was a few hundred feet from the roadblock when suddenly Westley thought he saw something moving behind the trucks, "See that," he shouted to Anderson, pointing. "There! Behind the trucks. I saw something."

"What?" Anderson yelled back, unable to hear.

"There!" Westley shouted again, this time seeing something move behind a broken down cottonwood tree at the edge of the wash just a few feet away.

"Over there!" Anderson shouted, "Two men! There!" He pointed across the road to his right. "See 'em?"

Suddenly, from behind trees and rocks and from down in the wash, nearly two hundred EarthIslanders popped up and formed two skirmish lines, one in front of the other, and two hundred feet long. They moved toward the bulldozer in a disciplined military way. They wielded clubs and baseball bats and wore a type of urban civil disobedience uniform including hard hats, goggles, football and hockey pads, heavy steel-toed boots, and thick elbow, arm and knee pads. Some even wore high-tech, army flack jackets. In unison, they pounded their shields and shouted obscenities. From behind rocks on the hillside above, more appeared throwing rocks and firing ball bearings from sling shots.

Westley, Anderson and the outlaws were bombarded and took a beating as the projectiles rained down on them. The bulldozer continued forward and its occupants hunkered down, except for Anderson who stood his ground against the barrage, rifle raised to his shoulder as if ready to fire. He targeted one EarthIsland fighter after another, attempting to intimidate them but they kept coming. They were determined, if necessary, to die for this cause. Anderson held his fire, knowing his gun was useless unless someone fired on him first.

From the left McVey and his men emerged from behind a small hill and encircled the bulldozer. Anderson was knocked to his knees by a fist-sized boulder thrown by McVey, striking him at the temple. He stutter-stepped back and forth, blood gushing from his head, before dropping to his knees. Three fighters carrying a long metal bar jammed it into the bulldozer's track, hoping to disable the behemoth. Instead, the bar was ripped from their hands as it ground into the gears then came back around swatting two of them in the head.

Despite the terrible beating, the outlaws repelled the enviro-patriots' attempts to climb aboard. Finally, McVey was successful and rushed at Becker, who saw him coming and pulled his six-shooter from his holster and was about to fire when Anderson, still reeling from his head wound, lunged forward and knocked the gun away. McVey tackled Becker and the two adversaries tumbled backwards off the bulldozer and onto the ground.

The cowboys waiting above at the trucks ran down the hill to the rescue. They carried ax handles, tire irons, chains and picked up rocks and deadwood they found along the way - anything they could use as a weapon. They ran wild and headlong into the riot line of EarthIslanders, crashing into the lines' middle and nearly collapsing it. The environmentalists took the brunt and held their ground, even moving forward a few feet until the next wave of cowboys smashed in. The cowboys threw themselves into the line like human cannonballs, attempting to break through at all cost and paying dearly for it. Wave after wave of cowboys and enviros streamed down the opposite sides of the wash, all running full tilt smack into the fight. Men were down everywhere as the battle doubled and redoubled in size.

The skirmish line between the two groups of patriots moved forward and backward across an invisible line in the sand. The better prepared and protected enviros took everything thrown at them, keeping their shields high, their protective equipment saving them again and again. Man for man, the cowboys were stronger and crazier, willing to take the horrendous punishment meted out and come back for more. It was as if they wanted to take shots in some macho show of how much they could take. The enviros responded with viciousness, but were surprised and frightened by their adversaries' courage and recklessness. While perhaps less strong, the enviros were equally game and more experienced fighters. They benefited from working as a unit and many had fought pitched battles against trained riot police in the streets of Seattle and Genoa and Washington. They used shields and clubs expertly. Like a rowing or sculling captain, one man shouted, "Step, hit, stand!" Round and round they went, swinging their clubs in near unison, lunging out with one foot to gain maximum force, hitting their mark squarely, then standing back a half step and bringing their shields high. "Step, hit, stand!" - round and round they went, delivering blows and then taking them on the helmet, shield or thick pads.

The battle raged and at its height more than 400 men were involved. It was nearly a standoff until cowboys mounted on horses charged down the hill and broke easily through the EarthIsland battle line. As the line collapsed chaos broke out, it was man to man, hand to hand. Some enviros formed circles of six to eight fighters in each, backs to the center. This tactic worked until the horsemen began riding back and forth through the circles effortlessly, knocking down and trampling their opponents. The enviros retaliated with long arcing streams of pepper spray into the horsemen's faces. They ripped the blinded riders from the saddle and beat them mercilessly. Frightened and out of control, the horses made the scene even more chaotic and dangerous. Men on both sides were trampled, yet the ranks weren't deterred and kept hammering away.

As the battle slogged on, Westley rolled forward, hunkering down, bleeding, taking hits from rocks and long stout bamboo poles swung from the ground. Sheriff Anderson huddled next to him holding his head as Billy defended against anyone climbing aboard. If they could just hold out, they would break the roadblock. Medics from EarthIsland, wearing red cross helmets and tee shirts, carried the injured out on stretchers, while the cowboys hoisted their injured over their shoulders and carried them up the hill and away from the battle.

Westley finally reached the blockade, lowering his blade and crashing into the first truck, one of two large old water trucks. As the water truck crumbled inward, pushing into the vehicles behind it, his bulldozer lugged down and struggled forward, its tracks digging into the soft gravel for traction. Westley was surprised, instead of easily pushing through the roadblock, the obstacle held together. The designers of the blockade had anticipated this, and all the vehicles were all chained together, frame to frame, using heavy marine anchor chain. Putting it into reverse, Westley backed up and came at the blockade again from another direction, hoping to find a weak spot and hasten its collapse, but again it held firm. Finding better traction on the tabletop, he pressed forward, his powerful earth-mover literally pushing all ten trucks further and further into the bottleneck, wedging them tighter and tighter between the narrow canyon walls. Putting his blade squarely between the two water trucks, he hoped to rip the chain apart. At the point his bulldozer could go no further, the chain finally burst apart and he surged forward.

"Alright!" he screamed.

He had done it. He jammed the caterpillar into reverse and pulled the truck wrapped about his blade backward, and as he did the entire line began pulling apart. He pushed forward again, this time driving over the top of a small truck, crushing it flat.

"You've done it!" Anderson shouted.

"We showed the mutherfuckers!" Westley hollered.

At the moment the roadblock gave way, the fighters on both sides stopped fighting. For an instant, everyone stood and watched. The cowboys cheered and the enviros groaned, their disappointment palpable.

As both sides started fighting again, an air-raid siren sounded from above on the south side of the wash. Immediately, the EarthIsland fighters systematically retreated, falling back to the road leading up the steep south side of the wash. They rushed up the hill. The cowboys were confused and elated. They won! The chicken-shit radical environmentalists couldn't take the heat. Some pursued the enviros, but soon broke off their pursuit, satisfied to let the cowards escape. They felt a deep sense of vindication, it was a fair fight and they had proven their superiority. They cheered each other and Thomas Westley, who continued working; pushing the destroyed trucks back and forth like an Israeli army tank crushing Palestinian cars.

When Jonah, standing atop the south side of the wash, could see the last EarthIsland fighter was safely out of harm's way, he picked up a bull-horn and pointed it down into the gulch.

"Fire in the hole!" he announced. "Get out now! This is your only warning! Fire in the hole. Leave now or suffer the consequences!"

The cowboys stopped celebrating, looked at each other with a mixture of confusion and fear. They searched the cliff line above but did not move, as if so surprised to be paralyzed.

"Fire in the Hole!" Jonah said one more time and added, "This one's for you, Ian!"

High on the north side of the ravine in a section of enormous tilting rock slabs came a deafening explosion. The ground shook and the concussion knocked some off their feet. The canyon quaked, rumbled and trembled. A cloud of white smoke appeared at the base of a house-sized slab near the top of a high ledge. The ground groaned, rumbled, made cracking sounds and shook. The giant boulder rocked back and forth slightly for what seemed a long time before a small patch of ground beneath it gave way and it started down.

The five-hundred-ton slab picked up speed as it plummeted down, rolling end over end into the narrows. The cowboys bolted for cover, some running one way, others going the opposite direction, some diving into the dry wash bed for cover. Westley, Anderson and Billy jumped from atop the still moving bulldozer and ran for their lives. Halfway down the hill, the boulder smashed into a rock ridge and broke into three spectacular pieces. The ground shuddered again, this time much more deeply causing a great shelf of the sandy ridge to give way and come crashing down into the wash. The sound was thunderous and a dust cloud rolled and billowed outward, engulfing everyone in its path.

One of the enormous pieces of the boulder landed in the flats, digging an eight foot hole before careening toward a group of cowboys. They dove away, some under a ledge in the wash, hoping the boulder would jump over them, others climbing the north side of the gully. The second piece came straight down into the gulch, rolling end-over-end, creating deep divots where it landed and rolling up the other side of the wash before stopping and rolling back down into the gulch. The largest chunk of rock, the size of a cabin, ramped up a small ridge and was catapulted high into the air. It crashed down directly atop Westley's still moving bulldozer, crushing it.

At the same time, a one hundred foot high and two hundred foot long shelf came roaring down, piling debris thirty feet high in the bottleneck and completely burying what was left of the bulldozer and the giant boulder that killed it. After a few minutes, the smoke and dust began to clear and the cowboys, struggling to breathe, covering their mouths and noses with bandanas and shirts, could see the results. Through the deadly-thick dust cloud, Westley walked to the place where his bulldozer was buried. He held his fists in the air and shouted, "You'll pay for this!"

Men on each side of the wash suffered serious injuries but luckily no one was killed. Above the wash on the south ridge, Jonah and the medics met the confrontation force fighters as they topped the hill and emerged out of the dust. He counted each man, making sure no one was missing. His trap worked as planned and while he didn't want to use the dynamite it was imperative to hold the Sagebrushers back. Jonah received word the day before from one of his many contacts that Westley intended to cut a second road out onto Four Mile Bench and Jonah didn't waste a minute devising a defensive plan, and moving his men into place.

He expected the cowboys to put up a strong fight but no one expected the "do or die" intensity they showed. While his men performed admirably, he watched from above as the cowboys threw themselves into the battle with a unanticipated ferocity. He feared they just might be crazy enough to mount a counterattack - now! His adversaries would not be intimidated nor would they be turned back. He had no idea how it would end and it scared him. It was easy to see the consequences of the battle as his fighters crested the hill. Many were injured and bleeding, all were exhausted and some could barely walk. "Good job," he told them, "I'm proud of you."

There was still plenty of fight in them and the battle seemed to ignite a deeper burning commitment. "We fucked 'em up good!" one announced.

"Those pee-brained mutherfuckers don't know when to quit!" another proclaimed.

The medics rushed about attending to the injured as Jonah directed every able-bodied man to stand at the ridge line, hoping to give the enemy the impression that hundreds more fighters were waiting. Wounded fighters lay everywhere, on the tabletop sandstone, in truck beds, on the ground, in the sand. Many were too tired or beaten to seek medical help. The two men struck by the metal bar jammed into the bulldozer's track were in the most serious condition. Their skulls had taken a hit and a medic packed their heads in sacks of ice and sat with them, constantly checking their vital signs. Later, they were loaded into the bed of a truck and with a few others were evacuated down The Gut, destined for Highway 89 and Page, Arizona, more than seventy miles away.

On the opposite ridge, the Sagebrushers regrouped. They were no better off than their enemy, in fact, they were worse. Their heroic recklessness resulted in many serious injuries. Those who could refused medical help, denying they were injured badly enough to deserve it. One man took an ax handle to the head and was unconscious; another was thrown from his horse and had severely broken his leg when it tangled in the stirrup; Becker, who nearly shot McVey, suffered a deep stab wound to the chest, dangerously near his heart. A local veterinarian from Panguitch desperately tried to keep him alive, giving him transfusions of blood donated on the spot. Anderson had a large gash on his temple and was helped back to the trucks where he laid on a horse blanket. He was delirious one moment, lucid and sharp the next, then talking rubbish and muttering to himself.

Thomas Westley sat on his bulldozer's trailer, bruised and bleeding. He suffered broken ribs and more broken bones in his left hand. He wrapped his hand with an old oily rag, then went to be with his men. He was proud of each of them and told them so. Strangely, although he would never say it, Westley begrudgingly admired the environmentalists. He figured the pot-smoking, just-do-it urbanites would break and run like a bunch of spoiled children at the first sign of a real fight, but he was wrong.

Billy found Sheriff Anderson sitting on the blanket and confronted him. "If Becker dies," he pointed, "I'm blaming you! You stopped him from defending himself and now he's going to die."

Anderson's head pulsed with pain, "I'm sorry," he repeated.

"Sorry ain't good enough, Sheriff. Becker's laying over there dying." He pointed in the direction.

"If Becker had plugged that guy plenty of us would be dead right now!" Anderson argued.

"That's what we're here for, ain't it?"

"You think we're the only ones with guns?"

"That don't cut no ice with me," Billy screamed, "I'm here to kill the mutherfuckers!" He lunged forward as if to hit the sheriff, "I want 'em dead - every last one of 'em!"

Westley heard the commotion and came running. "The Sheriff's right, Billy," he said. "We did the honorable thing." He placed his hand on Billy's shoulder in an attempt to calm him, "We kicked their asses, man to man."

"What about the dynamite?" Billy stammered, "You call that a fair fight? We could'a been killed!"

"It's not over!"

Westley spoke to the men standing around. "We'll make 'em pay but we need to keep our heads and do it our way. We'll make them pay all right." He looked around, "I guarantee it."

"I'll tell you what I'm going to do," Billy shouted, "I'm killing myself a few of them." With that he turned and stomped off.

The outlaws huddled at the ridge line, watching the radicals across the gully with spotting scopes attached to high powered rifles and talking of vengeance. If the sheriff and Westley didn't have the balls for a real fight they did. No one was going to kill one of them and get away with it. They drank whiskey straight and joked it was for medicinal purposes. If the chicken-shit radicals hadn't blown the gully out, we'd have them on the run, they told each other.

Anderson sat alone, lost in delusions. He replayed the battle over and over again in his mind. But it was not the battle that just occurred but a battle that happened fifty years earlier and a half world away. He was a young soldier in Korea and the Chinese overran his company's position and many men died. Afterwards, he helped carry the frozen bodies of his fallen brothers to awaiting trucks and piled the bodies of the Chinese atop each other and doused them with kerosene and torched them. He was eighteen-years-old and straight from his family's dairy farm.

By five o'clock the will to take up the battle hadn't returned as both sides licked their wounds and settled in. They nervously watched their enemy across the one-thousand-foot chasm in a deadly face off. Things were quiet but tense, each side worried about what would happen next. Both Jonah and Westley wanted a way out. They brought this on them-selves but now that it was happening, the stakes seemed too high. They used satellite phones to call for reinforcements, but the air waves were mysteriously jammed. Shon told Jonah he had never seen anything like it. "Someone's doing it intentionally," he told him. "Someone wants us to fight it out!" Jonah remembered what von Bank and his visitors had warned him, no one would be there to intervene. Tomorrow at dawn, if not sooner, the battle would turn deadly. Guards were posted in both camps and they gathered wood for bonfires to protect them against the coming night. Each was worried, not knowing what, if anything, the enemy had planned for the darkness.

Sunset filled the western desert sky with a cauldron of fiery red light before the quiet dusk sent shadows into the wash and filled it up with darkness. Sweet sage-scented winds slowed time and created the magical otherworldly atmosphere famous on the sandstone landscape.

In off moments, Jonah tried to come up with another workable scenario for dealing with the situation and each time he came back to the same conclusion. He had made the right decision. They were at the right place at the right time. Destiny brought them to this spiritual homeland to stop its destruction and destiny would be played out. He knew he was going to die and many others would perish with him. The tragic thing was nothing would change and the only result would be more destruction and more violence.

After nightfall, he paced back and forth from one end of his defensive line to the other, looking out into the darkness and wondering what the rednecks were up to. Would they be foolish enough to attack at night? It was their country, he thought, they knew every trail, every draw, every hill and every flat. He called for McVey.

"Take a few men and do a recon," Jonah instructed him. "We can't afford to be caught with our pants down."

McVey relished the idea. "Good, man. I agree." Both McVey's hands were bandaged heavily in white gauze. Blood soaked to the surface creating large red circles.

"What happened? You okay?" Jonah asked.

"Slipped on my knife"

"With both hands?"

"No problem, man. Look," he said, moved his fingers painfully. "I'm mobile." "You're going to have to do something about those white bandages." Jonah picked up a handful of dirt. "This will cover them up so no one can see them."

"Right," McVey answered, washing his hands with the dirt as Jonah poured it over them.

They had been adversaries for years but it was clear, they were on the same side. "We'll use the night vision goggles," McVey added.

"Get fitted with communications, too."

"Right."

"And make sure you're armed," Jonah said, looking directly into McVey's eyes.

"Right. Of course. I couldn't agree more."

After the quarter moon dropped behind the White Cliffs to the west, McVey and four of his best men slipped off the ridge. They wore Special

Forces night camouflage, faces were smeared in grease paint. Only an odd selection of head-gear, earrings and facial piercing might alert an enemy.

Across the ravine, a handful of outlaws moved west out of camp along the ridge line. They worked around a bend and a half mile further, climbed down into the wash and then came back toward the battle site. Westley knew he had been outmaneuvered, and walked right into their trap. It wasn't going to happen again. He sent the men to probe the enemy's defensive lines and to check to see if they were preparing an attack. The men stripped naked to the waist and smeared grease on their faces and torsos. They carried rifles and handguns and wore night vision goggles.

Somewhere in the darkness below, the two groups of warriors found one another and shots rang out. On the ridge line above, men from both sides rushed to peer down into the blackness. One shot after another cracked the silence until someone opened up with an automatic rifle, rattling off fifty rounds in one burst. The sound was deafening and its implication terrifying. Everyone grabbed a gun, expecting the enemy to appear at any moment. The firefight continued sporadically, an occasional tracer shot lighting the wash, before the shooting fell off and was silent.

When McVey and his men returned, they carried one wounded man. "Don't shoot," he whispered, coming out of the darkness. "It's us! We're alone!" They helped the injured man to the ground where medics took over. "He'll live. It's not bad," McVey told them.

"We thought you were dead!" Jonah cried out, his voice nearly breaking, "What happened?"

"Don't know," McVey said, shaking his head, "It was close! All I knew was all hell broke loose."

"They fired on you?"

"Yeah. Away from me, down in the gully."

"They take the first shot?" Jonah demanded.

"Yeah," McVey answered, nonchalantly.

"Good. Good," Jonah said, searching the night. "Kill anyone?"

"Don't know. I think we got one of 'em."

Across the wash at the cowboys' camp, the outlaws stumbled back up the road, one carrying a wounded man over his shoulder.

"He needs a doctor," they told Westley, who was waiting. "It's not bad, a flesh wound."

"Right. What happened?" Westley asked.

"We ran right into them," another said.

"Who started it?" Sheriff Anderson asked.

"They fired first."

"Get any of 'em?" Westley asked.

"Yeah, one. I think."

"They follow you back here?"

"No. No one followed us."

The first shots of the first full scale battle of the redrock land war had been fired.

The doorway to a bloody full scale battle was wide open. Both groups of patriots now had justification for shooting first and asking questions later.

Hours later at midnight, a deadly calm had taken control. Except for the sentries, most fighters slept, exhausted and unable to stay awake. Jonah walked from one sentry post to the next, making sure his men were awake and keeping an eye on the canyon and camp across from them. On the other side, Thomas Westley paced the ridge line too, wondering what the radicals were planning and how his men could take Tyler Wash. No matter what he decided, he knew people would lose their lives. He waited and had talked about this day for years - "The day we stand up and take our land back. If men have to die, so be it. It's a just and worthy cause."

CHAPTER THIRTY-ONE

With her back to the open door, Lessel Opel's long auburn hair was tangled and disheveled. She stood with legs apart and hands on her hips. She had spotted Garrett coming down the long hallway to her office and was waiting for him.

"Glad to see you're still here!" Garrett said tensely, at the door and without pausing moved behind her, wrapping his hands around her waist. She was stiff. Turning her by the hips to face him, he tried to kiss her but her firm breasts were cold against his chest.

"What does that mean?" she asked, pulling back. "How dare you?"

"What?"

"Glad you're still here! What kind of comment is that?"

"Finals? Remember, ten days ago you were spending all your time here."

" So?" she snapped and turned to face her desk, leaving him standing close behind her.

"And since you haven't seen fit to return my calls," he continued, "I assumed you were so busy you couldn't . . ."

"I know what you came for," she interrupted. "It's here somewhere. Let me see, where is it?" She went through piles of papers on her desk, then a stack of files laying on a coffee table. "I hope I haven't lost it."

"That makes two of us," he muttered, unable to keep his true agitation and fear hidden any longer. "Why didn't you return my calls? I left messages . . . I was worried . . . This is important. . . " he raised his eyebrows ". . . A matter of life and death . . . the best story I've ever had . . . You wouldn't believe what is . . . "

"Why should I care?" she asked frankly. "I got what I wanted and you got what you wanted." Her voice was warmer but still distant. "Oh yeah, here it is," she turned to face him. "For you."

He stood tall and shook his head, "I don't get it."

"That's the problem." She pointed an index finger close to his face.

"You never have and you never will." Her fingernails looked wet and shiny and blood red; suddenly, he thought of Ushi Binder. Lessel reached for a half burned Samson cigarette sitting in the ashtray, lit it and took a long drag, "I knew you'd be back for this." She said exhaling and handing him the report in the same yellow manilla envelope.

"Thank you, thank you, thank you." he said bowing formally from the waist. "I don't know what's wrong . . . I thought we were okay."

"Okay?" she questioned, sarcastically. "Yes. Okay."

"What's going on?"

"Business as usual," she shot back. "You needed to get laid and you needed to have your precious oil reserve exploration paper translated and you wanted them both right now - but hey, this time you had to wait for one. What's the problem? You come and you go. You want me to open my arms anytime you decide to just drop in. I told you I would do the translation and here it is."

Garrett looked at Lessel for a long time.

"Aren't you even going to look at it?" she asked, uncomfortable. "Life and death remember? Interesting stuff, I must say, if you like reading about oil."

"Oil?" It finally penetrated.

"The discovery of oil."

"Oil?" he repeated. "You mean coal?"

"If I meant coal, I would have said coal." She crossed her arms, leaned back, looked past him and exhaled. "The subject of the report is the discovery of a sizable oil reserve, technical data mostly, but from what I gather, it's a significant discovery, estimated at perhaps between two and five billion barrels under the Kaiparowits."

"There's no oil under Kaiparowits!" he exclaimed. "There's high quality coal but no oil!"

"Interesting," she pointed to the report, "that's not what this says."

"No," he smiled, bemused. "I don't believe it!" His eyes darted back and forth. "Let me see it, show me."

She laid the report on her desk and thumbed through it. He leaned over, straight arms, next to her.

"See," she pointed, "check it out."

Lessel recognized the document's importance and possible implications within fifteen minutes of starting the translation. She decided not to return his calls knowing he would lie to her about its significance and request she fax it to him. She knew if she did that she would never see him again. For the first time she possessed something he truly wanted and she knew he would be back for it - and soon. It all excited her immensely. She had long admired Garrett for his dogged pursuit of corporate and governmental wrongdoing. He was a fighter and she admired men who stood up for what they believed. He spent years ferreting out scum-bags and sticking it to them until suddenly something inexplicable happened and he was changed. He had always been a brooder but she could sense some growing defeat and insidious sadness a year before his break. The man she fell in love with was courageous to a fault, always moving forward, always taking risks. She hoped the real Garrett was back, and if he was, she wouldn't let him or the excitement of this investigation get away from her. She had never seen him so jumpy.

"Important?" she demurred, "Yes?"

"This could be it . . ." he muttered. "This could be the answer . . . Yes, yes!" He sat in her chair and poured over the document. As its significance sunk in, his excitement and even utter joy over the discovery were simultaneously overshadowed by the weight of its implications. He paced back and forth as Lessel stood next to the wall, arms folded, intently watching. He sat down like a defeated chess champion, analyzing his missteps and missed opportunities. "I should have figured it out sooner," he said to himself, shaking his head.

"Oil on Kaiparowits!" he finally announced, looking up. "If it's true and this information can be corroborated, it explains a lot. It's going to mean big trouble in the West. If it's true, this scam is shrewd beyond belief. The dirty, greedy bastards. This explains everything!"

"What?"

More to himself than Lessel, "No wonder they wanted us dead."

"Someone wants you dead?"

"I can just see it!" he said looking past her. "All the pieces are coming together." Turning to her, "It's a conspiracy. A most ambitious and evil conspiracy! It probably goes all the way to the top. It has to."

Now Garrett was acting like the man she remembered.

"Oil! Billions of dollars locked away forever in the national monument! Think about it! What better way to get at it than pitting two groups of extremists at each other's throats? Brilliant! While the fanatics go at it, they use it as a diversion - a reason for closing down the monument." He laughed sardonically, "Alright! I wish I had come up with it."

"I realized its importance," Lessel admitted nervously, unable to play stupid any longer and wanting to share in the discovery.

"You did?" he exclaimed. "Why didn't you call?"

"Someone wants you dead?"

"I don't know exactly who they are, but now I know why."

"To stop your investigation?"

"Ateen could be dead now!" Garrett jumped up, a realization swept over him. "Have you shown this to anyone?"

"Ateen?"

"You haven't told anyone?"

"Of course not."

"Jesus! At least three people are dead because of this!" He held the report up, "It may not look like it, but this is a bona fide smoking gun." He turned to her, "You're positive no one has . . ."

"I told you, no one!"

"Good. Good!" He looked around nervously, "We need to get out of here. We need to get this to the right people - now!"

With Lessel protesting and demanding to know more, they drove to Ricco's restaurant where he told her everything. She was excited by the whole unbelievable tale and felt her blood pounding. Every molecule of her existence was alive. The only time she ever felt this way since coming to America was having sex. In her homeland, she was raised with the fear of the Stazi, the hated East German Secret Police, and of political intrigue and unexplained disappearances of beloved professors and writers and even average citizens who spoke out, then disappeared. In America with its wall-to-wall phony idealism, she suffocated.

"As far as I know no one followed me, but we can't be sure," he told her, looking around. "We can't underestimate these people, they are professionals with resources and connections. They would definitely kill us for this report."

Later, from a pay phone, Garrett called David Horowitz, a one-time investigative journalist and now national news editor of the New York Times. Horowitz and Garrett covered the Contra Rebel war in Nicaragua in 1983 and survived a desperate week together alone in the jungle hunted by the Contras after traveling by boat to a rebel encampment to interview a resistance leader when the government attacked. They barely escaped into the jungle and for four days were lost until, exhausted and terrified, they stumbled onto a road and were picked up by a farmer on his way to market.

By midnight, Opel and Garrett and the geological report were aboard a late flight to New York City. Lessel leaned into him, laying her head on his shoulder. She was no longer the cold, raging Aryan intellectual and he was no longer the defeated and lost man she once admired.

When Ateen finally made it to the Bonanza Cafe the place was deserted; Nez, Natani, Tahonnie, Sekiqua and the rest were gone. The waitresses and kitchen help sat disheartened at the counter. Nez's wife, Lena, an influential matriarch who managed the cafe, gave him a message, "Pow wow at Endeshi!"

"What is it?"

Lena pointed to a newspaper laying open on the counter. The headline read: Land War Inevitable as Radicals and Extremists Converge. President backs plan for Temporary Closure of Grand Staircase National Monument.

Ateen arrived at Endeshi at dusk and was amazed to find nearly a thousand braves there ahead of him. They were dancing and chanting and milling around. He was struck that only half of the warriors were Dineh, the rest were Hopis, Paiutes, Utes and a contingent of two hundred braves from the American Indian Movement including Sioux, Shoshone and Nez Perce. Some wore traditional dress and war paint. The magic created when history is in the making enveloped the night and Ateen's heart pounded. Dust devils, brought by the spirits of the ancestors, danced with the braves. He had never seen or heard or felt anything like it. A long dormant spiritual power of the American natives was awakened as they chanted and danced.

Despite their territorial disputes, created in large part by the federal government, they were all brothers and shared equally in the stewardship of the land since the beginning of the Fourth World. The Place of Emergence belonged to each and all of them - and even to the foolish Anglo if they could only wake up and understand its importance. It was the secretive Hopi traditionalists including Alan Sekiqua who watched over the Place of Emergence for eight hundred years. The Hopi were the spiritual guides and authorities. They fostered the Plan and kept its many stories alive and powerful.

The warriors mixed and danced and sang and prepared for battle. They fasted and prayed and some inflicted pain on themselves by piercing their chest with sharpened eagle talons, letting the blood run down their chests. Hundreds raced onto the mountain at dusk, testing their courage against the night, dazzling the gods with their daring. They ran into the darkening dusk as far as possible before sprinting back through the oncoming night. They feasted on mutton and beef and turkeys roasting over open fires, and partook in ceremonial fry bread, then purified themselves in sweat lodges.

Above the gathering, on a high sandstone shelf, the most powerful elders and medicine men from each tribe held council. The bluff overlooked a million square miles of jumbled sandstone canyons and buttes and ridges and rounded domes lifting their heads upward as if to ask the heavens for answers. To the west, the citadel of the Kaiparowits loomed twenty miles away, the mighty fortress's high walls reflecting the last light while its feet were submerged in blue dusk. Behind the leaders, Navajo Mountain's ever-receeding pinnacles and ridges rose into the sky and melted into the heavens.

Each leader spoke his mind and they all listened. They could not let Kaiparowits be endangered or lose its protected monument status. Alan Sakiqua told them that for hundreds of years only the purest elders visited the remote escarpment. Taiwa, the Godhead, he told them had located The Place of Emergence at the end of the world and surrounded it by towers and ramparts and barriers and a vast entanglement of cliffs and canyons and embankments. The Hopi spiritual leaders made pilgrimages twice a year, in spring and fall, and had done so since leaving Chaco Canyon for the Three Mesas eight hundred years ago.

Over the last one hundred years, the big pieces of the American West were cut up into ever smaller sections until only the dry and inhospitable redrock country remained untouched - but that was not to last long. For many generations, the spiritual leaders listened to Anglos' endless talk of commerce. They talked and talked and talked about developing the coal reserves on Kaiparowits liked they talked about developing everything else; but there were always better coal fields and closer markets and less expensive ventures; plus the difficulty in removing and transporting the coal made Kaiparowits an unattractive proposition. It wasn't until the 1980s and 1990s, before the monument's designation, when the European conglomerate Anaxalrad started nosing around and spending millions exploring and test drilling and making preparations to move forward with a huge coal mine, that they really became worried.

At the time, they even considered divulging the truth about the Place of Emergence to the rest of the tribes and even the American public, in essence, to publicize it in an effort to save it. But Natani convinced them it was not a good idea, "This would not guarantee its safety or stop the coal mine. It will only create a giant anthill of Anglo fanning out over the land and combing every canyon until they found it. We must not forget the Anglo scavenge better than any other people. They would quickly find the holy site and - true to their souless nature - steal everything."

They discussed fighting for it and drew up plans for its defense. Located on one of three prongs or fingers of the mighty Kaiparowits, the escarpment was surrounded on three sides by two thousand foot cliffs and situated where no road could encroach. Fortunately, in 1996, they got wind that the President of the United States was considering creating The Grand Staircase, a three million acre national monument, with Kaiparowits at its center. Their prayers were answered and the Place of Emergence was saved. The Gods made it so, and the Place of Emergence would remain hidden until Taiwa swept away the Fourth World to construct the Fifth World - a place where only the most righteous, humble and worthy peoples would reside.

But now, seemingly, everything was changed. Two militant extremist groups of American patriots, the Sagebrushers and the environmentalists, were poised to fight it out over the future of the land and because of it, the sneaky politicians were now talking of decommissioning the monument. If that were to happen, the secrecy and safety of the Place of Emergence would again be in jeopardy.

When Ateen arrived, he was surrounded and taken to the elders' council. They sat Indian style, cross-legged on beautiful Navajo rugs and listened to his report. Standing at the center of the ring, he told them of the downing of the helicopter and how he was saved. "The Gods sent out the warriors to save me," he told them and theatrically recounted how the entire incident played out, finishing up with the braves bringing down the helicopter and it bursting into flames and plummeting into a hidden side canyon. "The Gods came to my assistance and now I know the Gods have been leading me and helping me and giving me clues."

The elders rocked back and forth smiling, some even laughing out loud. He told them about his investigation into the crimes in the monument and in the surrounding Anglo communities. He told them about Las Vegas Air Tours. "The men behind these crimes have no souls. They are mercenaries, killers who work for government and corporations. They work to destabilize weak governments so their rich and greedy bosses can steal their resources."

Pointing to the mountain behind him, he told them what happened on the night the apparition came to him. "The apparition led me higher and higher to a place where I could see the Kaiparowits clearly below me, then it pulled the ground out from underneath me and I fell into a pool of oil. It was a message - a clue - but I failed to see it."

He turned in a circle looking at each elder. "Later, near the Place of Emergence I discovered another pool of the crude oil. Again, it was a clue yet I still did not see or understand it." He spoke with authority, "It is my belief that the Gods were telling me that there is oil under the Kaiparowits. The oil men and politicians know this. They are creating a land war as a smokescreen, a diversion so they can steal it. We cannot underestimate them." He paused, "If we do not stop them they will destroy us."

The elders listened impassively, as if they already knew the truth of his words. Natani, the true leader of the Dineh, stood and walked slowly around the circle before speaking in the staccato of the high Dineh elders.

"One hundred and forty years ago, Kit Carson and his army swept through here," he made a large sweeping gesture with his arm, "killing and imprisoning all our peoples. It was a cruel treatment, punishment for crimes we did not commit. We were open and welcoming as the Creator taught us, but our people were wiped out and no one has ever stood responsible for these crimes. Many were forced onto small reservations, our cultures destroyed by Christianity, our lands pilfered and ruined and expropriated by the federal government; our people's hearts and minds poisoned with liquor, drugs and ideas of material goods - all from the Anglo.

"We now see a new and evil encroachment by the white man. They will stop at nothing to get this oil! If we do not stop them, they will destroy us and take our destiny away. We have lost so much already but the most important possessions, our families, our tribes, our religion and our sacred places have remained safe - until now.

"We are proud and peace loving peoples. We leave others alone because we want to be left alone to live and celebrate life our own way. The Creator gave us this land - not as our own - but as caretakers and we have done a good job. We have kept our end of the bargain and the circle of life has remained unbroken.

"Now we must stand on our own two feet and say No More! No more hand outs, no more government programs, no more mining leases and water giveaways, no more accounting errors and millions lost in trust funds. No more poisoning Dineh in Anglo uranium mines. No more stealing the Hopis' mineral and water rights. No more hiding the truth about the history of the Paiutes at Kanab. No more fighting and dying for oil.

"I say we will protect our land, our people and our sacred places. I say we are a peace loving people but we are stronger than we have ever been before, and now it is time to confront those who attempt to destroy us. We have learned the many lessons of the white man, and now we can play his game - a game we must win.

"We have learned that right now, the two Anglo armies - the rednecks and the radical environmentalists - are fighting it out over on the Cottonwood road. They are the foolish marionettes of those pulling their strings. Blood has been shed and it flows over our sacred lands. It is a sign we cannot ignore. The prophesy is clear."

CHAPTER THIRTY-TWO

By midnight most of the fighters in both camps were dead asleep. Earlier, Jonah and a handful of his lieutenants, Shon, McVey and forty or so members of EarthFirst!, the Greens, and Greenpeace sat in a circle around a bonfire wanting - needing - to talk but were unable, each locked in some personal twilight dimension. All they could muster was to sit together and stare quietly into the fire's embers. Jonah did what he could to comfort them; retrieving protein bars or bottles of water or checking wounds and changing bandages. He imprinted the nuances of each man's face into his memory. He knew some would not make it and it seemed important to get a good look now. They were brothers, a family forged on the anvil of devotion and purpose. They risked all they had or ever would have for a principle. No matter the outcome, they were patriots standing at the vanguard of an important movement. How many of his countrymen, Jonah wondered, would be willing to do the same?

Shoulder to shoulder, hip to jowl, they sat cradling their weapons, anticipating the new dawn as men have done before battles down through the ages. Many replayed the day's events over and over again as if it were a video game. McVey was nervous and relived the fear he felt during the fight. He could still feel the sensation of his knife hitting bone - ribs - as it plunged into Becker's abdomen on the bulldozer. Just for an instant, as the two tumbled to the ground, their eyes met and through some strange ethos of battle, they acknowledged their partnership in this primal dance.

No one knew but Jonah considered ordering a retreat; they could load up and leave, making it down The Gut to fight another day. Who could blame them? The rednecks couldn't follow and it would temporarily solve their problem. He tried to make it work in his head but ultimately nixed the idea, concluding the events of the day were a fulfillment of decisions and actions set into motion years ago. It had to play out as planned - the movement needed martyrs. Besides, he considered, each man set himself on the pathway leading to Tyler Wash. Who was he to interfere with their destiny?

At the fire ring, Jonah passed out cold beer. "We did what we said we'd do and we kept our cool. We fought as a unit, just as we trained." Raising his beer, "we showed them."

For a few minutes the heaviness evaporated and they laughed and raised their bottles to the awaiting night. "Two beers per man," Jonah finally joked. "We need clear-heads for tomorrow." With his mention of tomorrow, the mood darkened and everyone went silent. One by one they fell silent and dropped off to sleep where they sat.

Jonah checked on the guards encircling the camp. He admonished each to drink lots of water and "No matter what, never sit down." When he finished his rounds he began again. The starry night was quiet and liquid and carried with it a strong sleeping potion. On both sides of the wash everyone was exhausted, and as each minute passed it became more difficult not to succumb to sleep. Even Jonah, tirelessly walking the perimeter, was not immune from the night's intoxication and as dawn approached, he ignored his own advice and sat on a sandstone shelf. He needed a minute to gather his thoughts but within a few seconds fell into a deep sleep.

Across the wash, the Sagebrushers spent the evening tending to their wounds, preparing for the upcoming battle and resting. Westley, Anderson and a few others discussed tactics and battle plans, always second-guessing themselves because their opponent had outsmarted them. They were convinced EarthIsland had more surprises waiting for them. Anderson was weak and dizzy and had to sit down several times.

The men congregated in small groups of friends, family and neighbors. The Nevada contingent, thirty or more, circled their trucks wagon train-style on a piece of tabletop sandstone just off the road. Most lost themselves in the fire's flames but, unlike their counterparts across the wash, they exhibited less psychological trauma. The fact was, bitchin' and cryin' didn't get anybody anywhere. The matter was cut and dried.

In the Manhattan editorial offices of the New York Times, editor David Horowitz asked several senior editors and writers into his office. Garrett showed them the geological report and personnel files recovered from Las Vegas Air Tours' computer files and outlined what he believed was occurring. "There are still holes in the fabric of this conspiracy," he began, "but I'm convinced you'll see clearly what is going down there. Imagine, if this report is correct and two to five billion barrels of oil is under Kaiparowits," He paused, "Just imagine what some Americans might do to get at it.

"As I was explaining to David before you arrived, it was not EarthIsland or even the cowboys trying to gain sympathy, as some have claimed, who started the conflict by killing the cows and burning the historic line shack. It was ex-military and ex-CIA mercenaries working for as yet unknown parties at Las Vegas Air Tours who did the crimes. We can prove they are involved. These mercenaries are conducting a well planned and well financed terror campaign designed to put the two rival groups, the Sagebrushers and EarthIslanders, at each other's throats and start a land war. Their objective has been to get the ball rolling and then let the fanatics on both sides run with it. Once that has been accomplished, the politicians move to decommission the monument and clear the way for oil development. So far, as we've seen, they have done an excellent job. From what I'm hearing, EarthIsland and the Sagebrushers are facing off right now down on the Kaiparowits. I'm convinced that after the confrontation is over and a few patriots are martyred, the politicians and the behind-the-scenes power players will push for a temporary, then permanent closure of the monument."

Turning to Horowitz, "In a real way, David, although unwittingly, the Times has been drawn into the conspiracy. A few days ago you ran a guest editorial from Senator Kimball, who opposed the monument and has been a vocal proponent of developing domestic oil, calling for the temporary closure of the Grand Staircase. This so-called "trial balloon" was scoffed at and marginalized until the President publicly said he was considering the idea."

"Are you implying the President of the United States is involved in this so-called conspiracy?" Horowitz challenged.

"Make your own assessment. The President's history and views are well known. He's an oil man from Texas."

"Do you have evidence linking him?"

"That's where I hope you come in." He glanced around the room. "He's buddy-buddy with one of the owners of Las Vegas Air Tours and before being elected he sat on the board of directors of the company who owned Las Vegas Air Tours until it was sold recently."

Two editors, who had been investigating the President's oil connections for months, exchanged quick glances and everyone shifted in their seat.

Garrett continued, "I believe that if the confrontation gets bloody -

creating another generation of hatred and deceit - the monument will be temporarily or permanently closed. Then, "Surprise!" someone will announce that oil has been discovered and push to develop it - in the name of national security.

"In another ugly chapter of American patriotic blood lust, conservatives and oil men will see an honorable way out. They'll argue we should develop the oil so America can be more self sufficient and less dependent on our enemies in the Middle East. This will also set up a showdown with the environmentalists, one they believe they can win."

Garrett stopped, then continued, "Until Ateen and I got involved, everything was going as planned. Until then, their plan was working perfectly. Ambitious? Certainly. Doable? Certainly plausible when considering how easy it is to fool the American people. They shot the cows! They burned the line shack! They are responsible for most of the serious crimes and vandalism, including the bombing of the historic courthouse in Panguitch, Utah!"

"They killed Ian McCarthey and raped the two girls?" Horowitz quizzed.

Garrett admitted he didn't know. "I'm not certain which of the crimes were committed by the mercenaries and which were committed by the environmentalists and cowboys. Once the mercenaries got the ball rolling, I'm convinced the two parties took it from there - that will all have to be figured out on a case by case basis. Personally, I'm not convinced they had anything to do with the crime. It was too messy, not like them. These guys are professionals, they wouldn't leave witnesses.

"What I am certain of is, that although their plan was working like clockwork, the conspiracy had to take out a few people who got in their way. No big deal in an operation as ambitious as this - so much is at stake. They shot a Navajo sheepherder, Leon Nemelka, because he witnessed the cow killing and could identify them. We buried him on his uncle's land on the Utah Arizona strip. We arrived minutes after the murder. We watched the Huey helicopter used in the commission of the crime leaving. Ultimately, after a lot of groundwork - taking us to Amsterdam and Anaxalrad, who leaked the geological report to us, we traced the helicopter back to Las Vegas Air Tours. They also killed the archaeologist, Professor Cameron Longmire, because he innocently got too close and discovered a seeping pool of oil on the Kaiparowits. Finally, they killed an employee of Las Vegas Air Tours, a navigator by the name of Robert

Laramie, because they feared he discovered their operation and was about to go to the authorities."

"The geological report came from Anaxalrad?" an editor queried.

"They discovered the oil deposit."

"What's Anaxalrad's part in all this?" Horowitz asked.

"They discovered the oil! Anaxalrad owned all the mining leases to Kaiparowits until the outgoing president proclaimed Kaiparowits and a million acres surrounding it a national monument. Once that happened, they decided to withhold the information. Subsequently, someone leaked knowledge of the discovery and then after the cows were shot and tensions mounted, Anaxalrad put two and two together - knowing they were being cut out of the picture."

"If these guys are so professional, how is it you're here? Why aren't you dead?"

Garrett kicked back in his seat. "When my partner Ateen and I got too close they came after us, too." Raising his arm, he pointed west, "I left Ateen, twenty-four hours ago facing off with a van load of them. I have no idea whether he is dead or alive right now. I suspect someone is searching for me, too."

It was a fascinating and intriguing, if farfetched, story. If it were true and the geological report was accurate, the implications were ground shaking. The scam would rival Nixon's Watergate or Reagan and Oliver North's dirty little war run out of the White House basement; or even Enron and the white-collar corporate scandals. It could have a profound impact on national and international economics, environment, national parks, not to mention governmental ethics.

The hard-bitten editors were skeptical, but assigned senior writers and investigators to immediately track down leads and make enquiries. By the day's end, they learned enough to know something huge was up and the newsroom was tense and excited; history was in the making. They had enough to run a front page exclusive. The rest of the story would unfold as it may, bit by bit, one piece at a time over weeks, months and perhaps through congressional hearings, special prosecutors and Supreme Court proceedings. Where it would ultimately lead, no one was certain.

CHAPTER THIRTY-THREE

The Milky Way formed a pulsating belt from north to south, expanding and contracting like some cosmic timepiece. The creatures of Tyler Wash stayed in hiding, going hungry, knowing it was not safe out on this night. Gusts blew up from somewhere on the endless plateau, picking up speed and barreling into the squat cedars and junipers and making a great whooshing sound.

At the rear of EarthIsland's camp, where few guards were posted, a man moved to its edge, testing the security and looking for weak spots. He moved one way, then the other, stopping every few feet, listening and looking. He crept closer, from rock to tree to bush, until he was within the camp's perimeter. No one spotted him, in fact, the only guard was fast asleep. Cupping his hands around his mouth and turning in the direction of Hackberry Canyon, he called out, "Whoo Whoo - whoo whoo," the familiar call of the Great Horned Desert Owl. Jonah rustled and partially acknowledged the owl's call, before dropping back into an exhausted slumber.

One by one, a line of heavily armed men emerged from a slit in the canyon wall called Hackberry Canyon. The narrows of Hackberry were explored many times and were considered impassable. Each man moved silently from bush to tree to rock, a distance of five hundred yards, and then inside the camp. Even loaded down with weapons and ammunition, each man moved silently as if he belonged to the land; like a wily nocturnal coyote moving through its own territory, navigating the landscape as if it were the contents of his own soul. The line of men continued for a long time until they were all inside the EarthIsland battle camp.

Without waking a person, the intruders disarmed the sleeping sentries. They systematically found the fighters where they slept; in their sleeping bags, in the back seats and beds of vehicles, laying in the sand and on tabletop outcroppings. They relieved each fighter of his weapons and quietly stood guard over them. At the dying bonfire, they discovered fifty men spread out sleeping. Going from one to the next, they confiscated their guns, knives and clubs - all without a sound.

Dawn broke over the horizon and Thomas Westley awoke with a start, sensing someone standing over him. Instinctively, he reached for his six-shooter in its holster on his hip, but to his utter dismay it was gone. Rolling over like the wrestler he once was in high school, he expertly got to his feet in a crouching position, prepared to fight. He tried to clear his head to assess what was happening - somehow he was looking down the barrel of a gun - his gun!

"What the hell?" he cried out.

At the other end of the gun was an enormous Indian, six-foot-seven and three hundred and fifty pounds. His face was masked in war paint, the image was the American stars and stripes - red, white and blue. His eyes blinked like an exotic bird.

"What the . . . hell?" Westley screamed, shaking his head to clear the nightmarish sight. "Who in the hell . . ."

The commotion awakened everyone and they jumped up, groping for their weapons and believing the environmentalists staged a sneak attack, but to their dismay their weapons were gone! Frantically, they realized they were surrounded by armed Native Americans with rifles.

"Nobody moves!" the big man in the red, white and blue war paint shouted. "Nobody moves and nobody gets hurt!"

Anderson rushed at the man but was tripped by a brave who stuck out his foot. Anderson sprawled helplessly to the ground.

"No more of that!" the man demanded. He shouted to the scores of warriors whose rifles were at the ready. "Shoot to kill!"

He went on, "Settle down! Listen up! Everybody needs to settle down and no body gets hurt!"

"What the . . . who are you?" Anderson demanded, trying to get to his feet.

"My name is Brigham Joseph Ateen. Who am I speaking to?"

"By god, it's none of your business who we are . . . " Westley responded.

"What do you think you're doing here?" Anderson hollered.

"What does it look like?" Ateen retorted, and continued, "We're stopping you from getting yourselves killed."

"You have no right to . . ."

"Quiet!" Ateen ordered, "You are the ones with no rights! Look around! We control the situation. You're cornered."

"Where did you come from?" Westley asked, still unable to fully grasp the situation.

"It doesn't matter. What matters is we're here." He looked at the man, "What's your name?"

Westley stood impassively, "You're going to get yourselves in a hell of a lot of trouble if you contin. . . "

Ateen cocked the hammer on the six shooter and took a bead on Westley's head. "I asked your name, Anglo."

"The name's Thomas Westley - if it's any of your business."

"Smart move."

"What is this?"

"Just so you know, you are all under arrest." Ateen spoke loudly to the entire encampment, "You are all under arrest. We've confiscated every gun in camp. They are now the property of the Navajo Nation as are your horses and vehicles." He repeated again, "You are all under arrest. The environmentalists too!"

"By what authority?" Sheriff Anderson insisted.

"By the authority of the Dineh Nation and the Native American Defense Force. You men are trespassing and breaking the law. We are here to see you stop."

"What right do you have?"

"By the right of the Creator and the authority of the Dineh Nation."

"This isn't reservation land!" he protested.

"It is the Creator's land," Ateen nodded his head. "We have been its caretakers for six hundred years before you and your greedy little European ancestors arrived with your bloodthirsty Christianity and your phony papers of ownership."

CHAPTER THIRTY-FOUR

A convoy of school buses, escorted by Federal Marshals, left the pavement of Highway 12, and crossed onto the inadequate Cottonwood Canyon dirt road. Surprisingly, the Cottonwood was more congested than the highway. It was lined with hundreds of supporters and curiosity seekers. Scores of media SUVs and vans equipped with satellite dishes were parked everywhere and garishly colored dome tents seemed to sprout from the edge of a sagebrush covered hillside. A few media crews - the most desperate - rushed the empty buses, pushing and shoving and trying to get a look inside. They demanded to know what the buses were doing. Had an agreement been struck? Was the standoff over?

Law enforcement and national guardsmen waved the buses through the road block. Troop transport trucks and armored personnel carriers draped in camouflage were hidden in coves and dry washes. Helicopter gun ships circled at the middle horizon, keeping far enough away not to create problems but close enough to make their presence known. Soldiers sat in the shade or milled around near their trucks. The buses passed law enforcement agents from state and federal agencies, and various overlapping jurisdictions. The National Park Service bickered with county and state officials as federal agents belittled both and took charge - listening to neither. Every agency was armed to the teeth and paraded around in a scene resembling a Rambo-style national swat team competition.

In the week since Ateen and the Native American Defense Force used the little known trail in Hackberry Canyon to successfully end the confrontation between the rednecks and environmentalists, they found themselves in a standoff with the local, state and federal officials. By the time law enforcement finally responded, Ateen and his men had dug in and fortified defensive positions on the south side of the wash in what was the EarthIsland camp. Their prisoners - not a single man escaped - were safe and sound, sitting in a secure enclosure at the camp's center.

Negotiators moved between the two armed camps, walking down

what was left of the road into the wash and then up a deer trail on the other side. Ateen insisted on mediators from Amnesty International and Human Rights Watch - experts more accustomed to negotiating the release of prisoners from African strong men than working a North American hotspot. They went from camp to camp speaking of diplomacy and carrying lists of demands and drafts of potential agreements. Russell Means of the American Indian Movement, helped negotiate a deal and one hundred Sioux Indians shuttled food and water to Ateen's warriors. Ateen's defense forces continued to grow, well-armed fighters filtering in on little known remote back country trails. They numbered nearly a thousand heavily armed braves.

The situation remained tense and fluid. On the first day, Utah authorities made a tactical error by demanding the Natives give up their hostages and surrender immediately, threatening force if they didn't. The authorities gave them two hours. When the deadline came and went and nothing happened, the feds took control of the negotiations. This was not going to be another Ruby Ridge or Waco. This was much bigger and the stakes higher.

The Natives were ready to fight. Two hundred and fifty years of genocide, war crimes, lies, defeats and land thefts would end here. It was the new millennium and the slaughter and abuse they suffered at the hands of the "civilized" white-man were over. It was payback time. They claimed the sacred Kaiparowits Plateau and all of the Grand Staircase, annexing it into the Dineh Reservation. No one would take the land without a costly and determined fight. If change had to issue from the barrel of a gun, so be it.

With the marshals and buses came an agreement signed by the Secretary of the Interior, essentially allowing the Natives to occupy, secure and maintain the Kaiparowits and Grand Staircase as long as they coordinated with park authorities, in exchange for the release of all the hostages, an agreement to continue negotiations and the immediate cessation of all hostilities. Ateen conferred with the elders by satellite phone and after receiving assurances from the human rights representatives, the first new peace treaty in one hundred years between Native Americans and the U.S. government was signed. Within an hour, the prisoners were freed to be bused off and all local, state and federal law enforcement agencies fell back, except for the park service authorities.

As the cowed prisoners walked single file out of the wash to be loaded onto the buses, each was required to give his name. Becker, who was carried out on a stretcher, and four other "outlaws" were pulled aside, taken to an armored vehicle, searched, handcuffed and arrested for the beating death of Ian McCarthey and the brutal rapes of Lana and Summer. McVey and three of his men suffered the same fate, arrested on a federal warrant for the crime of arson and the bombing the Garfield County Maintenance Facility.

As the buses made it back to Highway 12, thousands of well-wishers from both camps waved American flags, sounded horns, sang impromptu versions of "God Bless America," and held up signs, "You are our Hero!" and "Way To Go!"

CHAPTER THIRTY-FIVE

Since before sun up, Cody and a new ranch-hand struggled to repair the hitch of a horse trailer in the tack room. The job required three men but there were only two of them and it had to be done. They were late already, the herd needed lower pasture a week ago and they struggled to get the repair finished, load the horses and be on the mountain by midday.

Lonnie carried a platter of hot cakes and black coffee out to the two men and as she approached, Cody hit his finger with a hammer and cried out in pain. She listened as he rattled-off a line of cuss words.

"Gawd damned, son-of-a-bitch, shit, dirty sack of lousy bastard . . ." He danced around the room, shaking his bloodied hand.

"Well, good morning!" Lonnie interrupted, shouting over the commotion.

"Oh, gawd-damn it! Sorry mom," Cody offered, squeezing the wrist of his bleeding hand with his other hand. "Gawwdd damn it!"

"You hurt, son?" she asked, not really concerned.

"Naw. Nope. Merely a flesh wound," he told her, wiping away the blood with his bandana then wrapping it around the smashed appendix.

Despite Cody being hurt Lonnie was in a particularly good mood. She felt truly blessed to see her son standing there. Things could be so much worse.

Two weeks earlier, she, Cody and their lawyer, Julie Bryant, the ex-assistant attorney general, met with FBI Special Agents at the regional offices in Salt Lake City. Cody was there to come clean about his involvement in the beating death of Ian McCarthey and the rapes. It was difficult for him to implicate others but he knew it was the right thing to do. He should have done it earlier and felt ashamed for waiting. The agents were cordial and polite at first and taped the meeting. It started out friendly enough but ended up an intense interrogation.

After a brief break for lunch, they were surprised to find Lana, one of two surviving victims at the conference table with the special agents waiting for them. She was accompanied by her father and attorney. It was the first time Lana had returned to the West from her East coast home since Ian's death and the brutal assault. She was frightened and did not look at Cody. When Bryant protested Lana's presence, saying no one informed them she'd be there and saying it was a dirty trick, Cody interrupted her, saying Lana had every right to be there.

Appearing small and fragile at the huge conference table, Lana recounted the horrific attack and torture. She broke down and cried time and again. When she got to the point where the perpetrators were about to kill them, she sat straight up and faced Cody. Staring at him she said, "This man saved my life. Without his help Summer and I would be dead. They were going to kill us both."

Lonnie burst out in tears.

She continued, "A minute more and it would have been all over." Lana, too, broke down and sobbed uncontrollably. The agents comforted her and told her she did not need to continue, but she wanted to finish. "When he showed up in his truck he, like, basically, took on the other men. He stood between us and wouldn't let them get to us - and kill us."

Lonnie and Bryant were now crying. Cody sat straight up; he wanted to comfort the women but fixed his gaze on a building outside the window and did not take his eyes from it.

"They were going to kill him, too," she finally went on. "He reached for his gun and told them not to try anything. He grabbed Ian and dragged him to the car and told us to get him inside and leave. As we drove off, I could see him in a shoving match with one of them."

Later that day, Cody signed a statement outlining what happened, naming those who were involved and promising to testify in court. Lana left without looking at Cody again. Turning to the group, she said, "I don't ever want to see any of you again."

Back in Panguitch, Lonnie resigned her job as County Commissioner effective immediately and she and Cody kept close to home, doing chores around the ranch that were long overdue.

"Morning, Commissioner," the new ranch hand, Thomas Westley, offered.

"Oh no, I'm just a private citizen now! Call me Lonnie." She stood in the doorway and held out her arms, gesturing to Westley to take the coffee and flapjacks. "You finding the beds in the bunk house to your liking?"

"Yes, ma'am," he smiled, "suits me just fine." Looking at the golden brown hot cakes, "Home cookin'! Beats jail food any day. Thanks!"

"It's just good ole rib-stickin' ranch food. Been a long time since you've had home cooking? I suspect your mother made you a pancake or two."

"Yes ma'am," he said, embarrassed. "I can still smell 'em. That's how good they were."

"The commissioner here makes the best damned pancakes in the county," Cody offered about his mother.

"I'm your mother, Cody. Don't you go calling me commissioner, either."

They laughed.

Lonnie stood at the shed entryway, hands in the back pockets of her faded jeans, not knowing whether to enter or not. "You going to get that thing fixed?"

"Got to," Cody answered, shoving down a pancake. "Need to get up on the mountain before afternoon."

Westley shuffled around and stood tall. He had something to say. "I sure want you two to know how much I appreciate all that you're doing for me." He turned to Lonnie and nodded, "Without the good word you put in for me with Judge Braithwaite, I'd still be in jail."

"Jail's no place for a man like you," Lonnie replied, smiling. "You need to be out doing what you know best - ranching. We'll be working you hard enough you won't be thanking us in a few weeks."

After the Native American Defense Force turned Westley and the others over to the authorities, he was arrested for inciting a riot, trespassing, and constructing an illegal road onto National Park Service land. Bail was set at a half million dollars and people from around the country came up with the money, and after Bullock promised to be responsible for him, he was released.

Since the confrontation, the media transformed him into a true John Wayne-style American hero. Big, strong, brave and silent. He was truly a rare breed, an American man not afraid to take a stand and risk it all for love of country. A popular western singer penned a song about Thomas Westley, and traditional land users tacked up pictures of him sitting atop his bulldozer across the West. A New York publishing company assigned a famous Western writer to assist him in generating a book.

By afternoon, the trailer was repaired and Cody and Lonnie, along with their hired hands including Westley all loaded into trucks and went to the mountain. For the next ten days they lived on the mountain, working 14 hour days, rounding up and moving the cows to lower range on the ranch. In the evenings, after Lonnie fed the men, they sat at the campfire and swapped stories of the old and new West.

In Boulder, Colorado at EarthIsland's headquarters, Jonah sat with a journalist from the Rolling Stone Magazine. He refused to answer questions about the confrontation pending the outcome of his trial which was not scheduled until early next year. There were various charges but most significant among them - and the one that would most likely put him behind bars - was using an explosives device in a terroristic manner.

"Just a hundred miles from here," he told the writer, "in Telluride and up near Vail, crimes against nature and wildlife are occurring as we speak. These crimes are perpetrated by the ski industry expansion into pristine forest." He demanded to know, "Where are all your readers? Sitting at their Playstation? Ridin' their skateboards? Just Doing It? We've got a President in the White House who wants to steal our national heritage - the great parks. He was willing to start a war between American patriots so he could line the pockets of his oil field buddies. Isn't anyone in your audience going to do something about it?"

Since the incident at Tyler Wash, Petra took over the day to day operation of EarthIsland. She fielded calls from the media and leaders of environmental organizations around the world. Jonah seemed overwhelmed most of the time. EarthIsland's stand in the redrocks spawned other firebrand leaders and organizations to do likewise. A new day dawned on a new breed of environmental activists.

In Washington D. C., hundreds of thousands of protesters chanted Jonah's name and filled the Washington Monument Plaza to protest the embattled president's anti-environment policies. They carried placards showing pictures of Monument Valley and Ian McCarthey. The words read, "Don't Let Him Die in Vain." Spectators and well-wishers thronged to Boulder as if Jonah were the Dali Lama. To millions of admiring Americans, Jonah represented the best America has to offer.

Privately, Jonah suffered post traumatic stress. One morning he wrote his resignation, packed his old pickup truck with camping gear and supplies and drove off. It was time to reconnect with the land. He visited the mountains and seashores and ended up editing a small local newspaper in the big sky country of Montana while awaiting his trial.

After leaving Lessel standing on the front porch of her apartment, Garrett spent the day driving from Boulder, Colorado to Blanding, Utah and then onto Cedar Mesa. The drive will cleanse my palate, he thought, especially the frenzy of Manhattan, the tumultuous nights with Lessel and all the remarkable events of the last few weeks. He had not lost his touch and now he felt he could have his old life back if he wanted it. I'll deal with that later, he thought.

It was midnight when he arrived on the high desert mesa. Slowly, he worked along a forgotten dirt road winding deep into the remote outback. Garrett knew the area well, it had been his secret hiding place for years. The sprawling cedar covered mesa was one of the last strongholds of great solitude and unbroken silence in America.

At his favorite campsite, at the edge of a ridge overlooking some mysterious canyons below, he rolled out of his truck, arced his back and took in the night. The air was fresh and the silence soothing. He laid his mat and sleeping bag on some soft sand and collapsed into it, watching the Milky Way swirl above before dropping off to sleep like a baby.

In the morning, loaded with food and water for a long stay, he cut a path towards some alabaster ridgelines at a misty blue horizon. By sunset he reached his secret campsite, one he constructed many years earlier. With its perfect fire ring, stone bench and wooden lean-to, this loner's camp was home. Over many visits' time, he lined the camp with rounded rocks and decorated the surrounding trees with feathers and tufts of fur he found on his meanderings. Some years came and went without a visit, but when he finally returned it was all exactly as he left it.

Garrett's outpost sat at the far-edge of an Anasazi burial ground where hundreds of mounds populated a broken ridgeline. Most of the mounds were desecrated but many more remained untouched and spirits resided at the site. He spent his days aimlessly wandering the forest, following his muse and the meander of the land. He left in the morning and returned at night. He made many discoveries - ruins, pottery, bones and arrowheads. Once, he found a broken seam in a line of sandstone ledges where a family of Anasazi mummies waited out eternity.

At night he sat at the campfire, burning in the flames of his recollections and reveries. One night late a gust of wind blew up and out of the canyon and with it Garrett heard dogs barking, men shouting, children calling-out and women crying. He jumped to his feet, turned in a circle and faced the direction of the wind. The silence was so overwhelming he didn't know if the cries were real or came from somewhere within. After listening for a long time, he finally turned away. Suddenly, from the left he heard his dead friend Mick's horse laugh, the one he hated when Mick was alive. It was coming from somewhere out in the vacuous darkness.

Garrett sat back down and smiled - he felt relaxed and finally at ease. At last he was home. There, among the peace and tranquility of this desert land, the reunion with his lost loved-ones was complete.

One hundred miles north and west as the crow flies, on Cottonwood Canyon road, the Native American Defense Force continued its tense but respectful standoff with the Anglo authorities. At every entrance to the Grand Staircase, the defense force had taken up positions. They allowed ranchers and locals and visitors to come and go as they pleased but no U.S. government personnel and no oil company exploration people were allowed to set foot inside. They warned state and federal authorities about over-flights, telling them they were at risk of being shot down and starting a full scale war.

No one mentioned the Place of Emergence. For the first time, natives were aware that the legend they were raised on was indeed true and that one day the prophesy would be fulfilled. Tribes from around the country, Canada and Mexico sent delegations to Navajo Mountain. Pilgrims from the two hundred native tribes sojourned there. In Washington D. C., for the first time in American history, negotiators at the Interior Department were drafting a bill allowing the Dineh and their allies to administer and manage the Grand Staircase - they could even rename the monument. It would be the first Indigenous People's National Park.

As everyday brought new revelations and allegations about the conspiracy to close the monument and develop the oil, the noose tightened around the necks of the president and his influential oil friends from Texas. One by one, low level Las Vegas Air Tours operatives were arrested and some were identifying their bosses and naming names. At the Bonanza Cafe, Nez, Natani, Tahonnie, Crank and Allan Sakiqua were skeptical and worried. In the two hundred years of dealing with the Anglo, the politicians had never kept their word - not once. Even if a Special Prosecutor was named and the president resigned, they knew full well that sooner or later, when the breast-beating died away and the political scandal moved into history, the question of the oil would remain. Some Anglo politicians already charged the Indian takeover had nothing to do with sacred lands and everything to do with controlling the oil.

On Navajo Mountain, Ateen found his granny making fry bread in the crisp autumn air. Every day the night lingered a little longer and Granny stoked her fire in the darkness.

"Grandson," she said, seeing Ateen approach, "are you back from the war?"

"Yes, Granny."

She stood slowly, placing one hand in the small of her back and using it to support herself. "Did we win?"

"Yes, Granny. We won the first battle but this war will last a long time."

"Yes. The Place of Emergence." She looked around satisfied at her grandson's presence and smiled.

"Yes, Granny." Ateen gathered tiny bits of kindling scattered around and made a pile next to Granny's cook stove.

"Grandfather told me you were coming," She announced, taking a cigarette from behind her ear and lighting it. "We were worried when you did not return from Nam." She shook her finger as if telling someone off, "I told them all you'd be back. I said, 'It is a long path into manhood and the journey to leadership is even longer.' I told them, 'He'll be back when his lessons are learned. He is no good to us until then anyway.' I told them, 'Mark my words, he'll save us one day. That's right! Mark my words!' I was right."

Ateen took a deep breath and straightened, taking in the fresh mountain air and looking around with deep satisfaction. He loved the mountain and his people; he wished he could spend the rest of his life there, caring for his granny and mother. He would build a new hogan for his mother, a big one, and tend the sheep and even buy a new truck. Home is a truly sacred place and for those who do not have one, they can never find peace or feel complete.

Behind Granny and Ateen, Lena Tsosie approached and stood next to a small pine tree. She was beautiful in the morning light and hugged herself to fend-off the chilly morning. Ateen and Granny noticed her at the same time.

"You need more firewood," Ateen announced quickly, moving off.

"I'll go chop some."

"You can't get away that easy, my brave grandson," Granny said, kneeling down and turning her attention to her fry bread.

Tsosie followed him a few feet behind.

"Where are you going?" he asked, perturbed.

"I'm coming to be with you."